THE LAW AND THE LADY

WILKIE COLLINS was born in London in 1824, the eldest son of the landscape painter William Collins. In 1846, having spent five years in the tea business, he was entered to read for the bar at Lincoln's Inn, where he gained the legal knowledge that was to give him much material for his writing. From the early fifties, he was a friend of Charles Dickens, acting with him, contributing to *Household Words*, travelling with him on the Continent. Dickens produced and acted in two melodramas written by Collins, *The Lighthouse* (1855) and *The Frozen Deep* (1857). Collins is best remembered for his novels, particularly *The Woman in White* (1860) and *The Moonstone* (1868), which T. S. Eliot called 'the first, the longest, and the best of modern English detective novels'. His later, and at the time rather sensational, novels include *The New Magdalen* (1873) and *The Law and the Lady* (1875). Collins also braved the moral censure of the Victorian age by keeping two women (and their households) while marrying neither. He died in 1889.

DAVID SKILTON was educated at King's College, Cambridge, and at the University of Copenhagen. After holding posts at the universities of Stockholm, Glasgow and Lampeter, he is now Professor of English at Cardiff University. His books include *Anthony Trollope and His Contemporaries* (1972; 1996), *Defoe to the Victorians* (Penguin, 1985), *The Early and Mid-Victorian Novel* (1993) and editions of numerous Victorian novels. For the Penguin Classics he has also edited Hardy's *Tess of the D'Urbervilles* and Trollope's *The Prime Minister* and *Autobiography*, and he has co-edited *Framley Parsonage*.

WILKIE COLLINS

THE LAW AND THE LADY

Edited with an Introduction and Notes by
DAVID SKILTON

PENGUIN BOOKS

PENGUIN BOOKS

Published by the Penguin Group
Penguin Books Ltd, 80 Strand, London WC2R 0RL, England
Penguin Putnam Inc., 375 Hudson Street, New York, New York 10014, USA
Penguin Books Australia Ltd, 250 Camberwell Road, Camberwell, Victoria 3124, Australia
Penguin Books Canada Ltd, 10 Alcorn Avenue, Toronto, Ontario, Canada M4V 3B2
Penguin Books India (P) Ltd, 11 Community Centre, Panchsheel Park, New Delhi – 110 017, India
Penguin Books (NZ) Ltd, Cnr Rosedale and Airborne Roads, Albany, Auckland, New Zealand
Penguin Books (South Africa) (Pty) Ltd, 24 Sturdee Avenue, Rosebank 2196, South Africa

Penguin Books Ltd, Registered Offices: 80 Strand, London WC2R 0RL, England

www.penguin.com

First published in book form 1875
Published in Penguin Classics 1998

5

Editorial matter copyright © David Skilton, 1998
All rights reserved

The moral right of the editor has been asserted

Set in 10/12.5 pt Monotype Baskerville
Typeset by Rowland Phototypesetting Ltd, Bury St Edmunds, Suffolk
Printed in England by Clays Ltd, St Ives plc

CONTENTS

INTRODUCTION

William Wilkie Collins, reputed inventor of the detective novel, friend and collaborator of Charles Dickens, and a domestic nonconformist supporting two unsanctified *ménages*, published *The Law and the Lady* in 1875. 'My friend Wilkie Collins is generally supposed to be sensational,' wrote Anthony Trollope shortly after the publication of this novel, adverting simultaneously to Collins's style of fiction and (for the benefit of those in the know) to his unorthodox domestic relations. Collins was a leading practitioner of a species of writing called 'the sensation novel', which he and other novelists such as Mary Braddon had made fashionable in the past decade and a half, while Trollope, by his own confession, was one of those 'generally called realistic'.[1] The Trollopian nudge in the ribs about the sensational nature of Collins's life of course refers to the fact that, unlike the monogamous Trollope, Collins kept two separate women with their respective families, and was married to neither. Although Collins's choice of living this way inevitably leads us to ask whether he was one who also rejected Victorian proprieties in his fiction, the precise details of these bohemian *ménages* do not much matter for the understanding of his fiction, even if they fascinate historians of social mores, and would in a later century have been deemed excellent copy in the nation's newspapers.

Victorian writers and many of their successors are fond of relating artists' lives point by point to their art, but such connections are rarely satisfying to the modern literary critic. When proved, they usually show little about the works of art concerned, as works of art, and are more useful in supporting biographical speculations. In the case of Wilkie Collins, however, the qualities of his life and work *are* mutually relevant even to today's critic, though not because certain events, personages or beliefs in the one can be simply paralleled in the other, but because each enacts a response to the dire shortcomings of Victorian marriage, with the implication that behind the conventional front of many a respectable household lie secrets that would not shame a gothic novel, and that at times of crisis these can provoke conflict as fierce as Greek tragedy. Unfortunately motives for such choices as Collins's could not be written about at the time, and can only be guessed at now. Certainly there is little to suggest that his partners were anything other than willing and largely contented participants in his unusual domestic arrangements, although we now easily recognize that the whole sexual system at the time, marital and non-marital, was heavily weighted against women's interests. It is unprofitable to judge the behaviour of one age against the standards of another, saying that if so-and-so were to do such-and-such a thing nowadays we should construe it in a certain, modern way, and, with little to go on about Collins's extra-legal family arrangements, we should not assume that we understand them.

What we do know is that Wilkie Collins had occasion to *think* about the domestic and legal position of women in a way that his friend and contemporary Charles Dickens did not.[2] The result was that among male novelists of the period, Collins took an unsurpassed interest in women characters, and particularly in their intellects and ambitions, and the social restrictions imposed on them. In contrast, for most of *his* career Dickens presented female characters as dolls, termagants, good sisters or stereotypical fallen women, and it is unlikely that Wilkie Collins enriched the nation's art when he encouraged Dickens to supplement the sexual infantilism this implies with a practical acquaintance with Parisian prostitutes. The point, however, is that Collins simply *knew* more about how women lived and thought than many men of the time. Among novelists, Anthony Trollope is the other who stands out as seriously interested in the mental life of women and their sense of identity, and again it is tempting to point to circumstances which had forced him to notice flaws in the accepted views of the different responsibilities of men and women. Trollope had learnt from hard experience that a father can ruin a family, while a mother can enter economic life and save it.[3] What the 'realistic' Trollope and the 'sensational' Wilkie Collins had in common was the ability to look at relations between the sexes with rather less rigidity of mind than most of their male contemporaries, even if neither measured up to the more strenuous standards of our day. Of course Collins probably avoided the pitfalls of conventional marriage only to generate an entirely new set of problems about which surviving documents are reticent, but he certainly seems to have tried to avoid the contradictions of middle-class marriage, which invested many a Victorian household with the dramatic potential of the House of Atreus, or, to use a lighter and historically more relevant example, *A Doll's House*, which Ibsen wrote soon after in 1879. All in all Collins was one of the writers of the period who best appreciated the problematic nature of orthodox mid-Victorian domesticity, even if he had absorbed the lessons of J. S. Mill's *The Subjection of Women* (1869) less thoroughly than his more radical Scandinavian contemporary.[4]

Wilkie Collins's reputation had been made with a string of good novels, including *Basil* (1852), *Hide and Seek* (1854) and *The Dead Secret* (1857), and his place in the literary record books was assured by *The Woman in White* (1859–60) and *The Moonstone* (1868), which enjoyed gigantic popularity. By common consent *The Law and the Lady* is not one of those of his novels which influenced the course of English fiction, as these two did. It is less complex and less ingeniously planned than these masterworks, but it shares their close attention to detail and their combination of detective work and abnormal psychology. And how accomplished it is! The riches of mid-Victorian fiction are so great that they obscure many a fine work such as this.

Novelists and their public were acutely aware of the existence of a literary market-place, and it was crowded with high-quality literary goods. Anthony Trollope describes readers going to well-known authors for their reading, basing their choice on the reputation for quality those authors have established, and he rightly names Wilkie Collins as one of these reliable suppliers: 'It is as natural that a novel reader wanting novels should send to a library for those by George Eliot or Wilkie Collins, as that a lady when she wants a pie for a picnic should go to Fortnum and Mason.'[5] Fortnum and Mason have retained their reputation, and fortunately the novelists of the period have largely kept theirs too, even if critics have from time to time announced that certain of them should be out of favour for various modish reasons, now largely forgotten. Among the high-quality pies on offer at the time in competition with *The Law and the Lady* were Charles Dickens's last novel, *Edwin Drood* (1870), George Eliot's *Middlemarch* (1871–2), Anthony Trollope's *The Eustace Diamonds* (1871–3), *The Way We Live Now* (1874–5) and *The Prime Minister* (1875–6), George Meredith's *Harry Richmond* (1870–71), Thomas Hardy's *Far from the Madding Crowd* (1874), Disraeli's *Lothair* (1870), and Samuel Butler's *Erewhon* (1872), as well as works by Braddon, Broughton, Annie Thackeray, Walter Besant and Sheridan LeFanu, not to mention Henry James. This was a literary pie-shop of which dreams could be made, and one can only agree with those Victorians who wrote that theirs was the age of the novel, as Shakespeare's had been the age of drama.

If, therefore, critics have been content to assume that *The Law and the Lady* is prominent neither among Wilkie Collins's works nor the novels of the eighteen-seventies, this may reflect no discredit on the work. After all, most novels are less intellectual than *Middlemarch*, less witty than *The Eustace Diamonds*, less strange than *Erewhon*, surrounded less by public attention than *Edwin Drood*, written by less prominent citizens than *Lothair*, and less clear as pointers to new directions in fiction than *Harry Richmond* and *Far from the Madding Crowd*. As an unfortunate result *The Law and the Lady* has often been relegated to the category of minor fiction, and few commentators have known what to do with it, though changes in the way in which we construe the world and literature should now make it increasingly approachable. The handles by which critics have usually sought to obtain a hold on the novel are threefold: as a detective story containing an early example of a woman detective; as a novel campaigning against what the author saw as a fertile source of injustice – the verdict of 'Not Proven', which is available to a jury under Scots law; and as a vehicle for the presentation of eccentricity, madness and idiocy through the characters of Miserrimus Dexter and his cousin 'Ariel'.

The last of these will be discussed later in this Introduction, while the second can be easily dismissed. Admittedly some of the novels which Collins wrote in the same decade as *The Law and the Lady*, such as *Man and Wife* (1870), *The New Magdalen* (1873) and *The Fallen Leaves* (1879), can be judged to have more 'mission' than fictional interest, as though after the death of his friend Dickens, Collins had lost the balance between campaigning and credibility, justifying Swinburne's couplet:

> What brought good Wilkie's genius nigh perdition?
> Some demon whispered – Wilkie! have a mission.[6]

The narrator (and, one suspects, the author) of *The Law and the Lady* may get a little heated from time to time over the supposed cowardly inadequacies of Scottish juries, hiding behind the 'Not Proven' verdict, but the story is never impeded, and Swinburne's demon has failed in this instance.

It is as a detective story that the stature of the novel is to be recognized; but as a detective story of a special kind, with some particularly modern aspects. The fact that the amateur detective is a woman, Valeria Woodville, is important, of course. Collins's first such character appeared in 1856 in the story 'The Diary of Anne Redway', and by 1875 there was a richer context of public discussion of the status of women for the fiction to resonate with. During the intervening years the philosopher and member of Parliament, John Stuart Mill, had proposed an unsuccessful amendment to the Reform Bill of 1867 to extend the franchise to women, and two years later had published his highly influential book, *The Subjection of Women*. Though far from adequate, the first Married Women's Property Acts of 1870 and 1874 had materially increased a married woman's control over property which she brought to her marriage, though Valeria Woodville still controls the money which she had before her marriage, not because of these new laws but because it has been legally settled on her in time-honoured fashion. (It was not until 1882 that the law recognized a married woman's property as hers separately.) Over the same period women began to have some limited access to higher education, and in 1874, just before publication of *The Law and the Lady*, Sophia Jex-Blake initiated medical training for women, and shortly after it, in 1877, established the right of women to practise as doctors. Valeria's conservative friend, Benjamin, says that 'the new generation is beyond my fathoming', while her clergyman uncle reproaches her with behaving like a lawyer 'in petticoats' (Ch. XIV). As so often, Collins is highly topical: University College, London had just admitted women to its Jurisprudence class in 1873, though the first woman law graduate from the College was not to take her degree until 1917.[7] Even if we find Valeria a too deferential wife in all matters but one, she is perceived by the other characters as distinctly 'advanced', and, whether she is made to articulate them or not, her actions strongly evoke major gender issues of the day.

Our 'detective in petticoats' suffers repeated discouragement from those she meets, who all suppose that as a woman she will lack the strength of mind and body necessary to carry through what she has undertaken. Indeed in the course of her investigations she runs real risks, which arise from a general assumption that a willingness to step beyond the social norms implies a readiness for illicit sexual adventure. At one point a man is so presumptuous (or out of control) as physically to take hold of her, but she escapes this assault by showing the affronted dignity of a virtuous woman. For a while she finds it an advantage to appear to inhabit the borderline between respectability and vice. Such, she explains, is 'the disordered and desperate condition' of her mind that she seeks a chambermaid's assistance in the application of cosmetics, in order to transform her appearance from that of a respectable middle-class woman into something calculated to appeal to an elderly *roué*. The maid recognizes that '[t]here is a gentleman in the case', and draws the wrong and worst conclusion. Yet such is Valeria's determination to assume this disreputable disguise that she bravely bears the servant's 'knowing' remarks. While going into the world as this travesty of her true, moral self, she meets a young soprano, a lower-class girl who is maintained by a well-to-do man, and actually is, in Victorian phrase, 'no better than she should be'. Even this young woman gives herself airs, and considers herself morally superior to continental singers, singling out *their* excessive use of make-up as indicative of their vices. When she refers to them as 'painted Jezebels', she recalls to the Victorian (though perhaps not the modern) mind the grisly end which that queen meets with in the Second Book of

Kings, when, having painted her face, she is trodden under foot, eaten by dogs, and her carcase is 'as dung upon the face of the field' (2 Kings 9:32–37). It can be hard to recreate the intensity of symbolic meaning which still surrounded the use of cosmetics, and we must remember that it was only a few years before, in 1868, that an impostor, 'Madame Rachel', had been condemned to five years' penal servitude for claiming that her products were made from such ingredients as water from the River Jordan, and could make women 'beautiful for ever'. When Valeria is deeply offended when a man physically takes hold of her, the insult must be seen in the context of the many ways in which she is dangerously stepping outside the domain of the respectable woman of the period. The use of make-up is symbolic of the daring involved in the total of her social transgressions throughout the story.

By her boldness and unconventionality in investigating a mystery which she should have left to the men, Valeria Woodville achieves much, but as a character she is ultimately disappointing to the modern reader, who regrets this admirable woman's exaggerated respect and consideration for her unimpressive husband. Nevertheless the mere fact of a female detective remains fascinating in the reactions it provokes from the men she has to win over to assist or inform her. All this produces a really worthwhile addition to the investigator as amateur male detective, as seen in Walter Hartright in *The Woman in White*. This, however, is not the only factor which clearly singles out *The Law and the Lady* from most other detective fiction.

One interpretation of the detective story is that it presents a fictional world out of kilter because of an unsolved mystery, usually a crime. The story, which is necessarily self-aware, acts out the solution to the enigma, and when the truth is out, the problem posed by the fiction is resolved and stability returns to the fictional world. The earliest and most famous detective in Western literature is Oedipus, who in systematically seeking to discover what is wrong with the kingdom of Thebes discovers that he is the criminal who must be expelled to purge the realm, having killed his father in a fit of road-rage, and unknowingly married his mother. As this is Greek tragedy, the opening situation can be grandly described (as it was by Hegel) as instability in 'the ethical substance', but the principle is in a way common to the detective story. Against this model *The Law and the Lady* does not score well. The solution to the mystery which Valeria Woodville identifies at the outset does not fully resolve the difficulties between the characters: no truth is revealed publicly, the world is not purged of error, and relationships within the fictional society are potentially as unstable as ever.

Oedipus continues with his investigations despite the forebodings of his mother-wife, and Valeria too is repeatedly warned not to proceed, since she risks thereby destroying her own marriage and peace of mind. The old undergraduate joke that the course of Greek culture would have been different if Oedipus had heeded his mother's call to stop asking questions and come in because his tea was ready shows up a quality of all fictional detection: detectives may have doubts, but there is no real question of their abandoning their quests or they will die, because the works in which they appear will instantly cease. So their stories are predicated on the action of continuing to solve the enigma, and doubts as to their constancy of purpose are embellishments, serving to manipulate the reader's response and leave the narrative less bald and unconvincing than it might otherwise be.

In the *Oedipus Tyrannus* there is no doubt, and hope is banished from a world ruled by Fate. The atmosphere of Wilkie Collins's stories suggests a greater freedom of choice, somewhat at odds with the portentous chapter headings, such as 'The Man's Decision', 'The Woman's Answer', and 'Nemesis at Last!', which suggest a representative quality in the characters concerned, and hence a diminished personal responsibility and an onward impulsion beyond their control. In an age which believed in individual freedom and individual moral responsibility, the suggestion that Fate might rule was one of the thrills of sensationalism. Perhaps this is why his contemporaries saw a clear distinction between 'sensationalism' and 'realism' in terms of dominance respectively of plot and character. Though the assumptions of Greek drama are quite different from those of the novel, Sophocles could be seen as having it both ways in the *Oedipus Tyrannus* and the *Oedipus at Colonus*, in that he develops an intense focus on a single figure by having him at once the offender, the inquiring mind, and the guilty, tortured subject. It is true that Valeria Woodville does not seriously harm herself by her detective work, as her counterpart in

Collins's *The Dead Secret* does when she discovers her own illegitimacy. Neither does she find herself to be the guilty party, like Franklin in *The Moonstone*, who, having sworn that '[i]f time, pains, and money can do it, I will lay my hand on the thief', finds that 'on the unanswerable evidence of the paint-stain, I had discovered Myself as the Thief'.[8] However, Collins does notably find means of endowing Valeria with an importance beyond the operation of her inquiring mind. At the end of the novel she is left in a unique position of power, elevated by her superior understanding above the husband she has set out to save.

That understanding is based on the possession of better information, and a close scrutiny of *The Law and the Lady* reveals that this is a novel in which not revelation but information is crucial. In that respect the novel should be at home in an age obsessed with information, for it bears a stronger resemblance to Le Carré's spy fiction than to most detective stories. There is indeed a considerable stress on who possesses or is believed to possess important information, and there is minute description of how information is obtained, and literally pieced together from fragments of paper or the disjointed utterances of a disintegrating mind; and what distinguishes this novel from many another is that the processes of information-gathering do not lead to revelation, but to another concealment, which is the nearest we reach to a 'solution'. In the process we are shown how secrets lurk not just behind the marriage whose stresses have ended in death, but also behind the partnership we are invited to see at the end as satisfactory. Indeed we are implicitly invited by extension to consider repression and concealment as endemic to marriage in general. In a form which invites closure, this story leaves almost as much open at the end as there was at the beginning, and in no way parallels the quasi-tragic pattern of restoring ethical balance to the world. Unlike many fictional couples in literature, Valeria and Eustace were from the start not likely to live happily ever after, and it is not clear to the modern reader that their chances are much better at the end than they were at the outset. The novel's ending asks us to believe that pregnancy and awakening parental instincts will cement the relationship, and that Valeria has 'everything a woman could want to make her happy' as she faces 'the glorious perils of childbirth' (Chs. XLIV and XXXVII). Victorian literary conventions are hereby satisfied; but for us, many alternative possibilities remain open.

The problematic narrative which Collins has produced prevents closure, which he would in all probability have liked to have achieved. To the modern reader, however, it is curiously satisfying to find that a woman who steps out of line, even if she never lets us forget her conventional deference to her husband, cannot be accommodated within the ideologically dominant narrative form. The lady doth protest her respect for her husband too much, we think, and we seize on every hint we can discover of a potential for marital disharmony, likely to stem from the psychological strains arising on the one hand from the revelations we have witnessed, and on the other imposed by the novel's conclusion. It is the book's principal strength that it demonstrates the prevalence and powerful effects of the repression so deeply ingrained in Victorian society and culture. In the case of this novel, sensationalism reaches a point where it is unable to carry its own implications through to their conclusion, because the analysis of the fictional situation in which the story ends requires a different fictional method from sensationalism's own. The workings of a marriage and the consciousness of the partners in it form an excellent subject for a different kind of novel – the species of novel which Victorian critics assumed was based on the painstaking development of individual character.

Yet when we look more closely at some of the gender assumptions in mid-Victorian characterization, we see how far Collins has come in terms of other aspects of characterization. One of the most influential literary critics among his contemporaries was Richard Holt Hutton, Literary Editor of the *Spectator*. In an essay on Browning, Hutton explains that different techniques are required for the presentation of male and female characters:

Educated *men's* characters are naturally *in position*, and most vigorous masculine characters of any kind have a defined bearing on the rest of the world, a characteristic attitude, a personal latitude and longitude on the map of human affairs, which an intellectual eye can seize and mark out at once. But it is not so usually with women's characters. They are best expressed not by attitude and outline, but by essence and indefinite tone. As an odour expresses and characterizes a flower even better than its shape and colour, as the note of a bird is in some sense a more personal expression of it than its form and feathers; so there is something of vital essence in a great poet's delineations of women which is far more expressive than any outline or colour.[9]

Valeria adopts an attitude *vis-à-vis* the world, and effectively asserts 'a personal latitude and longitude on the map of human affairs'. She is therefore presented in what Hutton elsewhere calls 'the dramatic mode', as opposed to the 'lyrical cry',[10] which would better express the 'inwardness' of a female character. At the time only George Eliot was held to be able to combine the two in a unified social and psychological account of women characters.

The sensation novel itself automatically produced problems in this regard by introducing active female characters, and these problems, like most Victorian issues, had a moral dimension. The best critic writing in *The Times*, Eneas Sweetland Dallas – like Collins a lover of women but not of feminism – explains the phenomenon humorously as follows:

When women are . . . put forward to lead the action of a plot, they must be urged into a false position. . . . [T]he novelist finds that to make an effect he has to give up his heroine to bigamy, to murder, to child-bearing by stealth in the Tyrol, and to all sorts of adventures which can only signify her fall. . . . [This] leads . . . to their appearing in a light which is not good.[11]

The difficulty was compounded by a carefully crafted story-line, which, it was always assumed, took attention away from psychological motivation, since characters' actions seemed to be called for less by any conceivable human motivation, than by the exigencies of the plot. Trollope's formulation of this assumption is useful:

The readers who prefer [realistic fiction] are supposed to take delight in the elucidation of character. Those who hold by [sensational fiction] are charmed by the construction and gradual development of a plot. All this is I think a mistake, – which mistake arises from the inability of the imperfect artist to be at the same time realistic and sensational. A good novel should be both, – and both in the highest degree.[12]

However strong Trollope's wish for the reconciliation of characterization and plot in a higher form which should be both sensational and realistic, the fact remains that the novel of mystery and detection did not in general provide the best vehicle for studies of any but extreme mental states, and Victorian moralists never tired of complaining that sensationalism sprang out of, represented and resulted in, an over-excitation of the brain and nervous system, as though it were an exemplification of Cabanis's dictum that 'the whole man' is in the nerves.[13]

Eccentricity, madness and idiocy feature prominently in *The Law and the Lady*, as in many of Collins's other novels. Swinburne quipped that the last was such a habit with Collins that he needed at least one character per novel 'abnormally and constitutionally deficient in nerve and brain'.[14] In *The Law and the Lady*, the idiot is there as a foil to the eccentric and brilliant Miserrimus Dexter, and is also apparently generated by the psychiatric theories of the day:

Constitutional tendency to nervous instability once established in a family may make itself felt in various directions, – epilepsy, hysteria, hypochondriasis, neuralgia, certain forms of paralysis, insanity, eccentricity. It is asserted that exceptional genius in an individual member is a phenomenal indication.

Confined to the question of insanity, this morbid inheritance may manifest itself in two directions, – in defective brain organization manifest from birth, or from the age at which its faculties are potential, *i.e.*, congenital insanity, or in the neurotic diathesis, which may be present in a brain to all appearance congenitally perfect, and may present itself merely by a tendency to break down under circumstances which would not affect a person of originally healthy constitution.[15]

It is tactless to give away too much about the story of a novel in an introduction, and so only the most general remarks can be made here, but they must centre on the man-machine, Miserrimus Dexter, born without legs, who identifies so strongly with his wheelchair that he exclaims 'My chair is Me' (Ch. XVII), and whose bodily build would have been Roman if he had had legs (Ch. XXV). In literary evolution he is a link between the centaur and the cyborg, and represents an alarmed fascination with the growing presence of machines and Western civilization's dependence upon them. His interest from a psychological point of view is that he compensates for his disability by taking on fantastic imaginary existences as the great heroes of history, such as 'Napoleon at the sunrise of Austerlitz' (Ch. XXIV). This habit, it turns out, is a symptom of monomania, which was defined by Henry Maudsley as present when a patient 'exhibits insane delusions on one subject or in regard to certain trains of thought, and talks sensibly in other respects'. The foil to this extraordinary character is a female cousin whom he has ironically dubbed 'Ariel', presumably to cast himself in the role of the great magician, Prospero. Valeria describes 'the girl's round fleshy inexpressive face, her rayless and colourless eyes, her coarse nose and heavy chin', and concludes that she is '[A] creature half alive; an imperfectly-developed animal in shapeless form . . .' (Ch. XXV).

Henry Maudsley, one of the great pioneers in the treatment of the insane, describes what was then held to be the likely outcome of this condition, and further reinforces the link between Ariel and Dexter, as the monomaniac and the congenital idiot meet in demented fellowship:

When . . . insanity has lasted for some time, without amendment taking place, the mind is often weakened, and the person, passing through degrees of craziness, falls finally into a condition of what is called *dementia*. It is the destruction of mind by disease, and may of course be more or less general and complete; in the worst cases demented patients have as little intelligence as the complete idiot, from whom, however, they differ in having lost what he never possessed.

In this condition 'his memory is impaired, his feelings quenched, his intelligence enfeebled or extinct'.[16] Dexter admits that he is full of nervous excitement, and, in his manic phases, exhausts his brain and nerves. In contrast, Ariel, he says, 'has no nerves' (Ch. XL). The change which the catastrophe of Dexter's story brings on her is that she now has nobody to bring out her 'latent intelligence, affection, pride, fidelity' (Ch. XXV).

Meeting earlier in this novel with an extraordinarily confident and exact prognosis along these lines of the course of Dexter's mental derangement, modern readers may be surprised at the self-assurance of Victorian psychiatrists, knowing so much less than their modern counterparts, yet pronouncing with such authority. As more becomes known about mental states, we increasingly distrust the judgements of such practitioners, but for the sake of the fiction and in order not to impede the forward impulsion of the plot, we must suspend disbelief and realize that Collins was consciously up-to-date in his understanding of insanity. Psychological disorder of any kind was treated by the medical establishment of the day as principally physical in its causes, and subject to forces which enabled its progress to be described in terms of physical deterioration or recovery of the brain or nerves, with little understanding needed of the mental processes involved. The strangeness of this restrictive conception of psychiatric disorder reminds us that what is missing from the novel, as much as from the medical analysis of insanity, is the close investigation of individual states of mind. We recognize an awareness of repression and even, perhaps, the subconscious, which seems vitally important, since we know that it would later revolutionize the diagnosis and treatment of mental disorders and provide powerful new tools for understanding cultural phenomena. But in this novel the awareness is not brought to bear on the non-lunatics amongst us, and what Freud dubbed their 'psychopathology of everyday life'. A novelist with the analytic tools to look at the states of mind and the self-deceptions of our happy couple at the conclusion of the novel would offer a plurality of possible implications to the ending of this story, and would effectively destabilize the sense of closure which Victorian convention had imposed.

In the absence of this dimension of psychoanalytic understanding, however, Collins could not exploit the promising situation he finally got his characters into, as his novel found itself in territory alien to its founding principles. On the other hand, a novelist devoted to 'the elucidation of character' (to use Trollope's phrase) would have had time to develop fictional personalities in far more complex mode.

Trollope and George Eliot give over considerable portions of their fictions to examining their characters' consciences, and when their characters come under psychological strain they painstakingly present their internal narratives about themselves and their situations, giving us not so much a proto-Freudian view of the subconscious as a post-Freudian phenomenological account of the characters' mental states. These people *are* their narratives, and an understanding of these states, even without a systematic, medical account of them, can lead to more satisfying psychological results than can be achieved by following, as Collins did, the latest scientific publications.

In breaking new fictional ground *The Law and the Lady* and other sensational fiction shifted attention away from what was known as 'inward portraiture'. But there are considerable compensations. Large cultural patterns of repression and insanity are laid bare, and there is the spectacle of a mental breakdown which provides the best suspense of the novel, as our detective has to work out whether, and if so how, sense can be made of the ramblings of someone in the grip of acute mania. After Freud and R. D. Laing, modern readers assume they know the answer, and are fascinated to witness the way in which the nineteenth century will solve a twentieth-century problem.

This is just one way in which Collins enacts the advances in forensic methods which we take for granted. Where a modern detective deploys squads of police in fingertip searches and sends potential clues to a forensic laboratory for analysis, Victorian detectives require individual effort and ingenuity to solve problems, not having a tradition of well-tried methods at their service. The science of detection is in its infancy, and after all it is only twenty years before that the word 'clew' or 'clue' shifted its principal meaning from 'ball of thread' to 'piece of evidence'. To present a woman pioneer helping to create the modern world is virtue enough in a novel. If in pursuing her inquiry into her husband's past, with the supplementary questions of what her married name really is, and therefore who she is in society, Valeria neglects the psychological dynamics of marriage, and has no anxieties about the straightforwardness of her own feelings for her husband, we know that we can turn for these things to other novels that were in the literary market-place in the eighteen-seventies, such as *Daniel Deronda*.

The Law and the Lady holds its own in other ways, and the literary pie-shop of the time – as well as that of today – would be very much the poorer without it.

NOTES

1. Anthony Trollope, *An Autobiography*, ed. David Skilton (Penguin Books, Harmondsworth, 1996), p. 146; written between October 1875 and April 1876.

2. Details of Collins's domestic life and of his relationship with Dickens are found in C. Peters, *The King of Inventors: a Life of Wilkie Collins* (Secker & Warburg, London, 1991).

3. Trollope's own account of his childhood is found in the first two chapters of *An Autobiography*.

4. Ibsen, like J. P. Jacobsen and a number of other important Scandinavian writers, was more clearly guided towards systematic feminism by the Danish critic Georg Brandes (the 'Great Dane' whom Joyce's Stephen Dedalus quotes), who translated and propagated Mill's feminist work. In Norwegian, Ibsen's play is more provocatively entitled 'A Doll's Home'.

5. *An Autobiography*, p. 133.

6. A. Swinburne, 'Wilkie Collins', in *Studies in Prose and Poetry* (1894), pp. 110–28.

7. See John H. Baker, 'University College and Legal Education 1826–1976', *Current Legal Problems*, 30 (1977), 1–13. There were no women barristers or solicitors until the two branches of the legal profession were compelled by the Sex Disqualification (Removal) Act of 1919 to admit them.

8. *The Moonstone*, Chapter 3.

9. Richard Holt Hutton, *Essays Theological and Literary* (2 vols., 1871), ii, 205–6.

10. Review of Trollope's *Sir Harry Hotspur of Humblethwaite*, *Spectator* xliii (26 November 1870), 1415; the identity of the reviewer is unknown, but its style, preoccupations and argument are those of the Literary Editor.

11. E. S. Dallas, *The Gay Science* (2 vols., 1866), ii, 297.

12. *An Autobiography*, p. 146.

13. Georges Cabanis (1757–1808): '*les nerfs, voilà tout l'homme*'.

14. Swinburne, op. cit.

15. 'Insanity', *Encyclopaedia Britannica* (9th ed., 1881), viii, 96.

16. Henry Maudsley, *Responsibility in Mental Disease* (International Scientific Series vol. 8, 1872), pp. 72–3.

FURTHER READING

Until recently Wilkie Collins was inadequately dealt with by academic critics. He was treated as a lesser friend and associate of Dickens, or as an exponent of a widespread but justly neglected genre, the sensation novel. In the last quarter of the twentieth century the situation has changed, although most books and articles on Wilkie Collins still have little or nothing to say about *The Law and the Lady*. The notable exception is Jenny Bourne Taylor, *In the Secret Theatre of the Home: Wilkie Collins, Sensation Narrative and Nineteenth Century Psychology* (Routledge, London, 1988), which deals most adequately with the social and intellectual background to the fiction.

Recent critical books which deal with Collins's better-known fiction include R. V. Andrew, *Wilkie Collins: a Critical Survey of His Prose Fiction* (Garland, New York, 1979); Richard Barickman, Susan MacDonald and Myra Stark, *Corrupt Relations: Dickens, Thackeray, Trollope, Collins, and the Victorian Sexual System* (Columbia University Press, New York, 1982); Tamar Heller, *Dead Secrets: Wilkie Collins and the Female Gothic* (Yale University Press, New Haven and London, 1992); Sue Lonoff de Cuevas, *Wilkie Collins and His Victorian Readers: a Study in the Rhetoric of Authorship* (AMS Press, New York, 1982); William Marshall, *Wilkie Collins* (Twayne Publishers, New York, 1970); Philip O'Neill, *Wilkie Collins: Women, Property and Propriety* (Macmillan, Basingstoke, 1988); Nicholas Rance, *Wilkie Collins and Other Sensation Novelists: Walking the Moral Hospital* (Macmillan, Basingstoke, 1991); Nelson Smith and R. C. Terry, *Wilkie Collins to the Forefront: Some Reassessments* (AMS Press, New York, 1994); Peter Thoms, *The Winding of the Labyrinth: Quest and Structure in the Major Novels of Wilkie Collins* (Ohio University Press, Athens, Ohio, 1992).

Since details of Collins's unorthodox domestic arrangements have been uncovered fairly recently, earlier biographical works are obviously seriously incomplete. The most reliable sources of biographical information are William M. Clarke, *The Secret Life of Wilkie Collins* (Allison & Busby, London, 1988), and Catherine Peters, *The King of Inventors: a Life of Wilkie Collins* (Minerva, London, 1992), both of which give useful and revealing extracts from his unpublished letters.

Of older material, essays by Swinburne in his *Studies in Prose and Poetry* (Chatto & Windus, London, 1894) and Dorothy Sayers in her *Wilkie Collins: a Critical and Biographical Study* (completed by E. R. Gregory) (Friends of the University of Toledo Libraries, Toledo, Ohio, 1977) are of more than historical interest.

Examples of the contemporary reception of some of Collins's other works are collected in Norman Page (ed.), *Wilkie Collins: the Critical Heritage* (Routledge & Kegan Paul, London, 1974), and some of the issues concerning mid-Victorian sensational fiction are discussed in David Skilton, *The Early and Mid-Victorian Novel* (Routledge, London, 1993).

A useful annotated bibliography of critical works can be found in Kirk H. Beetz, *Wilkie Collins: an Annotated Bibliography, 1889–1976* (The Scarecrow Author Bibliographies, no. 5, Scarecrow Press, Folkestone, 1978).

A NOTE ON THE TEXT

The Law and the Lady was serialized weekly in the *Graphic* from 26September 1874 to 13 March 1875, with an illustration to each instalment. Collins resisted the attempt of the Editor to bowdlerize Chapter XXXV in the interests of a family readership. The novel was published in three unillustrated volumes by Chatto & Windus in 1875. The present edition follows this three-volume edition, retaining Collins's individual habits of capitalization.

THE LAW & THE LADY

A NOVEL

BY

WILKIE COLLINS

IN THREE VOLUMES

VOL. I.

London

CHATTO AND WINDUS, PICCADILLY

1875

The Right of Translation is reserved.

NOTE:

Addressed to the Reader

In offering this book to you, I have no Preface to write. I have only to request that you will bear in mind certain established truths, which occasionally escape your memory when you are reading a work of fiction. Be pleased, then, to remember (First): That the actions of human beings are not invariably governed by the laws of pure reason. (Secondly): That we are by no means always in the habit of bestowing our love on the objects which are the most deserving of it, in the opinions of our friends. (Thirdly and Lastly): That characters which may not have appeared, and Events which may not have taken place, within the limits of our own individual experience, may nevertheless be perfectly natural Characters and perfectly probable Events, for all that. Having said these few words, I have said all that seems to be necessary at the present time, in presenting my new Story to your notice.

W. C.
LONDON, *February* 1, 1875.

CONTENTS

VOLUME I

VOLUME II

CONTENTS

VOLUME III

VOLUME I

CHAPTER I

The Bride's Mistake

'For after this manner in the old time the holy women also, who trusted in God, adorned themselves, being in subjection unto their own husbands; even as Sarah obeyed Abraham, calling him lord: whose daughters ye are as long as ye do well, and are not afraid with any amazement.'[1]

Concluding the Marriage Service of the Church of England in those well-known words, my Uncle Starkweather shut up his book, and looked at me across the altar rails with a hearty expression of interest on his broad red face. At the same time my aunt, Mrs Starkweather, standing by my side, tapped me smartly on the shoulder, and said,

'Valeria,[2] you are married!'

Where were my thoughts? What had become of my attention? I was too bewildered to know. I started and looked at my new husband. He seemed to be almost as much bewildered as I was. The same thought had, as I believe, occurred to us both at the same moment. Was it really possible – in spite of his mother's opposition to our marriage – that we were Man and Wife? My Aunt Starkweather settled the question by a second tap on my shoulder.

'Take his arm!' she whispered, in the tone of a woman who had lost all patience with me.

I took his arm.

'Follow your uncle.'

Holding fast by my husband's arm, I followed my uncle and the curate who had assisted him at the marriage.

The two clergymen led us into the vestry. The church was in one of the dreary quarters of London, situated between the City and the West End; the day was dull; the atmosphere was heavy and damp. We were a melancholy little wedding-party, worthy of the dreary neighbourhood and the dull day. No relatives or friends of my husband's were present; his family, as I have already hinted, disapproved of his marriage. Except my uncle and my aunt, no other relations appeared on my side. I had lost both my parents, and I had but few friends. My dear father's faithful old clerk, Benjamin, attended the wedding to 'give me away,' as the phrase is. He had known me from a child, and, in my forlorn position, he was as good as a father to me.

The last ceremony left to be performed was, as usual, the signing of the marriage-register. In the confusion of the moment (and in the absence of any information to guide me) I committed a mistake – ominous, in my Aunt Starkweather's opinion, of evil to come. I signed my married instead of my maiden name.

'What!' cried my uncle, in his loudest and cheeriest tones, 'you have forgotten your own name already? Well! well! let us hope you will never repent parting with it so readily. Try again, Valeria – try again.'

With trembling fingers I struck the pen through my first effort, and wrote my maiden name, very badly indeed, as follows:—

Valeria Brinton

When it came to my husband's turn I noticed, with surprise, that *his* hand trembled too, and that *he* produced a very poor specimen of his customary signature:—

Eustace Woodville

My aunt, on being requested to sign, complied under protest. 'A bad beginning!' she said, pointing to my first unfortunate signature with the feather-end of her pen. 'I say with my husband – I hope you may not live to regret it.'

Even then, in the days of my ignorance and my innocence, that curious outbreak of my aunt's superstition produced a certain uneasy sensation in my mind. It was a consolation to me to feel the reassuring pressure of my husband's hand. It was an indescribable relief to hear my uncle's hearty voice wishing me a happy life at parting. The good man had left his north-country Vicarage (my home since the death of my parents) expressly to read the service at my marriage; and he and my aunt had arranged to return by the midday train. He folded me in his great strong arms, and he gave me a kiss which must certainly have been heard by the idlers waiting for the bride and bridegroom outside the church door.

'I wish you health and happiness, my love, with all my heart. You are old enough to choose for yourself, and – no offence, Mr Woodville, you and I are new friends – and I pray God, Valeria, it may turn out that you have chosen well. Our house will be dreary enough without you; but I don't complain, my dear. On the contrary, if this change in your life makes you happier, I rejoice. Come! come! don't cry, or you will set your aunt off – and it's no joke at her time of life. Besides, crying will spoil your beauty. Dry your eyes and look in the glass there, and you will see that I am right. Goodbye, child – and God bless you!'

He tucked my aunt under his arm, and hurried out. My heart sank a little, dearly as I loved my husband, when I had seen the last of the true friend and protector of my maiden days.

The parting with old Benjamin came next. 'I wish you well, my dear; don't forget me,' was all he said. But the old days at home came back on me at those few words. Benjamin always dined with us on Sundays in my father's time, and always brought some little present with him for his master's child. I was very near to 'spoiling my beauty' (as my uncle had put it) when I offered the old man my cheek to kiss, and heard him sigh to himself, as if he too was not quite hopeful about my future life.

My husband's voice roused me, and turned my mind to happier thoughts.

'Shall we go, Valeria?' he asked.

I stopped him on our way out, to take advantage of my uncle's advice. In other words, to see how I looked in the glass over the vestry fireplace.

What does the glass show me?

The glass shows a tall and slender young woman of three-and-twenty years of age. She is not at all the sort of person who attracts attention in the street, seeing that she fails to exhibit the popular yellow hair and the popular painted cheeks. Her hair is black; dressed, in these later days (as it was dressed years since to please her father), in broad ripples drawn back from the forehead, and gathered into a simple knot behind (like the hair of the Venus de' Medici),[3] so as to show the neck beneath. Her complexion is pale: except in moments of violent agitation there is no colour to be seen in her face. Her eyes are of so dark a blue that they are generally mistaken for black. Her eyebrows are well enough in form, but they are too dark, and too strongly marked. Her nose just inclines towards the aquiline bend, and is considered a little too large by persons difficult to please in the matter of noses. The mouth, her best feature, is very delicately shaped, and is capable of presenting great varieties of expression. As to the face in general, it is too narrow and too long at the lower part; too broad and too low in the higher regions of the eyes and the head. The whole picture, as reflected in the glass, represents a woman of some elegance, rather too pale, and rather too sedate and serious in her moments of silence and repose – in short, a person who fails to strike the ordinary observer at first sight; but who gains in general estimation, on a second, and sometimes even on a third, view. As for her dress, it studiously conceals, instead of proclaiming, that she has been married that morning. She wears a grey Cashmere tunic trimmed with grey silk, and having a skirt of the same material and colour beneath it. On her head is a bonnet to match, relieved by a quilling of white muslin, with one deep red rose, as a morsel of positive colour, to complete the effect of the whole dress.

Have I succeeded or failed in describing the picture of myself which I see in the glass? It is not for me to say. I have done my best to keep clear of the two vanities – the vanity of depreciating, and the vanity of praising, my own personal appearance. For the rest, well written or badly written, thank Heaven it is done!

And whom do I see in the glass, standing by my side?

I see a man who is not quite so tall as I am and who has the misfortune of looking older than his years. His forehead is prematurely bald. His big chestnut-coloured beard and his long overhanging moustache are already streaked with grey. He has the colour in his face which my face wants, and the firmness in his figure which my figure wants. He looks at me with the tenderest and gentlest eyes (of a light brown) that I ever saw in the countenance of a man. His smile is rare and sweet; his manner, perfectly quiet and retiring, has yet a latent persuasiveness in it, which is (to women) irresistibly winning. He just halts a little in his walk, from the effect of an injury received in past years, when he was a soldier serving in India, and he carries a thick bamboo cane, with a curious crutch handle (an old favourite), to help himself along whenever he gets on his feet, indoors or out. With this one little drawback (if it *is* a drawback), there is nothing infirm or old or awkward about him; his slight limp when he walks has (perhaps to my partial eyes) a certain quaint grace of its own, which is pleasanter to see than the unrestrained activity of other men. And last, and best of all, I love him! I love him! I love him! And there is an end of my portrait of my husband on our wedding-day.

The glass has told me all I want to know. We leave the vestry at last.

The sky, cloudy since the morning, has darkened while we have been in the church, and the rain is beginning to fall heavily. The idlers outside stare at us grimly under their umbrellas, as we pass through their ranks, and hasten into our carriage. No cheering; no sunshine; no flowers strewn in our path; no grand breakfast; no genial speeches; no bridesmaids; no father's or mother's blessing. A dreary wedding – there is no denying it – and (if Aunt Starkweather is right) a bad beginning as well!

A *coupé*[4] has been reserved for us at the railway station. The attentive porter, on the look-out for his fee, pulls down the blinds over the side windows of the carriage, and shuts out all prying eyes in that way. After what seems to be an interminable delay the train starts. My husband winds his arm round me. 'At last!' he whispers, with love in his eyes that no words can utter, and presses me to him gently. My arm steals round his neck; my eyes answer his eyes. Our lips meet in the first long lingering kiss of our married life.

Oh, what recollections of that journey rise in me as I write! Let me dry my eyes, and shut up my paper for the day.

CHAPTER II

The Bride's Thoughts

We had been travelling for a little more than an hour, when a change passed insensibly over us both.

Still sitting close together, with my hand in his, with my head on his shoulder, little by little we fell insensibly into silence. Had we already exhausted the narrow yet eloquent vocabulary of love? Or had we determined by unexpressed consent, after enjoying the luxury of passion that speaks, to try the deeper and finer rapture of passion that thinks? I can hardly determine; I only know that a time came when under some strange influence our lips were closed towards each other. We travelled along, each of us absorbed in our own reverie. Was he thinking exclusively of me – as I was thinking exclusively of him? Before the journey's end I had my doubts. At a little later time I knew for certain, that his thoughts, wandering far away from his young wife, were all turned inward on his own unhappy self.

For me, the secret pleasure of filling my mind with him while I felt him by my side, was a luxury in itself.

I pictured in my thoughts our first meeting in the neighbourhood of my uncle's house.

Our famous north-country trout-stream wound its flashing and foaming way through a ravine in the rocky moorland. It was a windy, shadowy evening. A heavily clouded sunset lay low and red in the west. A solitary angler stood casting his fly, at a turn in the stream, where the backwater lay still and deep under an overhanging bank. A girl (myself) standing on the bank, invisible to the fisherman beneath, waited eagerly to see the trout rise.

The moment came; the fish took the fly.

Sometimes on the little level strip of sand at the foot of the bank; sometimes (when the stream turned again) in the shallower water rushing over its rocky bed, the angler followed the captured trout, now letting the line run out, and now winding it in again, in the difficult and delicate process of 'playing' the fish. Along the bank I followed, to watch the contest of skill and cunning between the man and the trout. I had lived long enough with my uncle Starkweather to catch some of his enthusiasm for field sports, and to learn something, especially, of the angler's art. Still following the stranger, with my eyes intently fixed on every movement of his rod and line, and with not so much as a chance fragment of my attention to spare for the rough path along which I was walking, I stepped by chance on the loose overhanging earth at the edge of the bank, and fell into the stream in an instant.

The distance was trifling; the water was shallow; the bed of the river was (fortunately for me) of sand. Beyond the fright and the wetting I had nothing to complain of. In a few moments I was out of the water and up again, very much ashamed of myself, on the firm ground. Short as the interval was, it proved long enough to favour the escape of the fish. The angler had heard my first instinctive cry of alarm, had turned, and had thrown aside his rod to help me. We confronted each other for the first time, I on the bank and he in the shallow water below. Our eyes encountered, and I verily believe our hearts encountered at the same moment. This I know for certain, we forgot our breeding as lady and gentleman; we looked at each other in barbarous silence.

I was the first to recover myself. What did I say to him?

I said something about my not being hurt, and then something more, urging him to run back, and try if he might not yet recover the fish.

He went back unwillingly. He returned to me – of course, without the fish. Knowing how bitterly disappointed my uncle would have been in his place, I apologised very earnestly. In my eagerness to make atonement I even offered to show him a spot where he might try again, lower down the stream.

He would not hear of it; he entreated me to go home and change my wet dress. I cared nothing for the wetting, but I obeyed him without knowing why.

He walked with me. My way back to the Vicarage was his way back to the inn. He had come to our parts, he told me, for the quiet and retirement as much as for the fishing. He had noticed me once or twice from the window of his room at the inn. He asked if I was not the Vicar's daughter.

I set him right. I told him that the Vicar had married my mother's sister, and that the two had been father and mother to me since the death of my parents. He asked if he might venture to call on Doctor Starkweather the next day: mentioning the name of a friend of his, with whom he believed the Vicar to be acquainted. I invited him to visit us, as if it had been my house; I was spell-bound under his eyes and under his voice. I had fancied, honestly fancied, myself to have been in love, often and often before this time. Never, in any other man's company, had I felt as I now felt in the presence of *this* man. Night seemed to fall suddenly over the evening landscape when he left me. I leaned against the Vicarage gate. I could not breathe; I could not think; my heart fluttered as if it would fly out of my bosom – and all this for a stranger! I burned with shame; but oh, in spite of it all, I was so happy!

And now, when little more than a few weeks had passed since that first meeting, I had him by my side; he was mine for life! I lifted my head from his bosom to look at him. I was like a child with a new toy – I wanted to make sure that he was really my own.

He never moved in his corner of the carriage. Was he deep in his own thoughts? and were they thoughts of Me?

I laid down my head again softly, so as not to disturb him. My mind wandered backward once more, and showed me another picture in the golden gallery of the past.

The garden at the Vicarage formed the new scene. The time was night. We had met together in secret. We were walking slowly to and fro, out of sight of the house; now in the shadowy paths of the shrubbery, now in the lovely moonlight on the open lawn.

We had long since owned our love, and devoted our lives to each other. Already our interests were one; already we shared the pleasures and the pains of life. I had gone out to meet him that night with a heavy heart, to seek comfort in his presence, and to find encouragement in his voice. He noticed that I sighed when he first took me in his arms, and he gently turned my head towards the moonlight, to read my trouble in my face. How often he had read my happiness there in the earlier days of our love!

'You bring bad news, my angel,' he said, lifting my hair tenderly from my forehead as he spoke. 'I see the lines here which tell me of anxiety and distress. I almost wish I loved you less dearly, Valeria.'

'Why?'

'I might give you back your freedom. I have only to leave this place, and your uncle would be satisfied, and you would be relieved from all the cares that are pressing on you now.'

'Don't speak of it, Eustace! If you want me to forget my cares, say you love me more dearly than ever.'

He said it in a kiss. We had a moment of exquisite forgetfulness of the hard ways of life – a moment of delicious absorption in each other. I came back to realities, fortified and composed, rewarded for all that I had gone through, ready to go through it all over again for another kiss. Only give a woman love, and there is nothing she will not venture, suffer, and do.

'Have they been raising fresh objections to our marriage?' he asked, as we slowly walked on again.

'No; they have done with objecting. They have remembered at last that I am of age, and that I can choose for myself. They have been pleading with me, Eustace, to give you up. My aunt, whom I thought rather a hard woman, has been crying – for the first time in my experience of her. My uncle, always kind and good to me, has been kinder and better than ever. He has told me that if I persist in becoming your wife I shall not be deserted on my wedding-day. Wherever we may marry he will be there to read the service, and my aunt will go to the church with me. But he entreats me to consider seriously what

I am doing – to consent to a separation from you for a time – to consult other people on my position towards you, if I am not satisfied with his opinion. Oh, my darling, they are as anxious to part us, as if you were the worst, instead of the best, of men!'

'Has anything happened since yesterday to increase their distrust of me?' he asked.

'Yes.'

'What is it?'

'You remember referring my uncle to a friend of yours and of his?'

'Yes. To Major Fitz-David.'

'My uncle has written to Major Fitz-David.'

'Why?'

He pronounced that one word in a tone so utterly unlike his natural tone that his voice sounded quite strange to me.

'You won't be angry, Eustace, if I tell you?' I said. 'My uncle, as I understood him, had several motives for writing to the Major. One of them was to enquire if he knew your mother's address.'

Eustace suddenly stood still.

I paused at the same moment, feeling that I could venture no further without the risk of offending him.

To speak the truth, his conduct, when he first mentioned our engagement to my uncle, had been (so far as appearances went) a little flighty and strange. The Vicar had naturally questioned him about his family. He had answered that his father was dead; and he had consented, though not very readily, to announce his contemplated marriage to his mother. Informing us that she too lived in the country, he had gone to see her – without more particularly mentioning her address. In two days he had returned to the Vicarage with a very startling message. His mother intended no disrespect to me or my relatives; but she disapproved so absolutely of her son's marriage that she (and the members of her family, who all agreed with her) would refuse to be present at the ceremony, if Mr Woodville persisted in keeping his engagement with Doctor Starkweather's niece. Being asked to explain this extraordinary communication, Eustace had told us that his mother and his sisters were bent on his marrying another lady, and that they were bitterly mortified and disappointed by his choosing a stranger to the family. This explanation was enough for me; it implied, so far as I was concerned, a compliment to my superior influence over Eustace, which a woman always receives with pleasure. But it failed to satisfy my uncle and my aunt. The Vicar expressed to Mr Woodville a wish to write to his mother, or to see her, on the subject of her strange message. Eustace obstinately declined to mention his mother's address, on the ground that the Vicar's interference would be utterly useless. My uncle at once drew the conclusion that the mystery about the address indicated something wrong. He refused to favour Mr Woodville's renewed proposal for my hand; and he wrote the same day to make enquiries of Mr Woodville's reference, and of his own friend – Major Fitz-David.

Under such circumstances as these, to speak of my uncle's motives was to venture on very delicate ground. Eustace relieved me from further embarrassment by asking a question to which I could easily reply.

'Has your uncle received any answer from Major Fitz-David?' he enquired.

'Yes.'

'Were you allowed to read it?' His voice sank as he said those words; his face betrayed a sudden anxiety which it pained me to see.

'I have got the answer with me to show you,' I said.

He almost snatched the letter out of my hand; he turned his back on me to read it by the light of the moon. The letter was short enough to be soon read. I could have repeated it at the time. I can repeat it now.

'DEAR VICAR, – Mr Eustace Woodville is quite correct in stating to you that he is a gentleman by birth and position, and that he inherits (under his deceased father's will) an independent fortune of two thousand a year.

'Always yours,
'LAWRENCE FITZ-DAVID.'

'Can anyone wish for a plainer answer than that?' Eustace asked, handing the letter back to me.

21

'If *I* had written for information about you,' I answered, 'it would have been plain enough for me.'

'Is it not plain enough for your uncle?'

'No.'

'What does he say?'

'Why need you care to know, my darling?'

'I want to know, Valeria. There must be no secret between us in this matter. Did your uncle say anything when he showed you the Major's letter?'

'Yes.'

'What was it?'

'My uncle told me that his letter of enquiry filled three pages, and he bade me observe that the Major's answer contained one sentence only. He said, "I volunteered to go to Major Fitz-David and talk the matter over. You see, he takes no notice of my proposal. I asked him for the address of Mr Woodville's mother. He passes over my request, as he has passed over my proposal – he studiously confines himself to the shortest possible statement of bare facts. Use your own common sense, Valeria. Isn't this rudeness rather remarkable on the part of a man who is a gentleman by birth and breeding, and who is also a friend of mine?"'

Eustace stopped me there.

'Did you answer your uncle's question?' he asked.

'No,' I replied. 'I only said that I did not understand the Major's conduct.'

'And what did your uncle say next? If you love me, Valeria, tell me the truth.'

'He used very strong language, Eustace. He is an old man; you must not be offended with him.'

'I am not offended. What did he say?'

'He said, "Mark my words! There is something under the surface in connection with Mr Woodville, or with his family, to which Major Fitz-David is not at liberty to allude. Properly interpreted, Valeria, that letter is a warning. Show it to Mr Woodville, and tell him (if you like) what I have just told you—"'

Eustace stopped me again.

'You are sure your uncle said those words?' he asked, scanning my face attentively in the moonlight.

'Quite sure. But I don't say what my uncle says. Pray don't think that!'

He suddenly pressed me to his bosom, and fixed his eyes on mine. His look frightened me.

'Goodbye, Valeria!' he said. 'Try and think kindly of me, my darling, when you are married to some happier man.'

He attempted to leave me. I clung to him in an agony of terror that shook me from head to foot.

'What do you mean?' I asked, as soon as I could speak. 'I am yours and yours only. What have I said, what have I done, to deserve those dreadful words?'

'We must part, my angel,' he answered, sadly. 'The fault is none of yours; the misfortune is all mine. My Valeria! how can you marry a man who is an object of suspicion to your nearest and dearest friends? I have led a dreary life. I have never found in any other woman the sympathy with me, the sweet comfort and companionship, that I find in you. Oh, it is hard to lose you! it is hard to go back again to my unfriended life! I must make the sacrifice, love, for your sake. I know no more why that letter is what it is than you do. Will your uncle believe me? Will your friends believe me? One last kiss, Valeria! Forgive me for having loved you – passionately, devotedly loved you. Forgive me – and let me go!'

I held him desperately, recklessly. His eyes put me beside myself; his words filled me with a frenzy of despair.

'Go where you may,' I said, 'I go with you! Friends – reputation – I care nothing who I lose, or what I lose. Oh, Eustace, I am only a woman – don't madden me! I can't live without you. I must and will be your wife!' Those wild words were all I could say before the misery and madness in me forced their way outward in a burst of sobs and tears.

He yielded. He soothed me with his charming voice; he brought me back to myself with his tender caresses. He called the bright heaven above us to witness that he devoted his whole life to me. He vowed – oh, in such solemn, such eloquent words! – that his one thought, night

23

and day, should be to prove himself worthy of such love as mine. And had he not nobly redeemed the pledge? Had not the betrothal of that memorable night been followed by the betrothal at the altar, by the vows before God? Ah, what a life was before me! What more than mortal happiness was mine!

Again, I lifted my head from his bosom to taste the dear delight of seeing him by my side – my life, my love, my husband, my own!

Hardly awakened yet from the absorbing memories of the past to the sweet realities of the present, I let my cheek touch his cheek, I whispered to him softly, 'Oh, how I love you! how I love you!'

The next instant I started back from him. My heart stood still. I put my hand up to my face. What did I feel on my cheek? (*I* had not been weeping – I was too happy.) What did I feel on my cheek? A tear!

His face was still averted from me. I turned it towards me, with my own hands, by main force.

I looked at him – and saw my husband, on our wedding-day, with his eyes full of tears.

CHAPTER III

Ramsgate Sands

Eustace succeeded in quieting my alarm. But I can hardly say that he succeeded in satisfying my mind as well.

He had been thinking, he told me, of the contrast between his past and his present life. Bitter remembrances of the years that had gone had risen in his memory, and had filled him with melancholy misgivings of his capacity to make my life with him a happy one. He had asked himself if he had not met me too late? if he was not already a man soured and broken by the disappointments and disenchantments of the past? Doubts such as these, weighing more and more heavily on his mind, had filled his eyes with the tears which I had discovered – tears which he now entreated me, by my love for him, to dismiss from my memory for ever.

I forgave him, comforted him, revived him – but there were moments when the remembrance of what I had seen troubled me in secret, and when I asked myself if I really possessed my husband's full confidence as he possessed mine.

We left the train at Ramsgate.

The favourite watering-place was empty; the season was just over. Our arrangements for the wedding-tour included a cruise to the Mediterranean in a yacht lent to Eustace by a friend. We were both fond of the sea, and we were equally desirous, considering the circumstances under which we had married, of escaping the notice of friends and acquaintances. With this object in view, having celebrated our marriage privately in London, we had decided on instructing the sailing-master of the yacht to join us at Ramsgate. At this port (when the season for visitors was at an end) we could embark far more privately than at the popular yachting stations situated in the Isle of Wight.

Three days passed – days of delicious solitude, of exquisite happiness, never to be forgotten, never to be lived over again, to the end of our lives!

Early on the morning of the fourth day, just before sunrise, a trifling incident happened, which was noticeable, nevertheless, as being strange to me in my experience of myself.

I awoke, suddenly and unaccountably, from a deep and dreamless sleep, with an all-pervading sensation of nervous uneasiness, which I had never felt before. In the old days at the Vicarage, my capacity as a sound sleeper had been the subject of many a little harmless joke. From the moment when my head was on the pillow I had never known what it was to wake until the maid knocked at my door. At all seasons and times the long and uninterrupted repose of a child was the repose that I enjoyed.

And now I had awakened, without any assignable cause, hours before my usual time. I tried to compose myself to sleep again. The effort was useless. Such a restlessness possessed me that I was not even able to lie still in the bed. My husband was sleeping soundly by my side. In the fear of disturbing him I rose, and put on my dressing-gown and slippers.

I went to the window. The sun was just rising over the calm grey sea. For a while, the majestic spectacle before me exercised a tranquillising influence on the irritable condition of my nerves. But, ere long, the old restlessness returned upon me. I walked slowly to and fro in the room, until I was weary of the monotony of the exercise. I took up a book and laid it aside again. My attention wandered; the author was powerless to recall it. I got on my feet once more, and looked at Eustace, and admired him and loved him in his tranquil sleep. I went back to the window, and wearied of the beautiful morning. I sat down before the glass, and looked at myself. How haggard and worn I was already, through waking before my usual time! I rose again, not knowing what to do next. The confinement to the four walls of the room began to be intolerable to me. I opened the door that led into my husband's dressing-room; and entered it, to try if the change would relieve me.

The first object that I noticed was his dressing-case, open on the toilette table.

I took out the bottles and pots and brushes and combs, the knives and scissors in one compartment, the writing materials in another. I smelt the perfumes and pomatums; I busily cleaned and dusted the bottles with my handkerchief as I took them out. Little by little I completely emptied the dressing-case. It was lined with blue velvet. In one corner I noticed a tiny strip of loose blue silk. Taking it between my finger and my thumb, and, drawing it upward, I discovered that there was a false bottom to the case, forming a secret compartment for letters and papers. In my strange condition – capricious, idle, inquisitive – it was an amusement to me to take out the papers, just as I had taken out everything else.

I found some receipted bills, which failed to interest me; some letters, which it is needless to say I laid aside, after only looking at the addresses; and, under all, a photograph, face downwards, with writing on the back of it. I looked at the writing, and saw these words:

'To my dear son, Eustace.'

His mother! the woman who had so obstinately and so mercilessly opposed herself to our marriage!

I eagerly turned the photograph, expecting to see a woman with a stern, ill-tempered, forbidding countenance. To my surprise, the face showed the remains of great beauty; the expression, though remarkably firm, was yet winning, tender, and kind. The grey hair was arranged in rows of little quaint old-fashioned curls on either side of the head, under a plain lace cap. At one corner of the mouth there was a mark, apparently a mole, which added to the characteristic peculiarity of the face. I looked and looked, fixing the portrait thoroughly in my mind. This woman, who had almost insulted me and my relatives, was, beyond all doubt or dispute, so far as appearances went, a person possessing unusual attractions – a person whom it would be a pleasure and a privilege to know.

I fell into deep thought. The discovery of the photograph quieted me as nothing had quieted me yet.

The striking of a clock downstairs in the hall warned me of the flight of time. I carefully put back all the objects in the dressing-case (beginning with the photograph) exactly as I had found them, and returned to the bedroom. As I looked at my husband still sleeping peacefully, the question forced itself into my mind, What had made that genial, gentle mother of his so sternly bent on parting us? so harshly and pitilessly resolute in asserting her disapproval of our marriage?

Could I put my question openly to Eustace when he woke? No; I was afraid to venture that length. It had been tacitly understood between us that we were not to speak of his mother – and, besides, he might be angry if he knew that I had opened the private compartment in his dressing-case.

After breakfast that morning we had news at last of the yacht. The vessel was safely moored in the inner harbour, and the sailing-master was waiting to receive my husband's orders on board.

Eustace hesitated at asking me to accompany him to the yacht. It would be necessary for him to examine the inventory of the vessel, and to decide questions, not very interesting to a woman, relating to charts and barometers, provisions and water. He asked me if I would wait for his return. The day was enticingly beautiful, and the tide was on the ebb. I pleaded for a walk on the sands; and the landlady at our lodgings, who happened to be in the room at the time, volunteered to accompany me and take care of me. It was agreed that we should walk as far as we felt inclined, in the direction of Broadstairs, and that Eustace should follow and meet us on the sands, after having completed his arrangements on board the yacht.

In half an hour more, the landlady and I were out on the beach.

The scene on that fine autumn morning was nothing less than enchanting. The brisk breeze, the brilliant sky, the flashing blue sea, the sun-bright cliffs and the tawny sands at their feet, the gliding procession of ships on the great marine highway of the English Channel – it was all so exhilarating, it was all so delightful, that I really believe if I had been by myself I could have danced for joy like a child. The one drawback to my happiness was the landlady's untiring tongue. She was a forward, good-natured, empty-headed woman, who persisted in talking, whether I listened or not; and who had a habit of perpetually addressing me as 'Mrs Woodville,' which I thought a little over-familiar as an assertion of equality from a person in her position to a person in mine.

We had been out, I should think, more than half-an-hour when we overtook a lady walking before us on the beach.

Just as we were about to pass the stranger she took her handkerchief from her pocket, and accidentally drew out with it a letter which fell, unnoticed by her, on the sand. I was nearest to the letter, and I picked it up and offered it to the lady.

The instant she turned to thank me, I stood rooted to the spot. There was the original of the photographic portrait in the dressing-case! there was my husband's mother, standing face to face with me! I recognised the quaint little grey curls, the gentle genial expression, the mole at the corner of the mouth. No mistake was possible. His mother herself!

The old lady, naturally enough, mistook my confusion for shyness. With perfect tact and kindness she entered into conversation with me. In another minute I was walking side by side with the woman who had sternly repudiated me as a member of her family; feeling, I own, terribly discomposed, and not knowing in the least whether I ought, or ought not, to assume the responsibility, in my husband's absence, of telling her who I was.

In another minute my familiar landlady, walking on the other side of my mother-in-law, decided the question for me. I happened to say that I supposed we must by that time be near the end of our walk – the little watering-place called Broadstairs. 'Oh, no, Mrs Woodville!' cried the irrepressible woman, calling me by my name, as usual; 'nothing like so near as you think!'

I looked with a beating heart at the old lady.

To my unutterable amazement, not the faintest gleam of recognition appeared in her face. Old Mrs Woodville went on talking to young Mrs Woodville just as composedly as if she had never heard her own name before in her life!

My face and manner must have betrayed something of the agitation that I was suffering. Happening to look at me at the end of her next sentence, the old lady started, and said in her kindly way,

'I am afraid you have over-exerted yourself. You are very pale – you are looking quite exhausted. Come and sit down here; let me lend you my smelling-bottle.'

I followed her, quite helplessly, to the base of the cliff. Some fallen fragments of chalk offered us a seat. I vaguely heard the voluble landlady's expressions of sympathy and regret; I mechanically took the smelling-bottle which my husband's mother offered to me, *after hearing my name,* as an act of kindness to a stranger.

If I had only had myself to think of, I believe I should have provoked an explanation on the spot. But I had Eustace to think of. I was entirely ignorant of the relations, hostile or friendly, which existed between his mother and himself. What could I do?

In the mean time, the old lady was still speaking to me with the most considerate sympathy. She too was fatigued, she said. She had passed a weary night at the bedside of a near relative, staying at Ramsgate. Only the day before, she had received a telegram announcing that one of her sisters was seriously ill. She was herself, thank God, still active and strong; and she had thought it her duty to start at once for Ramsgate. Towards the morning the state of the patient had improved. 'The doctor assures me, ma'am, that there is no immediate danger; and I thought it might revive me, after my long night at the bedside, if I took a little walk on the beach.'

I heard the words – I understood what they meant – but I was still too bewildered and too intimidated by my extraordinary position to be able to continue the conversation. The landlady had a sensible suggestion to make; the landlady was the next person who spoke.

'Here is a gentleman coming,' she said to me, pointing in the direction of Ramsgate. 'You can never walk back. Shall we ask him to send a chaise from Broadstairs to the gap in the cliff?'

The gentleman advanced a little nearer.

The landlady and I recognised him at the same moment. It was Eustace coming to meet us, as we had arranged. The irrepressible landlady gave the freest expression to her feelings. 'Oh, Mrs Woodville, ain't it lucky? here is Mr Woodville himself!'

Once more I looked at my mother-in-law. Once more the name failed to produce the slightest effect on her. Her sight was not so keen as ours; she had not recognised her son yet. *He* had young eyes like us, and he recognised his mother. For a moment he stopped like a man thunderstruck. Then he came on – his face white with suppressed emotion, his eyes fixed on his mother.

'You here!' he said to her.

'How do you do, Eustace?' she quietly rejoined. 'Have *you* heard of your aunt's illness, too? Did you know she was staying at Ramsgate?'

He made no answer. The landlady, drawing the inevitable inference from the words that she had just heard, looked from me to my mother-in-law in a state of amazement, which paralysed even *her* tongue. I waited, with my eyes on my husband, to see what he would do. If he had delayed acknowledging me another moment, the whole future course of my life might have been altered – I should have despised him.

He did *not* delay. He came to my side and took my hand.

'Do you know who this is?' he said to his mother.

She answered, looking at me with a courteous bend of her head:

'A lady I met on the beach, Eustace, who kindly restored to me a letter that I dropped. I think I heard the name' (she turned to the landlady): 'Mrs Woodville, was it not?'

My husband's fingers unconsciously closed on my hand with a grasp that hurt me. He set his mother right, it is only just to say, without one cowardly moment of hesitation.

'Mother,' he said to her, very quietly, 'this lady is my wife.'

She had hitherto kept her seat. She now rose slowly and faced her son in silence. The first expression of surprise passed from her face. It was succeeded by the most terrible look of mingled indignation and contempt that I ever saw in a woman's eyes.

'I pity your wife,' she said.

With those words, and no more, lifting her hand she waved him back from her, and went on her way again, as we had first found her, alone.

CHAPTER IV

On the Way Home

Left by ourselves, there was a moment of silence amongst us. Eustace spoke first.

'Are you able to walk back?' he said to me. 'Or shall we go on to Broadstairs, and return to Ramsgate by the railway?'

He put those questions as composedly, so far as his manner was concerned, as if nothing remarkable had happened. But his eyes and his lips betrayed him. They told me that he was suffering keenly in secret. The extraordinary scene that had just passed, far from depriving me of the last remains of my courage, had strung up my nerves and restored my self-possession. I must have been more or less than woman if my self-respect had not been wounded, if my curiosity had not been wrought to the highest pitch, by the extraordinary conduct of my husband's mother when Eustace presented me to her. What was the secret of her despising him, and pitying me? Where was the explanation

31

of her incomprehensible apathy when my name was twice pronounced in her hearing? Why had she left us, as if the bare idea of remaining in our company was abhorrent to her? The foremost interest of my life was now the interest of penetrating these mysteries. Walk? I was in such a fever of expectation that I felt as if I could have walked to the world's end, if I could only keep my husband by my side, and question him on the way!

'I am quite recovered,' I said. 'Let us go back, as we came, on foot.'

Eustace glanced at the landlady. The landlady understood him.

'I won't intrude my company on you sir,' she said, sharply. 'I have some business to do at Broadstairs – and, now I am so near, I may as well go on. Good morning, Mrs Woodville.'

She laid a marked emphasis on my name; and she added one significant look at parting, which (in the preoccupied state of my mind at that moment) I entirely failed to comprehend. There was neither time nor opportunity to ask her what she meant. With a stiff little bow, addressed to Eustace, she left us as his mother had left us; taking the way to Broadstairs, and walking rapidly.

At last, we were alone.

I lost no time in beginning my enquiries; I wasted no words in prefatory phrases. In the plainest terms, I put the question to him:

'What does your mother's conduct mean?'

Instead of answering, he burst into a fit of laughter – loud, coarse, hard laughter, so utterly unlike any sound I had ever yet heard issue from his lips, so strangely and shockingly foreign to his character as *I* understood it, that I stood still on the sands, and openly remonstrated with him.

'Eustace! you are not like yourself,' I said. 'You almost frighten me.'

He took no notice. He seemed to be pursuing some pleasant train of thought just started in his mind.

'So like my mother!' he exclaimed, with the air of a man who felt irresistibly diverted by some humorous idea of his own. 'Tell me all about it, Valeria!'

'Tell *you*?' I repeated. 'After what has happened, surely it is your duty to enlighten *me*.'

'You don't see the joke?' he said.

'I not only fail to see the joke,' I rejoined, 'I see something in your mother's language and your mother's behaviour which justifies me in asking you for a serious explanation.'

'My dear Valeria! if you understood my mother as well as I do, a serious explanation of her conduct would be the last thing in the world that you would expect from me. The idea of taking my mother seriously!' He burst out laughing again. 'My darling! you don't know how you amuse me.'

It was all forced; it was all unnatural. He, the most delicate, the most refined of men – a gentleman in the highest sense of the word – was coarse and loud and vulgar! My heart sank under a sudden sense of misgiving which, with all my love for him, it was impossible to resist. In unutterable distress and alarm I asked myself: 'Is my husband beginning to deceive me? is he acting a part, and acting it badly, before we have been married a week?'

I set myself to win his confidence in a new way. He was evidently determined to force his own point of view on me. I determined, on my side, to accept his point of view.

'You tell me I don't understand your mother,' I said, gently. 'Will you help me to understand her?'

'It is not easy to help you to understand a woman who doesn't understand herself,' he answered. 'But I will try. The key to my poor dear mother's character is, in one word – Eccentricity.'

If he had picked out the most inappropriate word in the whole Dictionary to describe the lady whom I had met on the beach, 'Eccentricity' would have been that word. A child who had seen what I saw, who had heard what I heard, would have discovered that he was trifling – grossly, recklessly trifling – with the truth.

'Bear in mind what I have said,' he proceeded; 'and, if you want to understand my mother, do what I asked you to do a minute since – tell me all about it. How came you to speak to her, to begin with?'

'Your mother told you, Eustace. I was walking just behind her, when she dropped a letter by accident—'

'No accident,' he interposed. 'The letter was dropped on purpose.'

'Impossible!' I exclaimed. 'Why should your mother drop the letter on purpose?'

'Use the key to her character, my dear. Eccentricity! My mother's odd way of making acquaintance with you.'

'Making acquaintance with me? I have just told you that I was walking behind her. She could not have known of the existence of such a person as myself until I spoke to her first.'

'So you suppose, Valeria.'

'I am certain of it.'

'Pardon me – you don't know my mother as I do.'

I began to lose all patience with him.

'Do you mean to tell me,' I said, 'that your mother was out on the sands to-day for the express purpose of making acquaintance with Me?'

'I have not the slightest doubt of it,' he answered, coolly.

'Why she didn't even recognise my name!' I burst out. 'Twice over, the landlady called me Mrs Woodville in your mother's hearing – and, twice over, I declare to you on my word of honour, it failed to produce the slightest impression on her. She looked, and acted, as if she had never heard her own name before in her life.'

' "Acted" is the right word,' he said, just as composedly as before. 'The women on the stage are not the only women who can act. My mother's object was to make herself thoroughly acquainted with you, and to throw you off your guard by speaking in the character of a stranger. It is so like her to take that roundabout way of satisfying her curiosity about a daughter-in-law whom she disapproves of! If I had not joined you when I did, you would have been examined and cross-examined about yourself and about me; and you would inno-cently have answered under the impression that you were speaking to a chance acquaintance. There is my mother all over! She is your enemy, remember – not your friend: she is not in search of your merits but of your faults. And you wonder why no impression was produced on her when she heard you addressed by your name! Poor innocent! I can tell you this – you only discovered my mother in her own character, when I put an end to the mystification by presenting you to each other. You saw how angry she was; and now you know why.'

I let him go on without saying a word. I listened – oh, with such a heavy heart! with such a crushing sense of disenchantment and despair!

The idol of my worship; the companion, guide, protector of my life – had he fallen so low? could he stoop to such shameless prevarication as this?

Was there one word of truth in all that he had said to me? Yes! If I had not discovered his mother's portrait, it was certainly true that I should not have known, not even vaguely suspected, who she really was. Apart from this, the rest was lying; clumsy lying which said one thing at least for him, that he was not accustomed to falsehood and deceit. Good Heavens – if my husband was to be believed, his mother must have tracked us to London; tracked us to the church; tracked us to the railway station; tracked us to Ramsgate! To assert that she knew me by sight as the wife of Eustace, and that she had waited on the sands, and dropped her letter for the express purpose of making acquaintance with me, was also to assert every one of these monstrous improbabilities to be facts that had actually happened!

I could say no more. I walked by his side in silence, feeling the miserable conviction that there was an abyss in the shape of a family secret between my husband and me. In the spirit, if not in the body, we were separated – after a married life of barely four days!

'Valeria,' he asked, 'have you nothing to say to me?'

'Nothing.'

'Are you not satisfied with my explanation?'

I detected a slight tremor in his voice as he put that question. The tone was, for the first time since we had spoken together, a tone that my experience associated with him in certain moods of his which I had already learnt to know well. Among the hundred thousand mysterious influences which a man exercises over the woman who loves him, I doubt if there is any more irresistible to her than the influence of his voice. I am not one of those women who shed tears on the smallest provocation: it is not in my temperament, I suppose. But when I heard that little natural change in his tone, my mind went back (I can't say why) to the happy day when I first owned that I loved him. I burst out crying.

He suddenly stood still, and took me by the hand. He tried to look at me.

I kept my head down and my eyes on the ground. I was ashamed of my weakness and my want of spirit. I was determined not to look at him.

In the silence that followed, he suddenly dropped on his knees at my feet, with a cry of despair that cut through me like a knife.

'Valeria! I am vile – I am false – I am unworthy of you. Don't believe a word of what I have been saying – lies, lies, cowardly contemptible lies! You don't know what I have gone through; you don't know how I have been tortured. Oh, my darling, try not to despise me! I must have been beside myself when I spoke to you as I did. You looked hurt; you looked offended; I didn't know what to do. I wanted to spare you even a moment's pain – I wanted to hush it up, and have done with it. For God's sake don't ask me to tell you any more! My love! my angel! it's something between my mother and me; it's nothing that need disturb you, it's nothing to anybody now. I love you, I adore you; my whole heart and soul are yours. Be satisfied with that. Forget what has happened. You shall never see my mother again. We will leave this place to-morrow. We will go away in the yacht. Does it matter where we live, so long as we live for each other? Forgive and forget! Oh, Valeria, Valeria, forgive and forget!'

Unutterable misery was in his face; unutterable misery was in his voice. Remember this. And remember that I loved him.

'It is easy to forgive,' I said, sadly. 'For your sake, Eustace, I will try to forget.'

I raised him gently as I spoke. He kissed my hands, with the air of a man who was too humble to venture on any more familiar expression of his gratitude than that. The sense of embarrassment between us, as we slowly walked on again, was so unendurable that I actually cast about in my mind for a subject of conversation as if I had been in the company of a stranger! In mercy to *him*, I asked him to tell me about the yacht.

He seized on the subject as a drowning man seizes on the hand that rescues him.

On that one poor little topic of the yacht, he talked, talked, talked, as if his life depended upon his not being silent for an instant on the rest of the way back. To me, it was dreadful to hear him. I could estimate what he was suffering, by the violence which he – ordinarily a silent and thoughtful man – was now doing to his true nature and to the prejudices and habits of his life. With the greatest difficulty I preserved my self-control, until we reached the door of our lodgings. There, I was obliged to plead fatigue, and ask him to let me rest for a little while in the solitude of my own room.

'Shall we sail to-morrow?' he called after me suddenly, as I ascended the stairs.

Sail with him to the Mediterranean the next day? Pass weeks and weeks absolutely alone with him, in the narrow limits of a vessel, with his horrible secret parting us in sympathy further and further from each other day by day? I shuddered at the thought of it.

'To-morrow is rather a short notice,' I said. 'Will you give me a little longer time to prepare for the voyage?'

'Oh, yes – take any time you like,' he answered, not (as I thought) very willingly. 'While you are resting – there are still one or two little things to be settled – I think I will go back to the yacht. Is there anything I can do for you, Valeria, before I go?'

'Nothing – thank you, Eustace.'

He hastened away to the harbour. Was he afraid of his own thoughts, if he were left by himself in the house? Was the company of the sailing-master and the steward better than no company at all?

It was useless to ask. What did I know about him or his thoughts? I locked myself into my room.

CHAPTER V

The Landlady's Discovery

I sat down, and tried to compose my spirits. Now, or never, was the time to decide what it was my duty to my husband and my duty to myself to do next.

The effort was beyond me. Worn out in mind and body alike, I was perfectly incapable of pursuing any regular train of thought. I vaguely felt – if I left things as they were – that I could never hope to remove the shadow which now rested on the married life that had begun so brightly. We might live together, so as to save appearances. But to forget what had happened, or to feel satisfied with my position, was beyond the power of my will. My tranquillity as a woman – perhaps my dearest interests as a wife – depended absolutely on penetrating the mystery of my mother-in-law's conduct, and on discovering the true meaning of the wild words of penitence and self-reproach which my husband had addressed to me on our way home.

So far I could advance towards realising my position – and no farther. When I asked myself what was to be done next, hopeless confusion, maddening doubt, filled my mind, and transformed me into the most listless and helpless of living women.

I gave up the struggle. In dull, stupid, obstinate despair, I threw myself on my bed, and fell, from sheer fatigue, into a broken, uneasy sleep.

I was awakened by a knock at the door of my room.

Was it my husband? I started to my feet as the idea occurred to me. Was some new trial of my patience and my fortitude at hand? Half nervously, half irritably, I asked who was there.

The landlady's voice answered me.

'Can I speak to you for a moment, if you please?'

I opened the door. There is no disguising it – though I loved him so dearly; though I had left home and friends for his sake – it was a relief to me, at that miserable time, to know that Eustace had not returned to the house.

The landlady came in, and took a seat, without waiting to be invited, close by my side. She was no longer satisfied with merely asserting herself as my equal. Ascending another step on the social ladder, she took her stand on the platform of patronage, and charitably looked down on me as an object of pity.

'I have just returned from Broadstairs,' she began. 'I hope you will do me the justice to believe that I sincerely regret what has happened?'

I bowed, and said nothing.

'As a gentlewoman myself,' proceeded the landlady – 'reduced by family misfortunes to let lodgings, but still a gentlewoman – I feel sincere sympathy with you. I will even go further than that. I will take it on myself to say that I don't blame *you*. No, no. I noticed that you were as much shocked and surprised at your mother-in-law's conduct as I was; and that is saying a great deal, a great deal indeed. However, I have a duty to perform. It is disagreeable, but it is not the less a duty on that account. I am a single woman; not from want of opportunities of changing my condition – I beg you will understand that – but from choice. Situated as I am, I receive only the most respectable persons into my house. There must be no mystery about the positions of *my* lodgers. Mystery in the position of a lodger carries with it – what shall I say? I don't wish to offend you – I will say, a certain Taint. Very well. Now I put it to your own common sense. Can a person in my position be expected to expose herself to – Taint? I make these remarks in a sisterly and Christian spirit. As a lady yourself (I will even go the length of saying a cruelly-used lady) you will, I am sure, understand—'

I could endure it no longer. I stopped her there.

'I understand,' I said, 'that you wish to give us notice to quit your lodgings. When do you want us to go?'

The landlady held up a long, lean, red hand, in sorrowful and sisterly protest.

'No,' she said. 'Not that tone! not those looks! It's natural you should be annoyed; it's natural you should be angry. But do – now do please try and control yourself. I put it to your own common sense (we will say a week for the notice to quit) – why not treat me like a friend? You don't know what a sacrifice, what a cruel sacrifice, I have made – entirely for your sake.'

'You!' I exclaimed. 'What sacrifice?'

'What sacrifice?' repeated the landlady. 'I have degraded myself as a gentlewoman. I have forfeited my own self-respect.' She paused for a moment, and suddenly seized me by the hand, in a perfect frenzy of friendship. 'Oh, my poor dear,' cried this intolerable person, 'I have discovered everything! A villain has deceived you. You are no more married than I am!'

I snatched my hand out of hers, and rose angrily from my chair.

'Are you mad?' I asked.

The landlady raised her eyes to the ceiling, with the air of a person who had deserved martyrdom, and who submitted to it cheerfully.

'Yes,' she said. 'I begin to think I *am* mad – mad to have devoted myself to an ungrateful woman, to a person who doesn't appreciate a sisterly and Christian sacrifice of self. Well! I won't do it again. Heaven forgive me – I won't do it again!'

'Do what again?' I asked.

'Follow your mother-in-law,' cried the landlady, suddenly dropping the character of a martyr, and assuming the character of a vixen in its place. 'I blush when I think of it. I followed that most respectable person every step of the way to her own door.'

Thus far, my pride had held me up. It sustained me no longer. I dropped back again into my chair, in undisguised dread of what was coming next.

'I gave you a look when I left you on the beach,' pursued the landlady; growing louder and louder, and redder and redder as she went on. 'A grateful woman would have understood that look. Never mind! I won't do it again. I overtook your mother-in-law at the gap in the cliff. I followed her – oh, how I feel the disgrace of it *now*! – I followed her to the station at Broadstairs. She went back by train to Ramsgate. *I* went back by train to Ramsgate. She walked to her lodgings. *I* walked to her lodgings. Behind her. Like a dog. Oh, the disgrace of it! Providentially as I then thought – I don't know what to think of it now – the landlord of the house happened to be a friend of mine, and happened to be at home. We have no secrets from each other, where lodgers are concerned. I am in a position to tell you, madam, what your mother-in-law's name really is. She knows nothing about any such person as Mrs Woodville, for an excellent reason. Her name is *not* Woodville. Her name (and consequently her son's name) is Macallan. Mrs Macallan, widow of the late General Macallan. Yes! your husband is *not* your husband. You are neither maid, wife, nor widow. You are worse than nothing, madam – and you leave my house.'

I stopped her as she opened the door to go out. She had roused *my* temper by this time. The doubt that she had cast on my marriage was more than mortal resignation could endure.

'Give me Mrs Macallan's address,' I said.

The landlady's anger receded into the background, and the land-lady's astonishment appeared in its place.

'You don't mean to tell me you are going to the old lady yourself?' she said.

'Nobody but the old lady can tell me what I want to know,' I answered. 'Your discovery (as you call it) may be enough for *you*; it is not enough for *me*. How do we know that Mrs Macallan may not have been twice married; and that her first husband's name may not have been Woodville?'

The landlady's astonishment subsided in its turn, and the landlady's curiosity succeeded as the ruling influence of the moment. Substantially, as I have already said of her, she was a goodnatured woman. Her fits of temper (as is usual with goodnatured people) were of the hot and the short-lived sort; easily roused and easily appeased.

'Stop a bit!' she stipulated. 'If I give you the address, will you promise to tell me everything your mother-in-law says to you when you come back?'

I gave the required promise, and received the address in return.

'No malice,' said the landlady, suddenly resuming all her old familiarity with me.

'No malice,' I answered, with all possible cordiality on my side.

In ten minutes more I was at my mother-in-law's lodgings.

CHAPTER VI

My Own Discovery

Fortunately for me, the landlord did not open the door when I rang. A stupid maid-of-all-work, who never thought of asking me for my name, let me in. Mrs Macallan was at home, and had no visitors with her. Giving me this information, the maid led the way upstairs, and showed me into the drawing-room without a word of announcement.

My mother-in-law was sitting alone, near a work-table, knitting.

The moment I appeared in the doorway, she laid aside her work; and, rising, signed to me with a commanding gesture of her hand to let her speak first.

'I know what you have come for,' she said. 'You have come here to ask questions. Spare yourself, and spare me. I warn you beforehand that I will not answer any questions relating to my son.'

It was firmly, but not harshly, said. I spoke firmly in my turn.

'I have not come here, madam, to ask questions about your son,' I answered. 'I have come – if you will excuse me – to ask you a question about yourself.'

She started, and looked at me keenly over her spectacles. I had evidently taken her by surprise.

'What is the question?' she enquired.

'I now know for the first time, madam, that your name is Macallan,' I said. 'Your son has married me under the name of Woodville. The only honourable explanation of this circumstance, so far as I know, is that my husband is your son by a first marriage. The happiness of my life is at stake. Will you kindly consider my position? Will you let me ask if you have been twice married, and if the name of your first husband was Woodville?'

She considered a little before she replied.

'The question is a perfectly natural one, in your position,' she said. 'But I think I had better not answer it.'

'May I ask why?'

'Certainly. If I answered you, I should only lead to other questions; and I should be obliged to decline replying to them. I am sorry to disappoint you. I repeat what I said on the beach – I have no other feeling than a feeling of sympathy towards *you*. If you had consulted me before your marriage, I should willingly have admitted you to my fullest confidence. It is now too late. You are married. I recommend you to make the best of your position, and to rest satisfied with things as they are.'

'Pardon me, madam,' I remonstrated. 'As things are, I don't know that I *am* married. All I know, unless you enlighten me, is that your son has married me under a name that is not his own. How can I be sure whether I am, or am not, his lawful wife?'

'I believe there can be no doubt that you are lawfully my son's wife,' Mrs Macallan answered. 'At any rate it is easy to take a legal opinion on the subject. If the opinion is that you are *not* lawfully married, my son (whatever his faults and failings may be) is a gentleman. He is incapable of wilfully deceiving a woman who loves and trusts him; he will do you justice. On my side, I will do you justice too. If the legal opinion is adverse to your rightful claims, I will promise to answer any questions which you may choose to put to me. As it is, I believe you to be lawfully my son's wife; and I say again, make the best of your position. Be satisfied with your husband's affectionate devotion to you. If you value your peace of mind, and the happiness of your life to come, abstain from attempting to know more than you know now.'

She sat down again with the air of a woman who had said her last word.

Further remonstrance would be useless – I could see it in her face; I could hear it in her voice. I turned round to open the drawing-room door.

'You are hard on me, madam,' I said, at parting. 'I am at your mercy, and I must submit.'

She suddenly looked up, and answered me with a flush on her kind and handsome old face.

'As God is my witness, child, I pity you from the bottom of my heart!'

After that extraordinary outburst of feeling, she took up her work with one hand, and signed to me with the other to leave her.

I bowed to her in silence, and went out.

I had entered the house, far from feeling sure of the course I ought to take in the future. I left the house, positively resolved, come what might of it, to discover the secret which the mother and son were hiding from me. As to the question of the name, I saw it now in the light in which I ought to have seen it from the first. If Mrs Macallan *had* been twice married (as I had rashly chosen to suppose) she would certainly have shown some signs of recognition, when she heard me addressed by her first husband's name. Where all else was mystery, there was no mystery here. Whatever his reasons might be, Eustace had assuredly married me under an assumed name.

Approaching the door of our lodgings, I saw my husband walking backwards and forwards before it, evidently waiting for my return. If he asked me the question, I decided to tell him frankly where I had been, and what had passed between his mother and myself.

He hurried to meet me with signs of disturbance in his face and manner.

'I have a favour to ask of you, Valeria,' he said. 'Do you mind returning with me to London by the next train?'

I looked at him. In the popular phrase, I could hardly believe my own ears.

'It's a matter of business,' he went on, 'of no interest to any one but myself; and it requires my presence in London. You don't wish to sail just yet, as I understand? I can't leave you here by yourself. Have you any objection to going to London for a day or two?'

I made no objection. I too was eager to go back.

In London, I could obtain the legal opinion which would tell me whether I was lawfully married to Eustace or not. In London, I should be within reach of the help and advice of my father's faithful old clerk. I could confide in Benjamin as I could confide in no one else. Dearly as I loved my uncle Starkweather, I shrank from communicating with him in my present need. His wife had told me that I had made a bad beginning, when I signed the wrong name in the marriage register. Shall I own it? My pride shrank from acknowledging, before the honeymoon was over, that his wife was right.

In two hours more we were on the railway again. Ah, what a contrast that second journey presented to the first! On our way to Ramsgate, everybody could see that we were a newly-wedded couple. On our way to London, nobody noticed us; nobody would have doubted that we had been married for years.

We went to a private hotel in the neighbourhood of Portland Place.

After breakfast, the next morning, Eustace announced that he must leave me to attend to his business. I had previously mentioned to him that I had some purchases to make in London. He was quite willing to let me go out alone – on the condition that I should take a carriage provided by the hotel.

My heart was heavy that morning: I felt the unacknowledged estrangement that had grown up between us very keenly. My husband opened the door to go out – and came back to kiss me before he left me by myself. That little afterthought of tenderness touched me. Acting on the impulse of the moment, I put my arm round his neck, and held him to me gently.

'My darling,' I said, 'give me all your confidence. I know that you love me. Show that you can trust me too.'

He sighed bitterly, and drew back from me – in sorrow, not in anger.

'I thought we had agreed, Valeria, not to return to that subject again,' he said. 'You only distress yourself and distress me.'

He left the room abruptly, as if he dare not trust himself to say more. It is better not to dwell on what I felt after this last repulse. I ordered the carriage at once. I was eager to find a refuge from my own thoughts in movement and change.

I drove to the shops first, and made the purchases which I had mentioned to Eustace by way of giving a reason for going out. Then I devoted myself to the object which I really had at heart. I went to old Benjamin's little villa, in the byeways of St John's Wood.

As soon as he had got over the first surprise of seeing me, he noticed that I looked pale and careworn. I confessed at once that I was in trouble. We sat down together by the bright fire-side in his little library (Benjamin, as far as his means would allow, was a great collector of books) – and there I told my old friend, frankly and truly, all that I have told here.

He was too distressed to say much. He fervently pressed my hand; he fervently thanked God that my father had not lived to hear what he had heard. Then, after a pause, he repeated my mother-in-law's name to himself, in a doubting, questioning tone.

'Macallan?' he said. 'Macallan? Where have I heard that name? Why does it sound as if it wasn't strange to me?'

He gave up pursuing the lost recollection, and asked, very earnestly, what he could do for me. I answered that he could help me in the first place to put an end to the doubt – an unendurable doubt to *me* – whether I was lawfully married or not. His energy of the old days, when he had conducted my father's business, showed itself again, the moment I said those words.

'Your carriage is at the door, my dear,' he answered. 'Come with me to my own lawyer, without wasting another moment.'

We drove to Lincoln's Inn Fields.

At my request, Benjamin put my case to the lawyer, as the case of a friend in whom I was interested. The answer was given without hesitation. I had married, honestly believing my husband's name to be the name under which I had known him. The witnesses to my marriage – my uncle, my aunt, and Benjamin – had acted, as I had acted, in perfect good faith. Under those circumstances, there was no doubt about the law. I was legally married. Macallan or Woodville, I was his wife.

This decisive answer relieved me of a heavy anxiety. I accepted my old friend's invitation to return with him to St John's Wood, and to make my luncheon at his early dinner.

On our way back I reverted to the one other subject which was now uppermost in my mind. I reiterated my resolution to discover why Eustace had not married me under the name that was really his own.

My companion shook his head, and entreated me to consider well beforehand what I proposed doing. His advice to me – so strangely do extremes meet! – was my mother-in-law's advice, repeated almost word for word. 'Leave things as they are, my dear. In the interest of your own peace of mind, be satisfied with your husband's affection. You know that you are his wife, and you know that he loves you. Surely that is enough?'

I had but one answer to this. Life, on such conditions as my good friend had just stated, would be simply unendurable to me. Nothing could alter my resolution – for this plain reason, that nothing could reconcile me to living with my husband on the terms on which we were living now. It only rested with Benjamin to say whether he would give a helping hand to his master's daughter or not.

The old man's answer was thoroughly characteristic of him.

'Mention what you want of me, my dear,' was all he said.

We were then passing a street in the neighbourhood of Portman Square. I was on the point of speaking again, when the words were suspended on my lips. I saw my husband.

He was just descending the steps of a house – as if leaving it after a visit. His eyes were on the ground: he did not look up when the carriage passed. As the servant closed the door behind him, I noticed that the number of the house was sixteen. At the next corner I saw the name of the street. It was Vivian Place.

'Do you happen to know who lives at number sixteen, Vivian Place?' I enquired of my companion.

Benjamin started. My question was certainly a strange one, after what he had just said to me.

'No,' he replied. 'Why do you ask?'

'I have just seen Eustace, leaving that house.'

'Well, my dear, and what of that?'

'My mind is in a bad way, Benjamin. Everything my husband does that I don't understand, rouses my suspicion now.'

Benjamin lifted his withered old hands, and let them drop on his knees again in mute lamentation over me.

'I tell you again,' I went on, 'my life is unendurable to me. I won't answer for what I may do, if I am left much longer to live in doubt of the one man on earth whom I love. You have had experience of the world. Suppose you were shut out from Eustace's confidence, as I am? Suppose you were as fond of him as I am, and felt your position as bitterly as I feel it – what would you do?'

The question was plain. Benjamin met it with a plain answer.

'I think I should find my way, my dear, to some intimate friend of your husband's,' he said, 'and make a few discreet enquiries in that quarter first.'

Some intimate friend of my husband's? I considered with myself. There was but one friend of his whom I knew of – my uncle's correspondent, Major Fitz-David. My heart beat fast as the name recurred to my memory. Suppose I followed Benjamin's advice? Suppose I applied to Major Fitz-David? Even if he too refused to answer my questions, my position would not be more helpless than it was now. I determined to make the attempt. The only difficulty in the way, so far, was to discover the Major's address. I had given back his letter to Doctor Starkweather, at my uncle's own request; I remembered that the address from which the Major wrote was somewhere in London; and I remembered no more.

'Thank you, old friend; you have given me an idea already,' I said to Benjamin. 'Have you got a Directory in your house?'

'No, my dear,' he rejoined, looking very much puzzled. 'But I can easily send out and borrow one.'

We returned to the villa. The servant was sent at once to the nearest stationer's to borrow a Directory. She returned with the book, just as we sat down to dinner. Searching for the Major's name, under the letter F, I was startled by a new discovery.

'Benjamin!' I said. 'This is a strange coincidence. Look here!'

He looked where I pointed. Major Fitz-David's address was Number Sixteen, Vivian Place – the very house which I had seen my husband leaving as we passed in the carriage!

CHAPTER VII

On the Way to the Major

'Yes,' said Benjamin. 'It *is* a coincidence certainly. Still—'

He stopped and looked at me. He seemed a little doubtful how I might receive what he had it in his mind to say to me next.

'Go on,' I said.

'Still, my dear, I see nothing suspicious in what has happened,' he resumed. 'To my mind, it is quite natural that your husband, being in London, should pay a visit to one of his friends. And it's equally natural that we should pass through Vivian Place, on our way back here. This seems to be the reasonable view. What do *you* say?'

'I have told you already that my mind is in a bad way about Eustace,' I answered. '*I* say there is some motive at the bottom of his visit to

Major Fitz-David. It is not an ordinary call. I am firmly convinced it is not an ordinary call!'

'Suppose we get on with our dinner?' said Benjamin, resignedly. 'Here is a loin of mutton, my dear – an ordinary loin of mutton. Is there anything suspicious in *that*? Very well, then. Show me you have confidence in the mutton; please eat. There's the wine, again. No mystery, Valeria, in that claret – I'll take my oath it's nothing but innocent juice of the grape. If we can't believe in anything else, let's believe in juice of the grape. Your good health, my dear.'

I adapted myself to the old man's genial humour as readily as I could. We ate and we drank, and we talked of bygone days. For a little while I was almost happy in the company of my fatherly old friend. Why was I not old too? Why had I not done with love – with its certain miseries; its transient delights; its cruel losses; its bitterly doubtful gains? The last autumn flowers in the window basked brightly in the last of the autumn sunlight. Benjamin's little dog digested his dinner in perfect comfort on the hearth. The parrot in the next house screeched his vocal accomplishments cheerfully. I don't doubt that it is a great privilege to be a human being. But may it not be the happier destiny to be an animal or a plant?

The brief respite was soon over; all my anxieties came back. I was once more a doubting, discontented, depressed creature, when I rose to say goodbye.

'Promise, my dear, you will do nothing rash,' said Benjamin, as he opened the door for me.

'Is it rash to go to Major Fitz-David?' I asked.

'Yes – if you go by yourself. You don't know what sort of man he is; you don't know how he may receive you. Let me try first, and pave the way, as the saying is. Trust my experience, my dear. In matters of this sort there is nothing like paving the way.'

I considered a moment. It was due to my good friend to consider before I said No.

Reflection decided me on taking the responsibility, whatever it might be, upon my own shoulders. Good or bad, compassionate or cruel, the Major was a man. A woman's influence was the safest influence to trust with him – where the end to be gained was such an end as I had in view. It was not easy to say this to Benjamin, without the danger of mortifying him. I made an appointment with the old man to call on me the next morning at the hotel, and talk the matter over again. Is it very disgraceful to me to add, that I privately determined (if the thing could be accomplished) to see Major Fitz-David in the interval?

'Do nothing rash, my dear. In your own interests, do nothing rash!'

Those were Benjamin's last words, when we parted for the day.

I found Eustace waiting for me in our sitting-room at the hotel. His spirits seemed to have revived since I had seen him last. He advanced to meet me cheerfully, with an open sheet of paper in his hand.

'My business is settled, Valeria, sooner than I had expected,' he began, gaily. 'Are your purchases all completed, fair lady? Are *you* free, too?'

I had learnt already (God help me!) to distrust his fits of gaiety. I asked cautiously,

'Do you mean free for to-day?'

'Free for to-day, and to-morrow, and next week, and next month – and next year, too, for all I know to the contrary,' he answered, putting his arm boisterously round my waist. 'Look here!'

He lifted the open sheet of paper which I had noticed in his hand, and held it for me to read. It was a telegram to the sailing master of the yacht; informing him that we had arranged to return to Ramsgate that evening, and that we should be ready to sail for the Mediterranean with the next tide.

'I only waited for your return,' said Eustace, 'to send the telegram to the office.'

He crossed the room, as he spoke, to ring the bell. I stopped him.

'I am afraid I can't go to Ramsgate to-day,' I said.

'Why not?' he asked, suddenly changing his tone and speaking sharply.

I dare say it will seem ridiculous to some people – but it is really true that he shook my resolution to go to Major Fitz-David, when he put his arm round me. Even a mere passing caress, from *him*, stole away my heart, and softly tempted me to yield. But the ominous alteration in his tone made another woman of me. I felt once more, and felt more strongly than ever, that, in my critical position, it was useless to stand still, and worse than useless to draw back.

'I am sorry to disappoint you,' I answered. 'It is impossible for me (as I told you at Ramsgate) to be ready to sail at a moment's notice. I want time.'

'What for?'

Not only his tone, but his look, when he put that second question, jarred on every nerve in me. He roused in my mind – I can't tell how or why – an angry sense of the indignity that he had put upon his wife in marrying her under a false name. Fearing that I should answer rashly, that I should say something which my better sense might regret, if I spoke at that moment, I said nothing. Women alone can estimate what it cost me to be silent. And men alone can understand how irritating my silence must have been to my husband.

'You want time?' he repeated. 'I ask you again – what for?'

My self-control, pushed to its extremest limits, failed me. The rash reply flew out of my lips, like a bird set free from a cage.

'I want time,' I said, 'to accustom myself to my right name.'

He suddenly stepped up to me with a dark look.

'What do you mean by your "right name"?'

'Surely you know,' I answered. 'I once thought I was Mrs Woodville. I have now discovered that I am Mrs Macallan.'

He started back at the sound of his own name, as if I had struck him – he started back and turned so deadly pale that I feared he was going to drop at my feet in a swoon. Oh, my tongue! my tongue! Why had I not controlled my miserable, mischievous woman's tongue?

'I didn't mean to alarm you, Eustace,' I said. 'I spoke at random. Pray forgive me.'

He waved his hand impatiently, as if my penitent words were tangible things – ruffling, worrying things like flies in summer – which he was putting away from him.

'What else have you discovered?' he asked, in low, stern tones.

'Nothing, Eustace.'

'Nothing?' He paused as he repeated the word, and passed his hand over his forehead in a weary way. 'Nothing, of course,' he resumed, speaking to himself, 'or she would not be here.'

He paused once more, and looked at me searchingly. 'Don't say again what you said just now,' he went on. 'For your own sake, Valeria, as well as for mine.' He dropped into the nearest chair, and said no more.

I certainly heard the warning; but the only words which really produced an impression on my mind were the words preceding it, which he had spoken to himself. He had said: 'Nothing, of course, *or she would not be here.*' If I had found out some other truth besides the truth about the name, would it have prevented me from ever returning to my husband? Was that what he meant? Did the sort of discovery that he contemplated, mean something so dreadful that it would have parted us at once and for ever? I stood by his chair in silence; and tried to find the answer to those terrible questions in his face. It used to speak to me so eloquently when it spoke of his love. It told me nothing now.

He sat for some time without looking at me, lost in his own thoughts. Then he rose on a sudden, and took his hat.

'The friend who lent me the yacht is in town,' he said. 'I suppose I had better see him, and say our plans are changed.' He tore up the telegram with an air of sullen resignation as he spoke. 'You are evidently determined not to go to sea with me,' he resumed. 'We had better give it up. I don't see what else is to be done. Do you?'

His tone was almost a tone of contempt. I was too depressed about myself, too alarmed about *him*, to resent it.

'Decide as you think best, Eustace,' I said, sadly. 'Every way, the prospect seems a hopeless one. As long as I am shut out from your confidence, it matters little whether we live on land or at sea – we cannot live happily.'

'If you could control your curiosity,' he answered, sternly, 'we might live happily enough. I thought I had married a woman who was superior to the vulgar failings of her sex. A good wife should know better than to pry into affairs of her husband's with which she has no concern.'

Surely it was hard to bear this? However, I bore it.

'Is it no concern of mine?' I asked, gently, 'when I find that my husband has not married me under his family name? Is it no concern of mine when I hear your mother say, in so many words, that she pities your wife? It is hard, Eustace, to accuse me of curiosity, because I cannot accept the unendurable position in which you have placed me. Your cruel silence is a blight on my happiness, and a threat to my future. Your cruel silence is estranging us from each other, at the beginning of our married life. And you blame me for feeling this? You tell me I am prying into affairs which are yours only? They are *not* yours only: I have my interest in them too. Oh, my darling, why do you trifle with our love and our confidence in each other? Why do you keep me in the dark?'

He answered with a stern and pitiless brevity,

'For your own good.'

I turned away from him in silence. He was treating me like a child.

He followed me. Putting one hand heavily on my shoulder, he forced me to face him once more.

'Listen to this,' he said. 'What I am now going to say to you, I say for the first, and last time. Valeria! if you ever discover what I am now keeping from your knowledge – from that moment you live a life of torture; your tranquillity is gone. Your days will be days of terror; your nights will be full of horrid dreams – through no fault of mine, mind! through no fault of mine! Every day of your life, you will feel some new distrust, some growing fear of me – and you will be doing me the vilest injustice all the time. On my faith as a Christian, on my honour as a man, if you stir a step further in this matter there is an end of your happiness for the rest of your life! Think seriously of what I have said to you; you will have time to reflect. I am going to tell my friend that our plans for the Mediterranean are given up. I shall not be back before the evening.' He sighed, and looked at me with unutterable sadness. 'I love you, Valeria,' he said. 'In spite of all that has passed, as God is my witness, I love you more dearly than ever.'

So he spoke. So he left me.

I must write the truth about myself, however strange it may appear. I don't pretend to be able to analyse my own motives; I don't pretend even to guess how other women might have acted in my place. It is true of *me*, that my husband's terrible warning – all the more terrible in its mystery and its vagueness – produced no deterrent effect on my mind: it only stimulated my resolution to discover what he was hiding from me. He had not been gone two minutes before I rang the bell, and ordered the carriage to take me to Major Fitz-David's house in Vivian Place.

Walking to and fro while I was waiting – I was in such a fever of excitement that it was impossible for me to sit still – I accidentally caught sight of myself in the glass.

My own face startled me: it was so haggard and so wild. Could I present myself to a stranger, could I hope to produce the necessary impression in my favour, looking as I looked at that moment? For all I knew to the contrary, my whole future might depend upon the effect which I produced on Major Fitz-David at first sight. I rang the bell again, and sent a message to one of the chambermaids to follow me to my room.

I had no maid of my own with me: the stewardess of the yacht would have acted as my attendant, if we had held to our first arrangement. It mattered little, so long as I had a woman to help me. The chambermaid appeared. I can give no better idea of the disordered and desperate condition of my mind at that time, than by owning that I actually consulted this perfect stranger on the question of my personal appearance. She was a middle-aged woman, with a large experience of the world and its wickedness written legibly on her manner and on her face. I put money into the woman's hand, enough of it to surprise her. She thanked me with a cynical smile, evidently placing her own evil interpretation on my motive for bribing her.

'What can I do for you, ma'am?' she asked, in a confidential whisper. 'Don't speak loud! There is somebody in the next room.'

'I want to look my best,' I said; 'and I have sent for you to help me.'

'I understand, ma'am.'

'What do you understand?'

She nodded her head significantly, and whispered to me again.

'Lord bless you, I'm used to this!' she said. 'There is a gentleman in the case. Don't mind me, ma'am. It's a way I have. I mean no harm.' She stopped and looked at me critically. 'I wouldn't change my dress, if I were you,' she went on. 'The colour becomes you.'

It was too late to resent the woman's impertinence. There was no help for it but to make use of her. Besides, she was right about the dress. It was of a delicate maize colour, prettily trimmed with lace. I could wear nothing which suited me better. My hair, however, stood in need of some skilled attention. The chambermaid rearranged it, with a ready hand which showed that she was no beginner in the art of dressing hair. She laid down the combs and brushes, and looked at me – then looked at the toilette table, searching for something which she apparently failed to find.

'Where do you keep it?' she asked.

'What do you mean?'

'Look at your complexion, ma'am. You will frighten him if he sees you like that. A touch of colour you *must* have. Where do you keep it? What! you haven't got it? you never use it? Dear, dear, dear me!'

For a moment, surprise fairly deprived her of her self-possession! Recovering herself, she begged permission to leave me for a minute. I let her go, knowing what her errand was. She came back with a box of paints and powders; and I said nothing to check her. I saw, in the glass, my skin take a false fairness, my cheeks a false colour, my eyes a false brightness – and I never shrank from it. No! I let the odious deceit go on; I even admired the extraordinary delicacy and dexterity with which it was all done. 'Anything' (I thought to myself, in the madness of that miserable time), 'so long as it helps me to win the Major's confidence! Anything so long as I discover what those last words of my husband's really mean!'

The transformation of my face was accomplished. The chambermaid pointed with her wicked forefinger in the direction of the glass.

'Bear in mind, ma'am, what you looked like when you sent for me,' she said. 'And just see for yourself how you look now. You're the prettiest woman (of your style) in London. Ah, what a thing pearl powder[1] is, when one knows how to use it!'

CHAPTER VIII

The Friend of the Women

I find it impossible to describe my sensations while the carriage was taking me to Major Fitz-David's house. I doubt, indeed, if I really felt or thought at all, in the true sense of those words.

From the moment when I had resigned myself into the hands of the chambermaid, I seemed in some strange way to have lost my ordinary identity – to have stepped out of my own character. At other times, my temperament was of the nervous and anxious sort, and my tendency was to exaggerate any difficulties that might place themselves in my way. At other times, having before me the prospect of a critical interview with a stranger, I should have considered with myself what it might be wise to pass over, and what it might be wise to say. Now, I never gave my coming interview with the Major a thought; I felt an unreasoning confidence in myself, and a blind faith in *him*. Now, neither the past nor the future troubled me; I lived unreflectingly in the present. I looked at the shops as we drove by them, and at the other carriages as they passed mine. I noticed – yes! and enjoyed – the glances of admiration which chance foot-passengers on the pavement cast at me. I said to myself, 'This looks well for my prospect of making a friend of the Major!' When we drew up at the door in Vivian Place, it is no exaggeration to say that I had but one anxiety – anxiety to find the Major at home.

The door was opened by a servant out of livery, an old man who looked as if he might have been a soldier in his earlier days. He eyed me with a grave attention, which relaxed little by little into sly approval. I asked for Major Fitz-David. The answer was not altogether encouraging; the man was not sure whether his master was at home or not.

I gave him my card. My cards, being part of my wedding outfit, necessarily had the false name printed on them – *Mrs Eustace Woodville*. The servant showed me into a front room on the ground floor, and disappeared with my card in his hand.

Looking about me, I noticed a door in the wall opposite the window, communicating with some inner room. The door was not of the ordinary kind. It fitted into the thickness of the partition wall, and worked in grooves. Looking a little nearer, I saw that it had not been pulled out so as completely to close the doorway. Only the merest chink was left; but it was enough to convey to my ears all that passed in the next room.

'What did you say, Oliver, when she asked for me?' enquired a man's voice, pitched cautiously in a low key.

'I said I was not sure you were at home, sir,' answered the voice of the servant who had let me in.

There was a pause. The first speaker was evidently Major Fitz-David himself. I waited to hear more.

'I think I had better not see her, Oliver,' the Major's voice resumed.

'Very good, sir.'

'Say I have gone out, and you don't know when I shall be back again. Beg the lady to write, if she has any business with me.'

'Yes, sir.'

'Stop, Oliver!'

Oliver stopped. There was another and longer pause. Then the master resumed the examination of the man.

'Is she young, Oliver?'

'Yes, sir.'

'And – pretty?'

'Better than pretty, sir, to my thinking.'

'Aye? aye? What you call a fine woman – eh, Oliver?'

'Certainly, sir.'

'Tall?'

'Nearly as tall as I am, Major.'

'Aye? aye? aye? A good figure?'

'As slim as a sapling, sir, and as upright as a dart.'

'On second thoughts I am at home, Oliver. Show her in! show her in!'

So far, one thing at least seemed to be clear. I had done well in sending for the chambermaid. What would Oliver's report of me have been, if I had presented myself to him with my colourless cheeks and my ill-dressed hair?

The servant reappeared; and conducted me (by way of the hall) to the inner room. Major Fitz-David advanced to welcome me. What was the Major like?

Well – he was like a finely-preserved gentleman of (say) sixty years old; little and lean, and chiefly remarkable by the extraordinary length of his nose. After this feature, I noticed, next, his beautiful brown wig; his sparkling little grey eyes; his rosy complexion; his short military whiskers, dyed to match his wig; his white teeth and his winning smile; his smart blue frock-coat, with a camellia in the buttonhole;[1] and his splendid ring – a ruby, flashing on his little finger as he courteously signed to me to take a chair.

'Dear Mrs Woodville, how very kind of you this is! I have been longing to have the happiness of knowing you. Eustace is an old friend of mine. I congratulated him when I heard of his marriage. May I make a confession? – I envy him now I have seen his wife.'

The future of my life was, perhaps, in this man's hands. I studied him attentively; I tried to read his character in his face.

The Major's sparkling little grey eyes softened as they looked at me; the Major's strong and sturdy voice dropped to its lowest and tenderest tones when he spoke to me; the Major's manner expressed, from the moment when I entered the room, a happy mixture of admiration and respect. He drew his chair close to mine, as if it was a privilege to be near me. He took my hand, and lifted my glove to his lips, as if that glove was the most delicious luxury the world could produce. 'Dear Mrs Woodville,' he said, as he softly laid my hand back on my lap, 'bear with an old fellow who worships your enchanting sex. You really brighten this dull house. It is *such* a pleasure to see you!'

There was no need for the old gentleman to make his little confession. Women, children, and dogs proverbially know by instinct who the people are who really like them. The women had a warm friend – perhaps, at one time, a dangerously warm friend – in Major Fitz-David. I knew as much of him as that, before I had settled myself in my chair and opened my lips to answer him.

'Thank you, Major, for your kind reception and your pretty compliment,' I said; matching my host's easy tone as closely as the necessary restraints on my side would permit. 'You have made your confession. May I make mine?'

Major Fitz-David lifted my hand again from my lap, and drew his chair as close as possible to mine. I looked at him gravely, and tried to release my hand. Major Fitz-David declined to let go of it, and proceeded to tell me why.

'I have just heard you speak for the first time,' he said. 'I am under the charm of your voice. Dear Mrs Woodville, bear with an old fellow who is under the charm! Don't grudge me my innocent little pleasures. Lend me – I wish I could say *give* me – this pretty hand. I am such an admirer of pretty hands; I can listen so much better with a pretty hand in mine. The ladies indulge my weakness. Please indulge me too. Yes? And what were you going to say?'

'I was going to say, Major, that I felt particularly sensible of your kind welcome, because, as it happens, I have a favour to ask of you.'

I was conscious, while I spoke, that I was approaching the object of my visit a little too abruptly. But Major Fitz-David's admiration rose from one climax to another with such alarming rapidity, that I felt the importance of administering a practical check to it. I trusted to those ominous words, 'a favour to ask of you,' to administer the check – and I did not trust in vain. My aged admirer gently dropped my hand, and (with all possible politeness) changed the subject.

'The favour is granted, of course!' he said. 'And now – tell me – how is our dear Eustace?'

'Anxious and out of spirits,' I answered.

'Anxious and out of spirits!' repeated the Major. 'The enviable man who is married to You, anxious and out of spirits? Monstrous! Eustace fairly disgusts me. I shall take him off the list of my friends.'

'In that case, take me off the list with him, Major. I am in wretched spirits too. You are my husband's old friend. I may acknowledge to *you* that our married life is – just now – not quite a happy one.'

Major Fitz-David lifted his eyebrows (dyed to match his whiskers) in polite surprise.

'Already!' he exclaimed. 'What can Eustace be made of? Has he no appreciation of beauty and grace? Is he the most insensible of living beings?'

'He is the best and dearest of men,' I answered. 'But there is some dreadful mystery in his past life—'

I could get no further: Major Fitz-David deliberately stopped me. He did it with the smoothest politeness, on the surface. But I saw a look in his bright little eyes, which said plainly, 'If you *will* venture on delicate ground, madam, don't ask me to accompany you.'

'My charming friend!' he exclaimed. 'May I call you my charming friend? You have – among a thousand other delightful qualities which I can see already – a vivid imagination. Don't let it get the upper hand! Take an old fellow's advice; don't let it get the upper hand! What can I offer you, dear Mrs Woodville? A cup of tea?'

'Call me by my right name, sir,' I answered, boldly. 'I have made a discovery. I know, as well as you do, that my name is Macallan.'

The Major started, and looked at me very attentively. His manner became grave, his tone changed completely, when he spoke next.

'May I ask,' he said, 'if you have communicated to your husband the discovery which you have just mentioned to me?'

'Certainly!' I answered. 'I consider that my husband owes me an explanation. I have asked him to tell me what his extraordinary conduct means – and he has refused, in language that frightens me. I have appealed to his mother – and *she* has refused to explain, in language that humiliates me. Dear Major Fitz-David, I have no friends to take my part; I have nobody to come to but you! Do me the greatest of all favours – tell me why your friend Eustace has married me under a false name!'

'Do *me* the greatest of all favours,' answered the Major. 'Don't ask me to say a word about it.'

He looked, in spite of his unsatisfactory reply, as if he really felt for me. I determined to try my utmost powers of persuasion; I resolved not to be beaten at the first repulse.

'I *must* ask you,' I said. 'Think of my position. How can I live, knowing what I know – and knowing no more? I would rather hear the most horrible thing you can tell me than be condemned (as I am now) to perpetual misgiving and perpetual suspense. I love my husband with all my heart; but I cannot live with him on these terms: the misery of it would drive me mad. I am only a woman, Major. I can only throw myself on your kindness. Don't – pray, pray don't keep me in the dark!'

I could say no more. In the reckless impulse of the moment, I snatched up his hand and raised it to my lips. The gallant old gentleman started as if I had given him an electric shock.

'My dear, dear lady!' he exclaimed, 'I can't tell you how I feel for you! You charm me, you overwhelm me, you touch me to the heart. What can I say? What can I do? I can only imitate your admirable frankness, your fearless candour. You have told me what your position is. Let me tell you, in my turn, how I am placed. Compose yourself – pray compose yourself! I have a smelling-bottle here, at the service of the ladies. Permit me to offer it.'

He brought me the smelling-bottle; he put a little stool under my feet; he entreated me to take time enough to compose myself. 'Infernal fool!' I heard him say to himself, as he considerately turned away from me for a few moments. 'If *I* had been her husband – come what might of it, I would have told her the truth!'

Was he referring to Eustace? And was he going to do what he would have done in my husband's place – was he really going to tell me the truth?

The idea had barely crossed my mind, when I was startled by a loud and peremptory knocking at the street-door. The Major stopped, and listened attentively. In a few moments the door was opened, and the rustling of a woman's dress was plainly audible in the hall. The Major hurried to the door of the room, with the activity of a young man. He was too late. The door was violently opened from the outer side, just as he got to it. The lady of the rustling dress burst into the room.

CHAPTER IX

The Defeat of the Major

Major Fitz-David's visitor proved to be a plump, round-eyed, over-dressed girl, with a florid complexion and straw-coloured hair. After first fixing on me a broad stare of astonishment, she pointedly addressed her apologies for intruding on us to the Major alone. The creature evidently believed me to be the last new object of the old gentleman's idolatry; and she took no pains to disguise her jealous resentment on discovering us together. Major Fitz-David set matters right in his own irresistible way. He kissed the hand of the over-dressed girl, as devotedly as he had kissed mine; he told her she was looking charmingly. Then he led her, with his happy mixture of admiration and respect, back to the door by which she had entered – a second door communicating directly with the hall.

'No apology is necessary, my dear,' he said. 'This lady is with me on a matter of business. You will find your singing-master waiting for you upstairs. Begin your lesson; and I will join you in a few minutes. *Au revoir*, my charming pupil – *au revoir*.'

The young lady answered this polite little speech in a whisper – with her round eyes fixed distrustfully on me while she spoke. The door closed on her. Major Fitz-David was at liberty to set matters right with me, in my turn.

'I call that young person one of my happy discoveries,' said the old gentleman, complacently. 'She possesses, I don't hesitate to say, the finest soprano voice in Europe. Would you believe it, I met with her at a railway station? She was behind the counter in a refreshment-room, poor innocent, rinsing wine-glasses, and singing over her work. Good heavens, such singing! Her upper notes electrified me. I said to myself, "Here is a born prima-donna – I will bring her out!" She is the third I have brought out in my time. I shall take her to Italy when her education is sufficiently advanced, and perfect her at Milan. In that unsophisticated girl, my dear lady, you see one of the future Queens of Song. Listen! she is beginning her scales. What a voice! Brava! Brava! Bravissima!'

The high soprano notes of the future Queen of Song rang through the house as he spoke. Of the loudness of the young lady's voice there could be no sort of doubt. The sweetness and the purity of it admitted, in my opinion, of considerable dispute.

Having said the polite words which the occasion rendered necessary, I ventured to recall Major Fitz-David to the subject in discussion between us when his visitor had entered the room. The Major was very unwilling to return to the perilous topic on which he had just touched when the interruption occurred. He beat time with his fore-finger to the singing upstairs; he asked me about *my* voice, and whether I sang; he remarked that life would be intolerable to him without Love and Art. A man in my place would have lost all patience, and would have given up the struggle in disgust. Being a woman, and having my end in view, my resolution was invincible. I fairly wore out the Major's resistance, and compelled him to surrender at discretion. It is only justice to add that, when he did make up his mind to speak to me again of Eustace, he spoke frankly, and spoke to the point.

'I have known your husband,' he began, 'since the time when he was a boy. At a certain period of his past life, a terrible misfortune fell upon him. The secret of that misfortune is known to his friends, and is religiously kept by his friends. It is the secret that he is keeping from You. He will never tell it to you as long as he lives. And he has bound *me* not to tell it, under a promise given on my word of honour. You wished, dear Mrs Woodville, to be made acquainted with my position towards Eustace. There it is!'

'You persist in calling me Mrs Woodville,' I said.

'Your husband wishes me to persist,' the Major answered. 'He assumed the name of Woodville, fearing to give his own name, when he first called at your uncle's house. He will now acknowledge no other. Remonstrance is useless. You must do, what we do – you must give way to an unreasonable man. The best fellow in the world in other respects: in this one matter, as obstinate and self-willed as he can be. If you ask me my opinion, I tell you honestly that I think he was wrong in courting and marrying you under his false name. He trusted his honour and his happiness to your keeping, in making you his wife. Why should he not trust the story of his troubles to you as well? His mother quite shares my opinion in this matter. You must not blame her for refusing to admit you into her confidence, after your marriage: it was then too late. Before your marriage, she did all she could do – without betraying secrets which, as a good mother, she was bound to respect – to induce her son to act justly towards you. I commit no indiscretion when I tell you that she refused to sanction your marriage, mainly for the reason that Eustace declined to follow her advice, and to tell you what his position really was. On my part, I did all I could to support Mrs Macallan in the course that she took. When Eustace wrote to tell me that he had engaged himself to marry a niece of my good friend Dr Starkweather, and that he had mentioned me as his reference, I wrote back to warn him that I would have nothing to do with the affair, unless he revealed the whole truth about himself to his future wife. He refused to listen to me, as he had refused to listen to his mother; and he held me, at the same time, to my promise to keep his secret. When Starkweather wrote to me, I had no choice but to involve myself in a deception of which I thoroughly disapproved – or to answer in a tone so guarded and so brief as to stop the correspondence at the outset. I chose the last alternative; and I fear I have offended my good old friend. You now see the painful position in which I am placed. To add to the difficulties of that situation, Eustace came here, this very day, to warn me to be on my guard, in case of your addressing to me the very request which you have just made! He told me that you had met with his mother, by an unlucky accident, and that you had discovered the family name. He declared that he had travelled to London for the express purpose of speaking to me personally on this serious subject. "I know your weakness," he said, "where women are concerned. Valeria is aware that you are my old friend. She will certainly write to you; she may even be bold enough to make her way into your house. Renew your promise to keep the great calamity of my life a secret, on your honour, and on your oath." Those were his words, as nearly as I can remember them. I tried to treat the thing lightly; I ridiculed the absurdly theatrical notion of "renewing my promise," and all the rest of it. Quite useless! He refused to leave me – he reminded me of his unmerited sufferings, poor fellow, in the past time. It ended in his bursting into tears. You love him, and so do I. Can you wonder that I let him have his way? The result is that I am doubly bound to tell you nothing, by the most sacred promise that a man can give. My dear lady, I cordially side with you in this matter; I long to relieve your anxieties. But what can I do?'

He stopped, and waited – gravely waited – to hear my reply.

I had listened from beginning to end, without interrupting him. The extraordinary change in his manner, and in his way of expressing himself, while he was speaking of Eustace, alarmed me as nothing had alarmed me yet. How terrible (I thought to myself) must this untold story be, if the mere act of referring to it makes light-hearted Major Fitz-David speak seriously and sadly – never smiling; never paying me a compliment; never even noticing the singing upstairs! My heart sank in me as I drew that startling conclusion. For the first time since I had entered the house, I was at the end of my resources; I knew neither what to say nor what to do next.

And yet, I kept my seat. Never had the resolution to discover what my husband was hiding from me been more firmly rooted in my mind than it was at that moment! I cannot account for the extraordinary inconsistency in my character which this confession implies. I can only describe the facts as they really were.

The singing went on upstairs. Major Fitz-David still waited impenetrably to hear what I had to say – to know what I resolved on doing next.

Before I had decided what to say or what to do, another domestic incident happened. In plain words, another knocking announced a new visitor at the house door. On this occasion, there was no rustling of a woman's dress in the hall. On this occasion, only the old servant entered the room carrying a magnificent nosegay in his hand. 'With Lady Clarinda's kind regards. To remind Major Fitz-David of his appointment.' Another lady! This time, a lady with a title. A great lady who sent her flowers and her messages without condescending to concealment. The Major – first apologising to me – wrote a few lines of acknowledgment, and sent them out to the messenger. When the door was closed again, he carefully selected one of the choicest flowers in the nosegay. 'May I ask,' he said, presenting the flower to me with his best grace, 'whether you now understand the delicate position in which I am placed between your husband and yourself?'

The little interruption caused by the appearance of the nosegay, had given a new impulse to my thoughts, and had thus helped, in some degree, to restore me to myself. I was able at last to satisfy Major Fitz-David that his considerate and courteous explanation had not been thrown away upon me.

'I thank you, most sincerely, Major,' I said. 'You have convinced me that I must not ask you to forget, on my account, the promise which you have given to my husband. It is a sacred promise which I, too, am bound to respect – I quite understand that.'

The Major drew a long breath of relief, and patted me on the shoulder in high approval of what I had said to him.

'Admirably expressed!' he rejoined, recovering his light-hearted looks and his lover-like ways all in a moment. 'My dear lady, you have the gift of sympathy; you see exactly how I am situated. Do you know, you remind me of my charming Lady Clarinda? *She* has the gift of sympathy, and sees exactly how I am situated. I should so enjoy introducing you to each other,' said the Major, plunging his long nose ecstatically into Lady Clarinda's flowers.

I had my end still to gain; and being (as you will have discovered by this time) the most obstinate of living women, I still kept that end in view.

'I shall be delighted to meet Lady Clarinda,' I replied. 'In the mean time —'

'I will get up a little dinner,' proceeded the Major, with a burst of enthusiasm. 'You and I and Lady Clarinda. Our young prima-donna shall come in the evening, and sing to us. Suppose we draw out the *menu*? My sweet friend, what is your favourite autumn soup?'

'In the mean time,' I persisted, 'to return to what we were speaking of just now —'

The Major's smile vanished, the Major's hand dropped the pen, destined to immortalise the name of my favourite autumn soup.

'*Must* we return to that?' he asked, piteously.

'Only for a moment,' I said.

'You remind me,' pursued Major Fitz-David, shaking his head sadly, 'of another charming friend of mine – a French friend – Madame Mirliflore. You are a person of prodigious tenacity of purpose. Madame Mirliflore is a person of prodigious tenacity of purpose. She happens to be in London. Shall we have her at our little dinner?' The Major brightened at the idea, and took up the pen again. 'Do tell me,' he said, 'what *is* your favourite autumn soup?'

'Pardon me,' I began; 'we were speaking just now—'

'Oh, dear me!' cried Major Fitz-David. 'Is this the other subject?'

'Yes – this is the other subject.'

The Major put down his pen for the second time, and regretfully dismissed from his mind Madame Mirliflore and the autumn soup.

'Yes?' he said with a patient bow, and a submissive smile. 'You were going to say—?'

'I was going to say,' I rejoined, 'that your promise only pledges you not to tell the secret which my husband is keeping from me. You have given no promise not to answer me, if I venture to ask you one or two questions.'

Major Fitz-David held up his hand warningly, and cast a sly look at me out of his bright little grey eyes.

'Stop!' he said. 'My sweet friend, stop there! I know where your questions will lead me, and what the result will be if I once begin to answer them. When your husband was here to-day, he took occasion to remind me that I was as weak as water in the hands of a pretty woman. He is quite right. I *am* as weak as water; I can refuse nothing to a pretty woman. Dear and admirable lady, don't abuse your influence! don't make an old soldier false to his word of honour!'

I tried to say something here in defence of my motives. The Major clasped his hands entreatingly, and looked at me with a pleading simplicity wonderful to see.

'Why press it?' he asked. 'I offer no resistance. I am a lamb – why sacrifice me? I acknowledge your power; I throw myself on your mercy. All the misfortunes of my youth and my manhood have come to me through women. I am not a bit better in my age – I am just as fond of the women, and just as ready to be misled by them as ever, with one foot in the grave. Shocking, isn't it? But how true! Look at this mark.' He lifted a curl of his beautiful brown wig, and showed me a terrible scar at the side of his head. 'That wound (supposed to be mortal at the time) was made by a pistol bullet,' he proceeded. 'Not received in the service of my country – oh, dear no! Received in the service of a much-injured lady, at the hands of her scoundrel of a husband, in a duel abroad. Well, she was worth it!' He kissed his hand affectionately to the memory of the dead, or absent, lady, and pointed to a water-colour drawing of a pretty country house, hanging on the opposite wall. 'That fine estate,' he proceeded, 'once belonged to me. It was sold years and years since. And who had the money? The women – God bless them all! – the women. I don't regret it. If I had another estate, I have no doubt it would go the same way. Your adorable sex has made its pretty playthings of my life, my time, and my money – and welcome! The one thing I have kept to myself, is my honour. And now, *that* is in danger! Yes; if you put your clever little questions, with those lovely eyes and with that gentle voice, I know what will happen! You will deprive me of the last and best of all my possessions. Have I deserved to be treated in that way – and by you, my charming friend? by you of all people in the world? Oh fie! fie!'

He paused, and looked at me as before – the picture of artless entreaty, with his head a little on one side. I made another attempt to speak of the matter in dispute between us, from my own point of view. Major Fitz-David instantly threw himself prostrate on my mercy more innocently than ever.

'Ask of me anything else in the wide world,' he said; 'but don't ask me to be false to my friend. Spare me *that* – and there is nothing I will not do to satisfy you. I mean what I say, mind!' he went on, bending closer to me, and speaking more seriously than he had spoken yet. 'I think you are very hardly used. It is monstrous to expect that a woman placed in your situation, will consent to be left for the rest of her life in the dark. No! no! if I saw you, at this moment, on the point of finding out for yourself what Eustace persists in hiding from you, I should remember that my promise, like all other promises, has its limits and reserves. I should consider myself bound in honour not to help you – but I would not lift a finger to prevent you from discovering the truth for yourself.'

At last he was speaking in good earnest: he laid a strong emphasis on his closing words. I laid a stronger emphasis on them still, by suddenly leaving my chair. The impulse to spring to my feet was irresistible. Major Fitz-David had started a new idea in my mind.

'Now we understand each other!' I said. 'I will accept your own terms, Major, I will ask nothing of you but what you have just offered to me of your own accord.'

'What have I offered?' he enquired, looking a little alarmed.

'Nothing that you need repent of,' I answered; 'nothing which it is not easy for you to grant. May I ask a bold question? Suppose this house were mine, instead of yours?'

'Consider it yours,' cried the gallant old gentleman. 'From the garrets to the kitchen, consider it yours!'

'A thousand thanks, Major; I will consider it mine, for the moment. You know – everybody knows – that one of a woman's many weaknesses is curiosity. Suppose my curiosity led me to examine everything in my new house?'

'Yes?'

'Suppose I went from room to room, and searched everything, and peeped in everywhere? Do you think there would be any chance—?'

The quick-witted Major anticipated the nature of my question. He followed my example; he, too, started to his feet, with a new idea in his mind.

'Would there be any chance,' I went on, 'of my finding my own way to my husband's secret, in this house? One word of reply, Major Fitz-David! Only one word – Yes, or No?'

'Don't excite yourself!' cried the Major.

'Yes, or No?' I repeated, more vehemently than ever.

'Yes,' said the Major – after a moment's consideration.

It was the reply I had asked for; but it was not explicit enough – now I had got it – to satisfy me. I felt the necessity of leading him (if possible) into details.

'Does "Yes" mean that there is some sort of clue to the mystery?' I asked. 'Something, for instance, which my eyes might see, and my hands might touch, if I could only find it?'

He considered again. I saw that I had succeeded in interesting him, in some way unknown to myself; and I waited patiently until he was prepared to answer me.

'The thing you mention,' he said; 'the clue (as you call it) might be seen and might be touched – supposing you could find it.'

'In this house?' I asked.

The Major advanced a step nearer to me, and answered,

'In this room.'

My head began to swim; my heart throbbed violently. I tried to speak; it was in vain; the effort almost choked me. In the silence, I could hear the music lesson still going on in the room above. The future prima-donna had done practising her scales, and was trying her voice now in selections from Italian operas. At the moment when I first heard her, she was singing the lovely air from the *Sonnambula*, 'Come per me sereno.'[1] I never hear that delicious melody, to this day, without being instantly transported in imagination to the fatal back-room in Vivian Place.

The Major – strongly affected himself, by this time – was the first to break the silence.

'Sit down again,' he said; 'and pray take the easy chair. You are very much agitated; you want rest.'

He was right. I could stand no longer; I dropped into the chair. Major Fitz-David rang the bell, and spoke a few words to the servant at the door.

'I have been here a long time,' I said, faintly. 'Tell me if I am in the way.'

'In the way?' he repeated, with his irresistible smile. 'You forget that you are in your own house!'

The servant returned to us, bringing with him a tiny bottle of champagne, and a plate-full of delicate little sugared biscuits.

'I have had this wine bottled expressly for the ladies,' said the Major. 'The biscuits come to me direct from Paris. As a favour to *me* you must take some refreshment. And then—' he stopped, and looked at me very attentively. 'And then,' he resumed, 'shall I go to my young prima-donna upstairs, and leave you here alone?'

It was impossible to hint more delicately at the one request which I now had it in my mind to make to him. I took his hand and pressed it gratefully.

'The tranquillity of my whole life to come, is at stake,' I said. 'When I am left here by myself, does your generous sympathy permit me to examine everything in the room?'

He signed to me to drink the champagne, and to eat a biscuit, before he gave his answer.

'This is serious,' he said. 'I wish you to be in perfect possession of yourself. Restore your strength—and then I will speak to you.'

I did as he bade me. In a minute from the time when I drank it, the delicious sparkling wine had begun to revive me.

'Is it your express wish,' he resumed, 'that I should leave you here by yourself, to search the room?'

'It is my express wish,' I answered.

'I take a heavy responsibility on myself in granting your request. But I grant it for all that, because I sincerely believe – as you believe – that the tranquillity of your life to come depends on your discovering the truth.' Saying those words, he took two keys from his pocket, 'You will naturally feel a suspicion,' he went on, 'of any locked doors that you may find here. The only locked places in the room are the doors of the cupboards under the long bookcase, and the door of the Italian cabinet in that corner. The small key opens the bookcase cupboards; the long key opens the cabinet door.'

With that explanation, he laid the keys before me on the table.

'Thus far,' he said, 'I have rigidly respected the promise which I made to your husband. I shall continue to be faithful to my promise, whatever may be the result of your examination of the room. I am bound in honour not to assist you, by word or deed. I am not even at liberty to offer you the slightest hint. Is that understood?'

'Certainly!'

'Very good. I have now a last word of warning to give you – and then I have done. If you do by any chance succeed in laying your hand on the clue, remember this – *the discovery which follows will be a terrible one.* If you have any doubt about your capacity to sustain a shock which will strike you to the soul, for God's sake give up the idea of finding out your husband's secret, at once and for ever!'

'I thank you for your warning, Major. I must face the consequences of making the discovery, whatever they may be.'

'You are positively resolved?'

'Positively.'

'Very well. Take any time you please. The house, and every person in it, is at your disposal. Ring the bell once, if you want the man servant. Ring twice, if you wish the housemaid to wait on you. From time to time, I shall just look in myself to see how you are going on. I am responsible for your comfort and security, you know, while you honour me by remaining under my roof.'

He lifted my hand to his lips, and fixed a last attentive look on me.

'I hope I am not running too great a risk,' he said – more to himself than to me. 'The women have led me into many a rash action, in my time. Have *you* led me, I wonder, into the rashest action of all?'

With those ominous last words he bowed gravely, and left me alone in the room.

CHAPTER X

The Search

The fire burning in the grate was not a very large one; and the outer air (as I had noticed on my way to the house) had something of a wintry sharpness in it, that day.

Still, my first feeling when Major Fitz-David left me, was a feeling of heat and oppression – with its natural result, a difficulty of breathing freely. The nervous agitation of the time was, I suppose, answerable for these sensations. I took off my bonnet and mantle and gloves, and opened the window for a little while. Nothing was to be seen outside but a paved courtyard (with a skylight in the middle), closed at the farther end by the wall of the Major's stables. A few minutes at the window cooled and refreshed me. I shut it down again, and took my first step on the way to discovery. In other words, I began my first examination of the four walls round me, and of all that they enclosed.

I was amazed at my own calmness. My interview with Major Fitz-David had, perhaps, exhausted my capacity for feeling any strong emotion – for the time at least. It was a relief to me to be alone; it was a relief to me to begin the search. Those were my only sensations, so far.

The shape of the room was oblong. Of the two shorter walls, one contained the door in grooves which I have already mentioned as communicating with the front room; the other was almost entirely occupied by the broad window which looked out on the courtyard.

Taking the doorway wall first, what was there, in the shape of furniture, on either side of it? There was a card-table on either side. Above each card-table stood a magnificent china bowl, placed on a gilt and carved bracket fixed to the wall.

I opened the card-tables. The drawers beneath contained nothing but cards, and the usual counters and markers. With the exception of one pack, the cards in both tables were still wrapped in their paper covers exactly as they had come from the shop. I examined the loose pack, card by card. No writing – no mark of any kind – was visible on any one of them. Assisted by a library ladder which stood against the bookcase, I looked next into the two china bowls. Both were perfectly empty. Was there anything more to examine on that side of the room? In the two corners there were two little chairs of inlaid wood, with red silk cushions. I turned them up, and looked under the cushions; and still I made no discoveries. When I had put the chairs back in their places, my search on one side of the room was complete. So far, I had found nothing.

I crossed to the opposite wall – the wall which contained the window.

The window (occupying, as I have said, almost the entire length and height of the wall) was divided into three compartments, and was adorned at either extremity by handsome curtains of dark red velvet. The ample, heavy folds of the velvet, left just room at the two corners of the wall, for two antique upright cabinets in buhl; containing rows of drawers, and supporting two fine bronze reproductions (reduced in size) of the Venus Milo and the Venus Callipyge.[1] I had Major Fitz-David's permission to do just what I pleased. I opened the six drawers in each cabinet, and examined their contents without hesitation.

Beginning with the cabinet in the right hand corner, my investigations were soon completed. All the six drawers were alike occupied by a collection of fossils, which (judging by the curious paper inscriptions fixed on some of them) were associated with a past period of the Major's life when he had speculated, not very successfully, in mines. After satisfying myself that the drawers contained nothing but the fossils and their inscriptions, I turned to the cabinet in the left hand corner next.

Here, a variety of objects was revealed to view; and the examination accordingly occupied a much longer time.

The top drawer contained a complete collection of carpenter's tools in miniature; relics probably of the far distant time when the Major was a boy, and when parents or friends had made him a present of a set of toy-tools. The second drawer was filled with toys of another sort – presents made to Major Fitz-David by his fair friends. Embroidered braces, smart smoking-caps, quaint pincushions, gorgeous slippers, glittering purses, all bore witness to the popularity of the friend of the women. The contents of the third drawer were of a less interesting sort: the entire space was filled with old account books, ranging over a period of many years. After looking into each book, and opening and shaking it uselessly, in search of any loose papers which might be hidden between the leaves, I came to the fourth drawer, and found more relics of past pecuniary transactions in the shape of receipted bills, neatly tied together and each inscribed at the back. Among the bills, I found nearly a dozen loose papers, all equally unimportant. The fifth drawer was in sad confusion. I took out first a loose bundle of ornamental cards, each containing the list of dishes at past banquets given, or attended, by the Major, in London and Paris – next, a box full of delicately tinted quill pens (evidently a lady's gift) – next, a quantity of old invitation cards – next, some dog's-eared French plays and books of the opera – next, a pocket-corkscrew, a bundle of cigarettes, and a bunch of rusty keys – lastly, a passport, a set of luggage labels, a broken silver snuff-box, two cigar-cases, and a torn map of Rome. 'Nothing anywhere to interest *me*,' I thought, as I closed the fifth, and opened the sixth, and last, drawer.

The sixth drawer was at once a surprise and a disappointment. It literally contained nothing but the fragments of a broken vase.

I was sitting, at the time, opposite to the cabinet, in a low chair. In the momentary irritation caused by my discovery of the emptiness of the last drawer, I had just lifted my foot to push it back into its place – when the door communicating with the hall opened; and Major Fitz-David stood before me.

His eyes, after first meeting mine, travelled downwards to my foot. The instant he noticed the open drawer, I saw a change in his face. It was only for a moment; but, in that moment, he looked at me with a sudden suspicion and surprise – looked as if he had caught me with my hand on the clue.

'Pray don't let me disturb you,' he said. 'I have only looked in for a moment to ask you a question.'

'What is it, Major?'

'Have you met with any letters of mine, in the course of your investigations?'

'I have found none yet,' I answered. 'If I do discover any letters, I shall of course not take the liberty of examining them.'

'I wanted to speak to you about that,' he rejoined. 'It only struck me a moment since, upstairs, that my letters might embarrass you. In your place, I should feel some distrust of anything which I was not at liberty to examine. I think I can set this matter right, however, with very little trouble to either of us. It is no violation of any promises or pledges on my part, if I simply tell you that my letters will not assist the discovery which you are trying to make. You can safely pass them over as objects that are not worth examining from your point of view. You understand me, I am sure?'

'I am much obliged to you, Major – I quite understand.'

'Are you feeling any fatigue?'

'None whatever – thank you.'

'And you still hope to succeed? You are not beginning to be discouraged already?'

'I am not in the least discouraged. With your kind leave I mean to persevere for some time yet.'

I had not closed the drawer of the cabinet, while we were talking; and I glanced carelessly, as I answered him, at the fragments of the broken vase. By this time he had got his feelings under perfect command. He, too, glanced at the fragments of the vase, with an appearance of perfect indifference. I remembered the look of suspicion and surprise that had escaped him on entering the room; and I thought his indifference a little over-acted.

'*That* doesn't look very encouraging,' he said with a smile, pointing to the shattered pieces of china in the drawer.

'Appearances are not always to be trusted,' I replied. 'The wisest thing I can do, in my present situation, is to suspect everything – even down to a broken vase.'

I looked hard at him as I spoke. He changed the subject.

'Does the music upstairs annoy you?' he asked.

'Not in the least, Major.'

'It will soon be over now. The singing master is going; and the Italian master has just arrived. I am sparing no pains to make my young prima-donna a most accomplished person. In learning to sing, she must also learn the language which is especially the language of music. I shall perfect her in the accent when I take her to Italy. It is the height of my ambition to have her mistaken for an Italian when she sings in public. Is there anything I can do, before I leave you again? May I send you some more champagne? Please say yes!'

'A thousand thanks, Major. No more champagne for the present.'

He turned at the door, to kiss his hand to me at parting. At the same moment I saw his eyes wander slily towards the bookcase. It was only for an instant. I had barely detected him before he was out of the room.

Left by myself again, I looked at the bookcase – looked at it attentively for the first time.

It was a handsome piece of furniture in ancient carved oak; and it stood against the wall which ran parallel with the hall of the house. Excepting the space occupied, in the upper corner of the room, by the second door which opened into the hall, the bookcase filled the whole length of the wall down to the window. The top was ornamented by vases, candelabra, and statuettes, in pairs, placed in a row. Looking along the row, I noticed a vacant space on the top of the bookcase, at the extremity of it which was nearest to the window. The opposite extremity, nearest to the door, was occupied by a handsome painted vase of a very peculiar pattern. Where was the corresponding vase, which ought to have been placed at the corresponding extremity of the bookcase? I returned to the open sixth drawer of the cabinet, and looked in again. There was no mistaking the pattern on the fragments, when I examined them now. The vase which had been broken, was the vase which had stood in the place now vacant on the top of the bookcase, at the end nearest to the window.

Making this discovery, I took out the fragments down to the smallest morsel of the shattered china, and examined them carefully one after another.

I was too ignorant of the subject to be able to estimate the value of the vase, or the antiquity of the vase – or even to know whether it was of British or of foreign manufacture. The ground was of a delicate cream-colour. The ornaments traced on this were wreaths of flowers and cupids, surrounding a medallion on either side of the vase. Upon the space within one of the medallions was painted with exquisite delicacy a woman's head; representing a nymph, or a goddess, or perhaps a portrait of some celebrated person – I was not learned enough to say which. The other medallion enclosed the head of a man, also treated in the classical style. Reclining shepherds and shepherdesses, in Watteau costume, with their dogs and their sheep, formed the adornments of the pedestal. Such had the vase been in the days of its prosperity when it stood on the top of the bookcase. By what accident had it become broken? And why had Major Fitz-David's face changed when he found that I had discovered the remains of his shattered work of Art in the cabinet drawer?

The remains left those serious questions unanswered – the remains told me absolutely nothing. And yet, if my own observation of the

Major was to be trusted, the way to the clue of which I was in search, lay – directly or indirectly – through the broken vase!

It was useless to pursue the question, knowing no more than I knew now. I returned to the bookcase.

Thus far, I had assumed (without any sufficient reason) that the clue of which I was in search, must necessarily reveal itself through a written paper of some sort. It now occurred to me – after the movement which I had detected on the part of the Major – that the clue might quite as probably present itself in the form of a book.

I looked along the lower rows of shelves; standing just near enough to them to read the titles on the backs of the volumes. I saw Voltaire in red morocco; Shakespeare in blue; Walter Scott in green; the History of England in brown; the Annual Register in yellow calf.[2] There I paused, wearied and discouraged already by the long rows of volumes. How (I thought to myself) am I to examine all these books? And what am I to look for, even if I do examine them all?

Major Fitz-David had spoken of a terrible misfortune which had darkened my husband's past life. In what possible way could any trace of that misfortune, or any suggestive hint of something resembling it, exist in the archives of the Annual Register or in the pages of Voltaire? The bare idea of such a thing seemed absurd. The mere attempt to make a serious examination in this direction was surely a wanton waste of time?

And yet, the Major had certainly stolen a look at the bookcase. And again, the broken vase had once stood on the bookcase. Did these circumstances justify me in connecting the vase and the bookcase as twin landmarks on the way that led to discovery? The question was not an easy one to decide, on the spur of the moment.

I looked up at the higher shelves.

Here the collection of books exhibited a greater variety. The volumes were smaller, and were not so carefully arranged as on the lower shelves. Some were bound in cloth; some were only protected by paper covers. One or two had fallen, and lay flat on the shelves. Here and there I saw empty spaces from which books had been removed and not replaced. In short, there was no discouraging uniformity in these higher regions of the bookcase. The untidy top shelves looked suggestive of some lucky accident which might unexpectedly lead the way to success. I decided, if I did examine the bookcase at all, to begin at the top.

Where was the library ladder?

I had left it against the partition wall which divided the back room from the room in front. Looking that way, I necessarily looked also towards the door that ran in grooves – the imperfectly-closed door through which I had heard Major Fitz-David question his servant on the subject of my personal appearance, when I first entered the house. No one had moved this door, during the time of my visit. Everybody entering or leaving the room, had used the other door which led into the hall.

At the moment when I looked round, something stirred in the front room. The movement let the light in suddenly, through the small open space left by the partially-closed door. Had somebody been watching me through the chink? I stepped softly to the door, and pushed it back until it was wide open. There was the Major, discovered in the front room! I saw it in his face – he had been watching me at the bookcase!

His hat was in his hand. He was evidently going out; and he dexterously took advantage of that circumstance to give a plausible reason for being so near the door.

'I hope I didn't frighten you,' he said.

'You startled me a little, Major.'

'I am so sorry, and so ashamed! I was just going to open the door, and tell you that I am obliged to go out. I have received a pressing message from a lady. A charming person – I should so like you to know her! She is in sad trouble, poor thing. Little bills, you know, and nasty tradespeople who want their money, and a husband – oh, dear me, a husband who is quite unworthy of her! A most interesting creature. You remind me of her a little – you both have the same carriage of the head. I shall not be more than half-an-hour gone. Can I do anything for you? You are looking fatigued. Pray let me send for some more champagne! No? Promise to ring when you want it. That's right! *Au revoir*, my charming friend – *au revoir*!'

I pulled the door to again, the moment his back was turned; and sat down for a while to compose myself.

He had been watching me at the bookcase! The man who was in my husband's confidence, the man who knew where the clue was to be found, had been watching me at the bookcase! There was no doubt of it now. Major Fitz-David had shown me the hiding-place of the secret, in spite of himself!

I looked with indifference at the other pieces of furniture, ranged against the fourth wall, which I had not examined yet. I surveyed, without the slightest feeling of curiosity, all the little elegant trifles scattered on the tables and on the chimneypiece; each one of which might have been an object of suspicion to me under other circumstances. Even the water-colour drawings failed to interest me, in my present frame of mind. I observed languidly that they were most of them portraits of ladies – fair idols, no doubt, of the Major's facile adoration – and I cared to notice no more. *My* business in that room (I was certain of it now!) began and ended with the bookcase. I left my seat to fetch the library ladder; determining to begin the work of investigation on the top shelves.

On my way to the ladder I passed one of the tables, and saw the keys lying on it which Major Fitz-David had left at my disposal.

The smaller of the two keys instantly reminded me of the cupboards under the bookcase. I had strangely overlooked these. A vague distrust of the locked doors, a vague doubt of what they might be hiding from me, stole into my mind. I left the ladder in its place against the wall, and set myself to examine the contents of the cupboards first.

The cupboards were three in number. As I opened the first of them, the singing upstairs ceased. For a moment there was something almost oppressive in the sudden change from noise to silence. I suppose my nerves must have been over-wrought. The next sound in the house – nothing more remarkable than the creaking of a man's boots, descending the stairs – made me shudder all over. The man was no doubt the singing master, going away after giving his lesson. I heard the house door close on him – and started at the familiar sound as if it was something terrible which I had never heard before! Then there was silence again. I roused myself as well as I could, and began my examination of the first cupboard.

It was divided into two compartments.

The top compartment contained nothing but boxes of cigars, ranged in rows one on another. The under compartment was devoted to a collection of shells. They were all huddled together anyhow – the Major evidently setting a far higher value on his cigars than on his shells. I searched this lower compartment carefully for any object interesting to me which might be hidden in it. Nothing was to be found in any part of it, besides the shells.

As I opened the second cupboard, it struck me that the light was beginning to fail.

I looked at the window. It was hardly evening yet. The darkening of the light was produced by gathering clouds. Raindrops pattered against the glass; the autumn wind whistled mournfully in the corners of the courtyard. I mended the fire before I renewed my search. My nerves were in fault again, I suppose. I shivered when I went back to the bookcase. My hands trembled: I wondered what was the matter with me.

The second cupboard revealed (in the upper division of it) some really beautiful cameos; not mounted, but laid on cotton wool, in neat cardboard trays. In one corner, half hidden under one of the trays, there peeped out the white leaves of a little manuscript. The manuscript proved to be a descriptive catalogue of the cameos – nothing more!

Turning to the lower division of the cupboard, I found more costly curiosities, in the shape of ivory carvings from Japan, and specimens of rare silk from China. I began to feel weary of disinterring the Major's treasures. The longer I searched, the farther I seemed to remove myself from the one object that I had it at heart to attain. After closing the door of the second cupboard, I almost doubted whether it would be worth my while to proceed farther, and open the third and last door.

A little reflection convinced me that it would be as well, now that I had begun my examination of the lower regions of the bookcase, to go on with it to the end. I opened the last cupboard.

On the upper shelf there appeared, in solitary grandeur, one object only – a gorgeously-bound book.

It was of a larger size than usual, judging of it by comparison with the dimensions of modern volumes. The binding was of blue velvet, with clasps of silver worked in beautiful arabesque patterns, and with a lock of the same precious metal to protect the book from prying eyes. When I took it up, I found that the lock was not closed.

Had I any right to take advantage of this accident, and open the book? I have put the question, since, to some of my friends, of both sexes. The women all agree that I was perfectly justified – considering the serious interests that I had at stake – in taking any advantage of any book in the Major's house. The men differ from this view; and declare that I ought to have put back the volume in blue velvet, unopened; carefully guarding myself from any after-temptation to look at it again, by locking the cupboard door. I dare say the men are right.

Being a woman, however, I opened the book, without a moment's hesitation.

The leaves were of the finest vellum, with tastefully-designed illuminations all round them. And what did these highly ornamented pages contain? To my unutterable amazement and disgust, they contained locks of hair, let neatly into the centre of each page – with inscriptions beneath, which proved them to be love-tokens from various ladies, who had touched the Major's susceptible heart at different periods of his life. The inscriptions were written in other languages besides English; but they appeared to be equally devoted to the same curious purpose – namely, to reminding the Major of the dates at which his various attachments had come to an untimely end. Thus, the first page exhibited a lock of the lightest flaxen hair, with these lines beneath: 'My adored Madeline. Eternal constancy. Alas: July 22nd, 1839!' The next page was adorned by a darker shade of hair, with a French inscription under it: 'Clémence. Idole de mon âme. Toujours fidèle. Hélas: 2me Avril, 1840!'[3] A lock of red hair followed – with a lamentation in Latin under it; a note being attached to the date of dissolution of partnership, in this case, stating that the lady was descended from the ancient Romans, and was therefore mourned appropriately in Latin by her devoted Fitz-David. More shades of hair, and more inscriptions followed, until I was weary of looking at them. I put down the book disgusted with the creatures who had assisted in filling it – and then took it up again, by an after-thought. Thus far, I had thoroughly searched everything that had presented itself to my notice. Agreeable or not agreeable, it was plainly of serious importance to my own interests to go on as I had begun, and thoroughly to search the book.

I turned over the pages until I came to the first blank leaf. Seeing that they were all blank leaves from this place to the end, I lifted the volume by the back, and, as a last measure of precaution, shook it so as to dislodge any loose papers or cards which might have escaped my notice between the leaves.

This time, my patience was rewarded by a discovery which indescribably irritated and distressed me.

A small photograph, mounted on a card, fell out of the book. A first glance showed me that it represented the portraits of two persons.

One of the persons I recognised as my husband.

The other person was a woman.

Her face was entirely unknown to me. She was not young. The picture represented her seated on a chair, with my husband standing behind, and bending over her, holding one of her hands in his. The woman's face was hard-featured and ugly, with the marking lines of strong passions and resolute self-will plainly written on it. Still, ugly as she was, I felt a pang of jealousy as I noticed the familiarly-affectionate action by which the artist (with the permission of his sitters, of course) had connected the two figures in a group. Eustace had briefly told me, in the days of our courtship, that he had more than once fancied himself to be in love, before he met with me. Could this very unattractive woman have been one of the objects of his admiration? Had she been near enough and dear enough to him, to be photographed with her hand in his? I looked and looked at the portraits, until I could endure them no longer. Women are strange creatures; mysteries even to themselves. I threw the photograph from me into a corner of the cupboard. I was savagely angry with my husband; I hated – yes, hated with all my heart and soul! – the woman who had got his hand in hers; the unknown woman with the self-willed hard-featured face.

All this time the lower shelf of the cupboard was still waiting to be looked over.

I knelt down to examine it – eager to clear my mind, if I could, of the degrading jealousy that had got possession of me.

Unfortunately, the lower shelf contained nothing but relics of the Major's military life; comprising his sword and pistols, his epaulettes, his sash, and other minor accoutrements. None of these objects excited the slightest interest in me. My eyes wandered back to the upper shelf; and, like the fool I was (there is no milder word that can fitly describe me at that moment), I took the photograph out again, and enraged myself uselessly by another look at it. This time I observed, what I had not noticed before, that there were some lines of writing (in a woman's hand) at the back of the portraits. The lines ran thus: –

'To Major Fitz-David, with two vases. From his friends, S. and E. M.'

Was one of those two vases the vase that had been broken? And was the change that I had noticed in Major Fitz-David's face produced by some past association in connection with it, which in some way affected me? It might or might not be so. I was little disposed to indulge in speculation on this topic, while the far more serious question of the initials confronted me on the back of the photograph.

'S. and E. M.'? Those last two letters might stand for the initials of my husband's name – his true name – Eustace Macallan. In this case, the first letter ('S.'), in all probability, indicated *her* name. What right had she to associate herself with him in that manner? I considered a little – my memory exerted itself – I suddenly called to mind that Eustace had sisters. He had spoken of them more than once, in the time before our marriage. Had I been mad enough to torture myself with jealousy of my husband's sister? It might well be so; 'S.' might stand for his sister's Christian name. I felt heartily ashamed of myself, as this new view of the matter dawned on me. What a wrong I had done to them both, in my thoughts! I turned the photograph, sadly and penitently, to examine the portraits again with a kinder and truer appreciation of them.

I naturally looked now for a family likeness between the two faces. There was no family likeness: on the contrary, they were as unlike each other in form and expression as faces could be. *Was* she his sister after all? I looked at her hands, as represented in the portrait. Her right hand was clasped by Eustace: her left hand lay on her lap. On the third finger – distinctly visible – there was a wedding-ring. Were any of my husband's sisters married? I had myself asked him the question when he mentioned them to me; and I perfectly remembered that he had replied in the negative.

Was it possible that my first jealous instinct had led me to the right conclusion after all? If it had, what did the association of the three initial letters mean? What did the wedding-ring mean? Good Heavens! was I looking at the portrait of a rival in my husband's affections – and was that rival his Wife?

I threw the photograph from me with a cry of horror. For one terrible moment, I felt as if my reason was giving way. I don't know what would have happened – or what I should have done next – if my love for Eustace had not taken the uppermost place among the contending emotions that tortured me. That faithful love steadied my brain. That faithful love roused the reviving influences of my better and nobler sense. Was the man whom I had enshrined in my heart of hearts, capable of such base wickedness as the bare idea of his marriage to another woman implied? No! – mine was the baseness, mine the wickedness, in having even for a moment thought it of him!

I picked up the detestable photograph from the floor, and put it back in the book. I hastily closed the cupboard door, fetched the library ladder, and set it against the bookcase. My one idea, now, was the idea of taking refuge in employment of any sort from my own thoughts. I felt the hateful suspicion that had degraded me, coming back again in spite of my efforts to repel it. The books! the books! my only hope was to absorb myself, body and soul, in the books.

I had one foot on the ladder, when I heard the door of the room open – the door which communicated with the hall.

I looked round, expecting to see the Major. I saw instead the Major's future prima-donna, standing just inside the door, with her round eyes steadily fixed on me.

'I can stand a good deal,' the girl began, coolly; 'but I can't stand *this* any longer.'

'What is it that you can't stand any longer?' I asked.

'If you have been here a minute, you have been here two good hours,' she went on. 'All by yourself, in the Major's study. I am of a jealous disposition – *I* am. And I want to know what it means.' She advanced a few steps nearer to me, with a heightening colour and a threatening look. 'Is he going to bring *you* out on the stage?' she asked, sharply.

'Certainly not.'

'He ain't in love with you – is he?'

Under other circumstances, I might have told her to leave the room. In my position, at that critical moment, the mere presence of a human creature was a positive relief to me. Even this girl, with her coarse questions and her uncultivated manners, was a welcome intruder on my solitude: she offered me a refuge from myself.

'Your question is not very civilly put,' I said. 'However, I excuse you. You are probably not aware that I am a married woman.'

'What has that got to do with it?' she retorted. 'Married, or single, it's all one to the Major. That brazen-faced hussey who calls herself Lady Clarinda is married – and she sends him nosegays three times a week! Not that I care, mind you, about the old fool. But I've lost my situation at the railway, and I've got my own interests to look after, and I don't know what may happen if I let other women come between him and me. That's where the shoe pinches – don't you see? I'm not easy in my mind, when I see him leaving you mistress here to do just what you like. No offence! I speak out – *I* do. I want to know what you are about, all by yourself, in this room? How did you pick up with the Major? I never heard him speak of you before to-day.'

Under all the surface selfishness and coarseness of this strange girl, there was a certain frankness and freedom which pleaded in her favour – to my mind at any rate. I answered frankly and freely, on my side.

'Major Fitz-David is an old friend of my husband's,' I said; 'and he is kind to me for my husband's sake. He has given me permission to look about in this room—'

I stopped, at a loss how to describe my employment in terms which should tell her nothing, and which should at the same time successfully set her distrust of me at rest.

'To look about in this room – for what?' she asked. Her eye fell on the library ladder, beside which I was still standing. 'For a book?' she resumed.

'Yes,' I said, taking the hint. 'For a book.'

'Haven't you found it yet?'

'No.'

She looked hard at me; undisguisedly considering with herself whether I was, or was not, speaking the truth.

'You seem to be a good sort,' she said, making up her mind at last. 'There's nothing stuck-up about you. I'll help you if I can. I have rummaged among the books here over and over again, and I know more about them than you do. What book do you want?'

As she put that awkward question, she noticed for the first time Lady Clarinda's nosegay lying on the side table where the Major had left it. Instantly forgetting me and my book, this curious girl pounced like a fury on the flowers, and actually trampled them under her feet!

'There!' she cried. 'If I had Lady Clarinda here, I'd serve her in the same way.'

'What will the Major say?' I asked.

'What do I care? Do you suppose I'm afraid of *him*? Only last week I broke one of his fine gimcracks up there, and all through Lady Clarinda and her flowers!'

She pointed to the top of the bookcase – to the empty space on it, close by the window. My heart gave a sudden bound, as my eyes took the direction indicated by her finger. *She* had broken the vase! Was the way to discovery about to reveal itself to me through this girl? Not a word would pass my lips; I could only look at her.

'Yes!' she said. 'The thing stood there. He knows how I hate her flowers, and he put her nosegay in the vase out of my way. There was a woman's face painted on the china; and he told me it was the living image of *her* face. It was no more like her than I am. I was in such a rage that I up with the book I was reading at the time, and shied it at the painted face. Over the vase went, bless your heart – crash to the floor. Stop a bit! I wonder whether *that's* the book you have been looking after? Are you like me? Do you like reading Trials?'

Trials? Had I heard her aright? Yes: she had said, Trials.

I answered by an affirmative motion of my head. I was still speechless. The girl sauntered in her cool way to the fireplace, and taking up the tongs, returned with them to the bookcase.

'Here's where the book fell,' she said – 'in the space between the bookcase and the wall. I'll have it out in no time.'

I waited without moving a muscle, without uttering a word.

She approached me, with the tongs in one hand, and with a plainly-bound volume in the other.

'Is that the book?' she said. 'Open it, and see.'

I took the book from her.

'It's tremendously interesting,' she went on. 'I've read it twice over – I have. Mind you, *I* believe he did it, after all.'

Did it? Did what? What was she talking about? I tried to put the question to her. I struggled – quite vainly – to say only those words: 'What are you talking about?'

She seemed to lose all patience with me. She snatched the book out of my hand, and opened it before me on the table by which we were standing side by side.

'I declare you're as helpless as a baby!' she said, contemptuously. 'There! *Is* that the book?'

I read the first lines on the title-page: –

A COMPLETE REPORT OF

THE TRIAL OF

EUSTACE MACALLAN

I stopped, and looked up at her. She started back from me with a scream of terror. I looked down again at the title-page, and read the next lines: –

FOR THE ALLEGED POISONING

OF

HIS WIFE.

There, God's mercy remembered me. There, the black blank of a swoon swallowed me up.

CHAPTER XI

The Return to Life

My first remembrance, when I began to recover my senses, was the remembrance of Pain – agonising pain, as if every nerve in my body was being twisted and torn out of me. My whole being writhed and quivered under the dumb and dreadful protest of Nature against the effort to recall me to life. I would have given worlds to be able to cry out – to entreat the unseen creatures about me to give me back to death. How long that speechless agony held me, I never knew. In a longer or a shorter time there stole over me slowly, a sleepy sense of relief. I heard my own laboured breathing. I felt my hands moving feebly and mechanically like the hands of a baby. I faintly opened my eyes, and looked round me – as if I had passed through the ordeal of death, and had awakened to new senses, in a new world.

The first person I saw, was a man – a stranger. He moved quietly out of my sight; beckoning, as he disappeared, to some other person in the room.

Slowly and unwillingly, the other person advanced to the sofa on which I lay. A faint cry of joy escaped me; I tried to hold out my feeble hands. The other person who was approaching me was my husband!

I looked at him eagerly. He never looked at me in return. With his eyes on the ground, with a strange appearance of confusion and distress in his face, he, too, moved away out of my sight. The unknown man whom I had first noticed, followed him out of the room. I called after him faintly, 'Eustace!' He never answered; he never returned. With an effort I moved my head on the pillow, so as to look round on the other side of the sofa. Another familiar face appeared before me as if in a dream. My good old Benjamin was sitting watching me, with the tears in his eyes.

He rose and took my hand silently, in his simple, kindly way.

'Where is Eustace?' I asked. 'Why has he gone away and left me?'

I was still miserably weak. My eyes wandered mechanically round the room as I put the question. I saw Major Fitz-David. I saw the table on which the singing-girl had opened the book to show it to me. I saw the girl herself, sitting alone in a corner, with her handkerchief to her eyes as if she was crying. In one mysterious moment, my memory recovered its powers. The recollection of that fatal title-page came back to me in all its horror. The one feeling that it roused in me now, was a longing to see my husband – to throw myself into his arms, and tell him how firmly I believed in his innocence, how truly and dearly I loved him. I seized on Benjamin with feeble, trembling hands. 'Bring him back to me!' I cried, wildly. 'Where is he? Help me to get up!'

A strange voice answered, firmly and kindly:

'Compose yourself, madam. Mr Woodville is waiting until you have recovered, in a room close by.'

I looked at him, and recognised the stranger who had followed my husband out of the room. Why had he returned alone? Why was Eustace not with me, like the rest of them? I tried to raise myself, and get on my feet. The stranger gently pressed me back again on the pillow. I attempted to resist him; quite uselessly of course. His firm hand held me, as gently as ever, in my place.

'You must rest a little,' he said. 'You must take some wine. If you exert yourself now, you will faint again.'

Old Benjamin stooped over me, and whispered a word of explanation.

'It's the doctor, my dear. You must do as he tells you.'

The doctor? They had called the doctor in to help them! I began dimly to understand that my fainting-fit must have presented symptoms far more serious than the fainting-fits of women in general. I appealed to the doctor, in a helpless, querulous way, to account to me for my husband's extraordinary absence.

'Why did you let him leave the room?' I asked. 'If I can't go to him why don't you bring him here to me?'

The doctor appeared to be at a loss how to reply to me. He looked at Benjamin, and said, 'Will you speak to Mrs Woodville?'

Benjamin, in his turn, looked at Major Fitz-David, and said, 'Will *you?*' The Major signed to them both to leave us. They rose together, and went into the front room; pulling the door to after them in its grooves. As they left us, the girl who had so strangely revealed my husband's secret to me rose in her corner and approached the sofa.

'I suppose I had better go too?' she said, addressing Major Fitz-David.

'If you please,' the Major answered.

He spoke (as I thought) rather coldly. She tossed her head, and turned her back on him in high indignation. 'I must say a word for myself!' cried this strange creature, with an hysterical outbreak of energy. 'I must say a word, or I shall burst!'

With that extraordinary preface she suddenly turned my way, and poured out a perfect torrent of words on me.

'You hear how the Major speaks to me?' she began. 'He blames me – poor Me – for everything that has happened. I am as innocent as the new-born babe. I acted for the best. I thought you wanted the book. I don't know now what made you faint dead away when I opened it. And the Major blames Me! As if it was my fault! I am not one of the fainting sort myself; but I feel it, I can tell you. Yes! I feel it, though I don't faint about it. I come of respectable parents – *I* do. My name is Hoighty – Miss Hoighty.[1] I have my own self-respect; and it's wounded. I say my self-respect is wounded, when I find myself blamed without deserving it. You deserve it, if anybody does. Didn't you tell me you were looking for a book? And didn't I present it to you promiscuously, with the best intentions? I think you might say so yourself, now the doctor has brought you to again. I think you might speak up for a poor girl who is worked to death with singing and languages and what not – a poor girl who has nobody else to speak for her. I am as respectable as you are, if you come to that. My name is Hoighty. My parents are in business, and my mamma has seen better days, and mixed in the best of company.'

There, Miss Hoighty lifted her handkerchief again to her face, and burst modestly into tears behind it.

It was certainly hard to hold *her* responsible for what had happened. I answered as kindly as I could; and I attempted to speak to Major Fitz-David in her defence. He knew what terrible anxieties were oppressing me at that moment; and, considerately refusing to hear a word, he took the task of consoling his young prima-donna entirely on himself. What he said to her I neither heard, nor cared to hear: he spoke in a whisper. It ended in his pacifying Miss Hoighty, by kissing her hand, and leading her (as he might have led a duchess) out of the room.

'I hope that foolish girl has not annoyed you – at such a time as this?' he said, very earnestly, when he returned to the sofa. 'I can't tell you how grieved I am at what has happened. I was careful to warn you, as you may remember. Still, if I could only have foreseen—'

I let him proceed no farther. No human forethought could have provided against what had happened. Besides, dreadful as the discovery had been, I would rather have made it, and suffer under it, as I was suffering now, than have been kept in the dark. I told him this. And then I turned to the one subject that was now of any interest to me – the subject of my unhappy husband.

'How did he come to this house?' I asked.

'He came here with Mr Benjamin, shortly after I returned,' the Major replied.

'Long after I was taken ill?'

'No. I had just sent for the doctor – feeling seriously alarmed about you.'

'What brought him here? Did he return to the hotel, and miss me?'

'Yes. He returned earlier than he had anticipated; and he felt uneasy at not finding you at the hotel.'

'Did he suspect me of being with you? Did he come here from the hotel?'

'No. He appears to have gone first to Mr Benjamin, to enquire about you. What he heard from your old friend, I cannot say. I only know that Mr Benjamin accompanied him when he came here.'

This brief explanation was quite enough for me – I understood what had happened. Eustace would easily frighten simple old Benjamin about my absence from the hotel; and, once alarmed, Benjamin would be persuaded without difficulty to repeat the few words which had passed between us, on the subject of Major Fitz-David. My husband's presence in the Major's house was perfectly explained. But his extraordinary conduct in leaving the room, at the very time when I was just recovering my senses, still remained to be accounted for. Major

Fitz-David looked seriously embarrassed when I put the question to him.

'I hardly know how to explain it to you,' he said. 'Eustace has surprised and disappointed me.'

He spoke very gravely. His looks told me more than his words: his looks alarmed me.

'Eustace has not quarrelled with you?' I said.

'Oh, no!'

'He understands that you have not broken your promise to him?'

'Certainly. My young vocalist (Miss Hoighty) told the doctor exactly what had happened; and the doctor in her presence repeated the statement to your husband.'

'Did the doctor see the "Trial"?'

'Neither the doctor nor Mr Benjamin has seen the "Trial." I have locked it up; and I have carefully kept the terrible story of your connection with the prisoner a secret from all of them. Mr Benjamin evidently has his suspicions. But the doctor has no idea, and Miss Hoighty has no idea, of the true cause of your fainting fit. They both believe that you are subject to serious nervous attacks; and that your husband's name is really Woodville. All that the truest friend could do to spare Eustace, I have done. He persists, nevertheless, in blaming me for letting you enter my house. And worse, far worse than this, he persists in declaring that the event of to-day has fatally estranged you from him. "There is an end of our married life," he said to me, "now she knows that I am the man who was tried at Edinburgh for poisoning my wife!" '

I rose from the sofa in horror.

'Good God!' I cried, 'does Eustace suppose that I doubt his innocence?'

'He denies that it is possible for you, or for anybody, to believe in his innocence,' the Major replied.

'Help me to the door,' I said. 'Where is he? I must, and will, see him!'

I dropped back exhausted on the sofa as I said the words. Major Fitz-David poured out a glass of wine from the bottle on the table, and insisted on my drinking it.

'You shall see him,' said the Major. 'I promise you that. The doctor has forbidden him to leave the house, until you have seen him. Only wait a little! My poor dear lady, wait, if it is only for a few minutes, until you are stronger!'

I had no choice but to obey him. Oh, those miserable helpless minutes on the sofa! I cannot write of them without shuddering at the recollection – even at this distance of time.

'Bring him here!' I said. 'Pray, pray bring him here!'

'Who is to persuade him to come back?' asked the Major, sadly. 'How can I, how can anybody, prevail with a man – a madman I had almost said! – who could leave you at the moment when you first opened your eyes on him? I saw Eustace alone, in the next room, while the doctor was in attendance on you. I tried to shake his obstinate distrust of your belief in his innocence, and of my belief in his innocence, by every argument and every appeal that an old friend could address to him. He had but one answer to give me. Reason as I might, and plead as I might, he still persisted in referring me to the Scotch Verdict.'

'The Scotch Verdict?' I repeated. 'What is that?'

The Major looked surprised at the question.

'Have you really never heard of the Trial?' he said.

'Never.'

'I thought it strange,' he went on, 'when you told me you had found out your husband's true name, that the discovery appeared to have suggested no painful association to your mind. It is not more than three years since all England was talking of your husband. One can hardly wonder at his taking refuge, poor fellow, in an assumed name! Where could you have been at the time?'

'Did you say it was three years ago?' I asked.

'Yes.'

I understood my strange ignorance of what appeared to be so well known to other people. Three years since, my father was alive. I was living with him, in a country house in Italy – up in the mountains, near Siena. We never saw an English newspaper, or met with an English traveller, for weeks and weeks together. There might certainly have been some reference made to the famous Scotch Trial in my father's letters from England. If there was, he never told me of it. Or, if he did mention the case, I must have forgotten it in course of time. 'Tell me,' I said to the Major, 'what has the Verdict to do with my husband's horrible doubt of us? Eustace is a free man. The verdict was Not Guilty, of course?'

Major Fitz-David shook his head sadly.

'Eustace was tried in Scotland,' he said. 'There is a verdict allowed by the Scotch law, which (so far as I know) is not permitted by the laws of any other civilised country on the face of the earth. When the jury are in doubt whether to condemn or acquit the prisoner brought before them, they are permitted, in Scotland, to express that doubt by a form of compromise. If there is not evidence enough, on the one hand, to justify them in finding a prisoner guilty, and not evidence enough, on the other hand, to thoroughly convince them that a prisoner is innocent, they extricate themselves from the difficulty by finding a verdict of Not Proven.'

'Was that the verdict when Eustace was tried?' I asked.

'Yes.'

'The jury were not quite satisfied that my husband was guilty? and not quite satisfied that my husband was innocent? Is that what the Scotch Verdict means?'

'That is what the Scotch Verdict means. For three years that doubt about him in the minds of the jury who tried him, has stood on public record.'

Oh, my poor darling! my innocent martyr! I understood it at last. The false name in which he had married me; the terrible words he had spoken when he had warned me to respect his secret; the still more terrible doubt that he felt of me at that moment – it was all intelligible to my sympathies; it was all clear to my understanding, now. I got up again from the sofa, strong in a daring resolution which the Scotch Verdict had suddenly kindled in me – a resolution, at once too sacred and too desperate to be confided, in the first instance, to any other than my husband's ear.

'Take me to Eustace,' I said. 'I am strong enough to bear anything now.'

After one searching look at me, the Major silently offered me his arm. We left the room together.

95

CHAPTER XII

The Scotch Verdict

We walked to the far end of the hall. Major Fitz-David opened the door of a long narrow room, built out at the back of the house as a smoking-room, and extending along one side of the courtyard as far as the stable wall.

My husband was alone in the room; seated at the farther end of it, near the fireplace. He started to his feet, and faced me in silence as I entered. The Major softly closed the door on us, and retired. Eustace never stirred a step to meet me. I ran to him, and threw my arms round his neck, and kissed him. The embrace was not returned; the kiss was not returned. He passively submitted – nothing more.

'Eustace,' I said, 'I never loved you more dearly than I love you at this moment! I never felt for you as I feel for you now!'

He released himself deliberately from my arms. He signed to me, with the mechanical courtesy of a stranger, to take a chair.

'Thank you, Valeria,' he answered, in cold measured tones. 'You could say no less to me after what has happened; and you could say no more. Thank you.'

We were standing before the fireplace. He left me, and walked away slowly with his head down; apparently intending to leave the room. I followed him – I got before him – I placed myself between him and the door.

'Why do you leave me?' I said. 'Why do you speak to me in this cruel way? Are you angry, Eustace? My darling, if you *are* angry, I ask you to forgive me.'

'It is I who ought to ask *your* pardon,' he replied. 'I beg you to forgive me, Valeria, for having made you my wife.'

He pronounced those words with a hopeless, heart-broken humility, dreadful to see. I laid my hand on his bosom. I said, 'Eustace, look at me.'

He slowly lifted his eyes to my face – eyes cold and clear and tearless, looking at me in steady resignation, in immovable despair. In the utter wretchedness of that moment, I was like him; I was as quiet and as cold as my husband. He chilled, he froze me.

'Is it possible,' I said, 'that you doubt my belief in your innocence?'

He left the question unanswered. He sighed bitterly to himself. 'Poor woman!' he said, as a stranger might have said, pitying me. 'Poor woman!'

My heart swelled in me as if it would burst. I lifted my hand from his bosom, and laid it on his shoulder to support myself.

'I don't ask you to pity me, Eustace; I ask you to do me justice. You are not doing me justice. If you had trusted me with the truth in the days when we first knew that we loved each other – if you had told me all, and more than all, that I know now – as God is my witness, I would still have married you! *Now* do you doubt that I believe you are an innocent man?'

'I don't doubt it,' he said. 'All your impulses are generous. You are speaking generously, and feeling generously. Don't blame me, my poor child, if I look on farther than you do; if I see what is to come – too surely to come – in the cruel future.'

'The cruel future!' I repeated. 'What do you mean?'

'You believe in my innocence, Valeria. The Jury who tried me doubted it – and have left that doubt on record. What reason have *you* for believing, in the face of the Verdict, that I am an innocent man?'

'I want no reason! I believe, in spite of the Jury, in spite of the Verdict.'

'Will your friends agree with you? When your uncle and aunt know what has happened – and sooner or later they must know it – what will they say? They will say, "He began badly; he concealed from our niece that he had been a prisoner on his trial; he married our niece under a false name. He may say he is innocent; but we have only his word for it. When he was put on his trial, the verdict was Not Proven. Not Proven won't do for us. If the Jury have done him an injustice – if he *is* innocent – let him prove it." That is what the world thinks and says of me. That is what your friends will think and say of me. The time is coming, Valeria, when you – even You – will feel that your friends have reason to appeal to on their side, and that you have no reason on yours.'

97

'That time will never come!' I answered, warmly. 'You wrong me, you insult me, in thinking it possible!'

He put down my hand from him, and drew back a step, with a bitter smile.

'We have only been married a few days, Valeria. Your love for me is new and young. Time, which wears away all things, will wear away the first fervour of that love.'

'Never! never!'

He drew back from me a little farther still.

'Look at the world round you,' he said. 'The happiest husbands and wives have their occasional misunderstandings and disagreements; the brightest married life has its passing clouds. When those days come for *us*, the doubts and fears that you don't feel now, will find their way to you then. When the clouds rise on *our* married life – when I say my first harsh word, when you make your first hasty reply – then, in the solitude of your own room, in the stillness of the wakeful night, you will think of my first wife's miserable death. You will remember that I was held responsible for it, and that my innocence was never proved. You will say to yourself, "Did it begin, in *her* time, with a harsh word from him, and with a hasty reply from her? Will it one day end with me, as the Jury half feared that it ended with her?" Hideous questions for a wife to ask herself! You will stifle them; you will recoil from them, like a good woman, with horror. But, when we meet the next morning, you will be on your guard, and I shall see it, and know in my heart of hearts what it means. Embittered by that knowledge, my next harsh word may be harsher still. Your next thoughts of me may remind you, more vividly and more boldly, that your husband was once tried as a poisoner, and that the question of his first wife's death was never properly cleared up. Do you see what materials for a domestic hell are mingling for us here? Was it for nothing that I warned you, solemnly warned you, to draw back, when I found you bent on discovering the truth? Can I ever be at your bedside now, when you are ill, and not remind you, in the most innocent things I do, of what happened at that other bedside, in the time of that other woman whom I married first? If I pour out your medicine, I commit a suspicious action – they said I poisoned *her* in her medicine. If I bring you a cup of tea, I revive the remembrance of a horrid doubt – they said I put the arsenic in *her* cup of tea. If I kiss you when I leave the room – I remind you that the prosecution accused me of kissing *her*, to save appearances and produce an effect on the nurse. Can we live together on such terms as these? No mortal creatures could support the misery of it. This very day I said to you, "If you stir a step farther in this matter, there is an end of your happiness for the rest of your life." You have taken that step – and the end has come to your happiness and to mine. The doubt that kills love has cast its blight on you and on me, for the rest of our lives!'

So far I had forced myself to listen to him. At those last words, the picture of the future that he was placing before me became too hideous to be endured. I refused to hear more.

'You are talking horribly,' I said. 'At your age and at mine, have we done with love, and done with hope? It is blasphemy to love and hope to say it!'

'Wait till you have read the Trial,' he answered. 'You mean to read it, I suppose?'

'Every word of it! With a motive, Eustace, which you have yet to know.'

'No motive of yours, Valeria, no love and hope of yours, can alter the inexorable facts. My first wife died poisoned; and the verdict of the Jury has not absolutely acquitted me of the guilt of causing her death. As long as you were ignorant of that, the possibilities of happiness were always within our reach. Now you know it, I say again – our married life is at an end.'

'No,' I said. 'Now I know it, our married life has begun – begun with a new object for your wife's devotion, with a new reason for your wife's love!'

'What do you mean?'

I went near to him again, and took his hand.

'What did you tell me the world has said of you?' I asked. 'What did you tell me my friends would say of you? "Not Proven won't do for us. If the Jury have done him an injustice – if he *is* innocent – let him prove it." Those were the words you put into the mouths of my friends. I adopt them for mine! *I* say, Not Proven won't do for *me*.

Prove your right, Eustace, to a verdict of Not Guilty. Why have you let three years pass without doing it? Shall I guess why? You have waited for your wife to help you. Here she is, my darling, ready to help you with all her heart and soul. Here she is, with one object in life – to show the world, and to show the Scotch Jury, that her husband is an innocent man!'

I had roused myself; my pulses were throbbing, my voice rang through the room. Had I roused *him*? What was his answer?

'Read the Trial.' That was his answer.

I seized him by the arm. In my indignation and my despair, I shook him with all my strength. God forgive me, I could almost have struck him, for the tone in which he had spoken, and the look that he had cast on me!

'I have told you that I mean to read the Trial,' I said. 'I mean to read it, line by line, with you. Some inexcusable mistake has been made. Evidence in your favour, that might have been found, has not been found. Suspicious circumstances have not been investigated. Crafty people have not been watched. Eustace! the conviction of some dreadful oversight, committed by you or by the persons who helped you, is firmly settled in my mind. The resolution to set that vile Verdict right was the first resolution that came to me, when I first heard of it in the next room. We *will* set it right! We *must* set it right – for your sake, for my sake, for the sake of our children if we are blest with children. Oh, my own love, don't look at me with those cold eyes! Don't answer me in those hard tones! Don't treat me as if I was talking ignorantly and madly of something that can never be!'

Still, I failed to rouse him. His next words were spoken compassionately rather than coldly – that was all.

'My defence was undertaken by the greatest lawyers in the land,' he said. 'After such men have done their utmost, and have failed – my poor Valeria, what can you, what can I, do? We can only submit.'

'Never!' I cried. 'The greatest lawyers are mortal men; the greatest lawyers have made mistakes before now. You can't deny that.'

'Read the Trial.' For the third time, he said those cruel words, and said no more.

In utter despair of moving him – feeling keenly, bitterly (if I must own it), his merciless superiority to all that I had said to him in the honest fervour of my devotion and my love – I thought of Major Fitz-David as a last resort. In the disordered state of my mind, at that moment, it made no difference to me that the Major had already tried to reason with him, and had failed. In the face of the facts, I had a blind belief in the influence of his old friend, if his old friend could only be prevailed upon to support my view.

'Is there no persuading you?' I said. He looked away without answering. 'At least you can wait for me a moment,' I went on. 'I want you to hear another opinion, besides mine.'

I left him, and returned to the study. Major Fitz-David was not there. I knocked at the door of communication with the front room. It was opened instantly by the Major himself. The doctor had gone away. Benjamin still remained in the room.

'Will you come and speak to Eustace?' I began. 'If you will only say what I want you to say—'

Before I could add a word more, I heard the house door opened and closed. Major Fitz-David and Benjamin heard it too. They looked at each other in silence.

I ran back, before the Major could stop me, to the room in which I had seen Eustace. It was empty. My husband had left the house.

CHAPTER XIII

The Man's Decision

My first impulse was the reckless impulse to follow Eustace – openly, through the streets.

The Major and Benjamin both opposed this hasty resolution on my part. They appealed to my own sense of self-respect, without (so far as I remember it) producing the slightest effect on my mind. They were more successful when they entreated me next to be patient, for my husband's sake. In mercy to Eustace, they begged me to wait half-an-hour. If he failed to return in that time, they pledged themselves to accompany me in search of him to the hotel.

In mercy to Eustace, I consented to wait. What I suffered under the forced necessity for remaining passive at that crisis in my life, no words of mine can tell. It will be better if I go on with my narrative.

Benjamin was the first to ask me what had passed between my husband and myself.

'You may speak freely, my dear,' he said. 'I know what has happened since you have been in Major Fitz-David's house. No one has told me about it; I found it out for myself. If you remember, I was struck by the name "Macallan," when you first mentioned it to me at my cottage. I couldn't guess why, at the time. I know why, now.'

Hearing this, I told them both unreservedly what I had said to Eustace, and how he had received it. To my unspeakable disappointment, they both sided with my husband – treating my view of his position as a mere dream. They said it, as he had said it, 'You have not read the Trial.'

I was really enraged with them. 'The facts are enough for *me*,' I said. 'We know he is innocent. Why is his innocence not proved? It ought to be, it must be, it shall be! If the Trial tells me it can't be done, I refuse to believe the Trial. Where is the book, Major? Let me see for myself, if his lawyers have left nothing for his wife to do. Did they love him as I love him? Give me the book!'

Major Fitz-David looked at Benjamin.

'It will only additionally shock and distress her, if I give her the book,' he said. 'Don't you agree with me?'

I interposed before Benjamin could answer.

'If you refuse my request,' I said, 'you will oblige me, Major, to go to the nearest bookseller, and tell him to buy the Trial for me. I am determined to read it.'

This time, Benjamin sided with me.

'Nothing can make matters worse than they are, sir,' he said. 'If I may be permitted to advise, let her have her own way.'

The Major rose, and took the book out of the Italian cabinet – to which he had consigned it for safe keeping.

'My young friend tells me, that she informed you of her regrettable outbreak of temper a few days since,' he said, as he handed me the volume. 'I was not aware, at the time, what book she had in her hand when she so far forgot herself as to destroy the vase. When I left you in the study, I supposed the Report of the Trial to be in its customary place, on the top shelf of the bookcase; and I own I felt some curiosity to know whether you would think of examining that shelf. The broken vase – it is needless to conceal it from you now – was one of a pair presented to me by your husband and his first wife, only a week before the poor woman's terrible death. I felt my first presentiment that you were on the brink of discovery, when I found you looking at the fragments – and I fancy I betrayed to you that something of the kind was disturbing me. You looked as if you noticed it.'

'I did notice it, Major. And I, too, had a vague idea that I was on the way to discovery. Will you look at your watch? Have we waited half-an-hour yet?'

My impatience had misled me. The ordeal of the half-hour was not yet at an end.

Slowly and more slowly, the heavy minutes followed each other – and still there were no signs of my husband's return. We tried to continue our conversation, and failed. Nothing was audible; no sounds but the ordinary sounds of the street disturbed the dreadful silence. Try as I might to repel it, there was one foreboding thought that pressed closer and closer on my mind as the interval of waiting wore its weary way on. I shuddered as I asked myself, if our married life had come to an end – if Eustace had really left me?

The Major saw – what Benjamin's slower perception had not yet discovered – that my fortitude was beginning to sink under the unrelieved oppression of suspense.

'Come!' he said. 'Let us go to the hotel.'

It then wanted nearly five minutes to the half-hour. I *looked* my gratitude to Major Fitz-David for sparing me those last five minutes: I could not speak to him, or to Benjamin. In silence, we three got into a cab and drove to the hotel.

The landlady met us in the hall. Nothing had been seen or heard of Eustace. There was a letter waiting for me upstairs, on the table in our sitting-room. It had been left at the hotel by a messenger, only a few minutes since.

Trembling and breathless, I ran up the stairs; the two gentlemen following me. The writing on the address of the letter was in my husband's hand. My heart sank in me as I looked at the lines; there could be but one reason for his writing to me. That closed envelope held his farewell words. I sat with the letter on my lap, stupefied – incapable of opening it.

Kind-hearted Benjamin attempted to comfort and encourage me. The Major, with his larger experience of women, warned the old man to be silent.

'Wait!' I heard him whisper. 'Speaking to her will do no good, now. Give her time.'

Acting on a sudden impulse, I held out the letter to him as he spoke. Even moments might be of importance, if Eustace had indeed left me. To give me time, might be to lose the opportunity of recalling him.

'You are his old friend,' I said. 'Open his letter, Major, and read it for me.'

Major Fitz-David opened the letter, and read it through to himself. When he had done, he threw it on the table with a gesture which was almost a gesture of contempt.

'There is but one excuse for him,' he said. 'The man is mad.'

Those words told me all. I knew the worst; and, knowing it, I could read the letter. It ran thus: –

'MY BELOVED VALERIA, –

'When you read these lines, you read my farewell words. I return to my solitary unfriended life – my life before I knew you.

'My darling, you have been cruelly treated. You have been entrapped into marrying a man who has been publicly accused of poisoning his first wife – and who has not been honourably and completely acquitted of the charge. And you know it!

'Can you live on terms of mutual confidence and mutual esteem with me, when I have committed this fraud, and when I stand towards you in this position? It was possible for you to live with me happily, while you were in ignorance of the truth. It is *not* possible, now you know all.

'No! the one atonement I can make is – to leave you. Your one chance of future happiness is to be disassociated, at once and for ever, from my dishonoured life. I love you, Valeria – truly, devotedly, passionately. But the spectre of the poisoned woman rises between us. It makes no difference that I am innocent even of the thought of harming my first wife. My innocence has not been proved. In this world, my innocence can never be proved. You are young and loving, and generous and hopeful. Bless others, Valeria, with your rare attractions and your delightful gifts. They are of no avail with *me*. The poisoned woman stands between us. If you live with me now, you will see her as I see her. *That* torture shall never be yours. I love you. I leave you.

'Do you think me hard and cruel? Wait a little, and time will change that way of thinking. As the years go on, you will say to yourself, "Basely as he deceived me, there was some generosity in him. He was man enough to release me of his own free will."

'Yes, Valeria, I fully, freely release you. If it be possible to annul our marriage, let it be done. Recover your liberty by any means that you may be advised to employ; and be assured beforehand of my entire and implicit submission. My lawyers have the necessary instructions on this subject. Your uncle has only to communicate with them, and I think he will be satisfied of my resolution to do you justice. The one interest that I have now left in life, is my interest in your welfare and your happiness in the time to come. Your welfare and your happiness are no longer to be found in your union with Me.

'I can write no more. This letter will wait for you at the hotel. It will be useless to attempt to trace me. I know my own weakness. My heart is all yours: I might yield to you if I let you see me again.

'Show these lines to your uncle, and to any friends whose opinions you may value. I have only to sign my dishonoured name; and every one will understand, and applaud, my motive for writing as I do. The name justifies – amply justifies – the letter. Forgive me, and forget me. Farewell!

'EUSTACE MACALLAN.'

In those words, he took his leave of me. We had then been married – six days.

CHAPTER XIV

The Woman's Answer

Thus far, I have written of myself with perfect frankness, and, I think I may fairly add, with some courage as well. My frankness fails me, and my courage fails me, when I look back to my husband's farewell letter, and try to recall the storm of contending passions that it roused in my mind. No! I cannot tell the truth about myself – I dare not tell the truth about myself – at that terrible time. Men! consult your observation of women, and imagine what I felt. Women! look into your own hearts, and see what I felt, for yourselves.

What I *did*, when my mind was quiet again, is an easier matter to deal with. I answered my husband's letter. My reply to him shall appear in these pages. It will show, in some degree, what effect (of the lasting sort) his desertion of me produced on my mind. It will also reveal the motives that sustained me, the hopes that animated me, in the new and strange life which my next chapters must describe.

I was removed from the hotel, in the care of my fatherly old friend, Benjamin. A bedroom was prepared for me in his little villa. There, I passed the first night of my separation from my husband. Towards the morning, my weary brain got some rest – I slept.

At breakfast-time, Major Fitz-David called to enquire about me. He had kindly volunteered to go and speak for me to my husband's lawyers, on the preceding day. They had admitted that they knew where Eustace had gone; but they declared at the same time that they were positively forbidden to communicate his address to anyone. In other respects, their 'Instructions' in relation to the wife of their client were (as they were pleased to express it) 'generous to a fault.' I had only to write to them, and they would furnish me with a copy by return of post.

This was the Major's news. He refrained, with the tact that distinguished him, from putting any questions to me beyond questions relating to the state of my health. These answered, he took his leave of me for that day. He and Benjamin had a long talk together afterwards, in the garden of the villa.

I retired to my room, and wrote to my uncle Starkweather; telling him exactly what had happened, and enclosing him a copy of my husband's letter. This done, I went out for a little while to breathe the fresh air, and to think. I was soon weary, and went back again to my room to rest. My kind old Benjamin left me at perfect liberty to be alone as long as I pleased. Towards the afternoon, I began to feel a little more like my old self again. I mean, by this, that I could think of Eustace, without bursting out crying, and could speak to Benjamin, without distressing and frightening the dear old man.

That night, I had a little more sleep. The next morning, I was strong enough to confront the first and foremost duty that I now owed to myself – the duty of answering my husband's letter.

I wrote to him in these words: –

'I am still too weak and weary, Eustace, to write to you at any length. But my mind is clear. I have formed my own opinion of you and your letter; and I know what I mean to do now you have left me. Some women, in my situation, might think that you had forfeited all right to their confidence. I don't think that. So I write and tell you what is in my mind, in the plainest and fewest words that I can use.

'You say you love me – and you leave me. I don't understand loving a woman, and leaving her. For my part, in spite of the hard things you have said and written to me, and in spite of the cruel manner in which you have left me, I love you – and I won't give you up. No! As long as I live, I mean to live your wife.

'Does this surprise you? It surprises *me*. If another woman wrote in this manner to a man who had behaved to her as you have behaved, I should be quite at a loss to account for her conduct. I am quite at a loss to account for my own conduct. I ought to hate you – and yet I can't help loving you. I am ashamed of myself; but so it is.

'You need feel no fear of my attempting to find out where you are, and of my trying to persuade you to return to me. I am not quite foolish enough to do that. You are not in a fit state of mind to return to me. You are all wrong, all over, from head to foot. When you get right again, I am vain enough to think that you will return to me of your own accord. And shall I be weak enough to forgive you? Yes! I shall certainly be weak enough to forgive you.

'But how are you to get right again?

'I have puzzled my brains over this question by night and by day – and my opinion is that you will never get right again, unless I help you.

'How am I to help you?

'The question is easily answered. What the Law has failed to do for you, your Wife must do for you. Do you remember what I said, when we were together in the back room at Major Fitz-David's house? I told you that the first thought that came to me, when I heard what the Scotch Jury had done, was the thought of setting their vile Verdict right. Well! Your letter has fixed this idea more firmly in my mind than ever. The only chance that I can see of winning you back to me, in the character of a penitent and loving husband, is to change that underhand Scotch Verdict of Not Proven, into an honest English verdict of Not Guilty.

'Are you surprised at the knowledge of the law which this way of writing betrays in an ignorant woman? I have been learning, my dear: the Law and the Lady have begun by understanding one another. In plain English, I have looked into Ogilvie's Imperial Dictionary;[1] and Ogilvie tells me: "A verdict of Not Proven only indicates that, in the opinion of the Jury, there is a deficiency in the evidence to convict the prisoner. A verdict of Not Guilty imports the Jury's opinion that the prisoner is innocent." – Eustace! that shall be the opinion of the world in general, and of the Scotch Jury in particular, in your case. To that one object I dedicate my life to come, if God spares me!

'Who will help me, when I need help, is more than I yet know. There was a time when I had hoped that we should go hand in hand together in doing this good work. That hope is at an end. I no longer expect you, or ask you, to help me. A man who thinks as you think, can give no help to anybody – it is his miserable condition to have no hope. So be it! I will hope for two, and will work for two; and I shall find some one to help me – never fear – if I deserve it.

'I will say nothing about my plans – I have not read the Trial yet.

It is quite enough for me that I know you are innocent. When a man is innocent, there *must* be a way of proving it: the one thing needful is to find the way. Sooner or later, with or without assistance, I shall find it. Yes! before I know any single particular of the Case, I tell you positively – I shall find it!

'You may laugh over this blind confidence on my part, or you may cry over it. I don't pretend to know whether I am an object for ridicule or an object for pity. Of one thing only I am certain. I mean to win you back, a man vindicated before the world, without a stain on his character or his name – thanks to his Wife.

'Write to me sometimes, Eustace; and believe me, through all the bitterness of this bitter business, your faithful and loving

'VALERIA.'

There was my reply! Poor enough as a composition (I could write a much better letter now), it had, if I may presume to say so, one merit. It was the honest expression of what I really meant and felt.

I read it to Benjamin. He held up his hands with his customary gesture when he was thoroughly bewildered and dismayed. 'It seems the rashest letter that ever was written,' said the dear old man. 'I never heard, Valeria, of a woman doing what you propose to do. Lord help us! the new generation is beyond my fathoming. I wish your uncle Starkweather was here: I wonder what he would say? Oh, dear me, what a letter from a wife to a husband! Do you really mean to send it to him?'

I added immeasurably to my old friend's surprise, by not even employing the post-office. I wished to see the 'Instructions' which my husband had left behind him. So I took the letter to his lawyers myself.

The firm consisted of two partners. They both received me together. One was a soft lean man, with a sour smile. The other was a hard fat man, with ill-tempered eyebrows. I took a great dislike to both of them. On their side, they appeared to feel a strong distrust of me. We began by disagreeing. They showed me my husband's Instructions; providing, among other things, for the payment of one clear half of his income, as long as he lived, to his wife. I positively refused to touch a farthing of his money.

The lawyers were unaffectedly shocked and astonished at this decision. Nothing of the sort had ever happened before, in the whole course of their experience. They argued and remonstrated with me. The partner with the ill-tempered eyebrows wanted to know what my reasons were. The partner with the sour smile reminded his colleague satirically that I was a lady, and had therefore no reasons to give. I only answered, 'Be so good as to forward my letter, gentlemen' – and left them.

I have no wish to claim any credit to myself in these pages which I do not honestly deserve. The truth is that my pride forbade me to accept help from Eustace, now that he had left me. My own little fortune (eight hundred a year) had been settled on myself when I married.[2] It had been more than I wanted as a single woman, and I was resolved that it should be enough for me now. Benjamin had insisted on my considering his cottage as my home. Under these circumstances, the expenses in which my determination to clear my husband's character might involve me, were the only expenses for which I had to provide. I could afford to be independent – and independent I resolved that I would be.

While I am occupied in confessing my weakness and my errors, it is only right to add that, dearly as I still loved my unhappy misguided husband, there was one little fault of his which I found it not easy to forgive.

Pardoning other things, I could not pardon his concealing from me that he had been married to a first wife. Why I should have felt this so bitterly as I did, at certain times and seasons, I am not able to explain. Jealousy was at the bottom of it, I suppose. And yet, I was not conscious of being jealous – especially when I thought of the poor creature's miserable death. Still, at odd times when I was discouraged and out of temper, I used to say to myself, 'Eustace ought not to have kept *that* secret from me.' What would *he* have said, if I had been a widow, and had never told him of it?

It was getting on towards evening when I returned to the cottage. Benjamin appeared to have been on the look-out for me. Before I could ring at the bell he opened the garden gate.

'Prepare yourself for a surprise, my dear,' he said. 'Your uncle, the

Reverend Doctor Starkweather, has arrived from the North, and is waiting to see you. He received your letter this morning, and he took the first train to London as soon as he had read it.'

In another minute my uncle's strong arms were round me. In my forlorn position, I felt the good Vicar's kindness, in travelling all the way to London to see me, very gratefully. It brought the tears into my eyes – tears, without bitterness, that did me good.

'I have come, my dear child, to take you back to your old home,' he said. 'No words can tell how fervently I wish you had never left your aunt and me. Well! well! we won't talk about it. The mischief is done – and the next thing is to mend it as well as we can. If I could only get within arm's length of that husband of yours, Valeria – there! there! God forgive me, I am forgetting that I am a clergyman. What shall I forget next, I wonder? By-the-bye, your aunt sends you her dearest love. She is more superstitious than ever. This miserable business doesn't surprise her a bit. She says it all began with your making that mistake about your name in signing the church register. You remember? Was there ever such stuff? Ah, she's a foolish woman, that wife of mine! But she means well – a good soul at bottom. She would have travelled all the way here along with me, if I would have let her. I said, "No; you stop at home and look after the house and the parish; and I'll bring the child back." You shall have your old bedroom, Valeria, with the white curtains, you know, looped up with blue! We will return to the Vicarage (if you can get up in time) by the nine-forty train to-morrow morning.'

Return to the Vicarage! How could I do that? How could I hope to gain what was now the one object of my existence, if I buried myself in a remote north-country village? It was simply impossible for me to accompany Doctor Starkweather on his return to his own house.

'I thank you, uncle, with all my heart,' I said. 'But I am afraid I can't leave London for the present.'

'You can't leave London for the present?' he repeated. 'What does the girl mean, Mr Benjamin?'

Benjamin evaded a direct reply.

'She is kindly welcome here, Doctor Starkweather,' he said, 'as long as she chooses to stay with me.'

'That's no answer,' retorted my uncle, in his rough-and-ready way. He turned to me. 'What is there to keep you in London?' he asked. 'You used to hate London. I suppose there is some reason?'

It was only due to my good guardian and friend that I should take him into my confidence sooner or later. There was no help for it but to rouse my courage and tell him frankly what I had it in my mind to do. The Vicar listened in breathless dismay. He turned to Benjamin, with distress as well as surprise in his face, when I had done.

'God help her!' cried the worthy man. 'The poor thing's troubles have turned her brain!'

'I thought you would disapprove of it, sir,' said Benjamin, in his mild and moderate way. 'I confess I disapprove of it myself.'

' "Disapprove of it," isn't the word,' retorted the Vicar. 'Don't put it in that feeble way, if you please. An act of madness – that's what it is, if she really means what she says.' He turned my way, and looked as he used to look, at the afternoon service, when he was catechising an obstinate child. 'You don't mean it,' he said, 'do you?'

'I am sorry to forfeit your good opinion, uncle,' I replied. 'But I must own that I do certainly mean it.'

'In plain English,' retorted the Vicar, 'you are conceited enough to think that you can succeed where the greatest lawyers in Scotland have failed. *They* couldn't prove this man's innocence, all working together. And *you* are going to prove it single-handed? Upon my word, you are a wonderful woman,' cried my uncle, suddenly descending from indignation to irony. 'May a plain country parson, who isn't used to lawyers in petticoats,[3] be permitted to ask how you mean to do it?'

'I mean to begin by reading the Trial, uncle.'

'Nice reading for a young woman! You will be wanting a batch of nasty French novels next. Well, and when you have read the Trial – what then? Have you thought of that?'

'Yes, uncle. I have thought of that. I shall first try to form some conclusion (after reading the Trial) as to the guilty person who really committed the crime. Then, I shall make out a list of the witnesses who spoke in my husband's defence. I shall go to those witnesses, and tell them who I am, and what I want. I shall ask all sorts of questions which grave lawyers might think it beneath their dignity to put. I shall be guided, in what I do next, by the answers I receive. And I shall not be discouraged, no matter what difficulties are thrown in my way. Those are my plans, uncle, so far as I know them now.'

The Vicar and Benjamin looked at each other, as if they doubted the evidence of their own senses. The Vicar spoke.

'Do you mean to tell me,' he said, 'that you are going roaming about the country, to throw yourself on the mercy of strangers, and to risk whatever rough reception you may get in the course of your travels? You! A young woman! Deserted by your husband! With nobody to protect you! Mr Benjamin, do you hear her? And can you believe your ears? I declare to Heaven *I* don't know whether I am awake or dreaming. Look at her – just look at her! There she sits as cool and easy as if she had said nothing at all extraordinary, and was going to do nothing out of the common way! What am I to do with her – that's the serious question – what on earth am I to do with her?'

'Let me try my experiment, uncle, rash as it may look to you,' I said. 'Nothing else will comfort and support me; and God knows I want comfort and support. Don't think me obstinate. I am ready to admit that there are serious difficulties in my way.'

The Vicar resumed his ironical tone.

'Oh!' he said. 'You admit that, do you? Well, there is something gained, at any rate!'

'Many another woman before me,' I went on, 'has faced serious difficulties, and has conquered them – for the sake of the man she loved.'

Doctor Starkweather rose slowly to his feet, with the air of a person whose capacity of toleration had reached its last limits.

'Am I to understand that you are still in love with Mr Eustace Macallan?' he asked.

'Yes,' I answered.

'The hero of the great Poison Trial?' pursued my uncle. 'The man who has deceived and deserted you? You love him?'

'I love him more dearly than ever.'

'Mr Benjamin,' said the Vicar. 'If she recovers her senses between this and nine o'clock to-morrow morning, send her with her luggage to Loxley's Hotel, where I am now staying. Good night, Valeria. I shall consult with your aunt as to what is to be done next. I have no more to say.'

'Give me a kiss, uncle, at parting.'

'Oh, yes. I'll give you a kiss. Anything you like, Valeria. I shall be sixty-five next birthday; and I thought I knew something of women, at my time of life. It seems I know nothing. Loxley's Hotel is the address, Mr Benjamin. Good night.'

Benjamin looked very grave when he returned to me, after accompanying Doctor Starkweather to the garden gate.

'Pray be advised, my dear,' he said. 'I don't ask you to consider *my* view of this matter as good for much. But your uncle's opinion is surely worth considering?'

I did not reply. It was useless to say any more. I made up my mind to be misunderstood and discouraged, and to bear it. 'Good night, my dear old friend,' was all I said to Benjamin. Then I turned away – I confess with the tears in my eyes – and took refuge in my bedroom.

The window-blind was up; and the autumn moonlight shone brilliantly into the little room.

As I stood by the window, looking out, the memory came to me of another moonlight night – when Eustace and I were walking together in the Vicarage garden before our marriage. It was the night of which I have written, many pages back, when there were obstacles to our union, and when Eustace had offered to release me from my engagement to him. I saw the dear face again, looking at me in the moonlight; I heard once more his words, and mine. 'Forgive me' (he had said) 'for having loved you – passionately, devotedly loved you. Forgive me, and let me go.'

And I had answered, 'Oh, Eustace, I am only a woman – don't madden me! I can't live without you. I must, and will, be your wife!' And now, after marriage had united us, we were parted! Parted, still loving each other as passionately as ever. And why? Because he had been accused of a crime that he had never committed, and because a Scotch jury had failed to see that he was an innocent man.

I looked at the lovely moonlight, pursuing these remembrances and these thoughts. A new ardour burnt in me. 'No!' I said to myself.

'Neither relations nor friends shall prevail on me to falter and fail in my husband's cause. The assertion of his innocence is the work of my life – I will begin it to-night!'

I drew down the blind, and lit the candles. In the quiet night – alone and unaided – I took my first step on the toilsome and terrible journey that lay before me. From the title-page to the end, without stopping to rest and without missing a word, I read the Trial of my husband for the murder of his wife.

END OF THE FIRST VOLUME

VOLUME II

CHAPTER XV

The Story of the Trial. The Preliminaries

Let me confess another weakness, on my part, before I begin the story
of the Trial. I cannot prevail upon myself to copy, for the second
time, the horrible title-page which holds up to public ignominy my
husband's name. I have copied it once in my tenth chapter. Let once
be enough.

Turning to the second page of the Trial, I found a Note, assuring
the reader of the absolute correctness of the Report of the Proceedings.
The compiler described himself as having enjoyed certain privileges.
Thus, the presiding Judge had himself revised his charge to the Jury.
And, again, the chief lawyers for the prosecution and the defence,
following the Judge's example, had revised their speeches, for, and
against, the prisoner. Lastly, particular care had been taken to secure
a literally correct report of the evidence given by the various witnesses.
It was some relief to me to discover this Note, and to be satisfied at
the outset that the Story of the Trial was, in every particular, fully
and truly told.

The next page interested me more nearly still. It enumerated the
actors in the Judicial Drama – the men who held in their hands my
husband's honour, and my husband's life. Here is the List:

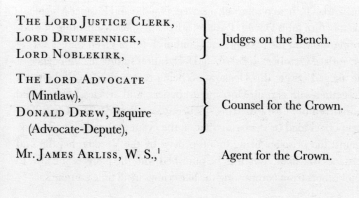

The Lord Justice Clerk, Lord Drumfennick, Lord Noblekirk,	Judges on the Bench.
The Lord Advocate (Mintlaw), Donald Drew, Esquire (Advocate-Depute),	Counsel for the Crown.
Mr. James Arliss, W. S.,[1]	Agent for the Crown.

THE DEAN OF FACULTY
   (Farmichael),   Counsel for the Panel
ALEXANDER CROCKET, Esquire   (otherwise the Prisoner).
   (Advocate),

Mr. THORNIEBANK, W. S.,
                              Agents for the Panel.
Mr. PLAYMORE, W. S.,

The Indictment against the Prisoner then followed. I shall not copy the uncouth language, full of needless repetitions (and, if I know anything of the subject, not guiltless of bad grammar as well), in which my innocent husband was solemnly and falsely accused of poisoning his first wife. The less there is of that false and hateful Indictment on this page, the better and the truer the page will look, to *my* eyes.

To be brief, then, Eustace Macallan was 'indicted and accused, at the instance of David Mintlaw, Esq., Her Majesty's Advocate, for Her Majesty's interest,' of the Murder of his Wife by poison, at his residence called Gleninch, in the county of Mid-Lothian. The poison was alleged to have been wickedly and feloniously given by the prisoner to his wife Sara, on two occasions, in the form of arsenic, administered in tea, medicine, 'or other article or articles of food or drink, to the prosecutor unknown, or in some other manner to the prosecutor unknown.' It was further declared that the prisoner's wife had died of the poison thus administered by her husband, on one or other, or both, of the stated occasions; and that she was thus murdered by her husband. The next paragraph asserted, that the said Eustace Macallan, taken before John Daviot, Esquire, advocate, sheriff-substitute of Mid-Lothian, did in his presence at Edinburgh (on a given date – viz.: – the 29th of October), subscribe a Declaration stating his innocence of the alleged crime: this Declaration being reserved in the Indictment – together with certain Documents, papers, and articles, enumerated in an Inventory – to be used in evidence against the prisoner. The Indictment concluded by declaring that, in the event of the offence charged against the prisoner being found proven by the Verdict, he, the said Eustace Macallan, 'ought to be punished with the pains of the law, to deter others from committing the like crimes in all time coming.'

So much for the Indictment! I have done with it – and I am rejoiced to have done with it.

An Inventory of papers, documents, and articles followed at great length, on the three next pages. This, in its turn, was succeeded by the list of the witnesses, and by the names of the jurors (fifteen in number) balloted for, to try the case. And then, at last, the Report of the Trial began. It resolved itself, to my mind, into three great Questions. As it appeared to me at the time, so let me present it here.

CHAPTER XVI

First Question – Did the Woman Die Poisoned?

The proceedings began at ten o'clock. The prisoner was placed at the Bar, before the High Court of Justiciary, at Edinburgh. He bowed respectfully to the Bench, and pleaded Not Guilty, in a low voice.

It was observed by everyone present, that the prisoner's face betrayed the traces of acute mental suffering. He was deadly pale. His eyes never once wandered to the crowd in the Court. When certain witnesses appeared against him, he looked at them with a momentary attention. At other times, he kept his eyes on the ground. When the evidence touched on his wife's illness and death, he was deeply affected, and covered his face with his hands. It was a subject of general remark and general surprise, that the prisoner, in this case (although a man), showed far less self-possession than the last prisoner tried in that Court for murder – a woman, who had been convicted on overwhelming evidence. There were persons present (a small minority only) who considered this want of composure on the part of the prisoner to be a sign in his favour. Self-possession, in his dreadful position, signified to their minds, the stark insensibility of a heartless and shameless criminal, and afforded in itself a presumption – not of innocence – but of guilt.

The first witness called was John Daviot, Esquire, Sheriff-Substitute of Mid-Lothian. He was examined by the Lord Advocate (as counsel for the prosecution); and said:

'The prisoner was brought before me on the present charge. He made, and subscribed, a Declaration, on the 29th of October. It was freely and voluntarily made; the prisoner having been first duly warned and admonished.'

Having identified the Declaration, the Sheriff-Substitute – being cross-examined by the Dean of Faculty (as counsel for the defence) – continued his evidence in these words:

'The charge against the prisoner was, Murder. This was communicated to him before he made the Declaration. The questions addressed to the prisoner were put, partly by me, partly by another officer, the Procurator-Fiscal. The answers were given distinctly, and, so far as I could judge, without reserve. The statements put forward in the Declaration, were all made in answer to questions asked by the Procurator-Fiscal or by myself.'

A clerk in the Sheriff-Clerk's office then officially produced the Declaration, and corroborated the evidence of the witness who had preceded him.

The appearance of the next witness created a marked sensation in the Court. This was no less a person than the nurse who had attended Mrs Macallan in her last illness – by name, Christina Ormsay.

After the first formal answers, the nurse (examined by the Lord Advocate) proceeded to say:

'I was first sent for, to attend the deceased lady, on the seventh of October. She was then suffering from a severe cold, accompanied by a rheumatic affection of the left knee-joint. Previous to this, I understood that her health had been fairly good. She was not a very difficult person to nurse, when you got used to her, and understood how to manage her. The main difficulty was caused by her temper. She was not a sullen person; she was headstrong and violent – easily excited to fly into a passion, and quite reckless, in her fits of anger, as to what she said or did. At such times, I really hardly think she knew what she was about. My own idea is, that her temper was made still more irritable by unhappiness in her married life. She was far from being a reserved person. Indeed, she was disposed (as I thought) to be a little too communicative about herself and her troubles, with persons, like me, who were beneath her in station. She did not scruple, for instance, to tell me (when we had been long enough together to get used to each other) that she was very unhappy, and fretted a good deal about her husband. One night, when she was wakeful and restless, she said to me—'

The Dean of Faculty here interposed; speaking on the prisoner's behalf. He appealed to the Judges to say whether such loose and unreliable evidence as this, was evidence which could be received by the Court?

The Lord Advocate (speaking on behalf of the Crown) claimed it as his right to produce the evidence. It was of the utmost importance, in this case, to show (on the testimony of an unprejudiced witness) on what terms the husband and wife were living. The witness was a most respectable woman. She had won, and deserved, the confidence of the unhappy lady whom she attended on her death-bed.

After briefly consulting together, the Judges unanimously decided that the evidence could not be admitted. What the witness had herself seen and observed of the relations between the husband and wife, was the only evidence that they could receive.

The Lord Advocate thereupon continued his examination of the witness. Christina Ormsay resumed her evidence as follows:

'My position as nurse led necessarily to my seeing more of Mrs Macallan than any other person in the house. I am able to speak, from experience, of many things not known to others who were only in her room at intervals.

'For instance, I had more than one opportunity of personally observing that Mr and Mrs Macallan did not live together very happily. I can give you an example of this, not drawn from what others told me, but from what I noticed for myself.

'Towards the latter part of my attendance on Mrs Macallan, a young widow lady, named Mrs Beauly – a cousin of Mr Macallan's – came to stay at Gleninch. Mrs Macallan was jealous of this lady; and she showed it, in my presence, only the day before her death, when Mr Macallan came into her room to enquire how she had passed the night. "Oh," she said, "never mind how *I* have slept! What do you care whether I sleep well or ill? How has Mrs Beauly passed the night? Is she more beautiful than ever this morning? Go back to her – pray go back to her! Don't waste your time with me." Beginning in that manner, she worked herself into one of her furious rages. I was brushing her hair at the time; and, feeling that my presence was an impropriety under the circumstances, I attempted to leave the room. She forbade me to go. Mr Macallan felt, as I did, that my duty was to withdraw; and he said so in plain words. Mrs Macallan insisted on my staying, in language so insolent to her husband that he said, "If you cannot control yourself, either the nurse leaves the room or I do." She refused to yield even then. "A good excuse," she said, "for getting back to Mrs Beauly. Go!" He took her at her word, and walked out of the room. He had barely closed the door, before she began reviling him to me in the most shocking manner. She declared, among other things she said of him, that the news of all others which he would be glad to hear would be the news of her death. I ventured, quite respectfully, on remonstrating with her. She took up the hairbrush, and threw it at me – and, then and there, dismissed me from my attendance on her. I left her; and waited below until her fit of passion had worn itself out. Then I returned to my place at the bedside, and, for a while, things went on again as usual.

'It may not be amiss to add a word which may help to explain Mrs Macallan's jealousy of her husband's cousin. Mrs Macallan was a very plain woman. She had a cast in one of her eyes, and (if I may use the expression) one of the most muddy, blotchy complexions it was ever my misfortune to see in a person's face. Mrs Beauly, on the other hand, was a most attractive lady. Her eyes were universally admired; and she had a most beautifully clear and delicate colour. Poor Mrs Macallan said of her, most untruly, that she painted.

'No; the defects in the complexion of the deceased lady were not in any way attributable to her illness. I should call them born and bred defects in herself.

'Her illness, if I am asked to describe it, I should say was troublesome – nothing more. Until the last day, there were no symptoms in the least degree serious about the malady that had taken her. Her rheumatic knee was painful, of course, acutely painful if you like, when she moved it; and the confinement to bed was irksome enough, no doubt. But otherwise there was nothing in the lady's condition, before the fatal attack came, to alarm her or anybody about her. She had her books, and her writing-materials, on an invalid table which worked on a pivot, and could be arranged in any position most agreeable to her. At times, she read and wrote a great deal. At other times, she lay quiet, thinking her own thoughts, or talking with me and with one or two lady friends in the neighbourhood who came regularly to see her.

'Her writing, so far as I knew, was almost entirely of the poetical sort. She was a great hand at composing poetry. On one occasion only, she showed me some of her poems. I am no judge of such things. Her poetry was of the dismal kind; despairing about herself, and wondering why she had ever been born, and nonsense like that. Her husband came in more than once for some hard hits at his cruel heart and his ignorance of his wife's merits. In short, she vented her discontent with her pen as well as with her tongue. There were times – and pretty often too – when an angel from heaven would have failed to have satisfied Mrs Macallan.

'Throughout the period of her illness the deceased lady occupied the same room – a large bedroom situated (like all the best bedrooms) on the first floor of the house.

'Yes: the plan of the room now shown to me is quite accurately taken, according to my remembrance of it. One door led into the great passage, or corridor, on which all the doors opened. A second door, at one side (marked B on the plan), led into Mr Macallan's sleeping room. A third door, on the opposite side (marked C on the plan), communicated with a little study or book-room, used, as I was told, by Mr Macallan's mother when she was staying at Gleninch, but seldom or never entered by anyone else. Mr Macallan's mother was not at Gleninch while I was there. The door between the bedroom and this study was locked, and the key was taken out. I don't know who had the key, or whether there were more keys than one in existence. The door was never opened, to my knowledge. I only got into the study, to look at it along with the housekeeper, by entering through a second door that opened on to the corridor.

'I beg to say that I can speak, from my own knowledge, positively about Mrs Macallan's illness, and about the sudden change which ended in her death. By the doctor's advice, I made notes, at the time, of dates and hours, and such like. I looked at my notes before coming here.

'From the seventh of October, when I was first called in to nurse her, to the twentieth of the same month, she slowly, but steadily, improved in health. Her knee was still painful, no doubt; but the inflammatory look of it was disappearing. As to the other symptoms, except weakness from lying in bed, and irritability of temper, there was really nothing the matter with her. She slept badly, I ought perhaps to add. But we remedied this, by means of composing-draughts, prescribed for that purpose by the doctor.

'On the morning of the twenty-first, at a few minutes past six, I got my first alarm that something was going wrong with Mrs Macallan.

'I was woke, at the time I have mentioned, by the ringing of the hand-bell which she kept on her bed-table. Let me say for myself that I had only fallen asleep on the sofa in the bedroom, at past two in the morning, from sheer fatigue. Mrs Macallan was then awake. She was in one of her bad humours with me. I had tried to prevail on her to let me remove her dressing-case from her bed-table, after she had used it in making her toilet for the night. It took up a great deal of room; and she could not possibly want it again before the morning. But no – she insisted on my letting it be. There was a glass inside the case; and, plain as she was, she never wearied of looking at herself in that glass! I saw that she was in a bad state of temper, so I gave her her way, and let the dressing-case be. Finding that she was too sullen to speak to me after that, and too obstinate to take her composing-draught from me when I offered it, I laid me down on the sofa at her bed-foot, and fell asleep, as I have said.

'The moment her bell rang, I was up and at the bedside, ready to make myself useful.

'I asked what was the matter with her. She complained of faintness and depression, and said she felt sick. I enquired if she had taken anything in the way of physic or food while I had been asleep. She answered that her husband had come in about an hour since, and, finding her still sleepless, had himself administered the composing-draught. Mr Macallan (sleeping in the next room) joined us while she was speaking. He, too, had been aroused by the bell. He heard what Mrs Macallan said to me about the composing-draught, and made no remark upon it. It seemed to me that he was alarmed at his wife's faintness. I suggested that she should take a little wine, or brandy-and-water. She answered that she could swallow nothing so strong as wine or brandy, having a burning pain in her stomach already. I put my hand on her stomach – quite lightly. She screamed when I touched her.

'This symptom alarmed us. We sent to the village for the medical man who had attended Mrs Macallan during her illness: one Mr Gale.

'The doctor seemed no better able to account for the change for the worse in his patient than we were. Hearing her complain of thirst, he gave her some milk. Not long after taking it, she was sick. The sickness appeared to relieve her. She soon grew drowsy, and slumbered. Mr Gale left us, with strict injunctions to send for him instantly if she was taken ill again.

'Nothing of the sort happened; no change took place for the next three hours or more. She roused up towards half-past nine, and enquired about her husband. I informed her that he had returned to his own room, and asked if I should send for him. She said, "No." I asked next, if she would like anything to eat or drink. She said, "No," again, in rather a vacant, stupefied way – and then told me to go downstairs and get my breakfast. On my way down, I met the housekeeper. She invited me to breakfast with her in her room, instead of in the servants' hall as usual. I remained with the housekeeper but a short time: certainly not more than half-an-hour.

'Going upstairs again, I met the under-housemaid, sweeping, on one of the landings.

'The girl informed me that Mrs Macallan had taken a cup of tea, during my absence in the housekeeper's room. Mr Macallan's valet had ordered the tea for his mistress, by his master's directions. The under-housemaid made it, and took it upstairs herself to Mrs Macallan's room. Her master (she said) opened the door, when she knocked, and took the teacup from her with his own hand. He opened the door widely enough for her to see into the bedroom, and to notice that nobody was with Mrs Macallan but himself.

'After a little talk with the under-housemaid, I returned to the bedroom. No one was there. Mrs Macallan was lying perfectly quiet, with her face turned away from me on the pillow. Approaching the bedside, I kicked against something on the floor. It was a broken teacup. I said to Mrs Macallan, "How comes the teacup to be broken, ma'am?" She answered, without turning towards me – in an odd, muffled kind of voice – "I dropped it." "Before you drank your tea, ma'am?" I asked. "No," she said; "in handing the cup back to Mr Macallan after I had done." I had put my question, wishing to know – in case she had spilt the tea when she dropped the cup – whether it would be necessary to get her any more. I am quite sure I remember correctly my question, and her answer. I enquired next if she had been long alone. She said, shortly, "Yes; I have been trying to sleep." I said, "Do you feel pretty comfortable?" She answered "Yes," again. All this time, she still kept her face sulkily turned from me towards the wall. Stooping over her to arrange the bed-clothes, I looked towards her table. The writing materials which were always kept on it, were disturbed; and there was wet ink on one of the pens. I said, "Surely you haven't been writing, ma'am?" "Why not?" she said; "I couldn't sleep." "Another poem?" I asked. She laughed to herself – a bitter, short laugh. "Yes," she said; "another poem." "That's good," I said; "it looks as if you were getting quite like yourself again. We shan't want the doctor any more to-day." She made no answer to this, except an impatient sign with her hand. I didn't understand the sign. Upon that, she spoke again – and crossly enough, too! "I want to be alone; leave me."

'I had no choice but to do as I was told. To the best of my observation, there was nothing the matter with her, and nothing for the nurse to do. I put the bell-rope within reach of her hand, and I went downstairs again.

'Half an hour more, as well as I can guess it, passed. I kept within hearing of the bell; but it never rang. I was not quite at my ease – without exactly knowing why. That odd muffled voice in which she had spoken to me hung on my mind, as it were. I was not quite satisfied about leaving her alone for too long a time together − and then, again, I was unwilling to risk throwing her into one of her fits of passion by going back before she rang for me. It ended in my venturing into the room on the ground floor, called the Morning Room, to consult Mr Macallan. He was usually to be found there in the forenoon of the day.

'On this occasion, however, when I looked into the Morning Room it was empty.

'At the same moment, I heard the master's voice on the terrace outside. I went out, and found him speaking to one Mr Dexter, an old friend of his, and (like Mrs Beauly) a guest staying in the house. Mr Dexter was sitting at the window of his room upstairs (he was a cripple, and could only move himself about in a chair on wheels); and Mr Macallan was speaking to him from the terrace below.

' "Dexter!" I heard Mr Macallan say. "Where is Mrs Beauly? Have you seen anything of her?"

'Mr Dexter answered, in his quick, off-hand way of speaking, "Not I! I know nothing about her."

'Then I advanced, and, begging pardon for intruding, I mentioned to Mr Macallan the difficulty I was in about going back or not to his wife's room, without waiting until she rang for me. Before he could advise me in the matter, the footman made his appearance, and informed me that Mrs Macallan's bell was then ringing − and ringing violently.

'It was close on eleven o'clock. As fast as I could mount the stairs, I hastened back to the bedroom.

'Before I opened the door, I heard Mrs Macallan groaning. She was in dreadful pain; feeling a burning heat in the stomach, and in the throat; together with the same sickness which had troubled her in the early morning. Though no doctor, I could see in her face that this second attack was of a far more serious nature than the first. After ringing the bell for a messenger to send to Mr Macallan, I ran to the door to see if any of the servants happened to be within call.

'The only person I saw in the corridor was Mrs Beauly. She was on her way from her own room, she said, to enquire after Mrs Macallan's health. I said to her, "Mrs Macallan is seriously ill again,

ma'am. Would you please tell Mr Macallan, and send for the doctor?"
She ran downstairs at once to do as I told her.

'I had not been long back at the bedside when Mr Macallan and
Mrs Beauly both came in together. Mrs Macallan cast a strange look
on them (a look I cannot at all describe), and made them leave her.
Mrs Beauly, looking very much frightened, withdrew immediately.
Mr Macallan advanced a step or two nearer to the bed. His wife
looked at him again, in the same strange way, and cried out – half as
if she was threatening him, half as if she was entreating him – "Leave
me with the nurse. Go!" He only waited to say to me in a whisper,
"The doctor is sent for" – and then he left the room.

'Before Mr Gale arrived, Mrs Macallan was violently sick. What
came from her was muddy and frothy, and faintly streaked with blood.
When Mr Gale saw it, he looked very serious; I heard him say to
himself, "What does this mean?" He did his best to relieve Mrs
Macallan, but with no good result that I could see. After a time, she
seemed to suffer less. Then more sickness came on. Then there was
another intermission. Whether she was suffering or not, I observed
that her hands and feet (whenever I touched them) remained equally
cold. Also, the doctor's report of her pulse was always the same –
"very small and feeble." I said to Mr Gale, "What is to be done, sir?"
And Mr Gale said to me, "I won't take the responsibility on myself
any longer; I must have a physician from Edinburgh."

'The fastest horse in the stables at Gleninch was put into a dog-cart;
and the coachman drove away full speed to Edinburgh, to fetch the
famous Doctor Jerome.

'While we were waiting for the physician, Mr Macallan came into
his wife's room, with Mr Gale. Exhausted as she was, she instantly
lifted her hand, and signed to him to leave her. He tried by soothing
words to persuade her to let him stay. No! She still insisted on sending
him out of her room. He seemed to feel it – at such a time, and in the
presence of the doctor. Before she was aware of him, he suddenly
stepped up to the bedside, and kissed her on the forehead. She shrank
from him with a scream. Mr Gale interfered, and led him out of the
room.

'In the afternoon, Dr Jerome arrived.

'The great physician came just in time to see her seized with another attack of sickness. He watched her attentively, without speaking a word. In the interval when the sickness stopped, he still studied her, as it were, in perfect silence. I thought he would never have done examining her. When he was at last satisfied, he told me to leave him alone with Mr Gale. "We will ring," he said, "when we want you here again."

'It was a long time before they rang for me. The coachman was sent for, before I was summoned back to the bedroom. He was despatched to Edinburgh, for the second time, with a written message from Doctor Jerome to his head-servant, saying that there was no chance of his returning to the city, and to his patients, for some hours to come. Some of us thought this looked badly for Mrs Macallan. Others said it might mean that the doctor had hopes of saving her, but expected to be a long time in doing it.

'At last I was sent for. On my presenting myself in the bedroom, Doctor Jerome went out to speak to Mr Macallan, leaving Mr Gale along with me. From that time, as long as the poor lady lived, I was never left alone with her. One of the two doctors was always in her room. Refreshments were prepared for them; but still they took it in turns to eat their meal – one relieving the other at the bedside. If they had administered remedies to their patient I should not have been surprised by this proceeding. But they were at the end of their remedies; their only business in the room seemed to be to keep watch. I was puzzled to account for this. Keeping watch was the nurse's business. I thought the conduct of the doctors very strange.

'By the time that the lamp was lit in the sick room, I could see that the end was near. Excepting an occasional feeling of cramp in her legs, she seemed to suffer less. But her eyes looked sunk in her head; her skin was cold and clammy; her lips had turned to a bluish paleness. Nothing roused her now – excepting the last attempt made by her husband to see her. He came in with Dr Jerome, looking like a man terror-struck. She was past speaking; but the moment she saw him, she feebly made signs and sounds which showed that she was just as resolved as ever not to let him come near her. He was so overwhelmed that Mr Gale was obliged to help him out of the room. No other person was allowed to see the patient. Mr Dexter and Mrs Beauly made their enquiries outside the door, and were not invited in. As the evening drew on, the doctors sat on either side of the bed, silently watching her, silently waiting for her death.

'Towards eight o'clock, she seemed to have lost the use of her hands and arms; they lay helpless outside the bedclothes. A little later, she sank into a sort of dull sleep. Little by little, the sound of her heavy breathing grew fainter. At twenty minutes past nine, Doctor Jerome told me to bring the lamp to the bedside. He looked at her, and put his hand on her heart. Then he said to me, "You can go downstairs, nurse: it is all over." He turned to Mr Gale. "Will you enquire if Mr Macallan can see us?" he said. I opened the door for Mr Gale, and followed him out. Doctor Jerome called me back for a moment, and told me to give him the key of the door. I did so, of course – but I thought this also very strange. When I got down to the servants' hall, I found there was a general feeling that something was wrong. We were all uneasy – without knowing why.

'A little later the two doctors left the house. Mr Macallan had been quite incapable of receiving them, and hearing what they had to say. In this difficulty, they had spoken privately with Mr Dexter, as Mr Macallan's old friend, and the only gentleman then staying at Gleninch.

'Before bedtime I went upstairs, to prepare the remains of the deceased lady for the coffin. The room in which she lay was locked; the door leading into Mr Macallan's room being secured, as well as the door leading into the corridor. The keys had been taken away by Mr Gale. Two of the men-servants were posted outside the bedroom to keep watch. They were to be relieved at four in the morning – that was all they could tell me.

'In the absence of any explanations or directions, I took the liberty of knocking at the door of Mr Dexter's room. From his lips I first heard the startling news. Both the doctors had refused to give the usual certificate of death! There was to be a medical examination of the body the next morning.'

There the examination of the nurse, Christina Ormsay, came to an end.

Ignorant as I was of the law, I could see what impression the evidence (so far) was intended to produce on the minds of the Jury. After first showing that my husband had had two opportunities of administering the poison – once in the medicine and once in the tea – the counsel for the Crown led the Jury to infer that the prisoner had taken those opportunities to rid himself of an ugly and jealous wife whose detestable temper he could no longer endure.

Having directed his examination to the attainment of this object, the Lord Advocate had done with the witness. The Dean of Faculty – acting in the prisoner's interests – then rose to bring out the favourable side of the wife's character by cross-examining the nurse. If he succeeded in this attempt, the Jury might reconsider their conclusion that the wife was a person who had exasperated her husband beyond endurance. In that case, where (so far) was the husband's motive for poisoning her? and where was the presumption of the prisoner's guilt?

Pressed by this skilful lawyer, the nurse was obliged to exhibit my husband's first wife under an entirely new aspect. Here is the substance of what the Dean of Faculty extracted from Christina Ormsay:

'I persist in declaring that Mrs Macallan had a most violent temper. But she was certainly in the habit of making amends for the offence that she gave by her violence. When she was quiet again, she always made her excuses to me; and she made them with a good grace. Her manners were engaging at such times as these. She spoke and acted like a well-bred lady. Then again, as to her personal appearance. Plain as she was in face, she had a good figure; her hands and feet, I was told, had been modelled by a sculptor. She had a very pleasant voice; and she was reported when in health to sing beautifully. She was also (if her maid's account was to be trusted) a pattern, in the matter of dressing, for the other ladies in the neighbourhood. Then, as to Mrs Beauly, though she was certainly jealous of the beautiful young widow, she had shown at the same time that she was capable of controlling that feeling. It was through Mrs Macallan that Mrs Beauly was in the house. Mrs Beauly had wished to postpone her visit, on account of the state of Mrs Macallan's health. It was Mrs Macallan herself – not her husband – who decided that Mrs Beauly should not be disappointed, and should pay her visit to Gleninch, then and there.

Further, Mrs Macallan (in spite of her temper) was popular with her friends, and popular with her servants. There was hardly a dry eye in the house when it was known she was dying. And, further still, in those little domestic disagreements at which the nurse had been present, Mr Macallan had never lost his temper, and had never used harsh language: he seemed to be more sorry than angry when the quarrels took place.' – Moral for the Jury: Was this the sort of woman who would exasperate a man into poisoning her? And was this the sort of man who would be capable of poisoning his wife?

Having produced that salutary counter-impression, the Dean of Faculty sat down; and the medical witnesses were called next.

Here, the evidence was simply irresistible.

Doctor Jerome and Mr Gale positively swore that the symptoms of the illness were the symptoms of poisoning by arsenic. The surgeon who had performed the post-mortem examination followed. He positively swore that the appearance of the internal organs proved Dr Jerome and Mr Gale to be right in declaring that their patient had died poisoned. Lastly, to complete this overwhelming testimony, two analytical chemists actually produced in Court the arsenic which they had found in the body, in a quantity admittedly sufficient to have killed two persons instead of one. In the face of such evidence as this, cross-examination was a mere form. The first Question raised by the Trial – Did the Woman Die Poisoned? – was answered in the affirmative, and answered beyond the possibility of doubt.

The next witnesses called were witnesses concerned with the question that now followed – the obscure and terrible question: Who Poisoned Her?

CHAPTER XVII

Second Question – Who Poisoned Her?

The evidence of the doctors and the chemists closed the proceedings, on the first day of the Trial.

On the second day, the evidence to be produced by the prosecution, was anticipated with a general feeling of curiosity and interest. The Court was now to hear what had been seen and done, by the persons officially appointed to verify such cases of suspected crime as the case which had occurred at Gleninch. The Procurator-Fiscal – being the person officially appointed to direct the preliminary investigations of the Law – was the first witness called, on the second day of the Trial.

Examined by the Lord Advocate, the Fiscal gave his evidence, as follows:

'On the twenty-sixth of October, I received a communication from Doctor Jerome of Edinburgh, and from Mr Alexander Gale, medical practitioner, residing in the village or hamlet of Dingdovie, near Edinburgh. The communication related to the death, under circumstances of suspicion, of Mrs Eustace Macallan, at her husband's house, hard by Dingdovie, called Gleninch. There was also forwarded to me, enclosed in the document just mentioned, two reports. One described the results of a post-mortem examination of the deceased lady; and the other stated the discoveries made, after a chemical analysis of certain of the interior organs of her body. The result, in both instances, proved to demonstration that Mrs Eustace Macallan had died of poisoning by arsenic.

'Under these circumstances, I set in motion a search and enquiry in the house at Gleninch, and elsewhere, simply for the purpose of throwing light on the circumstances which had attended the lady's death.

'No criminal charge, in connection with the death, was made at my office against any person, either in the communication which I received from the medical men, or in any other form. The investigations at Gleninch, and elsewhere, beginning on the twenty-sixth of October, were not completed until the twenty-eighth. Upon this latter date – acting on certain discoveries which were reported to me, and on my own examination of letters and other documents brought to my office – I made a criminal charge against the prisoner; and obtained a warrant for his apprehension. He was examined before the Sheriff, on the twenty-ninth of October, and was committed for Trial before this Court.'

The Fiscal having made his statement, and having been cross-examined (on technical matters only), the persons employed in his office were called next. These men had a story of startling interest to tell. Theirs were the fatal discoveries which had justified the Fiscal in charging my husband with the murder of his wife. The first of the witnesses was a sheriff's officer. He gave his name as Isaiah School-craft.

Examined by Mr Drew – Advocate-Depute, and counsel for the Crown with the Lord Advocate – Isaiah Schoolcraft said:

'I got a warrant on the twenty-sixth of October, to go to the country house near Edinburgh, called Gleninch. I took with me Robert Lorrie, Assistant to the Fiscal. We first examined the room in which Mrs Eustace Macallan had died. On the bed, and on a movable table which was attached to it, we found books and writing materials, and a paper containing some unfinished verses in manuscript; afterwards identified as being in the handwriting of the deceased. We enclosed these articles in paper, and sealed them up.

'We next opened an Indian cabinet in the bedroom. Here we found many more verses, on many more sheets of paper, in the same handwriting. We also discovered, first, some letters – and next a crumpled piece of paper thrown aside in a corner of one of the shelves. On closer examination, a chemist's printed label was discovered on this morsel of paper. We also found in the folds of it a few scattered grains of some white powder. The paper and the letters were carefully enclosed, and sealed up as before.

'Further investigation in the room revealed nothing which could throw any light on the purpose of our enquiry. We examined the clothes, jewellery, and books of the deceased. These we left under lock and key. We also found her dressing-case, which we protected by seals, and took away with us to the Fiscal's office, along with all the other articles that we had discovered in the room.

'The next day we continued our examination in the house; having received, in the interval, fresh instructions from the Fiscal. We began our work in the bedroom communicating with the room in which Mrs Macallan had died. It had been kept locked since the death. Finding nothing of any importance here, we went next to another room on the same floor, in which we were informed the prisoner was then lying, ill in bed.

'His illness was described to us as a nervous complaint, caused by the death of his wife, and by the proceedings which had followed it. He was reported to be quite incapable of exerting himself, and quite unfit to see strangers. We insisted nevertheless (in deference to our instructions) on obtaining admission to his room. He made no reply, when we enquired whether he had, or had not, removed anything from the sleeping-room next to his late wife's which he usually occupied, to the sleeping-room in which he now lay. All he did was to close his eyes, as if he was too feeble to speak to us or to notice us. Without further disturbing him, we began to examine the room and the different objects in it.

'While we were so employed, we were interrupted by a strange sound. We likened it to the rumbling of wheels in the corridor outside.

'The door opened, and there came swiftly in a gentleman – a cripple – wheeling himself along in a chair. He wheeled his chair straight up to a little table which stood by the prisoner's bedside, and said something to him in a whisper too low to be overheard. The prisoner opened his eyes, and quickly answered by a sign. We informed the crippled gentleman, quite respectfully, that we could not allow him to be in the room at this time. He appeared to think nothing of what we said. He only answered, "My name is Dexter. I am one of Mr Macallan's old friends. It is you who are intruding here; not I." We again notified to him that he must leave the room; and we pointed out particularly that he had got his chair in such a position against the bedside-table as to prevent us from examining it. He only laughed. "Can't you see for yourselves," he said; "that it is a table, and nothing more?" In reply to this, we warned him that we were acting under a legal warrant, and that he might get into trouble if he obstructed us in the execution of our duty. Finding there was no moving him by fair means, I took his chair and pulled it away, while Robert Lorrie laid hold of the table and carried it to the other end of the room. The crippled gentleman flew into a furious rage with me for presuming to touch his chair. "My chair is Me," he said: "how dare you lay hands on Me?" I first opened the door; and then, by way of accommodating him, gave the chair a good push behind with my stick, instead of my hand – and so sent It, and him, safely and swiftly out of the room.

'Having locked the door, so as to prevent any further intrusion, I joined Robert Lorrie in examining the bedside-table. It had one drawer in it, and that drawer we found secured.

'We asked the prisoner for the key.

'He flatly refused to give it to us, and said we had no right to unlock his drawers. He was so angry that he even declared it was lucky for us he was too weak to rise from his bed. I answered civilly that our duty obliged us to examine the drawer, and that, if he still declined to produce the key, he would only oblige us to take the table away and have the lock opened by a smith.

'While we were still disputing, there was a knock at the door of the room.

'I opened the door cautiously. Instead of the crippled gentleman, whom I had expected to see again, there was another stranger standing outside. The prisoner hailed him as a friend and neighbour, and eagerly called upon him for protection from us. We found this second gentleman pleasant enough to deal with. He informed us readily that he had been sent for by Mr Dexter, and that he was himself a lawyer – and he asked to see our warrant. Having looked at it, he at once informed the prisoner (evidently very much to the prisoner's surprise) that he must submit to have the drawer examined – under protest. And then, without more ado, he got the key, and opened the table drawer for us himself.

'We found inside several letters, and a large book, with a lock to it; having the words "My Diary" inscribed on it in gilt letters. As a matter of course, we took possession of the letters and the Diary, and sealed them up to be given to the Fiscal. At the same time, the gentleman wrote out a protest, on the prisoner's behalf, and handed us his card. The card informed us that he was Mr Playmore — now one of the agents for the prisoner. The card and the protest were deposited, with the other documents, in the care of the Fiscal. No other discoveries of any importance were made at Gleninch.

'Our next enquiries took us to Edinburgh — to the druggist whose label we had found on the crumpled morsel of paper, and to other druggists likewise whom we were instructed to question. On the twenty-eighth of October, the Fiscal was in possession of all the information that we could collect, and our duties for the time being came to an end.'

This concluded the evidence of Schoolcraft and Lorrie. It was not shaken on cross-examination; and it was plainly unfavourable to the prisoner.

Matters grew worse still when the next witnesses were called. The druggist whose label had been found on the crumpled bit of paper now appeared on the stand, to make the position of my unhappy husband more critical than ever.

Andrew Kinlay, druggist, of Edinburgh, deposed as follows:

'I keep a special registry-book of the poisons sold by me. I produce the book. On the date therein mentioned, the prisoner at the bar, Mr Eustace Macallan, came into my shop, and said that he wished to purchase some arsenic. I asked him what it was wanted for? He told me it was wanted by his gardener, to be used, in solution, for the killing of insects in the greenhouse. At the same time he mentioned his name — Mr Macallan, of Gleninch. I at once directed my assistant to put up the arsenic (two ounces of it); and I made the necessary entry in my book. Mr Macallan signed the entry; and I signed it afterwards as witness. He paid for the arsenic, and took it away with him wrapped up in two papers — the outer wrapper being labelled with my name and address, and with the word "Poison" in large letters; exactly like the label now produced on the piece of paper found at Gleninch.'

The next witness, Peter Stockdale (also a druggist of Edinburgh), followed, and said:

'The prisoner at the bar called at my shop, on the date indicated

on my register – some days later than the date indicated in the register
of Mr Kinlay. He wished to purchase sixpenny-worth of arsenic. My
assistant, to whom he had addressed himself, called me. It is a rule in
my shop that no one sells poisons but myself. I asked the prisoner
what he wanted the arsenic for. He answered that he wanted it for
killing rats at his house called Gleninch. I said, "Have I the honour
of speaking to Mr Macallan, of Gleninch?" He said that was his name.
I sold him the arsenic – about an ounce and a half – and labelled the
bottle in which I put it with the word "Poison," in my own handwriting.
He signed the Register, and took the arsenic away with him, after
paying for it.'

The cross-examination of these two men succeeded in asserting
certain technical objections to their evidence. But the terrible fact that
my husband himself had actually purchased the arsenic, in both cases,
remained unshaken.

The next witnesses – the gardener, and the cook, at Gleninch –
wound the chain of hostile evidence round the prisoner more mercilessly still.

On examination, the gardener said, on his oath:

'I never received any arsenic from the prisoner or from anyone else,
at the date to which you refer, or at any other date. I never used any
such thing as a solution of arsenic, or ever allowed the men working
under me to use it, in the conservatories, or in the garden, at Gleninch.
I disapprove of arsenic as a means of destroying noxious insects
infesting flowers and plants.'

The cook, being called next, spoke as positively as the gardener.

'Neither my master, nor any other person, gave me any arsenic to
destroy rats, at any time. No such thing was wanted. I declare, on my
oath, that I never saw any rats, in, or about, the house – or ever heard
of any rats infesting it.'

Other household servants at Gleninch gave similar evidence. Nothing could be extracted from them on cross-examination – except that
there might have been rats in the house, though they were not aware
of it. The possession of the poison was traced directly to my husband,
and to no one else. That he had bought it was actually proved; and
that he had kept it, was the one conclusion that the evidence justified.

The witnesses who came next did their best to press the charge against the prisoner home to him. Having the arsenic in his possession, what had he done with it? The evidence led the Jury to infer what he had done with it.

The prisoner's valet deposed that his master had rung for him at twenty minutes to ten, on the morning of the day on which his mistress died, and had ordered a cup of tea for her. The man had received the order at the open door of Mrs Macallan's room, and could positively swear that no other person but his master was there at the time.

The under-housemaid, appearing next, said that she had made the tea, and had herself taken it upstairs, before ten o'clock, to Mrs Macallan's room. Her master had received it from her at the open door. She could look in, and see that he was alone in her mistress's room.

The nurse, Christina Ormsay, being recalled, repeated what Mrs Macallan had said to her, on the day when that lady was first taken ill. She had said (speaking to the nurse at six o'clock in the morning), 'Mr Macallan came in about an hour since; he found me still sleepless, and gave me my composing-draught.' This was at five o'clock in the morning, while Christina Ormsay was asleep on the sofa. The nurse further swore that she had looked at the bottle containing the composing-mixture, and had seen, by the measuring marks on the bottle, that a dose had been poured out since the dose previously given, administered by herself.

On this occasion, special interest was excited by the cross-examination. The closing questions, put to the under-housemaid and the nurse, revealed for the first time what the nature of the defence was to be.

Cross-examining the under-housemaid, the Dean of Faculty said:

'Did you ever notice, when you were setting Mrs Eustace Macallan's room to rights, whether the water left in the basin was of a blackish or bluish colour?' The witness answered, 'I never noticed anything of the sort.'

The Dean of Faculty went on:

'Did you ever find, under the pillow of the bed, or in any other hiding-place in Mrs Macallan's room, any books or pamphlets, telling of remedies used for improving a bad complexion?' The witness answered, 'No.'

The Dean of Faculty persisted:

'Did you ever hear Mrs Macallan speak of arsenic, taken as a wash, or taken as a medicine, as a good thing to improve the complexion?' The witness answered, 'Never.'

Similar questions were next put to the nurse, and were all answered, by this witness also, in the negative.

Here, then – in spite of the negative answers – was the plan of the defence made dimly visible for the first time to the Jury and to the audience. By way of preventing the possibility of a mistake in so serious a matter, the Chief Judge (the Lord Justice Clerk) put this plain question, when the witnesses had retired, to the Counsel for the defence:

'The Court and the Jury,' said his lordship, 'wish distinctly to understand the object of your cross-examination of the housemaid and the nurse. Is it the theory of the defence, that Mrs Eustace Macallan used the arsenic which her husband purchased, for the purpose of improving the defects of her complexion?'

The Dean of Faculty answered:

'That is what we say, my lord, and what we propose to prove, as the foundation of the defence. We cannot dispute the medical evidence which declares that Mrs Macallan died poisoned. But we assert that she died of an overdose of arsenic, ignorantly taken, in the privacy of her own room, as a remedy for the defects – the proved and admitted defects – of her complexion. The prisoner's Declaration before the Sheriff, expressly sets forth that he purchased the arsenic at the request of his wife.'

The Lord Justice Clerk enquired, upon this, if there was any objection, on the part of either of the learned counsel, to have the Declaration read in Court, before the Trial proceeded further.

To this, the Dean of Faculty replied that he would be glad to have the Declaration read. If he might use the expression, it would usefully pave the way, in the minds of the Jury, for the defence which he had to submit to them.

The Lord Advocate (speaking on the other side) was happy to be able to accommodate his learned brother in this matter. So long as the mere assertions which the Declaration contained were not supported by proof, he looked upon that document as evidence for the prosecution, and he, too, was quite willing to have it read.

Thereupon, the prisoner's Declaration of his innocence – on being charged before the Sheriff with the murder of his wife – was read, in the following terms:

'I bought the two packets of arsenic, on each occasion, at my wife's own request. On the first occasion, she told me the poison was wanted by the gardener, for use in the conservatories. On the second occasion, she said it required by the cook for ridding the lower part of the house of rats.

'I handed both packets of arsenic to my wife immediately on my return home. I had nothing to do with the poison, after buying it. My wife was the person who gave orders to the gardener and the cook – not I. I never held any communication with either of them.

'I asked my wife no questions about the use of the arsenic; feeling no interest in the subject. I never entered the conservatories for months together; I care little about flowers. As for the rats, I left the killing of them to the cook and the other servants – just as I should have left any other part of the domestic business to the cook and the other servants.

'My wife never told me she wanted the arsenic to improve her complexion. Surely, I should be the last person admitted to the knowledge of such a secret of her toilet as that? I implicitly believed what she told me – viz., that the poison was wanted, for the purposes specified, by the gardener and the cook.

'I assert positively, that I lived on friendly terms with my wife; allowing, of course, for the little occasional disagreements and misunderstandings of married life. Any sense of disappointment, in connection with my marriage, which I might have felt privately, I conceived it to be my duty, as a husband and a gentleman, to conceal from my wife. I was not only shocked and grieved by her untimely death – I was filled with fear that I had not, with all my care, behaved affectionately enough to her in her lifetime.

'Furthermore, I solemnly declare that I know no more of how she took the arsenic found in her body than the babe unborn. I am innocent even of the thought of harming that unhappy woman. I administered the composing-draught, exactly as I found it in the bottle. I afterwards gave her the cup of tea, exactly as I received it from the under-housemaid's hand. I never had access to the arsenic, after I placed the two packages in my wife's possession. I am entirely ignorant of what she did with them, or of where she kept them. I declare, before God, I am innocent of the horrible crime with which I am charged.'

With the reading of those true and touching words, the proceedings on the second day of the Trial came to an end.

So far, I must own, the effect on me of reading the Report was to depress my spirits, and to lower my hopes. The whole weight of the evidence, at the close of the second day, was against my husband. Woman, as I was, and partisan as I was, I could plainly see that.

The merciless Lord Advocate (I confess I hated him!) had proved (1) that Eustace had bought the poison; (2) that the reason which he had given to the druggists for buying the poison was not the true reason; (3) that he had had two opportunities of secretly administering the poison to his wife. On the other side, what had the Dean of Faculty proved? As yet – nothing. The assertions in the prisoner's Declaration of his innocence were still, as the Lord Advocate had remarked, assertions not supported by proof. Not one atom of evidence had been produced to show that it was the wife who had secretly used the arsenic, and used it for her complexion.

My one consolation was, that the reading of the Trial had already revealed to me the helpful figures of two friends, on whose sympathy I might surely rely. The crippled Mr Dexter had especially shown himself to be a thorough good ally of my husband's. My heart warmed to the man who had moved his chair against the bedside-table – the man who had struggled to the last to defend Eustace's papers from the wretches who had seized them! I decided, then and there, that the first person to whom I would confide my aspirations and my hopes should be Mr Dexter. If he felt any difficulty about advising me, I would then apply next to the agent, Mr Playmore – the second good friend, who had formally protested against the seizure of my husband's papers.

Fortified by this resolution, I turned the page, and read the history of the third day of the Trial.

CHAPTER XVIII

Third Question – What Was His Motive?

The first question (Did the Woman die Poisoned?) had been answered, positively. The second question (Who Poisoned Her?) had been answered, apparently. There now remained the third and final question – What Was His Motive? The first evidence called, in answer to that enquiry, was the evidence of relatives and friends of the dead wife.

Lady Brydehaven, widow of Rear Admiral Sir George Brydehaven, examined by Mr Drew (counsel for the Crown with the Lord Advocate), gave evidence as follows:

'The deceased lady (Mrs Eustace Macallan) was my niece. She was the only child of my sister; and she lived under my roof after the time of her mother's death. I objected to her marriage – on grounds which were considered purely fanciful and sentimental by her other friends. It is extremely painful to me to state the circumstances in public; but I am ready to make the sacrifice, if the ends of justice require it.

'The prisoner at the Bar, at the time of which I am now speaking, was staying as a guest in my house. He met with an accident, while he was out riding, which caused a severe injury to one of his legs. The leg had been previously hurt, while he was serving with the army in India. This circumstance tended greatly to aggravate the injury received in the accident. He was confined to a recumbent position on a sofa for many weeks together: and the ladies in the house took it in turns to sit with him, and wile away the weary time by reading to him and talking to him. My niece was foremost among these volunteer nurses. She played admirably on the piano; and the sick man happened – most unfortunately as the event proved – to be fond of music.

'The consequences of the perfectly innocent intercourse thus begun, were deplorable consequences for my niece. She became passionately attached to Mr Eustace Macallan: without awakening any corresponding affection on his side.

'I did my best to interfere, delicately and usefully, while it was still possible to interfere with advantage. Unhappily, my niece refused to place any confidence in me. She persistently denied that she was actuated by any warmer feeling towards Mr Macallan than a feeling of friendly interest. This made it impossible for me to separate them, without openly acknowledging my reason for doing so, and thus producing a scandal which might have affected my niece's reputation. My husband was alive at that time; and the one thing I could do, under the circumstances, was the thing I did. I requested him to speak privately to Mr Macallan, and to appeal to his honour to help us out of the difficulty, without prejudice to my niece.

'Mr Macallan behaved admirably. He was still helpless. But he made an excuse for leaving us which it was impossible to dispute. In two days after my husband had spoken to him, he was removed from the house.

'The remedy was well intended; but it came too late, and it utterly failed. The mischief was done. My niece pined away visibly; neither medical help nor change of air and scene did anything for her. In course of time – after Mr Macallan had recovered from the effects of his accident – I found out that she was carrying on a clandestine correspondence with him, by means of her maid. His letters, I am bound to say, were most considerately and carefully written. Nevertheless, I felt it my duty to stop the correspondence.

'My interference – what else could I do but interfere? – brought matters to a crisis. One day, my niece was missing at breakfast time. The next day, we discovered that the poor infatuated creature had gone to Mr Macallan's chambers in London, and had been found hidden in his bedroom, by some bachelor friends who came to visit him.

'For this disaster Mr Macallan was in no respect to blame. Hearing footsteps outside, he had only time to take measures for saving her character by concealing her in the nearest room – and the nearest room happened to be his bedchamber. The matter was talked about of course, and motives were misinterpreted in the vilest manner. My husband had another private conversation with Mr Macallan. He again behaved admirably. He publicly declared that my niece had visited him as his betrothed wife. In a fortnight from that time, he silenced scandal in the one way that was possible – he married her.

'I was alone in opposing the marriage. I thought it at the time – what it has proved to be since – a fatal mistake.

'It would have been sad enough, if Mr Macallan had only married her without a particle of love on his side. But, to make the prospect more hopeless still, he was himself, at that very time, the victim of a misplaced attachment to a lady who was engaged to another man. I am well aware that he compassionately denied this – just as he compassionately affected to be in love with my niece when he married her. But his hopeless admiration of the lady whom I have mentioned, was a matter of fact notorious among his friends. It may not be amiss to add, that *her* marriage preceded *his* marriage. He had irretrievably lost the woman he really loved – he was without a hope or an aspiration in life – when he took pity on my niece.

'In conclusion, I can only repeat that no evil which could have happened (if she had remained a single woman) would have been comparable, in my opinion, to the evil of such a marriage as this. Never, I sincerely believe, were two more ill-assorted persons united in the bonds of matrimony, than the prisoner at the bar and his deceased wife.'

The evidence of this witness produced a strong sensation among the audience, and had a marked effect on the minds of the Jury. Cross-examination forced Lady Brydehaven to modify some of her opinions, and to acknowledge that the hopeless attachment of the prisoner to another woman was a matter of rumour only. But the facts in her narrative remained unshaken – and, for that one reason, they invested the crime charged against the prisoner with an appearance of possibility, which it had entirely failed to assume during the earlier part of the Trial.

Two other ladies (intimate friends of Mrs Eustace Macallan) were called next. They differed from Lady Brydehaven in their opinions on the propriety of the marriage; but on all the material points, they supported her testimony, and confirmed the serious impression which the first witness had produced on every person in Court.

The next evidence which the prosecution proposed to put in, was the silent evidence of the letters and the Diary found at Gleninch.

In answer to a question from the Bench, the Lord Advocate stated that the letters were written by friends of the prisoner and of his deceased wife, and that passages in them bore directly on the terms on which the two associated in their married life. The Diary was still more valuable as evidence. It contained the prisoner's daily record of domestic events, and of the thoughts and feelings which they aroused in him at the time.

A most painful scene followed this explanation.

Writing, as I do, long after the events took place, I still cannot prevail upon myself to describe in detail what my unhappy husband said and did, at this distressing period of the Trial. Deeply affected while Lady Brydehaven was giving her evidence, he had with difficulty restrained himself from interrupting her. He now lost all control over his feelings. In piercing tones which rang through the Court, he protested against the contemplated violation of his own most sacred secrets and his wife's most sacred secrets. 'Hang me, innocent as I am!' he cried, 'but spare me *that*!' The effect of this terrible outbreak on the audience, is reported to have been indescribable. Some of the women present were in hysterics. The Judges interfered from the Bench – but with no good result. Quiet was at length restored by the Dean of Faculty, who succeeded in soothing the prisoner – and who then addressed the Judges, pleading for indulgence to his unhappy client in most touching and eloquent language. The speech, a masterpiece of impromptu oratory, concluded with a temperate yet strongly-urged protest against the reading of the papers discovered at Gleninch.

The three Judges retired to consider the legal question submitted to them. The sitting was suspended for more than half an hour.

As usual in such cases, the excitement in the Court communicated itself to the crowd outside in the street. The general opinion here –

led, as it was supposed, by one of the clerks or other inferior persons connected with the legal proceedings – was decidedly adverse to the prisoner's chance of escaping a sentence of death. 'If the letters and the Diary are read,' said the brutal spokesmen of the mob, 'the letters and the Diary will hang him.'

On the return of the Judges into Court, it was announced that they had decided, by a majority of two to one, on permitting the documents in dispute to be produced in evidence. Each of the Judges, in turn, gave his reasons for the decision at which he had arrived. This done, the Trial proceeded. The reading of the extracts from the letters and the extracts from the Diary began.

The first letters produced were the letters found in the Indian cabinet, in Mrs Eustace Macallan's room. They were addressed to the deceased lady by intimate (female) friends of hers, with whom she was accustomed to correspond. Three separate Extracts, from letters written by three different correspondents, were selected to be read in Court.

First Correspondent: 'I despair, my dearest Sara, of being able to tell you how your last letter has distressed me. Pray forgive me, if I own to thinking that your very sensitive nature exaggerates or misinterprets, quite unconsciously of course, the neglect that you experience at the hands of your husband. I cannot say anything about *his* peculiarities of character, because I am not well enough acquainted with him to know what they are. But, my dear, I am much older than you, and I have had a much longer experience than yours of, what somebody calls, "the lights and shadows of married life." Speaking from that experience, I must tell you what I have observed. Young married women, like you, who are devotedly attached to their husbands, are apt to make one very serious mistake. As a rule, they all expect too much from their husbands. Men, my poor Sara, are not like *us*. Their love, even when it is quite sincere, is not like our love. It does not last, as it does with us. It is not the one hope and one thought of their lives, as it is with us. We have no alternative – even when we most truly respect and love them – but to make allowance for this difference between the man's nature and the woman's. I do not for one moment excuse your husband's coldness. He is wrong, for example, in never looking at you when he speaks to you, and in never noticing the efforts that you make to please him. He is worse than wrong – he is really cruel if you like – in never returning your kiss when you kiss him. But, my dear, are you quite sure that he is always *designedly* cold and cruel? May not his conduct be sometimes the result of troubles and anxieties which weigh on his mind, and which are troubles and anxieties that you cannot share? If you try to look at his behaviour in this light, you will understand many things which puzzle and pain you now. Be patient with him, my child. Make no complaints; and never approach him with your caresses, at times when his mind is preoccupied or his temper ruffled. This may be hard. advice to follow, loving him as ardently as you do. But rely on it, the secret of happiness for us women is to be found (alas, only too often!) in such exercise of restraint and resignation as your old friend now recommends. Think, my dear, over what I have written – and let me hear from you again.'

SECOND CORRESPONDENT: 'How can you be so foolish, Sara, as to waste your love on such a cold-blooded brute as your husband seems to be? To be sure, I am not married yet – or perhaps I should not be so surprised at you. But I shall be married one of these days; and if my husband ever treats me as Mr Macallan treats you, I shall insist on a separation. I declare I think I would rather be actually beaten, like the women among the lower orders, than be treated with the polite neglect and contempt which you describe. I burn with indignation when I think of it. It must be quite insufferable. Don't bear it any longer, my poor dear. Leave him, and come and stay with me. My brother is a law-student, as you know. I read to him portions of your letter; and he is of opinion that you might get, what he calls, a judicial separation.[1] Come and consult him.'

THIRD CORRESPONDENT: 'You know, my dear Mrs Macallan, what *my* experience of men has been. Your letter does not surprise me in the least. Your husband's conduct to you points to one conclusion. He is in love with some other woman. There is Somebody in the dark, who gets from him everything that he denies to you. I have been through it all – and I know! Don't give way. Make it the business of your life to find out who the creature is. Perhaps there may be more than one of them. It doesn't matter. One, or many, if you can only discover them, you may make his existence as miserable to him as he makes your existence to you. If you want my experience to help you, say the word, and it is freely at your service. I can come and stay with you, at Gleninch, any time after the fourth of next month.'

With those abominable lines the readings from the letters of the women came to an end. The first and longest of the Extracts produced the most vivid impression in Court. Evidently the writer was, in this case, a worthy and sensible person. It was generally felt, however, that all three of the letters – no matter how widely they might differ in tone – justified the same conclusion. The wife's position at Gleninch (if the wife's account of it was to be trusted) was the position of a neglected and an unhappy woman.

The correspondence of the prisoner, which had been found, with his Diary, in the locked bed-table drawer, was produced next. The letters in this case were, with one exception, all written by men. Though the tone of them was moderation itself, as compared with the second and third of the women's letters, the conclusion still pointed the same way. The life of the husband, at Gleninch, appeared to be just as intolerable as the life of the wife.

For example, one of the prisoner's male friends wrote, inviting him to make a yacht voyage round the world. Another suggested an absence of six months on the Continent. A third recommended field sports in India. The one object aimed at by all the writers was plainly to counsel a separation, more or less plausible and more or less complete, between the married pair.

The last letter read was addressed to the prisoner in a woman's handwriting, and was signed by a woman's Christian name only.

'Ah, my poor Eustace, what a cruel destiny is ours!' (the letter began). 'When I think of your life, sacrificed to that wretched woman, my heart bleeds for you! If *we* had been man and wife – if it had been *my* unutterable happiness to love and cherish the best, the dearest of men – what a paradise of our own we might have lived in, what delicious hours we might have known! But regret is vain; we are separated, in this life – separated by ties which we both mourn, and yet which we must both respect. My Eustace, there is a world beyond this! There, our souls will fly to meet each other, and mingle in one long heavenly embrace – in a rapture forbidden to us on earth. The misery described in your letter – oh! why, why did you marry her? – has wrung this confession of feeling from me. Let it comfort you; but let no other eyes see it. Burn my rashly-written lines, and look (as I look) to the better life which you may yet share with your own HELENA.'

The reading of this outrageous letter provoked a question from the Bench. One of the Judges asked if the writer had attached any date or address to her letter.

In answer to this, the Lord Advocate stated that neither the one nor the other appeared. The envelope showed that the letter had been posted in London. 'We propose,' the learned counsel continued, 'to read certain passages from the prisoner's Diary, in which the name signed at the end of the letter occurs more than once; and we may possibly find other means of identifying the writer, to the satisfaction of your lordships, before the Trial is over.'

The promised passages from my husband's private Diary were now read. The first extract related to a period of nearly a year before the date of Mrs Eustace Macallan's death. It was expressed in these terms:

'News, by this morning's post, which has quite overwhelmed me. Helena's husband died suddenly, two days since, of heart disease. She is free – my beloved Helena is free! And I?

'I am fettered to a woman with whom I have not a single feeling in common. Helena is lost to me, by my own act. Ah! I can understand now, as I never understood before, how irresistible temptation can be, and how easily, sometimes, crime may follow it. I had better shut up these leaves for the night. It maddens me to no purpose to think of my position or to write of it.'

The next passage, dated a few days later, dwelt on the same subject:

'Of all the follies that a man can commit, the greatest is acting on impulse. I acted on impulse when I married the unfortunate creature who is now my wife.

'Helena was then lost to me, as I too hastily supposed. She had married the man to whom she rashly engaged herself, before she met with me. He was younger than I, and, to all appearances, heartier and stronger than I. So far as I could see, my fate was sealed for life. Helena had written her farewell letter, taking leave of me in this world, for good. My prospects were closed; my hopes had ended. I had not an aspiration left; I had no necessity to stimulate me to take refuge in work. A chivalrous action, an exertion of noble self-denial, seemed to be all that was left to me, all that I was fit for.

'The circumstances of the moment adapted themselves, with a fatal facility, to this idea. The ill-fated woman who had become attached to me (Heaven knows without so much as the shadow of encouragement on my part!), had, just at that time, rashly placed her reputation at the mercy of the world. It rested with me to silence the scandalous tongues that reviled her. With Helena lost to me, happiness was not to be expected. All women were equally indifferent to me. A generous action would be the salvation of *this* woman. Why not perform it? I married her on that impulse – married her, just as I might have jumped into the water and saved her, if she had been drowning; just as I might have knocked a man down, if I had seen him ill-treating her in the street!

'And now, the woman for whom I have made this sacrifice stands between me and my Helena – my Helena, free to pour out all the treasures of her love on the man who adores the earth that she touches with her foot!

'Fool! Madman! Why don't I dash out my brains against the wall that I see opposite to me while I write these lines?

'My gun is there in the corner. I have only to tie a string to the trigger, and to put the muzzle to my mouth—No! My mother is alive; my mother's love is sacred. I have no right to take the life which she gave me. I must suffer and submit. Oh, Helena! Helena!'

The third extract – one among many similar passages – had been written about two months before the death of the prisoner's wife.

'More reproaches addressed to me! There never was such a woman for complaining; she lives in a perfect atmosphere of ill-temper and discontent.

'My new offences are two in number. I never ask her to play to me now; and, when she puts on a new dress expressly to please me, I never notice it. Notice it! Good Heavens! The effort of my life is *not* to notice her, in anything she does or says. How could I keep my temper, unless I kept as much as possible out of the way of private interviews with her? And I do keep my temper. I am never hard on her; I never use harsh language to her. She has a double claim on my forbearance – she is a woman; and the law has made her my wife. I remember this; but I am human. The less I see of her – except when visitors are present – the more certain I can feel of preserving my self-control.

'I wonder what it is that makes her so utterly distasteful to me. She is a plain woman; but I have seen uglier women than she, whose caresses I could have endured, without the sense of shrinking that comes over me when I am obliged to submit to *her* caresses. I keep the feeling hidden from her. She loves me, poor thing! – and I pity her. I wish I could do more; I wish I could return, in the smallest degree, the feeling with which she regards me. But, no – I can only pity her. If she would be content to live on friendly terms with me, and never to exact demonstrations of tenderness, we might get on pretty well. But she wants love. Unfortunate creature, she wants love!

'Oh, my Helena! I have no love to give her. My heart is yours.

'I dreamt last night, that this unhappy wife of mine was dead. The dream was so vivid that I actually got out of my bed, and opened the door of her room, and listened.

'Her calm regular breathing was distinctly audible in the stillness of the night. She was in a deep sleep. I closed the door again, and lit my candle and read. Helena was in all my thoughts; it was hard work to fix my attention on the book. But anything was better than going to bed again, and dreaming perhaps for the second time that I, too, was free.

'What a life mine is! what a life my wife's is! If the house was to take fire, I wonder whether I should make an effort to save myself, or to save her?'

The last two passages read, referred to later dates still.

'A gleam of brightness has shone over this dismal existence of mine at last.

'Helena is no longer condemned to the seclusion of widowhood. Time enough has passed to permit of her mixing again in society. She is paying visits to friends in our part of Scotland; and, as she and I are cousins, it is universally understood that she cannot leave the North without also spending a few days at my house. She writes me word that the visit, however embarrassing it may be to us privately, is nevertheless a visit that must be made, for the sake of appearances. Blessings on appearances! I shall see this angel in my purgatory – and all because Society in Mid-Lothian would think it strange that my cousin should be visiting in my part of Scotland, and not visit Me!

'But we are to be very careful. Helena says, in so many words, "I come to see you, Eustace, as a sister. You must receive me as a brother, or not receive me at all. I shall write to your wife to propose the day for my visit. I shall not forget – do you not forget – that it is by your wife's permission that I enter your house."

'Only let me see her! I will submit to anything to obtain the unutterable happiness of seeing her!'

The last Extract followed, and consisted of these lines only:

'A new misfortune! My wife has fallen ill. She has taken to her bed, with a bad rheumatic cold, just at the time appointed for Helena's visit to Gleninch. But, on this occasion (I gladly own it!), she has behaved charmingly. She has written to Helena to say that her illness is not serious enough to render a change necessary in the arrangements, and to make it her particular request that my cousin's visit shall take place upon the day originally decided on.

'This is a great sacrifice made to me, on my wife's part. Jealous of every woman, under forty, who comes near me, she is of course jealous of Helena – and she controls herself, and trusts me!

'I am bound to show my gratitude for this, and I will show it. From this day forth, I vow to live more affectionately with my wife. I tenderly embraced her this very morning – and, I hope, poor soul, she did not discover the effort that it cost me.'

There, the readings from the Diary came to an end.

The most unpleasant pages in the whole Report of the Trial were – to me – the pages which contained the extracts from my husband's Diary. There were expressions, here and there, which not only pained me, but which almost shook Eustace's position in my estimation. I think I would have given everything I possessed to have had the power of annihilating certain lines in that Diary. As for his passionate expressions of love for Mrs Beauly, every one of them went through me like a sting! He had whispered words quite as warm into my ears, in the days of his courtship. I had no reason to doubt that he truly and dearly loved me. But the question was – Had he, just as truly and dearly, loved Mrs Beauly, before me? Had she or I won the first of his heart? He had declared to me, over and over again, that he had only fancied himself to be in love, before the day when we met. I had believed him then. I determined to believe him still. I did believe him. But I hated Mrs Beauly!

As for the painful impression produced in Court by the readings from the letters and the Diary, it seemed to be impossible to increase it. Nevertheless, it *was* perceptibly increased. In other words, it was rendered more unfavourable still towards the prisoner, by the evidence of the next, and last, witness called on the part of the prosecution.

William Enzie, under-gardener at Gleninch, was sworn, and deposed as follows:

'On the twentieth of October, at eleven o'clock in the forenoon, I was at work in the shrubbery, on the side next to the garden called the Dutch Garden. There was a summer-house in the Dutch Garden, having its back set towards the shrubbery. The day was wonderfully fine and warm for the time of year.

'Passing to my work, I passed the back of the summer-house. I heard voices inside – a man's voice and a lady's voice. The lady's voice was strange to me. The man's voice I recognised as the voice of my master. The ground in the shrubbery was soft; and my curiosity was excited. I stepped up to the back of the summer-house, without being heard; and I listened to what was going on inside.

'The first words I could distinguish were spoken in my master's voice. He said, "If I could only have foreseen that you might one day be free, what a happy man I might have been!" The lady's voice answered, "Hush! you must not talk so." My master said upon that, "I must talk of what is in my mind; it is always in my mind that I have lost you." He stopped a bit there, and then he said on a sudden, "Do me one favour, my angel! Promise me not to marry again." The lady's voice spoke out, thereupon, sharply enough, "What do you mean?" My master said, "I wish no harm to the unhappy creature who is a burden on my life; but suppose—?" "Suppose nothing," the lady said; "come back to the house."

'She led the way into the garden, and turned round, beckoning my master to join her. In that position, I saw her face plainly; and I knew it for the face of the young widow lady who was visiting at the house. She was pointed out to me by the head-gardener, when she first arrived, for the purpose of warning me that I was not to interfere if I found her picking the flowers. The gardens at Gleninch were shown to tourists on certain days; and we made a difference, of course, in the matter of the flowers, between strangers and guests staying in the house. I am quite certain of the identity of the lady who was talking with my master. Mrs Beauly was a comely person – and there was no mistaking her for any other than herself. She and my master withdrew together on the way to the house. I heard nothing more of what passed between them.'

This witness was severely cross-examined as to the correctness of his recollection of the talk in the summer-house, and as to his capacity for identifying both the speakers. On certain minor points he was shaken. But he firmly asserted his accurate remembrance of the last words exchanged between his master and Mrs Beauly; and he personally described the lady, in terms which proved that he had correctly identified her.

With this, the answer to the third Question raised by the Trial – the question of the prisoner's Motive for poisoning his wife – came to an end.

The story for the prosecution was now a story told. The staunchest friends of the prisoner in Court were compelled to acknowledge that the evidence, thus far, pointed clearly and conclusively against him. He seemed to feel this himself. When he withdrew at the close of the third day of the Trial, he was so depressed and exhausted that he was obliged to lean on the arm of the governor of the jail.

CHAPTER XIX

The Evidence for the Defence

The feeling of interest excited by the Trial was prodigiously increased on the fourth day. The witnesses for the defence were now to be heard; and first and foremost among them was the prisoner's mother. She looked at her son as she lifted her veil to take the oath. He burst into tears. At that moment, the sympathy felt for the mother was generally extended to the unhappy son.

Examined by the Dean of Faculty, Mrs Macallan the elder gave her answers with remarkable dignity and self-control.

Questioned as to certain private conversations which had passed between her late daughter-in-law and herself, she declared that Mrs Eustace Macallan was morbidly sensitive on the subject of her personal appearance. She was devotedly attached to her husband; the great anxiety of her life was to make herself as attractive to him as possible. The imperfections in her personal appearance – and especially in her complexion – were subjects to her of the bitterest regret. The witness had heard her say, over and over again (referring to her complexion), that there was no risk she would not run, and no pain she would not suffer, to improve it. 'Men' (she had said) 'are all caught by outward appearances: my husband might love me better, if I had a better colour.'

Being asked next if the passages from her son's Diary were to be depended on as evidence – that is to say, if they fairly represented the peculiarities in his character, and his true sentiments towards his wife – Mrs Macallan denied it in the plainest and the strongest terms.

'The extracts from my son's Diary are a libel on his character,' she said. 'And not the less a libel, because they happen to be written by himself. Speaking from a mother's experience of him, I know that he must have written the passages produced, in moments of uncontrollable depression and despair. No just person judges hastily of a man by the rash words which may escape him in his moody and miserable moments. Is my son to be so judged, because he happens to have written *his* rash words, instead of speaking them? His pen has been his most deadly enemy, in this case – it has presented him at his very worst. He was not happy in his marriage – I admit that. But I say at the same time, that he was invariably considerate towards his wife. I was implicitly trusted by both of them; I saw them in their most private moments. I declare – in the face of what she appears to have written to her friends and correspondents – that my son never gave his wife any just cause to assert that he treated her with cruelty and neglect.'

These words, firmly and clearly spoken, produced a strong impression. The Lord Advocate – evidently perceiving that any attempt to weaken that impression would not be likely to succeed – confined himself, in cross-examination, to two significant questions.

'In speaking to you of the defects in her complexion,' he said, 'did your daughter-in-law refer in any way to the use of arsenic as a remedy?'

The answer to this was, 'No.'

The Lord Advocate proceeded:

'Did you yourself ever recommend arsenic, or mention it casually, in the course of the private conversations which you have described?'

The answer to this was, 'Never.'

The Lord Advocate resumed his seat. Mrs Macallan the elder withdrew.

An interest of a new kind was excited by the appearance of the next witness. This was no less a person than Mrs Beauly herself. The Report describes her as a remarkably attractive person; modest and ladylike in her manner, and, to all appearance, feeling sensitively the public position in which she was placed.

The first portion of her evidence was almost a recapitulation of the evidence given by the prisoner's mother – with this difference, that Mrs Beauly had been actually questioned by the deceased lady on the subject of cosmetic applications to the complexion. Mrs Eustace Macallan had complimented her on the beauty of her complexion, and had asked what artificial means she used to keep it in such good order. Using no artificial means (and knowing nothing whatever of cosmetics), Mrs Beauly had resented the question; and a temporary coolness between the two ladies had been the result.

Interrogated as to her relations with the prisoner, Mrs Beauly indignantly denied that she or Mr Macallan had ever given the deceased lady the slightest cause for jealousy. It was impossible for Mrs Beauly to leave Scotland, after visiting at the houses of her cousin's neighbours, without also visiting at her cousin's house. To take any other course would have been an act of downright rudeness, and would have excited remark. She did not deny that Mr Macallan had admired her in the days when they were both single people. But there was no further expression of that feeling, when she had married another man, and when he had married another woman. From that time, their intercourse was the innocent intercourse of a brother and sister. Mr Macallan was a gentleman: he knew what was due to his wife and to Mrs Beauly – she would not have entered the house, if experience had not satisfied her of that. As for the evidence of the under-gardener, it was little better than pure invention. The greater part of the conversation which he had described himself as overhearing had never taken place. The little that was really said (as the man reported it) was said jestingly; and she had checked it immediately – as the witness had himself confessed. For the rest, Mr Macallan's behaviour towards his wife was invariably kind and considerate. He was constantly devising means to alleviate her sufferings from the rheumatic affection which confined her to her bed; he had spoken of her, not once but many times, in terms of the sincerest sympathy. When she ordered her husband and witness to leave the room, on the day of her death, Mr Macallan said to witness afterwards, 'We must bear with her jealousy, poor soul: we know that we don't deserve it.' In that patient manner, he submitted to her infirmities of temper, from first to last.

The main interest in the cross-examination of Mrs Beauly, centred in a question which was put at the end. After reminding her that she had given her name, on being sworn, as 'Helena Beauly,' the Lord Advocate said:

'A letter addressed to the prisoner, and signed "Helena," has been read in Court. Look at it, if you please. Are you the writer of that letter?'

Before the witness could reply, the Dean of Faculty protested against the question. The Judges allowed the protest, and refused to permit the question to be put. Mrs Beauly thereupon withdrew. She had betrayed a very perceptible agitation on hearing the letter referred to, and on having it placed in her hands. This exhibition of feeling was variously interpreted among the audience. Upon the whole, however, Mrs Beauly's evidence was considered to have aided the impression which the mother's evidence had produced in the prisoner's favour.

The next witnesses – both ladies, and both school-friends of Mrs Eustace Macallan – created a new feeling of interest in Court. They supplied the missing link in the evidence for the defence.

The first of the ladies declared that she had mentioned arsenic, as a means of improving the complexion, in conversation with Mrs Eustace Macallan. She had never used it herself, but she had read of the practice of eating arsenic, among the Styrian peasantry, for the purpose of clearing the colour, and of producing a general appearance of plumpness and good health.[1] She positively swore that she had related this result of her reading to the deceased lady, exactly as she now related it in Court.

The second witness, present at the conversation already mentioned, corroborated the first witness in every particular; and added that she had procured the book relating to the arsenic-eating practices of the Styrian peasantry, and to their results, at Mrs Eustace Macallan's own request. This book she had herself despatched by post to Mrs Eustace Macallan at Gleninch.

There was but one assailable point in this otherwise conclusive evidence. The cross-examination discovered it.

Both the ladies were asked, in turn, if Mrs Eustace Macallan had expressed to them, directly or indirectly, any intention of obtaining arsenic, with a view to the improvement of her complexion. In each case the answer to that all-important question was, 'No.' Mrs Eustace Macallan had heard of the remedy, and had received the book. But of her own intentions in the future, she had not said one word. She had begged both the ladies to consider the conversation as strictly private – and there it had ended.

It required no lawyer's eye to discern the fatal defect which was now revealed in the evidence for the defence. Every intelligent person present could see that the prisoner's chance of an honourable acquittal depended on tracing the poison to the possession of his wife – or at least on proving her expressed intention to obtain it. In either of these cases, the prisoner's Declaration of his innocence would claim the support of testimony, which – however indirect it might be – no honest and intelligent men would be likely to resist. Was that testimony forthcoming? Was the counsel for the defence not at the end of his resources yet?

The crowded audience waited, in breathless expectation, for the appearance of the next witness. A whisper went round, among certain well-instructed persons, that the Court was now to see and hear the prisoner's old friend – already often referred to in the course of the Trial, as 'Mr Dexter.'

After a brief interval of delay, there was a sudden commotion among the audience, accompanied by suppressed exclamations of curiosity and surprise. At the same moment, the crier summoned the new witness by the extraordinary name of—

'MISERRIMUS DEXTER.'

CHAPTER XX

The End of the Trial

The calling of the witness produced a burst of laughter from the public seats – due partly, no doubt, to the strange name by which he had been summoned; partly, also, to the instinctive desire of all crowded assemblies, when their interest is painfully excited, to seize on any relief in the shape of the first excuse for merriment which may present itself. A severe rebuke from the Bench restored order among the audience. The Lord Justice Clerk declared that he would 'clear the Court' if the interruption to the proceedings was renewed.

During the silence which followed this announcement, the new witness appeared.

Gliding, self-propelled in his chair on wheels, through the opening made for him among the crowd, a strange and startling creature – literally the half of a man – revealed himself to the general view. A coverlid,[1] which had been thrown over his chair, had fallen off during his progress through the throng. The loss of it exposed to the public curiosity the head, the arms, and the trunk of a living human being: absolutely deprived of the lower limbs. To make this deformity all the more striking and all the more terrible, the victim of it was – as to his face and his body – an unusually handsome, and an unusually well-made man. His long silky hair, of a bright and beautiful chestnut colour, fell over shoulders that were the perfection of strength and grace. His face was bright with vivacity and intelligence. His large clear blue eyes, and his long delicate white hands, were like the eyes and hands of a beautiful woman. He would have looked effeminate, but for the manly proportions of his throat and chest; aided in their effect by his flowing beard and long moustache, of a lighter chestnut shade than the colour of his hair. Never had a magnificent head and body been more hopelessly ill-bestowed than in this instance! Never had Nature committed a more careless or a more cruel mistake than in the making of this man!

He was sworn, seated of course in his chair. Having given his name, he bowed to the Judges, and requested their permission to preface his evidence with a word of explanation.

'People generally laugh when they first hear my strange Christian name,' he said, in a low clear resonant voice which penetrated to the remotest corners of the Court. 'I may inform the good people here that many names, still common among us, have their significations, and that mine is one of them. "Alexander," for instance, means, in the Greek, "a helper of men." "David" means, in Hebrew, "well-beloved." "Francis" means, in German, "free." My name, "Miserrimus," means, in Latin, "most unhappy." It was given to me by my father, in allusion to the deformity which you all see – the deformity with which it was my misfortune to be born. You won't laugh at "Miserrimus" again, will you?' He turned to the Dean of Faculty, waiting to examine him for the defence. 'Mr Dean, I am at your service. I apologise for delaying, even for a moment, the proceedings of the Court.'

He delivered his little address with perfect grace and good humour. Examined by the Dean, he gave his evidence clearly, without the slightest appearance of hesitation or reserve.

'I was staying at Gleninch, as a guest in the house, at the time of Mrs Eustace Macallan's death,' he began. 'Doctor Jerome and Mr Gale desired to see me, at a private interview – the prisoner being then in a state of prostration which made it impossible for him to attend to his duties as master of the house. At this interview, the two doctors astonished and horrified me, by declaring that Mrs Eustace Macallan had died poisoned. They left it to me to communicate the dreadful news to her husband; and they warned me that a post-mortem examination must be held on the body.

'If the Fiscal had seen my old friend, when I communicated the doctors' message, I doubt if he would have ventured to charge the prisoner with the murder of his wife. To my mind the charge was nothing less than an outrage. I resisted the seizure of the prisoner's Diary and letters, animated by that feeling. Now that the Diary has been produced, I agree with the prisoner's mother in denying that it is fair evidence to bring against him. A Diary (when it extends beyond a bare record of facts and dates) is, in general, nothing but an expression of the weakest side in the character of the person who keeps it. It is, in nine cases out of ten, the more or less contemptible outpouring of vanity and conceit which the writer dare not exhibit to any mortal but himself. I am the prisoner's oldest friend. I solemnly declare that I never knew he could write downright nonsense, until I heard his Diary read in this Court!

'*He* kill his wife! *He* treat his wife with neglect and cruelty! I venture to say, from twenty years' experience of him, that there is no man in this assembly who is, constitutionally, more incapable of crime, and more incapable of cruelty, than the man who stands at that Bar. While I am about it, I go further still. I even doubt whether a man capable of crime, and capable of cruelty, could have found it in his heart to do evil to the woman whose untimely death is the subject of this enquiry.

'I have heard what the ignorant and prejudiced nurse, Christina Ormsay, has said of the deceased lady. From my own personal observation I contradict every word of it. Mrs Eustace Macallan – granting her personal defects – was nevertheless one of the most charming women I ever met with. She was highly bred, in the best sense of the word. I never saw, in any other person, so sweet a smile as hers, or such grace and beauty of movement as hers. If you liked music, she sang beautifully; and few professed musicians had such a touch on the piano as hers. If you preferred talking, I never yet met with the man (or even the woman, which is saying a great deal more) whom her conversation could not charm. To say that such a wife as this could be first cruelly neglected, and then barbarously murdered, by the man – no! by the martyr – who stands there, is to tell me that the sun never shines at noonday, or that the heaven is not above the earth.

'Oh, yes! I know that the letters of her friends show that she wrote to them in bitter complaint of her husband's conduct to her. But remember what one of those friends (the wisest and the best of them) says in reply. "I own to thinking," she writes, "that your sensitive nature exaggerates or misinterprets the neglect that you experience at the hands of your husband." There, in that one sentence, is the whole truth! Mrs Eustace Macallan's nature was the imaginative, self-tormenting nature of a poet. No mortal love could ever have been refined enough for *her*. Trifles which women of a coarser moral fibre would have passed over without notice, were causes of downright agony to that exquisitely sensitive temperament. There are persons born to be unhappy. That poor lady was one of them. When I have said this, I have said all.

'No! There is one word more still to be added.

'It may be as well to remind the prosecution that Mrs Eustace Macallan's death was, in the pecuniary sense, a serious loss to her husband. He had insisted on having the whole of her fortune settled on herself, and on her relatives after her, when he married. Her income from that fortune helped to keep in splendour the house and grounds at Gleninch. The prisoner's own resources (aided even by his mother's jointure) were quite inadequate fitly to defray the expenses of living at his splendid country seat. Knowing all the circumstances, I can positively assert that the wife's death has deprived the husband of two-thirds of his income. And the prosecution, viewing him as the basest and cruellest of men, declares that he deliberately killed her – with all his pecuniary interests pointing to the preservation of her life!

'It is useless to ask me whether I noticed anything in the conduct of the prisoner and Mrs Beauly, which might justify a wife's jealousy. I never observed Mrs Beauly with any attention; and I never encouraged the prisoner in talking to me about her. He was a general admirer of pretty women – so far as I know, in a perfectly innocent way. That he could prefer Mrs Beauly to his wife, is inconceivable to me – unless he was out of his senses. I never had any reason to believe that he was out of his senses.

'As to the question of the arsenic – I mean the question of tracing the poison to the possession of Mrs Eustace Macallan – I am able to give evidence, which may perhaps be worthy of the attention of the Court.

'I was present, in the Fiscal's office, during the examination of the papers, and of the other objects discovered at Gleninch. The dressing-case belonging to the deceased lady was shown to me, after its contents had been officially investigated by the Fiscal himself. I happen to have a very sensitive sense of touch. In handling the lid of the dressing-case, on the inner side, I felt something at a certain place, which induced me to examine the whole structure of the lid very carefully. The result was the discovery of a private repository, concealed in the space between the outer wood and the lining. In that repository I found the bottle which I now produce.'

The further examination of the witness was suspended, while the hidden bottle was compared with the bottles properly belonging to the dressing-case.

These last were of the finest cut glass, and of a very elegant form – entirely unlike the bottle found in the private repository, which was of the commonest manufacture, and of the shape ordinarily in use among chemists. Not a drop of liquid, not the smallest atom of any solid substance, remained in it. No smell exhaled from it – and, more unfortunately still for the interests of the defence, no label was found attached to the bottle when it had been discovered.

The chemist who had sold the second supply of arsenic to the prisoner was recalled, and examined. He declared that the bottle was exactly like the bottle in which he placed the arsenic. It was, however, equally like hundreds of other bottles in his shop. In the absence of the label (on which he had himself written the word 'Poison') it was impossible for him to identify the bottle. The dressing-case, and the deceased lady's bedroom, had been vainly searched for the chemist's missing label – on the chance that it might have become accidentally detached from the mysterious empty bottle. In both instances, the search had been without result. Morally, it was a fair conclusion that this might be really the bottle which had contained the poison. Legally, there was not the slightest proof of it.

Thus ended the last effort of the defence to trace the arsenic purchased by the prisoner to the possession of his wife. The book relating the practices of the Styrian peasantry (found in the deceased lady's room) had been produced. But could the book prove that she had asked her husband to buy arsenic for her? The crumpled paper, with the grains of powder left in it, had been identified by the chemist, and had been declared to contain grains of arsenic. But where was the proof that Mrs Eustace Macallan's hand had placed the packet in the cabinet, and had emptied it of its contents? No direct evidence anywhere! Nothing but conjecture!

The renewed examination of Miserrimus Dexter touched on matters of no general interest. The cross-examination resolved itself, in sub-stance, into a mental trial of strength between the witness and the Lord Advocate; the struggle terminating (according to the general opinion) in favour of the witness. One question, and one answer only, I will repeat here. They appeared to me of serious importance to the object that I had in view in reading the Trial.

'I believe, Mr Dexter,' the Lord Advocate remarked, in his most ironical manner, 'that you have a theory of your own, which makes the death of Mrs Eustace Macallan no mystery to *you*?'

'I may have my own ideas on that subject, as on other subjects,' the witness replied. 'But let me ask their lordships, the Judges – Am I here to declare theories or to state facts?'

I made a note of that answer. Mr Dexter's 'ideas' were the ideas of a true friend to my husband, and of a man of far more than average ability. They might be of inestimable value to me, in the coming time – if I could prevail on him to communicate them.

I may mention, while I am writing on the subject, that I added to this first note a second, containing an observation of my own. In alluding to Mrs Beauly, while he was giving his evidence, Mr Dexter had spoken of her so slightingly – so rudely, I might almost say – as to suggest that he had some private reasons for disliking (perhaps for distrusting) this lady. Here, again, it might be of vital importance to me to see Mr Dexter, and to clear up, if I could, what the dignity of the Court had passed over without notice.

The last witness had been now examined. The chair on wheels glided away, with the half-man in it, and was lost in a distant corner of the Court. The Lord Advocate rose to address the Jury for the prosecution.

I do not scruple to say that I never read anything so infamous as this great lawyer's speech. He was not ashamed to declare, at starting, that he firmly believed the prisoner to be guilty. What right had he to say anything of the sort? Was it for *him* to decide? Was he the Judge and Jury both, I should like to know? Having begun by condemning the prisoner, on his own authority, the Lord Advocate proceeded to pervert the most innocent actions of that unhappy man, so as to give them as vile an aspect as possible. Thus: When Eustace kissed his poor wife's forehead, on her death-bed, he did it to create a favourable impression in the minds of the doctor and the nurse! Again, when his grief under his bereavement completely overwhelmed him, he was triumphing in secret, and acting a part! If you looked into his heart, you would see there a diabolical hatred for his wife, and an infatuated passion for Mrs Beauly! In everything he had said, he had lied; in everything he had done, he had acted like a crafty and heartless wretch! So the chief counsel for the prosecution spoke of the prisoner, standing helpless before him at the Bar. In my husband's place, if I could have done nothing more, I would have thrown something at his head. As it was, I tore the pages which contained the speech for the prosecution out of the Report, and trampled them under my feet – and felt all the better, too, for having done it. At the same time, I am a little ashamed of having revenged myself on the harmless printed leaves, now.

The fifth day of the Trial opened with the speech for the defence. Ah, what a contrast to the infamies uttered by the Lord Advocate was the grand burst of eloquence by the Dean of Faculty, speaking on my husband's side!

This illustrious lawyer struck the right note at starting.

'I yield to no one,' he began, 'in the pity I feel for the wife. But I say, the martyr in this case, from first to last, is the husband. Whatever the poor woman may have endured, that unhappy man at the Bar has suffered, and is now suffering, more. If he had not been the kindest of men, the most docile and most devoted of husbands, he would never have occupied his present dreadful situation. A man of a meaner and harder nature would have felt suspicion of his wife's motives, when she asked him to buy poison – would have seen through the wretchedly commonplace excuses she made for wanting it – and would have wisely and cruelly said, "No." The prisoner is not that sort of man. He is too good to his wife, too innocent of any evil thought towards her, or towards anyone, to foresee the inconveniences and the dangers to which his fatal compliance may expose him. And what is the result? He stands there, branded as a murderer, because he was too high-minded and too honourable to suspect his wife.'

Speaking thus of the husband, the Dean was just as eloquent and just as unanswerable when he came to speak of the wife.

'The Lord Advocate,' he said, 'has asked, with the bitter irony for which he is celebrated at the Scottish Bar, why we have failed entirely to prove that the prisoner placed the two packets of poison in the possession of his wife? I say, in answer, we have proved, first, that the wife was passionately attached to the husband; secondly, that she felt bitterly the defects in her personal appearance, and especially the defects in her complexion; and, thirdly, that she was informed of arsenic as a supposed remedy for these defects, taken internally. To men who know anything of human nature, there is proof enough! Does my learned friend actually suppose, that women are in the habit of mentioning the secret artifices and applications by which they improve their personal appearance? Is it in his experience of the sex, that a woman who is eagerly bent on making herself attractive to a man, would tell that man, or tell anybody else who might communicate with him, that the charm by which she hoped to win his heart – say the charm of a pretty complexion – had been artificially acquired by the perilous use of a deadly poison? The bare idea of such a thing is absurd. Of course, nobody ever heard Mrs Eustace Macallan speak of arsenic. Of course, nobody ever surprised her in the act of taking arsenic. It is in the evidence, that she would not even confide her intention to try the poison to the friends who had told her of it as a remedy, and who had got her the book. She actually begged them to consider their brief conversation on the subject as strictly private. From first to last, poor creature, she kept her secret; just as she would have kept her secret, if she had worn false hair, or if she had been indebted to the dentist for her teeth. And there you see her husband, in peril of his life, because a woman acted *like* a woman – as your wives, Gentlemen of the Jury, would, in a similar position, act towards You.'

After such glorious oratory as this (I wish I had room to quote more of it!) the next, and last, speech delivered at the Trial – that is to say the Charge of the Judge to the Jury – is dreary reading indeed.

His lordship first told the Jury that they could not expect to have direct evidence of the poisoning. Such evidence hardly ever occurred in cases of poisoning. They must be satisfied with the best circumstantial evidence. All quite true, I dare say. But, having told the Jury they might accept circumstantial evidence, he turned back again on his own words, and warned them against being too ready to trust it! 'You must have evidence satisfactory and convincing to your own minds,' he said; 'in which you find no conjectures – but only irresistible and just inferences.' Who is to decide what is a just inference? And what does circumstantial evidence rest on, *but* conjecture?

After this specimen, I need give no further extracts from the summing-up. The Jury, thoroughly bewildered no doubt, took refuge in a compromise. They occupied an hour in considering and debating among themselves, in their own room. (A jury of women would not have taken a minute!) Then they returned into Court, and gave their timid and trimming Scotch Verdict in these words:

'Not Proven.'[2]

Some slight applause followed, among the audience, which was instantly checked. The prisoner was dismissed from the Bar with the formalities observed on such occasions. He slowly retired, like a man in deep grief; his head sunk on his breast – not looking at anyone, and not replying when his friends spoke to him. He knew, poor fellow, the slur that the Verdict left on him. 'We don't say you are innocent of the crime charged against you; we only say, there is not evidence enough to convict you.' In that lame and impotent conclusion the proceedings ended, at the time. And there they would have remained, for all time – but for Me.

CHAPTER XXI

I See My Way

In the grey light of the new morning, I closed the Report of my husband's Trial for the Murder of his first Wife.

No sense of fatigue overpowered me. I had no wish, after my long hours of reading and thinking, to lie down and sleep. It was strange, but it was so. I felt as if I *had* slept, and had now just awakened – a new woman, with a new mind.

I could almost understand Eustace's desertion of me. To a man of his refinement, it would have been a martyrdom to meet his wife, after she had read the things published of him to all the world, in the Report. I felt this, as he would have felt it. At the same time, I thought he might have trusted Me to make amends to him for the martyrdom, and might have come back. Perhaps, it might yet end in his coming back. In the meanwhile, and in that expectation, I pitied and forgave him with my whole heart.

One little matter only dwelt on my mind disagreeably, in spite of my philosophy. Did Eustace still secretly love Mrs Beauly? or had I extinguished that passion in him? To what order of beauty did this lady belong? Were we, by any chance, the least in the world like one another?

The window of my room looked to the east. I drew up the blind, and saw the sun rising grandly in a clear sky. The temptation to go out and breathe the fresh morning air was irresistible. I put on my hat and shawl, and took the Report of the Trial under my arm. The bolts of the back door were easily drawn. In another minute, I was out in Benjamin's pretty little garden.

Composed and strengthened by the inviting solitude and the delicious air, I found courage enough to face the serious question that now confronted me – the question of the future.

I had read the Trial. I had vowed to devote my life to the sacred object of vindicating my husband's innocence. A solitary defenceless woman, I stood pledged to myself to carry that desperate resolution through to an end. How was I to begin?

The bold way of beginning was surely the wise way, in such a position as mine. I had good reasons (founded, as I have already mentioned, on the important part played by this witness at the Trial) for believing that the fittest person to advise and assist me, was – Miserrimus Dexter. He might disappoint the expectations that I had fixed on him, or he might refuse to help me, or (like my uncle Starkweather) he might think I had taken leave of my senses. All these events were possible. Nevertheless, I held to my resolution to try the experiment. If he was in the land of the living, I decided that my first step at starting should take me to the deformed man, with the strange name.

Supposing he received me, sympathised with me, understood me? What would he say? The nurse, in her evidence, had reported him as speaking in an off-hand manner. He would say, in all probability, 'What do you mean to do? And how can I help you to do it?'

Had I answers ready, if those two plain questions were put to me? Yes! if I dared own to any human creature, what was, at that very moment, secretly fermenting in my mind. Yes! if I could confide to a stranger, a suspicion roused in me by the Trial, which I have been thus far afraid to mention even in these pages!

It must, nevertheless, be mentioned now. My suspicion led to results, which are part of my story, and part of my life.

Let me own then, to begin with, that I closed the record of the Trial actually agreeing, in one important particular, with the opinion of my enemy and my husband's enemy – the Lord Advocate! He had characterised the explanation of Mrs Eustace Macallan's death, offered by the defence, as 'a clumsy subterfuge, in which no reasonable being could discern the smallest fragment of probability.' Without going quite so far as this, I, too, could see no reason whatever in the evidence for assuming that the poor woman had taken an overdose of the poison, by mistake. I believed that she had the arsenic secretly in her possession, and that she had tried, or intended to try, the use of it internally, for the purpose of improving her complexion. But further than this I could not advance. The more I thought of it, the more plainly justified the lawyers for the prosecution seemed to me to be, in declaring that Mrs Eustace Macallan had died by the hand of a poisoner – although they were entirely and certainly mistaken in charging my husband with the crime.

My husband being innocent, somebody else, on my own showing, must be guilty. Who, among the persons inhabiting the house at the time, had poisoned Mrs Eustace Macallan? My suspicion, in answering that question, pointed straight to a woman. And the name of that woman was – Mrs Beauly!

Yes! To that startling conclusion I had arrived. It was, to my mind, the inevitable result of reading the evidence.

Look back for a moment to the letter produced in Court, signed 'Helena,' and addressed to Mr Macallan. No reasonable person can doubt (though the Judges excused her from answering the question) that Mrs Beauly was the writer. Very well. The letter offers, as I think, trustworthy evidence to show the state of the woman's mind when she paid her visit to Gleninch.

Writing to Mr Macallan, at a time when she was married to another man – a man to whom she had engaged herself before she met with Mr Macallan – what does she say? She says, 'When I think of your life sacrificed to that wretched woman, my heart bleeds for you.' And, again, she says, 'If it had been my unutterable happiness to love and cherish the best, the dearest of men, what a paradise of our own we might have lived in, what delicious hours we might have known!'

If this is not the language of a woman shamelessly and furiously in love with a man – not her husband – what is? She is so full of him, that even her idea of another world (see the letter) is the idea of 'embracing' Mr Macallan's 'soul.' In this condition of mind and morals, the lady one day finds herself and her embraces free, through the death of her husband. As soon as she can decently visit she goes visiting; and, in due course of time, she becomes the guest of the man whom she adores. His wife is ill in her bed. The one other visitor at Gleninch is a cripple, who can only move in his chair on wheels. The lady has the house and the one beloved object in it, all to herself. No obstacle stands between her, and 'the unutterable happiness of loving and cherishing the best, the dearest of men' – but a poor sick ugly wife, for whom Mr Macallan never has felt, and never can feel, the smallest particle of love.

Is it perfectly absurd to believe that such a woman as this, impelled by these motives, and surrounded by these circumstances, would be capable of committing a crime – if the safe opportunity offered itself?

What does her own evidence say?

She admits that she had a conversation with Mrs Eustace Macallan, in which that lady 'questioned her on the subject of cosmetic applications to the complexion.' Did nothing else take place at that interview? Did Mrs Beauly make no discoveries (afterwards turned to fatal account) of the dangerous experiment which her hostess was then trying, to improve her ugly complexion? All we know is, that Mrs Beauly said nothing about it.

What does the under-gardener say?

He heard a conversation between Mr Macallan and Mrs Beauly, which shows that the possibility of Mrs Beauly becoming Mrs Eustace Macallan had certainly presented itself to that lady's mind, and was certainly considered by her to be too dangerous a topic of discourse to be pursued. Innocent Mr Macallan would have gone on talking. Mrs Beauly is discreet, and stops him.

And what does the nurse (Christina Ormsay) tell us?

On the day of Mrs Eustace Macallan's death, the nurse is dismissed from attendance, and is sent downstairs. She leaves the sick woman, recovered from her first attack of illness, and able to amuse herself with writing. The nurse remains away for half an hour, and then gets uneasy at not hearing the invalid's bell. She goes to the Morning Room to consult Mr Macallan; and there she hears that Mrs Beauly is missing. Mr Macallan doesn't know where she is, and asks Mr Dexter if he has seen her. Mr Dexter has not set eyes on her. At what time does the disappearance of Mrs Beauly take place? At the very time when Christina Ormsay had left Mrs Eustace Macallan alone in her room!

Meanwhile, the bell rings at last, rings violently. The nurse goes back to the sick room at five minutes to eleven, or thereabouts, and finds that the bad symptoms of the morning have returned in a gravely aggravated form. A second dose of poison – larger than the dose administered in the early morning – has been given, during the absence of the nurse, and (observe) during the disappearance also of Mrs Beauly. The nurse, looking out into the corridor for help, encounters Mrs Beauly herself, innocently on her way from her own room – just up, we are to suppose, at eleven in the morning! – to enquire after the sick woman.

A little later, Mrs Beauly accompanies Mr Macallan to visit the invalid. The dying woman casts a strange look at both of them, and tells them to leave her. Mr Macallan understands this as the fretful outbreak of a person in pain, and waits in the room to tell the nurse that the doctor is sent for. What does Mrs Beauly do? She runs out panic-stricken, the instant Mrs Eustace Macallan looks at her. Even Mrs Beauly, it seems, has a conscience!

Is there nothing to justify suspicion in such circumstances as these – circumstances sworn to, on the oaths of the witnesses?

To me, the conclusion is plain. Mrs Beauly's hand gave that second dose of poison. Admit this; and the inference follows that she also gave the first dose in the early morning. How could she do it? Look again at the evidence. The nurse admits that she was asleep, from past two in the morning to six. She also speaks of a locked door of communication with the sick room, the key of which had been removed, nobody knew by whom. Some person must have stolen that key. Why not Mrs Beauly?

One word more, and all that I had in my mind at that time will be honestly revealed.

Miserrimus Dexter, under cross-examination, had indirectly admitted that he had ideas of his own on the subject of Mrs Eustace Macallan's death. At the same time, he had spoken of Mrs Beauly in a tone which plainly betrayed that he was no friend to that lady. Did *he* suspect her, too? My chief motive in deciding to ask his advice, before I applied to anyone else, was to find an opportunity of putting that question to him. If he really thought of her as I did, my course was clear before me. The next step to take would be carefully to conceal my identity – and then to present myself, in the character of a harmless stranger, to Mrs Beauly.

There were difficulties, of course, in my way. The first and greatest difficulty was to obtain an introduction to Miserrimus Dexter.

The composing influence of the fresh air in the garden had, by this time, made me readier to lie down and rest than to occupy my mind in reflecting on my difficulties. Little by little, I grew too drowsy to think – then too lazy to go on walking. My bed looked wonderfully inviting, as I passed by the open window of my room.

In five minutes more I had accepted the invitation of the bed, and had said farewell to my anxieties and my troubles. In five minutes more I was fast asleep.

A discreetly gentle knock at my door was the first sound that roused me. I heard the voice of my good old Benjamin speaking outside.

'My dear! I am afraid you will be starved if I let you sleep any longer. It is half-past one o'clock; and a friend of yours has come to lunch with us.'

A friend of mine? What friends had I? My husband was far away; and my uncle Starkweather had given me up in despair.

'Who is it?' I cried out from my bed, through the door.

'Major Fitz-David,' Benjamin answered – by the same medium.

I sprang out of bed. The very man I wanted was waiting to see me! Major Fitz-David, as the phrase is, knew everybody. Intimate with my husband, he would certainly know my husband's old friend – Miserrimus Dexter.

Shall I confess that I took particular pains with my toilet, and that I kept the luncheon waiting? The woman doesn't live who would have done otherwise – when she had a particular favour to ask of Major Fitz-David.

CHAPTER XXII

The Major Makes Difficulties

As I opened the dining-room door, the Major hastened to meet me. He looked the brightest and the youngest of living elderly gentlemen – with his smart blue frock-coat, his winning smile, his ruby ring, and his ready compliment. It was quite cheering to meet the modern Don Juan once more.

'I don't ask after your health,' said the old gentleman; 'your eyes answer me, my dear lady, before I can put the question. At your age a long sleep is the true beauty-draught. Plenty of bed – there is the simple secret of keeping your good looks and living a long life – plenty of bed!'

'I have not been so long in my bed, Major, as you suppose. To tell the truth, I have been up all night, reading.'

Major Fitz-David lifted his well-painted eyebrows, in polite surprise.

'What is the happy book which has interested you so deeply?' he asked.

'The book,' I answered, 'is the Trial of my husband for the murder of his first wife.'

The Major's smile vanished. He drew back a step, with a look of dismay.

'Don't mention that horrid book!' he exclaimed. 'Don't speak of that dreadful subject! What have beauty and grace to do with Trials, Poisonings, Horrors? Why, my charming friend, profane your lips by talking of such things? Why frighten away the Loves and the Graces that lie hid in your smile? Humour an old fellow who adores the Loves and the Graces, and who asks nothing better than to sun himself in your smile. Luncheon is ready. Let us be cheerful. Let us laugh, and lunch.'

He led me to the table and filled my plate and my glass, with the air of a man who considered himself to be engaged in one of the most important occupations of his life. Benjamin kept the conversation going on in the interval.

'Major Fitz-David brings you some news, my dear,' he said. 'Your mother-in-law, Mrs Macallan, is coming here to see you to-day.'

My mother-in-law coming to see me! I turned eagerly to the Major for further information.

'Has Mrs Macallan heard anything of my husband?' I asked. 'Is she coming here to tell me about him?'

'She has heard from him, I believe,' said the Major; 'and she has also heard from your uncle, the Vicar. Our excellent Starkweather has written to her – to what purpose I have not been informed. I only know that on receipt of his letter, she has decided on paying you a visit. I met the old lady last night at a party; and I tried hard to discover whether she was coming to you as your friend or your enemy. My powers of persuasion were completely thrown away on her. The fact is,' said the Major, speaking in the character of a youth of five-and-twenty, making a modest confession, 'I don't get on well with old women. Take the will for the deed, my sweet friend. I have tried to be of some use to you – and I have failed.'

Those words offered me the opportunity for which I was waiting. I determined not to lose it.

'You can be of the greatest use to me,' I said, 'if you will allow me to presume, Major, on your past kindness. I want to ask you a question: and I may have a favour to beg when you have answered me.'

Major Fitz-David set down his wine-glass on its way to his lips, and looked at me with an appearance of breathless interest.

'Command me, my dear lady – I am yours and yours only,' said the gallant old gentleman. 'What do you wish to ask me?'

'I wish to ask you if you know Miserrimus Dexter?'

'Good Heavens!' cried the Major; 'that *is* an unexpected question! Know Miserrimus Dexter? I have known him for more years than I like to reckon up. What *can* be your object—?'

'I can tell you what my object is in two words,' I interposed. 'I want you to give me an introduction to Miserrimus Dexter.'

My impression is that the Major turned pale under his paint. This, at any rate, is certain; his sparkling little grey eyes looked at me in undisguised bewilderment and alarm.

'You want to know Miserrimus Dexter?' he repeated, with the air of a man who doubted the evidence of his own senses. 'Mr Benjamin! have I taken too much of your excellent wine? Am I the victim of a delusion – or did our fair friend really ask me to give her an introduction to Miserrimus Dexter?'

Benjamin looked at me in some bewilderment on his side, and answered quite seriously—

'I think you said so, my dear.'

'I certainly said so,' I rejoined. 'What is there so very surprising in my request?'

'The man is mad!' cried the Major. 'In all England you could not have picked out a person more essentially unfit to be introduced to a lady – to a young lady especially – than Dexter. Have you heard of his horrible deformity?'

'I have heard of it – and it doesn't daunt me.'

'Doesn't daunt you? My dear lady, the man's mind is as deformed as his body. What Voltaire said satirically of the character of his countrymen in general, is literally true of Miserrimus Dexter. He is a mixture of the tiger and the monkey. At one moment, he would frighten you; and at the next, he would set you screaming with laughter. I don't deny that he is clever in some respects – brilliantly clever, I admit. And I don't say that he has ever committed any acts of violence, or ever willingly injured anybody. But, for all that, he is mad, if ever a man was mad yet. Forgive me if the enquiry is impertinent. What can your motive possibly be for wanting an introduction to Miserrimus Dexter?'

'I want to consult him.'

'May I ask on what subject?'

'On the subject of my husband's Trial.'

Major Fitz-David groaned, and sought a momentary consolation in his friend Benjamin's claret.

'That dreadful subject again!' he exclaimed. 'Mr Benjamin, why does she persist in dwelling on that dreadful subject?'

'I must dwell on what is now the one employment and the one hope of my life,' I said. 'I have reason to think that Miserrimus Dexter can help me to clear my husband's character of the stain which the Scotch Verdict has left on it. Tiger and monkey as he may be, I am ready to run the risk of being introduced to him. And I ask you again – rashly and obstinately as I fear you will think – to give me the introduction. It will put you to no inconvenience. I won't trouble you to escort me; a letter to Mr Dexter will do.'

The Major looked piteously at Benjamin, and shook his head. Benjamin looked piteously at the Major, and shook *his* head.

'She appears to insist on it,' said the Major.

'Yes,' said Benjamin. 'She appears to insist on it.'

'I won't take the responsibility, Mr Benjamin, of sending her alone to Miserrimus Dexter.'

'Shall I go with her, sir?'

The Major reflected. Benjamin, in the capacity of protector, did not appear to inspire our military friend with confidence. After a moment's consideration, a new idea seemed to strike him. He turned to me.

'My charming friend,' he said, 'be more charming than ever – consent to a compromise. Let us treat this difficulty about Dexter from a social point of view. What do you say to a little dinner?'

'A little dinner?' I repeated, not in the least understanding him.

'A little dinner,' the Major reiterated. 'At my house. You insist on my introducing you to Dexter; and I refuse to trust you alone with that crack-brained personage. The only alternative under the circumstances is to invite him to meet you, and to let you form your own opinion of him – under the protection of my roof. Who shall we have to meet you, besides?' pursued the Major, brightening with hospitable intentions. 'We want a perfect galaxy of beauty round the table, as a species of compensation, when we have got Miserrimus Dexter for one of the guests. Madame Mirliflore is still in London. You would be sure to like her – she is charming; she possesses your firmness, your extraordinary tenacity of purpose. Yes, we will have Madame Mirliflore. Who else? Shall we say Lady Clarinda? Another charming person, Mr Benjamin! You would be sure to admire her – she is so sympathetic, she resembles in so many respects our fair friend here. Yes, Lady Clarinda shall be one of us; and you shall sit next to her, Mr Benjamin, as a proof of my sincere regard for you. Shall we have my young prima donna to sing to us in the evening? I think so. She is pretty; she will assist in obscuring the deformity of Dexter. Very well; there is our party complete; I will shut myself up this evening, and approach the question of dinner with my cook. Shall we say this day week,' asked the Major, taking out his pocket-book – 'at eight o'clock?'

I consented to the proposed compromise – but not very willingly. With a letter of introduction, I might have seen Miserrimus Dexter that afternoon. As it was, the 'little dinner' compelled me to wait in absolute inaction, through a whole week. However, there was no help for it but to submit. Major Fitz-David, in his polite way, could be as obstinate as I was. He had evidently made up his mind; and further opposition on my part would be of no service to me.

'Punctually at eight, Mr Benjamin,' reiterated the Major. 'Put it down in your book.'

Benjamin obeyed – with a side look at me, which I was at no loss to interpret. My good old friend did not relish meeting a man at dinner, who was described as 'half tiger, half monkey'; and the privilege of sitting next to Lady Clarinda rather daunted than delighted him. It was all my doing, and he, too, had no choice but to submit. 'Punctually at eight, sir,' said poor old Benjamin, obediently recording his formidable engagement. 'Please to take another glass of wine.'

The Major looked at his watch, and rose – with fluent apologies for abruptly leaving the table.

'It is later than I thought,' he said. 'I have an appointment with a friend – a female friend; a most attractive person. You a little remind me of her, my dear lady – you resemble her in complexion; the same creamy paleness. I adore creamy paleness. As I was saying, I have an appointment with my friend; she does me the honour to ask my opinion on some very remarkable specimens of old lace. I have studied old lace. I study everything that can make me useful or agreeable to your enchanting sex. You won't forget our little dinner? I will send Dexter his invitation the moment I get home.' He took my hand, and looked at it critically, with his head a little on one side. 'A delicious hand,' he said; 'you don't mind my looking at it, you don't mind my kissing it – do you? A delicious hand is one of my weaknesses. Forgive my weaknesses. I promise to repent and amend, one of these days.'

'At your age, Major, do you think you have much time to lose?' asked a strange voice, speaking behind us.

We all three looked round towards the door. There stood my husband's mother, smiling satirically – with Benjamin's shy little maid-servant waiting to announce her.

Major Fitz-David was ready with his answer. The old soldier was not easily taken by surprise.

'Age, my dear Mrs Macallan, is a purely relative expression,' he said. 'There are some people who are never young; and there are other people who are never old. I am one of the other people. *Au revoir!*'

With that answer, the incorrigible Major kissed the tips of his fingers to us, and walked out. Benjamin, bowing with his old-fashioned courtesy, threw open the door of his little library, and, inviting Mrs Macallan and myself to pass in, left us together in the room.

CHAPTER XXIII

My Mother-in-law Surprises Me

I took a chair at a respectful distance from the sofa on which Mrs Macallan seated herself. The old lady smiled, and beckoned to me to take my place by her side. Judging by appearances, she had certainly not come to see me in the character of an enemy. It remained to be discovered whether she was really disposed to be my friend.

'I have received a letter from your uncle, the Vicar,' she began. 'He asks me to visit you; and I am happy – for reasons which you shall presently hear – to comply with his request. Under other circumstances, I doubt very much, my dear child – strange as the confession may appear – whether I should have ventured into your presence. My son has behaved to you so weakly, and (in my opinion) so inexcusably, that I am really, speaking as his mother, almost ashamed to face you.'

Was she in earnest? I listened to her, and looked at her, in amazement.

'Your uncle's letter,' pursued Mrs Macallan, 'tells me how you have behaved under your hard trial, and what you propose to do, now Eustace has left you. Doctor Starkweather, poor man, seems inexpressibly shocked by what you said to him when he was in London. He begs me to use my influence to induce you to abandon your present ideas, and to make you return to your old home at the Vicarage. I don't in the least agree with your uncle, my dear! Wild as I believe your plans to be – you have not the slightest chance of succeeding in carrying them out – I admire your courage; your fidelity; your unshaken faith in my unhappy son, after his unpardonable behaviour to you. You are a fine creature, Valeria! And I have come here to tell you so in plain words. Give me a kiss, child. You deserve to be the wife of a hero – and you have married one of the weakest of living mortals. God forgive me for speaking so of my own son! But it's in my mind, and it must come out!'

This way of speaking of Eustace was more than I could suffer –

even from his mother. I recovered the use of my tongue, in my husband's defence.

'I am sincerely proud of your good opinion, dear Mrs Macallan,' I said. 'But you distress me – forgive me if I own it plainly – when I hear you speak so disparagingly of Eustace. I cannot agree with you that my husband is the weakest of living mortals.'

'Of course not!' retorted the old lady. 'You are like all good women – you make a hero of the man you love, whether he deserves it or not. Your husband has hosts of good qualities, child – and perhaps I know them better than you do. But his whole conduct, from the moment when he first entered your uncle's house to the present time, has been (I say again) the conduct of an essentially weak man. What do you think he has done now by way of climax? He has joined a charitable brotherhood; and he is off to the war in Spain with a red cross on his arm[1] when he ought to be here on his knees asking his wife to forgive him. I say that is the conduct of a weak man. Some people might call it by a harder name.'

This news startled and distressed me. I might be resigned to his leaving me (for a time); but all my instincts as a woman revolted at his placing himself in a position of danger, during his separation from his wife. He had now deliberately added to my anxieties. I thought it cruel of him – but I would not confess what I thought to his mother. I affected to be as cool as she was; and I disputed her conclusions with all the firmness that I could summon to help me. The terrible old woman only went on abusing him more vehemently than ever.

'What I complain of in my son,' proceeded Mrs Macallan, 'is that he has entirely failed to understand you. If he had married a fool, his conduct would be intelligible enough. He would have done wisely to conceal from a fool that he had been married already, and that he had suffered the horrid public exposure of a Trial for the murder of his wife. Then, again, he would have been quite right, when this same fool had discovered the truth, to take himself off out of her way, before she could suspect him of poisoning her – for the sake of the peace and quiet of both parties. But you are not a fool. I can see that, after only a short experience of you. Why can't he see it, too? Why didn't he trust you with his secret from the first, instead of stealing his way into your affections under an assumed name? Why did he plan (as he confessed to me) to take you away to the Mediterranean, and to keep you abroad, for fear of some officious friends at home betraying him to you as the prisoner of the famous Trial? What is the plain answer to all these questions? What is the one possible explanation of this otherwise unaccountable conduct? There is only one answer, and one explanation. My poor wretched son – he takes after his father; he isn't the least like me! – is weak in his way of judging; weak in his way of acting; and, like all weak people, headstrong and unreasonable to the last degree. There is the truth! Don't get red and angry. I am as fond of him as you are. I can see his merits, too. And one of them is, that he has married a woman of spirit and resolution – so faithful, and so fond of him, that she won't even let his own mother tell her of his faults. Good child! I like you for hating me!'

'Dear madam, don't say that I hate you!' I exclaimed (feeling very much as if I did hate her, though, for all that!). 'I only presume to think that you are confusing a delicate-minded man with a weak-minded man. Our dear unhappy Eustace—'

'Is a delicate-minded man,' said the impenetrable Mrs Macallan, finishing my sentence for me. 'We will leave it there, my dear, and get on to another subject. I wonder whether we shall disagree about that, too?'

'What is the subject, madam?'

'I won't tell you, if you call me madam. Call me, mother. Say, "What is the subject, mother?"'

'What is the subject, mother?'

'Your notion of turning yourself into a Court of Appeal for a new Trial of Eustace, and forcing the world to pronounce a just verdict on him. Do you really mean to try it?'

'I do!'

Mrs Macallan considered for a moment grimly with herself.

'You know how heartily I admire your courage, and your devotion to my unfortunate son,' she said. 'You know, by this time, that *I* don't cant. But I cannot see you attempt to perform impossibilities; I cannot let you uselessly risk your reputation and your happiness, without warning you before it is too late. My child! the thing you have got it in your head to do, is not to be done by you or by anybody. Give it up.'

'I am deeply obliged to you, Mrs Macallan—'

'Mother!'

'I am deeply obliged to you, mother, for the interest that you take in me—but I cannot give it up. Right or wrong, risk or no risk, I must, and I will, try it!'

Mrs Macallan looked at me very attentively, and sighed as she looked.

'Oh, youth, youth!' she said to herself, sadly. 'What a grand thing it is to be young!' She controlled the rising regret, and turned on me suddenly, almost fiercely, with these words: 'What, in God's name, do you mean to do?'

At the instant when she put the question, the idea crossed my mind that Mrs Macallan could introduce me, if she pleased, to Miserrimus Dexter. She must know him, and know him well, as a guest at Gleninch and an old friend of her son.

'I mean to consult Miserrimus Dexter,' I answered, boldly.

Mrs Macallan started back from me, with a loud exclamation of surprise.

'Are you out of your senses?' she asked.

I told her, as I had told Major Fitz-David, that I had reason to think Mr Dexter's advice might be of real assistance to me at starting.

'And I,' rejoined Mrs Macallan, 'have reason to think that your whole project is a mad one, and that in asking Dexter's advice on it you appropriately consult a madman. You needn't start, child! There is no harm in the creature. I don't mean that he will attack you, or be rude to you. I only say that the last person whom a young woman, placed in your painful and delicate position, ought to associate herself with, is Miserrimus Dexter.'

Strange! Here was the Major's warning repeated by Mrs Macallan, almost in the Major's own words. Well! It shared the fate of most warnings. It only made me more and more eager to have my own way.

'You surprise me very much,' I said. 'Mr Dexter's evidence, given at the Trial, seems as clear and reasonable as evidence can be.'

'Of course it is!' answered Mrs Macallan. 'The shorthand writers and reporters put his evidence into presentable language, before they printed it. If you had heard what he really said, as I did, you would have been either very much disgusted with him, or very much amused by him, according to your way of looking at things. He began, fairly enough, with a modest explanation of his absurd Christian name, which at once checked the merriment of the audience. But as he went on, the mad side of him showed itself. He mixed up sense and nonsense in the strangest confusion: he was called to order over and over again; he was even threatened with fine and imprisonment for contempt of Court. In short, he was just like himself – a mixture of the strangest and the most opposite qualities; at one time, perfectly clear and reasonable, as you said just now; at another, breaking out into rhapsodies of the most outrageous kind, like a man in a state of delirium. A more entirely unfit person to advise anybody, I tell you again, never lived. You don't expect Me to introduce you to him, I hope?'

'I did think of such a thing,' I answered. 'But, after what you have said, dear Mrs Macallan, I give up the idea of course. It is not a great sacrifice – it only obliges me to wait a week for Major Fitz-David's dinner party. He has promised to ask Miserrimus Dexter to meet me.'

'There is the Major all over!' cried the old lady. 'If you pin your faith on that man, I pity you. He is as slippery as an eel. I suppose you asked him to introduce you to Dexter?'

'Yes.'

'Exactly! Dexter despises him, my dear. He knows as well as I do that Dexter won't go to his dinner. And he takes that roundabout way of keeping you apart – instead of saying No to you plainly, like an honest man.'

This was bad news. But I was, as usual, too obstinate to own myself defeated.

'If the worst comes to the worst,' I said, 'I can but write to Mr Dexter, and beg him to grant me an interview.'

'And go to him by yourself, if he does grant it?' enquired Mrs Macallan.

'Certainly. By myself.'

'You really mean it?'

'I do indeed.'

'I won't allow you to go by yourself.'

'May I venture to ask, ma'am, how you propose to prevent me?'

'By going with you, to be sure, you obstinate hussy! Yes, yes – I can be as headstrong as you are, when I like. Mind! I don't want to know what your plans are. I don't want to be mixed up with your plans. My son is resigned to the Scotch Verdict. And I am resigned to the Scotch Verdict. It is you who won't let matters rest as they are. You are a vain and foolhardy young person. But, somehow, I have taken a liking to you; and I won't let you go to Miserrimus Dexter by yourself. Put on your bonnet!'

'Now?' I asked.

'Certainly! My carriage is at the door. And the sooner it's over, the better I shall be pleased. Get ready – and be quick about it!'

I required no second bidding. In ten minutes more, we were on our way to Miserrimus Dexter.

Such was the result of my mother-in-law's visit!

CHAPTER XXIV

Miserrimus Dexter – First View

We had dawdled over our luncheon, before Mrs. Macallan arrived at Benjamin's cottage. The ensuing conversation between the old lady and myself (of which I have only presented a brief abstract) lasted until quite late in the afternoon. The sun was setting in heavy clouds when we got into the carriage; and the dreary twilight began to fall round us while we were still on the road.

The direction in which we drove took us (as well as I could judge) towards the great northern suburb of London.

For more than an hour, the carriage threaded its way through a dingy brick labyrinth of streets, growing smaller and smaller, and dirtier and dirtier, the further we went. Emerging from the labyrinth, I noticed in the gathering darkness dismal patches of waste ground which seemed to be neither town nor country. Crossing these, we passed some forlorn outlying groups of houses with dim little scattered shops among them, looking like lost country villages wandering on the way to London; disfigured and smoke-dried already by their journey! Darker and darker, and drearier and drearier, the prospect grew – until the carriage stopped at last, and Mrs Macallan announced, in her sharply-satirical way, that we had reached the end of our journey. 'Prince Dexter's Palace, my dear,' she said. 'What do you think of it?'

I looked round me – not knowing what to think of it, if the truth must be told.

We had got out of the carriage, and we were standing on a rough half-made gravel path. Right and left of me, in the dim light, I saw the half-completed foundations of new houses in their first stage of existence. Boards and bricks were scattered about us. At places, gaunt scaffolding-poles rose like the branchless trees of the brick-desert. Behind us, on the other side of the high road, stretched another plot of waste ground, as yet not built on. Over the surface of this second desert, the ghastly white figures of vagrant ducks gleamed at intervals in the mystic light. In front of us, at a distance of two hundred yards or so, as well as I could calculate, rose a black mass which gradually resolved itself, as my eyes became accustomed to the twilight, into a long, low, and ancient house, with a hedge of evergreens and a pitch-black paling in front of it. The footman led the way towards the paling, through the boards and the bricks, the oyster-shells[1] and the broken crockery, that strewed the ground. And this was 'Prince Dexter's Palace'!

There was a gate in the pitch-black paling, and a bell-handle – discovered with great difficulty. Pulling at the handle, the footman set in motion, to judge by the sound produced, a bell of prodigious size, fitter for a church than a house.

While we were waiting for admission, Mrs Macallan pointed to the low dark line of the old building.

'There is one of his madnesses!' she said. 'The speculators in this new neighbourhood have offered him, I don't know how many thousand pounds for the ground that house stands on. It was originally the manor-house of the district. Dexter purchased it, many years since, in one of his freaks of fancy. He has no old family associations with the place; the walls are all but tumbling about his ears; and the money offered would really be of use to him. But no! He refused the proposal of the enterprising speculators, by letter, in these words: "My house is a standing monument of the picturesque and beautiful, amid the mean, dishonest, and grovelling constructions of a mean, dishonest, and grovelling age. I keep my house, gentlemen, as a useful lesson to you. Look at it, while you are building round me – and blush, if you can, for your own work." Was there ever such an absurd letter written yet? Hush! I hear footsteps in the garden. Here comes his cousin. His cousin is a woman. I may as well tell you that, or you might mistake her for a man, in the dark.'

A rough deep voice, which I should certainly never have supposed to be the voice of a woman, hailed us from the inner side of the paling.

'Who's there?'

'Mrs Macallan,' answered my mother-in-law.

'What do you want?'

'We want to see Dexter.'

'You can't see him.'

'Why not?'

'What did you say your name was?'

'Macallan. Mrs Macallan. Eustace Macallan's mother. *Now* do you understand?'

The voice muttered and grunted behind the paling, and a key turned in the lock of the gate.

Admitted to the garden, in the deep shadow of the shrubs, I could see nothing distinctly of the woman with the rough voice, except that she wore a man's hat. Closing the gate behind us, without a word of welcome or explanation, she led the way to the house. Mrs Macallan followed her easily, knowing the place; and I walked in Mrs Macallan's footsteps as closely as I could. 'This is a nice family,' my mother-in-law whispered to me. 'Dexter's cousin is the only woman in the house, and Dexter's cousin is an idiot.'[2]

We entered a spacious hall, with a low ceiling – dimly lit at its further end by one small oil lamp. I could see that there were pictures on the grim brown walls – but the subjects represented were invisible in the obscure and shadowy light.

Mrs Macallan addressed herself to the speechless cousin with the man's hat.

'Now tell me,' she said. 'Why can't we see Dexter?'

The cousin took a sheet of paper off the hall table, and handed it to Mrs Macallan.

'The Master's writing!' said this strange creature, in a hoarse whisper, as if the bare idea of 'the Master' terrified her. 'Read it. And stay, or go, which you please.'

She opened an invisible side-door in the wall, masked by one of the pictures – disappeared through it like a ghost – and left us together, alone in the hall.

Mrs Macallan approached the oil lamp, and looked by its light at the sheet of paper which the woman had given to her. I followed, and peeped over her shoulder, without ceremony. The paper exhibited written characters, traced in a wonderfully large and firm handwriting. Had I caught the infection of madness in the air of the house? Or did I really see before me these words?

'NOTICE. – My immense imagination is at work. Visions of heroes unroll themselves before me. I re-animate in myself the spirits of the departed great. My brains are boiling in my head. Any persons who disturb me, under existing circumstances, will do it at the peril of their lives. – DEXTER.'

Mrs Macallan looked round at me quietly with her sardonic smile.

'Do you still persist in wanting to be introduced to him?' she asked.

The mockery in the tone of the question roused my pride. I determined that I would not be the first to give way.

'Not if I am putting you in peril of your life, ma'am,' I answered, pertly enough, pointing to the paper in her hand.

My mother-in-law returned to the hall-table, and put the paper back on it, without condescending to reply. She then led the way to an arched recess on our right hand, beyond which I dimly discerned a broad flight of oaken stairs.

'Follow me,' said Mrs Macallan, mounting the stairs in the dark. 'I know where to find him.'

We groped our way up the stairs to the first landing. The next flight of steps, turning in the reverse direction, was faintly illuminated, like the hall below, by one oil lamp, placed in some invisible position above us. Ascending the second flight of stairs, and crossing a short corridor, we discovered the lamp, through the open door of a quaintly-shaped circular room, burning on the mantelpiece. Its light illuminated a strip of thick tapestry, hanging loose from the ceiling to the floor, on the wall opposite to the door by which we had entered.

Mrs Macallan drew aside the strip of tapestry, and, signing to me to follow her, passed behind it.

'Listen!' she whispered.

Standing on the inner side of the tapestry, I found myself in a dark recess or passage, at the end of which a ray of light from the lamp showed me a closed door. I listened, and heard, on the other side of the door, a shouting voice, accompanied by an extraordinary rumbling and whistling sound travelling backwards and forwards, as well as I could judge, over a great space. Now the rumbling and the whistling would reach their climax of loudness, and would overcome the resonant notes of the shouting voice. Then, again, those louder sounds gradually retreated into distance, and the shouting voice made itself heard as the more audible sound of the two. The door must have been of prodigious solidity. Listen as intently as I might, I failed to catch the articulate words (if any) which the voice was pronouncing, and I was equally at a loss to penetrate the cause which produced the rumbling and whistling sounds.

'What can possibly be going on,' I whispered to Mrs Macallan, 'on the other side of that door?'

'Step softly,' my mother-in-law answered, 'and come and see.'

She arranged the tapestry behind us, so as completely to shut out the light in the circular room. Then, noiselessly turning the handle, she opened the heavy door.

We kept ourselves concealed in the shadow of the recess, and looked through the open doorway.

I saw (or fancied I saw, in the obscurity) a long room, with a low ceiling. The dying gleam of an ill-kept fire formed the only light by which I could judge of objects and distances. Redly illuminating the central portion of the room, opposite to which we were standing, the firelight left the extremities shadowed in almost total darkness. I had barely time to notice this, before I heard the rumbling and whistling sounds approaching me. A high chair on wheels moved by, through the field of red light, carrying a shadowy figure with floating hair, and arms furiously raised and lowered, working the machinery that propelled the chair at its utmost rate of speed. 'I am Napoleon, at the sunrise of Austerlitz!'[3] shouted the man in the chair as he swept past me, on his rumbling and whistling wheels, in the red glow of the firelight. 'I give the word; and thrones rock, and kings fall, and nations tremble, and men by tens of thousands fight and bleed and die!' The chair rushed out of sight, and the shouting man in it became another hero. 'I am Nelson!' the ringing voice cried now. 'I am leading the fleet at Trafalgar. I issue my commands, prophetically conscious of victory and death. I see my own apotheosis – my public funeral, my nation's tears, my burial in the glorious church. The ages remember me, and the poets sing my praise in immortal verse!' The strident wheels turned at the far end of the room, and came back. The fantastic and frightful apparition, man and machinery blended in one – the new Centaur, half man, half chair – flew by me again in the dying light. 'I am Shakspere!' cried the frantic creature, now. 'I am writing "Lear," the tragedy of tragedies. Ancients and moderns, I am the poet who towers over them all. Light! light! the lines flow out like lava from the eruption of my volcanic mind. Light! light! for the poet of all time to write the words that live for ever!' He ground and tore his way back towards the middle of the room. As he approached the fireplace, a last morsel of unburnt coal (or wood) burst into momentary flame, and showed the open doorway. In that moment, he saw us! The wheel-chair stopped with a shock that shook the crazy old floor of the room, altered its course, and flew at us with the rush of a wild animal. We drew back, just in time to escape it, against the wall of the recess. The chair passed on, and burst aside the hanging tapestry. The light of the lamp in the circular room poured in through the gap. The creature in the chair checked his furious wheels, and looked back over his shoulder with an impish curiosity horrible to see.

'Have I run over them? Have I ground them to powder for presuming to intrude on me?' he said to himself. As the expression of this amiable doubt passed his lips, his eyes lighted on us. His mind instantly veered back again to Shakspere and 'King Lear.' 'Goneril and Regan!' he cried. 'My two unnatural daughters, my she-devil children, come to mock at me!'

'Nothing of the sort,' said my mother-in-law, as quietly as if she was addressing a perfectly reasonable being, 'I am your old friend, Mrs Macallan; and I have brought Eustace Macallan's second wife to see you.'

The instant she pronounced those last words, 'Eustace Macallan's second wife,' the man in the chair sprang out of it with a shrill cry of horror, as if she had shot him. For one moment we saw a head and body in the air, absolutely deprived of the lower limbs. The moment after, the terrible creature touched the floor as lightly as a monkey, on his hands. The grotesque horror of the scene culminated in his hopping away, on his hands, at a prodigious speed, until he reached the fireplace in the long room. There he crouched over the dying embers, shuddering and shivering, and muttering, 'Oh, pity me, pity me!' dozens and dozens of times over to himself.

This was the man whose advice I had come to ask – whose assistance I had confidently counted on, in my hour of need!

CHAPTER XXV

Miserrimus Dexter – Second View

Thoroughly disheartened and disgusted, and (if I must honestly confess it) thoroughly frightened too, I whispered to Mrs Macallan, 'I was wrong, and you were right. Let us go.'

The ears of Miserrimus Dexter must have been as sensitive as the ears of a dog. He heard me say, 'Let us go.'

'No!' he answered. 'Bring Eustace Macallan's second wife in here. I am a gentleman – I must apologise to her. I am a student of human character – I wish to see her.'

The whole man appeared to have undergone a complete transformation. He spoke in the gentlest of voices – and he sighed hysterically when he had done, like a woman recovering from a burst of tears. Was it reviving courage or reviving curiosity? When Mrs Macallan said to me, 'The fit is over now; do you still wish to go away?' I answered, 'No; I am ready to go in.'

'Have you recovered your belief in him, already?' asked my mother-in-law, in her mercilessly satirical way.

'I have recovered from my terror of him,' I replied.

'I am sorry I terrified you,' said the soft voice at the fireplace. 'Some people think I am a little mad at times. You came, I suppose, at one of the times – if some people are right. I admit that I am a visionary. My imagination runs away with me, and I say and do strange things. On those occasions, anybody who reminds me of that horrible Trial, throws me back into the past, and causes me unutterable nervous suffering. I am a very tender-hearted man. As the necessary consequence (in such a world as this), I am a miserable wretch. Accept my excuses. Come in, both of you. Come in, and pity me.'

A child would not have been frightened of him now. A child would have gone in, and pitied him.

The room was getting darker and darker. We could just see the crouching figure of Miserrimus Dexter at the expiring fire – and that was all.

'Are we to have no light?' asked Mrs Macallan. 'And is this lady to see you, when the light comes, out of your chair?'

He lifted something bright and metallic, hanging round his neck, and blew on it a series of shrill, trilling, birdlike notes. After an interval, he was answered by a similar series of notes, sounding faintly in some distant region of the house.

'Ariel is coming,' he said. 'Compose yourself, Mama Macallan, Ariel will make me presentable to a lady's eyes.'

He hopped away on his hands into the darkness at the end of the room. 'Wait a little,' said Mrs Macallan; 'and you will have another surprise – you will see the "delicate Ariel."'

We heard heavy footsteps in the circular room.

'Ariel!' sighed Miserrimus Dexter out of the darkness, in his softest notes.

To my astonishment, the coarse masculine voice of the cousin in the man's hat – the Caliban's, rather than the Ariel's voice[1] – answered, 'Here!'

'My chair, Ariel!'

The person thus strangely misnamed drew aside the tapestry, so as to let in more light – then entered the room, pushing the wheeled chair before her. She stooped, and lifted Miserrimus Dexter from the floor, like a child. Before she could put him into the chair, he sprang out of her arms with a little gleeful cry, and alighted on his seat, like a bird alighting on its perch!

'The lamp,' said Miserrimus Dexter. 'And the looking-glass. Pardon me,' he added, addressing us, 'for turning my back on you. You mustn't see me until my hair is set to rights. Ariel! the brush, the comb, and the perfumes.'

Carrying the lamp in one hand, the looking-glass in the other, and the brush (with the comb stuck in it) between her teeth, Ariel the Second, otherwise Dexter's cousin, presented herself plainly before me for the first time. I could now see the girl's round fleshy inexpressive face, her rayless and colourless eyes, her coarse nose and heavy chin. A creature half alive; an imperfectly-developed animal in shapeless form, clad in a man's pilot jacket,[2] and treading in a man's heavy laced boots: with nothing but an old red flannel petticoat, and a broken comb in her frowsy flaxen hair, to tell us that she was a woman – such was the inhospitable person who had received us in the darkness, when we first entered the house.

This wonderful valet, collecting her materials for dressing her still more wonderful master's hair, gave him the looking-glass (a hand-mirror), and addressed herself to her work.

She combed, she brushed, she oiled, she perfumed the flowing locks and the long silky beard of Miserrimus Dexter, with the strangest mixture of dulness and dexterity that I ever saw. Done in brute silence, with a lumpish look and a clumsy gait, the work was perfectly well done, nevertheless. The imp in the chair superintended the whole proceeding critically by means of his hand-mirror. He was too deeply interested in this occupation to speak, until some of the concluding touches to his beard brought the misnamed Ariel in front of him, and so turned her full face towards the part of the room in which Mrs Macallan and I were standing. Then he addressed us – taking special care, however, not to turn his head our way while his toilet was still incomplete.

'Mama Macallan,' he said, 'what is the Christian name of your son's second wife?'

'Why do you want to know?' asked my mother-in-law.

'I want to know, because I can't address her as "Mrs Eustace Macallan."'

'Why not?'

'It recalls *the other* Mrs Eustace Macallan. If I am reminded of those horrible days at Gleninch, my fortitude will give way – I shall burst out screaming again.'

Hearing this, I hastened to interpose.

'My name is Valeria,' I said.

'A Roman name,' remarked Miserrimus Dexter. 'I like it. My own name has a Roman ring in it. My bodily build would have been Roman, if I had been born with legs. I shall call you, Mrs Valeria. Unless you disapprove of it?'

I hastened to say that I was far from disapproving of it.

'Very good,' said Miserrimus Dexter. 'Mrs Valeria, do you see the face of this creature in front of me?'

He pointed with the hand-mirror to his cousin, as unconcernedly as he might have pointed to a dog. His cousin, on her side, took no more notice than a dog would have taken of the contemptuous phrase by which he had designated her. She went on combing and oiling his beard as composedly as ever.

'It is the face of an idiot, isn't it?' pursued Miserrimus Dexter. 'Look at her! She is a mere vegetable. A cabbage in a garden has as much life and expression in it as that girl exhibits at the present moment. Would you believe there was latent intelligence, affection, pride, fidelity, in such a half-developed being as this?'

I was really ashamed to answer him. Quite needlessly! The impenetrable young woman went on with her master's beard. A machine could not have taken less notice of the life and the talk around it than this incomprehensible creature.

'*I* have got at that latent affection, pride, fidelity, and the rest of it,' resumed Miserrimus Dexter. '*I* hold the key to that dormant Intelligence. Grand thought! Now look at her, when I speak. (I named her, poor wretch, in one of my ironical moments. She has got to like her name, just as a dog gets to like his collar.) Now, Mrs Valeria, look and listen. Ariel!'

The girl's dull face began to brighten. The girl's mechanically-moving hand stopped, and held the comb in suspense.

'Ariel! you have learnt to dress my hair, and anoint my beard – haven't you?'

Her face still brightened. 'Yes! yes! yes!' she answered, eagerly. 'And you say I have learnt to do it well – don't you?'

'I say that. Would you like to let anybody else do it for you?'

Her eyes melted softly into light and life. Her strange unwomanly voice sank to the gentlest tones that I had heard from her yet.

'Nobody else shall do it for me,' she said, at once proudly and tenderly. 'Nobody, as long as I live, shall touch you but me.'

'Not even the lady there?' asked Miserrimus Dexter, pointing backward with his hand-mirror to the place at which I was standing.

Her eyes suddenly flashed, her hand suddenly shook the comb at me, in a burst of jealous rage.

'Let her try!' cried the poor creature, raising her voice again to its hoarsest notes. 'Let her touch you if she dares!'

Dexter laughed at the childish outbreak. 'That will do, my delicate Ariel,' he said. 'I dismiss your Intelligence for the present. Relapse into your former self. Finish my beard.'

She passively resumed her work. The new light in her eyes, the new expression in her face, faded little by little, and died out. In another minute, the face was as vacant and as lumpish as before: the hands did their work again with the lifeless dexterity which had so painfully impressed me when she first took up the brush. Miserrimus Dexter appeared to be perfectly satisfied with these results.

'I thought my little experiment might interest you,' he said. 'You see how it is? The dormant intelligence of my curious cousin is like the dormant sound in a musical instrument. I play upon it – and it answers to my touch. She likes being played upon. But her great delight is to hear me tell a story. I puzzle her to the verge of distraction; and the more I confuse her, the better she likes the story. It is the greatest fun; you really must see it some day.' He indulged himself in a last look at the mirror. 'Ah!' he said complacently, 'now I shall do. Vanish, Ariel!'

She tramped out of the room in her heavy boots, with the mute obedience of a trained animal. I said 'Good night' as she passed me. She neither returned the salutation nor looked at me: the words simply produced no effect on her dull senses. The one voice that could reach her was silent. She had relapsed once more into the vacant inanimate creature who had opened the gate to us – until it pleased Miserrimus Dexter to speak to her again.

'Valeria!' said my mother-in-law. 'Our modest host is waiting to see what you think of him.'

While my attention was fixed on his cousin, he had wheeled his chair round, so as to face me – with the light of the lamp falling full on him. In mentioning his appearance as a witness at the Trial, I find I have borrowed (without meaning to do so) from my experience of him at this later time. I saw plainly now the bright intelligent face, and the large clear blue eyes; the lustrous waving hair of a light chestnut colour; the long delicate white hands, and the magnificent throat and chest, which I have elsewhere described. The deformity which degraded and destroyed the manly beauty of his head and breast, was hidden from view by an Oriental robe of many colours, thrown over the chair like a coverlid. He was clothed in a jacket of black velvet, fastened loosely across his chest with large malachite buttons; and he wore lace ruffles at the ends of his sleeves, in the fashion of the last century. It may well have been due to want of perception on my part – but I could see nothing mad in him, nothing in any way repelling, as he now looked at me. The one defect that I could discover in his face was at the outer corners of his eyes, just under the temple. Here, when he laughed, and, in a lesser degree, when he smiled, the skin contracted into quaint little wrinkles and folds, which looked strangely out of harmony with the almost youthful appearance of the rest of his face. As to his other features, the mouth, so far as his beard and moustache permitted me to see it, was small and delicately formed. The nose – perfectly shaped on the straight Grecian model – was perhaps a little too thin, judged by comparison with the full cheeks and the high massive forehead. Looking at him as a whole (and speaking of him, of course, from a woman's, not a physiognomist's, point of view),[3] I can only describe him as being an unusually handsome man. A painter would have revelled in him as a model for St John. And a young girl, ignorant of what the Oriental robe hid from view, would have said to herself the instant she looked at him, 'Here is the hero of my dreams!'

'Well, Mrs Valeria,' he said, quietly, 'do I frighten you now?'

'Certainly not, Mr Dexter.'

His blue eyes – large as the eyes of a woman, clear as the eyes of a child – rested on my face with a strangely varying play of expression, which at once interested and perplexed me.

Now, there was doubt, uneasy painful doubt, in the look: and now again it changed brightly to approval, so open and unrestrained that a vain woman might have fancied she had made a conquest of him at first sight. Suddenly, a new emotion seemed to take possession of him. His eyes sank, his head drooped; he lifted his hands with a gesture of regret. He muttered and murmured to himself; pursuing some secret and melancholy train of thought, which seemed to lead him further and further away from present objects of interest, and to plunge him deeper and deeper in troubled recollections of the past. Here and there, I caught some of the words. Little by little, I found myself trying to fathom what was darkly passing in this strange man's mind.

'A far more charming face,' I heard him say. 'But no – not a more beautiful figure. What figure was ever more beautiful than hers? Something – but not all – of her enchanting grace. Where is the resemblance which has brought her back to me? In the pose of the figure, perhaps? In the movement of the figure, perhaps? Poor martyred angel! What a life! And what a death! what a death!'

Was he comparing me with the victim of the poison – with my husband's first wife? His words seemed to justify the conclusion. If I was right, the dead woman had been evidently a favourite with him. There was no misinterpreting the broken tones of his voice when he spoke of her; he had admired her, living; he mourned her, dead.

Supposing that I could prevail upon myself to admit this extraordinary person into my confidence, what would be the result? Should I be the gainer or the loser by the resemblance which he fancied he had discovered? Would the sight of me console him? or pain him? I waited eagerly to hear more on the subject of the first wife. Not a word more escaped his lips. A new change came over him. He lifted his head with a start, and looked about him, as a weary man might look if he was suddenly disturbed in a deep sleep.

'What have I done?' he said. 'Have I been letting my mind drift again?' He shuddered, and sighed. 'Oh, that house of Gleninch!' he murmured sadly to himself. 'Shall I never get away from it in my thoughts? Oh, that house of Gleninch!'

To my infinite disappointment, Mrs Macallan checked the further revelation of what was passing in his mind.

Something in the tone and manner of his allusion to her son's country house seemed to have offended her. She interposed sharply and decisively.

'Gently, my friend, gently!' she said. 'I don't think you quite know what you are talking about.'

His great blue eyes flashed at her fiercely. With one turn of his hand, he brought his chair close at her side. The next instant he caught her by the arm, and forced her to bend to him, until he could whisper in her ear. He was violently agitated. His whisper was loud enough to make itself heard where I was sitting at the time.

'I don't know what I am talking about?' he repeated − with his eyes fixed attentively, not on my mother-in-law, but on me. 'You short-sighted old woman! where are your spectacles? Look at her! Do you see no resemblance − the figure, not the face! − do you see no resemblance there to Eustace's first wife?'

'Pure fancy!' rejoined Mrs Macallan. 'I see nothing of the sort.'

He shook her impatiently.

'Not so loud,' he whispered. 'She will hear you.'

'I have heard you both,' I said. 'You need have no fear, Mr Dexter, of speaking before me. I know that my husband had a first wife; and I know how miserably she died. I have read the Trial.'

'You have read the life and death of a martyr!' cried Miserrimus

Dexter. He suddenly wheeled his chair my way; he bent over me, almost tenderly; his eyes filled with tears. 'Nobody appreciated her at her true value,' he said, 'but me. Nobody but me! nobody but me!'

Mrs Macallan walked away impatiently to the end of the room.

'When you are ready, Valeria, I am,' she said. 'We cannot keep the servants and the horses waiting much longer in this bleak place.'

I was too deeply interested in leading Miserrimus Dexter to pursue the subject on which he had touched, to be willing to leave him at that moment. I pretended not to have heard Mrs Macallan. I laid my hand, as if by accident, on the wheel-chair to keep him near me.

'You showed how highly you esteemed that poor lady in your evidence at the Trial,' I said. 'I believe, Mr Dexter, you have ideas of your own about the mystery of her death?'

He had been looking at my hand, resting on the arm of his chair, until I ventured on my question. At that, he suddenly raised his eyes, and fixed them with a frowning and furtive suspicion on my face.

'How do you know I have ideas of my own?' he asked, sternly.

'I know it from reading the Trial,' I answered. 'The lawyer who cross-examined you spoke almost in the very words which I have just used. I had no intention of offending you, Mr Dexter.'

His face cleared as rapidly as it had clouded. He smiled, and laid his hand on mine. His touch struck me cold. I felt every nerve in me shivering under it – I drew my hand away quickly.

'I beg your pardon,' he said, 'if I have misunderstood you. I *have* ideas of my own, about that unhappy lady.' He paused, and looked at me in silence, very earnestly. 'Have *you* any ideas?' he asked. 'Ideas about her life? or about her death?'

I was deeply interested; I was burning to hear more. It might encourage him to speak if I was candid with him. I answered, 'Yes.'

'Ideas which you have mentioned to anyone?' he went on.

'To no living creature,' I replied – 'as yet.'

'This is very strange!' he said, still earnestly reading my face. 'What interest can *you* have in a dead woman whom you never knew? Why did you ask me that question, just now? Have you any motive in coming here to see me?'

I boldly acknowledged the truth. I said, 'I have a motive.'

'Is it connected with Eustace Macallan's first wife?'

'It is.'

'With anything that happened in her lifetime?'

'No.'

'With her death?'

'Yes.'

He suddenly clasped his hands, with a wild gesture of despair – and then pressed them both on his head, as if he was struck by some sudden pain.

'I can't hear it to-night!' he said; 'I would give worlds to hear it – but I daren't; I should lose all hold over myself in the state I am in now. I am not equal to raking up the horror and the mystery of the past; I have not courage enough to open the grave of the martyred dead. Did you hear me, when you came here? I have an immense imagination. It runs riot at times. It makes an actor of me. I play the parts of all the heroes that ever lived. I feel their characters. I merge myself in their individualities. For the time, I *am* the man I fancy myself to be. I can't help it. I am obliged to do it. If I restrained my imagination, when the fit is on me, I should go mad. I let myself loose. It lasts for hours. It leaves me, with my energies worn out, with my sensibilities frightfully acute. Rouse any melancholy or terrible associations in me, at such times; and I am capable of hysterics, I am capable of screaming. You heard me scream. You shall *not* see me in hysterics. No, Mrs Valeria – no, you innocent reflection of the dead and gone – I would not frighten you for the world. Will you come here to-morrow in the daytime? I have got a chaise and a pony. Ariel, my delicate Ariel, can drive. She shall call at Mama Macallan's and fetch you. We will talk to-morrow, when I am fit for it. I am dying to hear you. I will be fit for you in the morning. I will be civil, intelligent, communicative in the morning. No more of it now! Away with the subject! The too-exciting, the too-interesting subject! I must compose myself, or my brains will explode in my head. Music is the true narcotic for excitable brains. My harp! my harp!'

He rushed away in his chair to the far end of the room – passing Mrs Macallan as she returned to me, bent on hastening our departure.

'Come!' said the old lady, irritably. 'You have seen him, and he has made a good show of himself. More of him might be tiresome. Come away.'

The chair returned to us more slowly. Miserrimus Dexter was working it with one hand only. In the other, he held a harp, of a pattern which I had hitherto only seen in pictures. The strings were few in number; and the instrument was so small that I could have held it easily on my lap. It was the ancient harp of the pictured Muses and the legendary Welsh Bards.

'Good night, Dexter,' said Mrs Macallan.

He held up one hand imperatively.

'Wait!' he said. 'Let her hear me sing.' He turned to me. 'I decline to be indebted to other people for my poetry and my music,' he went on. 'I compose my own poetry, and my own music. I improvise. Give me a moment to think. I will improvise for You.'

He closed his eyes, and rested his head on the frame of the harp. His fingers gently touched the strings while he was thinking. In a few minutes he lifted his head, looked at me, and struck the first notes – the prelude to the song.

Was it good music? or bad? I cannot decide whether it was music at all. It was a wild barbaric succession of sounds; utterly unlike any modern composition. Sometimes, it suggested a slow and undulating Oriental dance. Sometimes it modulated into tones which reminded me of the severer harmonies of the old Gregorian chants.[4] The words, when they followed the prelude, were as wild, as recklessly free from all restraint of critical rules, as the music. They were assuredly inspired by the occasion; I was the theme of the strange song. And thus – in one of the finest tenor voices I ever heard – my poet sang of me:

> Why does she come?
> She reminds me of the lost;
> She reminds me of the dead:
> > In her form like the other,
> > In her walk like the other:
> Why does she come?

> Does Destiny bring her?
>> Shall we range together
> The mazes of the past?
>> Shall we search together
> The secrets of the past?
> Shall we interchange thoughts, surmises, suspicions?
> Does Destiny bring her?
>
> The Future will show.
>> Let the night pass;
>> Let the day come.
> I shall see into Her mind:
> She will look into Mine.
>> The Future will show.

His voice sank, his fingers touched the strings more and more feebly as he approached the last lines. The over-wrought brain needed, and took, its re-animating repose. At the final words, his eyes slowly closed. His head lay back on the chair. He slept with his arms round his harp, as a child sleeps, hugging its last new toy.

We stole out of the room on tiptoe, and left Miserrimus Dexter – poet, composer, and madman – in his peaceful sleep.

CHAPTER XXVI

More of My Obstinacy

Ariel was downstairs in the shadowy hall, half asleep, half awake, waiting to see the visitors clear of the house. Without speaking to us, without looking at us, she led the way down the dark garden walk, and locked the gate behind us. 'Good night, Ariel,' I called out to her over the paling. Nothing answered me but the tramp of her heavy footsteps returning to the house, and the dull thump, a moment afterwards, of the closing door.

The footman had thoughtfully lit the carriage lamps. Carrying one of them to serve as a lantern, he lighted us over the wilds of the brick-desert, and landed us safely on the path by the high road.

'Well!' said my mother-in-law, when we were comfortably seated in the carriage again. 'You have seen Miserrimus Dexter; and I hope you are satisfied. I will do him the justice to declare that I never, in all my experience, saw him more completely crazy than he was to-night. What do *you* say?'

'I don't presume to dispute your opinion,' I answered. 'But, speaking for myself, I am not quite sure that he is mad.'

'Not mad!' cried Mrs Macallan, 'after those frantic performances in his chair? Not mad, after the exhibition he made of his unfortunate cousin? Not mad, after the song that he sang in your honour, and the falling asleep by way of conclusion? Oh, Valeria! Valeria! Well said the wisdom of our ancestors – there are none so blind as those who won't see!'

'Pardon me, dear Mrs Macallan – I saw everything that you mention; and I never felt more surprised, or more confounded, in my life. But now I have recovered from my amazement, and can think over it quietly, I must still venture to doubt whether this strange man is really mad, in the true meaning of the word. It seems to me that he openly expresses – I admit in a very reckless and boisterous way – thoughts and feelings which most of us are ashamed of as weaknesses, and which we keep to ourselves accordingly. I confess I have often fancied myself transformed into some other person, and have felt a certain pleasure in seeing myself in my new character. One of our first amusements as children (if we have any imagination at all) is to get out of our own characters, and to try the characters of other personages as a change – to be fairies, to be queens, to be anything, in short, but what we really are. Mr Dexter lets out the secret, just as the children do – and, if that is madness, he is certainly mad. But I noticed that when his imagination cooled down, he became Miserrimus Dexter again – he no more believed himself, than we believed him, to be Napoleon or Shakspere. Besides, some allowance is surely to be made for the solitary, sedentary life that he leads. I am not learned enough to trace the influence of that life in making him what he is. But I think I can see the result in an over-excited imagination; and I fancy I can trace his exhibiting his power over the poor cousin, and his singing of that wonderful song, to no more formidable cause than inordinate self-conceit. I hope the confession will not lower me seriously in your good opinion – but I must say I have enjoyed my visit; and, worse still, Miserrimus Dexter really interests me!'

'Does this learned discourse on Dexter mean that you are going to see him again?' asked Mrs Macallan.

'I don't know how I may feel about it to-morrow morning,' I said. 'But my impulse at this moment is decidedly to see him again. I had a little talk with him, while you were away at the other end of the room; and I believe he really can be of use to me—'

'Of use to you, in what?' interposed my mother-in-law.

'In the one object which I have in view – the object, dear Mrs Macallan, which I regret to say you do not approve.'

'And you are going to take him into your confidence? to open your whole mind to such a man as the man we have just left?'

'Yes – if I think of it to-morrow, as I think of it to-night. I dare say it is a risk: but I must run risks. I know I am not prudent; but prudence won't help a woman in my position, with my end to gain.'

Mrs Macallan made no further remonstrance, in words. She opened a capacious pocket in front of the carriage, and took from it a box of matches and a railway reading-lamp.

'You provoke me,' said the old lady, 'into showing you what your husband thinks of this new whim of yours. I have got his letter with me – his last letter from Spain. You shall judge for yourself, you poor deluded young creature, whether my son is worthy of the sacrifice, the useless and hopeless sacrifice, which you are bent on making of yourself, for his sake. Strike a light!'

I willingly obeyed her. Ever since she had informed me of Eustace's departure to Spain, I had been eager for more news of him – for something to sustain my spirits, after so much that had disappointed and depressed me. Thus far, I did not even know whether my husband thought of me sometimes in his self-imposed exile. As to his regretting already the rash act which had separated us, it was still too soon to begin hoping for that.

The lamp having been lit, and fixed in its place between the two front windows of the carriage, Mrs Macallan produced her son's letter. There is no folly like the folly of love. It cost me a hard struggle to restrain myself from kissing the paper on which the dear hand had rested.

'There!' said my mother-in-law. 'Begin on the second page; the page devoted to you. Read straight down to the last line at the bottom – and, in God's name, come back to your senses, child, before it is too late!'

I followed my instructions, and read these words:

'Can I trust myself to write of Valeria? I *must* write of her! Tell me how she is, how she looks, what she is doing. I am always thinking of her. Not a day passes but I mourn the loss of her. Oh, if she had only been contented to let matters rest as they were! Oh, if she had never discovered the miserable truth!

'She spoke of reading the Trial, when I saw her last. Has she persisted in doing so? I believe – I say this seriously, mother – I believe the shame and the horror of it would have been the death of me, if I had met her face to face, when she first knew of the ignominy that I have suffered, of the infamous suspicion of which I have been publicly made the subject. Think of those pure eyes looking at a man who has been accused (and never wholly absolved) of the foulest and the vilest of all murders – and then think of what that man must feel, if he has any heart and any sense of shame left in him. I sicken as I write of it.

'Does she still meditate that hopeless project – the offspring, poor angel, of her artless, unthinking generosity? Does she still fancy that it is in *her* power to assert my innocence before the world? Oh, mother (if she does), use your utmost influence to make her give up the idea! Spare her the humiliation, the disappointment, the insult perhaps, to which she may innocently expose herself. For her sake, for my sake, leave no means untried to attain this righteous, this merciful end.

'I send her no message – I dare not do it. Say nothing when you see her, which can recall me to her memory. On the contrary, help her to forget me as soon as possible. The kindest thing I can do – the one atonement I can make to her – is to drop out of her life.'

With those wretched words it ended. I handed his letter back to his mother in silence. She said but little, on her side.

'If *this* doesn't discourage you,' she remarked, slowly folding up the letter, 'nothing will. Let us leave it there, and say no more.'

I made no answer – I was crying behind my veil. My domestic prospect looked so dreary; my unfortunate husband was so hopelessly misguided, so pitiably wrong! The one chance for both of us (and the one consolation for poor Me) was to hold by my desperate resolution more firmly than ever. If I had wanted anything to confirm me in this view, and to arm me against the remonstrances of every one of my friends, Eustace's letter would have proved more than sufficient to answer the purpose. At least, he had not forgotten me; he thought of me, and he mourned the loss of me, every day of his life. That was encouragement enough – for the present. 'If Ariel calls for me in the pony-chaise tomorrow,' I thought to myself, 'with Ariel I go.'

Mrs Macallan set me down at Benjamin's door.

I mentioned to her, at parting – I stood sufficiently in awe of her to put it off till the last moment – that Miserrimus Dexter had arranged to send his cousin and his pony-chaise to her residence, on the next day; and I enquired thereupon whether my mother-in-law would permit me to call at her house to wait for the appearance of the cousin, or whether she would prefer sending the chaise on to Benjamin's cottage. I fully expected an explosion of anger to follow this bold avowal of my plans for the next day. The old lady agreeably surprised me. She proved that she had really taken a liking to me: she kept her temper.

'If you persist in going back to Dexter, you certainly shall not go to him from my door,' she said. 'But I hope you will *not* persist. I hope you will wake a wiser woman to-morrow morning.'

The morning came. A little before noon, the arrival of the pony-chaise was announced at the door, and a letter was brought in to me from Mrs Macallan.

'I have no right to control your movements,' my mother-in-law wrote. 'I send the chaise to Mr Benjamin's house; and I sincerely trust that you will not take your place in it. I wish I could persuade you, Valeria, how truly I am your friend. I have been thinking about you anxiously in the wakeful hours of the night. *How* anxiously, you will understand, when I tell you that I now reproach myself for not having done more than I did to prevent your unhappy marriage. And yet, what I could have done I don't really know. My son admitted to me that he was courting you under an assumed name – but he never told me what the name was, or who you were, or where your friends lived. Perhaps, I ought to have taken measures to find this out. Perhaps, if I had succeeded, I ought to have interfered and enlightened you, even at the sad sacrifice of making an enemy of my own son. I honestly thought I did my duty in expressing my disapproval, and in refusing to be present at the marriage. Was I too easily satisfied? It is too late to ask. Why do I trouble you with an old woman's vain misgivings and regrets? My child, if you come to any harm, I shall feel (indirectly) responsible for it. It is this uneasy state of mind which sets me writing, with nothing to say that can interest you. Don't go to Dexter! The fear has been pursuing me all night that your going to Dexter will end badly. Write him an excuse. Valeria! I firmly believe you will repent it if you return to that house.'

Was ever a woman more plainly warned, more carefully advised, than I? And yet, warning and advice were both thrown away on me!

Let me say for myself that I was really touched by the kindness of my mother-in-law's letter – though I was not shaken by it in the smallest degree. As long as I lived, moved, and thought, my one purpose now was to make Miserrimus Dexter confide to me his ideas on the subject of Mrs Eustace Macallan's death. To those ideas I looked as my guiding stars along the dark way on which I was going. I wrote back to Mrs Macallan, as I really felt, gratefully and penitently. And then I went out to the chaise.

CHAPTER XXVII

Mr Dexter at Home

I found all the idle boys in the neighbourhood collected round the pony-chaise, expressing, in the occult language of slang, their high enjoyment and appreciation of the appearance of 'Ariel' in her man's jacket and hat. The pony was fidgety – *he* felt the influence of the popular uproar. His driver sat, whip in hand, magnificently impenetrable to the jibes and jests that were flying round her. I said 'Good morning,' on getting into the chaise. Ariel only said 'Gee up!' and started the pony.

I made up my mind to perform the journey to the distant northern suburb in silence. It was evidently useless for me to attempt to speak; and experience informed me that I need not expect to hear a word fall from the lips of my companion. Experience, however, is not always infallible. After driving for half-an-hour in stolid silence, Ariel astounded me by suddenly bursting into speech.

'Do you know what we are coming to?' she asked, keeping her eyes straight between the pony's ears.

'No,' I answered. 'I don't know the road. What are we coming to?'

'We are coming to a canal.'

'Well?'

'Well! I have half a mind to upset you in the canal.'

This formidable announcement appeared to me to require some explanation. I took the liberty of asking for it.

'Why should you upset me?' I enquired.

'Because I hate you,' was the cool and candid reply.

'What have I done to offend you?' I asked next.

'What do you want with The Master?' Ariel asked, in her turn.

'Do you mean Mr Dexter?'

'Yes.'

'I want to have some talk with Mr Dexter.'

'You don't! You want to take my place. You want to brush his hair and oil his beard, instead of me. You wretch!'

I now began to understand. The idea which Miserrimus Dexter had jestingly put into her head, in exhibiting her to us on the previous night, had been ripening slowly in that dull brain, and had found its way outwards into words, about fifteen hours afterwards, under the irritating influence of my presence!

'I don't want to touch his hair or his beard,' I said. 'I leave that entirely to you.'

She looked round at me; her fat face flushing, her dull eyes dilating, with the unaccustomed effort to express herself in speech, and to understand what was said to her in return.

'Say that again,' she burst out. 'And say it slower this time.'

I said it again, and I said it slower.

'Swear it!' she cried, getting more and more excited.

I preserved my gravity (the canal was just visible in the distance), and swore it.

'Are you satisfied now?' I asked.

There was no answer. Her last resources of speech were exhausted. The strange creature looked back again straight between the pony's ears, emitted hoarsely a grunt of relief; and never more looked at me, never more spoke to me, for the rest of the journey. We drove past the banks of the canal; and I escaped immersion. We rattled, in our jingling little vehicle, through the streets and across the waste patches of ground, which I dimly remembered in the darkness, and which looked more squalid and more hideous than ever in the broad daylight. The chaise turned down a lane, too narrow for the passage of any larger vehicle, and stopped at a wall and a gate that were new objects to me. Opening the gate with her key, and leading the pony, Ariel introduced me to the back garden and yard of Miserrimus Dexter's rotten and rambling old house. The pony walked off independently to his stable, with the chaise behind him. My silent companion led me through a bleak and barren kitchen, and along a stone passage. Opening a door at the end, she admitted me to the back of the hall, into which Mrs Macallan and I had penetrated by the front entrance to the house. Here, Ariel lifted a whistle which hung round her neck, and blew the shrill trilling notes, with the sound of which I was already familiar as the means of communication between Miserrimus Dexter and his slave. The whistling over, the slave's unwilling lips struggled into speech, for the last time.

'Wait till you hear The Master's whistle,' she said. 'Then go upstairs.'

So! I was to be whistled for like a dog. And worse still, there was no help for it but to submit like a dog. Had Ariel any excuses to make? Nothing of the sort! She turned her shapeless back on me, and vanished into the kitchen region of the house.

After waiting for a minute or two, and hearing no signal from the floor above, I advanced into the broader and brighter part of the hall, to look by daylight at the pictures which I had only imperfectly discovered in the darkness of the night. A painted inscription in many colours, just under the cornice of the ceiling, informed me that the works on the walls were the production of the all-accomplished Dexter himself. Not satisfied with being poet and composer, he was painter as well. On one wall the subjects were described as 'Illustrations of the Passions'; on the other, as 'Episodes in the Life of the Wandering Jew'. Chance spectators like myself were gravely warned, by means of the inscription, to view the pictures as efforts of pure imagination. 'Persons who look for mere Nature in works of Art' (the inscription announced) 'are persons to whom Mr Dexter does not address himself with the brush. He relies entirely on his imagination. Nature puts him out.'

Taking due care to dismiss all ideas of Nature from my mind, to begin with, I looked at the pictures which represented the Passions, first.

Little as I knew critically of Art, I could see that Miserrimus Dexter knew still less of the rules of drawing, colour, and composition. His pictures were, in the strictest meaning of that expressive word – Daubs. The diseased and riotous delight of the painter in representing Horrors, was (with certain exceptions to be hereafter mentioned) the one remarkable quality that I could discover in the series of his works.

The first of the Passion-pictures illustrated Revenge. A corpse, in fancy costume, lay on the bank of a foaming river, under the shade of a giant tree. An infuriated man, also in fancy costume, stood astride over the dead body, with his sword lifted to the lowering sky, and watched, with a horrid expression of delight, the blood of the man whom he had just killed, dripping slowly in a procession of big red drops down the broad blade of his weapon. The next picture illustrated Cruelty, in many compartments. In one, I saw a disembowelled horse savagely spurred on by his rider at a bullfight. In another, an aged philosopher was dissecting a live cat, and gloating over his work. In a third, two Pagans politely congratulated each other on the torture of two saints: one saint was roasting on a gridiron; the other, hung up to a tree by his heels, had just been skinned, and was not quite dead yet. Feeling no great desire, after these specimens, to look at any more of the illustrated Passions, I turned to the opposite wall to be instructed in the career of the Wandering Jew. Here, a second inscription informed me that the painter considered the Flying Dutchman to be no other than the Wandering Jew, pursuing his interminable journey by sea.[1] The marine adventures of this mysterious personage were the adventures chosen for representation by Dexter's brush. The first picture showed me a harbour on a rocky coast. A vessel was at anchor, with the helmsman singing on the deck. The sea in the offing was black and rolling; thunder-clouds lay low on the horizon, split by broad flashes of lightning. In the glare of the lightning, heaving and pitching, appeared the misty form of the Phantom Ship approaching the shore. In this work, badly as it was painted, there were really signs of a powerful imagination, and even of a poetical feeling for the supernatural. The next picture showed the Phantom Ship, moored (to the horror and astonishment of the helmsman) behind the earthly vessel in the harbour. The Jew had stepped on shore. His boat was on the beach. His crew – little men with stony white faces, dressed in funereal black – sat in silent rows on the seats of the boat, with their oars in their lean long hands. The Jew, also in black, stood with his eyes and hands raised imploringly to the thunderous heaven. The wild creatures of land and sea – the tiger, the rhinoceros, the crocodile; the sea-serpent, the shark, and the devil-fish – surrounded the accursed Wanderer in a mystic circle, daunted and fascinated at the sight of him. The lightning was gone. The sky and sea had darkened to a great black blank. A faint and lurid light lit the scene, falling downward from a torch, brandished by an avenging Spirit that hovered over the Jew on outspread vulture-wings. Wild as the picture might be in its conception, there was a suggestive power in it which I confess strongly impressed me. The mysterious silence in the house, and my strange position at the moment, no doubt had their effect on my mind. While I was still looking at the ghastly composition before me, the shrill trilling sound of the whistle upstairs burst on the stillness. For the moment, my nerves were so completely upset, that I started with a cry of alarm. I felt a momentary impulse to open the door, and run out. The idea of trusting myself alone with the man who had painted those frightful pictures, actually terrified me; I was obliged to sit down on one of the hall chairs. Some minutes passed before my mind recovered its balance, and I began to feel like my ordinary self again. The whistle sounded impatiently for the second time. I rose, and ascended the broad flight of stairs which led to the ante-room. To draw back at the point which I had now reached would have utterly degraded me in my own estimation. Still, my heart did certainly beat faster than usual, when I found myself on the top of the stairs; and I honestly acknowledge that I saw my own imprudence, just then, in a singularly vivid light.

There was a glass over the mantelpiece in the ante-room. I lingered for a moment (nervous as I was) to see how I looked in the glass.

The hanging tapestry over the inner door had been left partially drawn aside. Softly as I moved, the dog's ears of Miserrimus Dexter caught the sound of my dress on the floor. The fine tenor voice, which I had last heard singing, called to me gently.

'Is that Mrs Valeria? Please don't wait there. Come in!'

I entered the inner room.

The wheeled chair advanced to meet me, so slowly and so softly that I hardly knew it again. Miserrimus Dexter languidly held out his hand. His head inclined pensively to one side; his large blue eyes looked at me piteously. Not a vestige seemed to be left of the raging, shouting creature of my first visit, who was Napoleon at one moment and Shakspere at another. Mr Dexter of the morning was a mild, thoughtful, melancholy man, who only recalled Mr Dexter of the night by the inveterate oddity of his dress. His jacket, on this occasion, was of pink quilted silk. The coverlid which hid his deformity matched the jacket in pale sea-green satin; and, to complete these strange vagaries of costume, his wrists were actually adorned with massive bracelets of gold, formed on the severely-simple models which have descended to us from ancient times!

'How good of you to cheer and charm me by coming here!' he said, in his most mournful and most musical tones. 'I have dressed, expressly to receive you, in the prettiest clothes I have. Don't be surprised. Except in this ignoble and material nineteenth century, men have always worn precious stuffs and beautiful colours as well as women. A hundred years ago, a gentleman in pink silk was a gentleman properly dressed. Fifteen hundred years ago, the patricians of the classic times wore bracelets exactly like mine. I despise the brutish contempt for beauty and the mean dread of expense which degrade a gentleman's costume to black cloth, and limit a gentleman's ornaments to a finger ring, in the age I live in. I like to be bright and beautiful, especially when brightness and beauty come to see me. You don't know how precious your society is to me. This is one of my melancholy days. Tears rise unbidden to my eyes. I sigh and sorrow over myself; I languish for pity. Just think of what I am! A poor solitary creature, cursed with a frightful deformity. How pitiable! how dreadful! My affectionate heart – wasted. My extraordinary talents – useless or misapplied. Sad! sad! sad! Please pity me.'

His eyes were positively filled with tears – tears of compassion for himself! He looked at me and spoke to me with the wailing querulous entreaty of a sick child wanting to be nursed. I was quite at a loss what to do. It was perfectly ridiculous – but I was never more embarrassed in my life.

'Please pity me!' he repeated. 'Don't be cruel. I only ask a little thing. Pretty Mrs Valeria, say you pity me!'

I said I pitied him – and I felt that I blushed as I did it.

'Thank you,' said Miserrimus Dexter, humbly. 'It does me good. Go a little further. Pat my hand.'

I tried to restrain myself; but my sense of the absurdity of this last petition (quite gravely addressed to me, remember!) was too strong to be controlled. I burst out laughing.

Miserrimus Dexter looked at me with a blank astonishment which only increased my merriment. Had I offended him? Apparently not.

Recovering from his astonishment, he laid his head luxuriously on the back of his chair, with the expression of a man who was listening critically to a performance of some sort. When I had quite exhausted myself, he raised his head, and clapped his shapely white hands, and honoured me with an 'encore.'

'Do it again,' he said, still in the same childish way. 'Merry Mrs Valeria, *you* have a musical laugh – *I* have a musical ear. Do it again.'

I was serious enough by this time. 'I am ashamed of myself, Mr Dexter,' I said. 'Pray forgive me.'

He made no answer to this; I doubt if he heard me. His variable temper appeared to be in course of undergoing some new change. He sat looking at my dress (as I supposed) with a steady and anxious attention, gravely forming his own conclusions, stedfastly pursuing his own train of thought.

'Mrs Valeria,' he burst out suddenly, 'you are not comfortable in that chair.'

'Pardon me,' I replied; 'I am quite comfortable.'

'Pardon *me*,' he rejoined. 'There is a chair of Indian basket-work at the end of the room, which is much better suited to you. Will you accept my apologies if I am rude enough to allow you to fetch it for yourself? I have a reason.'

He had a reason! What new piece of eccentricity was he about to exhibit? I rose, and fetched the chair: it was light enough to be quite easily carried. As I returned to him, I noticed that his eyes were still strangely employed in what seemed to me to be the closest scrutiny of my dress. And stranger still, the result of this appeared to be, partly to interest and partly to distress him.

I placed the chair near him, and was about to take my seat in it, when he sent me back again, on another errand, to the end of the room.

'Oblige me indescribably,' he said. 'There is a hand-screen hanging on the wall, which matches the chair. We are rather near the fire here. You may find the screen useful. Once more forgive me for letting you fetch it for yourself. Once more let me assure you that I have a reason.'

Here was his 'reason,' reiterated, emphatically reiterated, for the second time! Curiosity made me as completely the obedient servant of his caprices as Ariel herself. I fetched the hand-screen. Returning with it, I met his eyes still fixed with the same incomprehensible attention on my perfectly plain and unpretending dress, and still expressing the same curious mixture of interest and regret.

'Thank you a thousand times,' he said. 'You have (quite innocently) wrung my heart. But you have not the less done me an inestimable kindness. Will you promise not to be offended with me, if I confess the truth?'

He was approaching his explanation! I never gave a promise more readily in my life.

'I have rudely allowed you to fetch your chair and your screen for yourself,' he went on. 'My motive will seem a very strange one, I am afraid. Did you observe that I noticed you very attentively – too attentively, perhaps?'

'Yes,' I said. 'I thought you were noticing my dress.'

He shook his head, and sighed bitterly.

'Not your dress,' he said. 'And not your face. Your dress is not pretty. Your face is still strange to me. Dear Mrs Valeria, I wanted to see you walk.'

To see me walk! What did he mean? Where was that erratic mind of his wandering to now?

'You have a rare accomplishment for an Englishwoman,' he resumed; 'you walk well. *She* walked well. I couldn't resist the temptation of seeing her again, in seeing you. It was *her* movement, *her* sweet simple unsought grace (not yours) when you walked to the end of the room and returned to me. You raised her from the dead, when you fetched the chair and the screen. Pardon me for making use of you; the idea was innocent, the motive was sacred. You have distressed, and delighted me. My heart bleeds – and thanks you.'

He paused for a moment: he let his head droop on his breast – then suddenly raised it again.

'Surely we were talking about her last night,' he said. 'What did I say? what did you say? My memory is confused; I half remember, half forget. Please remind me. You're not offended with me – are you?'

I might have been offended with another man. Not with him. I was far too anxious to find my way into his confidence – now that he had touched of his own accord on the subject of Eustace's first wife – to be offended with Miserrimus Dexter.

'We were speaking,' I answered, 'of Mrs Eustace Macallan's death; and we were saying to one another—'

He interrupted me, leaning forward eagerly in his chair.

'Yes! yes!' he exclaimed. 'And I was wondering what interest *you* could have in penetrating the mystery of her death. Tell me! Confide in me! I am dying to know!'

'Not even you have a stronger interest in that subject than the interest that I feel,' I said. 'The happiness of my whole life to come depends on my clearing up the mystery of her death.'

'Good God! – why?' he cried. 'Stop! I am exciting myself. I mustn't do that. I must have all my wits about me; I mustn't wander. The thing is too serious. Wait a minute!'

An elegant little basket was hooked on to one of the arms of his chair. He opened it, and drew out a strip of embroidery partially finished, with the necessary materials for working, all complete. We looked at each other across the embroidery. He noticed my surprise.

'Women,' he said, 'wisely compose their minds, and help themselves to think quietly, by doing needlework. Why are men such fools as to deny themselves the same admirable resource – the simple and soothing occupation which keeps the nerves steady and leaves the mind calm and free? As a man, I follow the women's wise example. Mrs Valeria, permit me to compose myself.'

Gravely arranging his embroidery, this extraordinary being began to work with the patient and nimble dexterity of an accomplished needlewoman.

'Now,' said Miserrimus Dexter, 'if you are ready, I am. You talk – I work. Please begin.'

I obeyed him, and began.

CHAPTER XXVIII

In the Dark

With such a man as Miserrimus Dexter, and with such a purpose as I had in view, no half-confidences were possible. I must either risk the most unreserved acknowledgment of the interests that I really had at stake, or I must make the best excuse that occurred to me for abandoning my contemplated experiment at the last moment. In my present critical situation, no such refuge as a middle course lay before me – even if I had been inclined to take it. As things were, I ran all risks, and plunged headlong into my own affairs at starting.

'Thus far, you know little or nothing about me, Mr Dexter,' I said. 'You are, as I believe, quite unaware that my husband and I are not living together at the present time?'

'Is it necessary to mention your husband?' he asked, coldly, without looking up from his embroidery, and without pausing in his work.

'It is absolutely necessary,' I answered. 'I can explain myself to you in no other way.'

He bent his head, and sighed resignedly.

'You and your husband are not living together, at the present time?' he resumed. 'Does that mean that Eustace has left you?'

'He has left me, and has gone abroad.'

'Without any necessity for it?'

'Without the least necessity.'

'Has he appointed no time for his return to you?'

'If he perseveres in his present resolution, Mr Dexter, Eustace will never return to me.'

For the first time, he raised his head from his embroidery – with a sudden appearance of interest.

'Is the quarrel so serious as that?' he asked. 'Are you free of each other, pretty Mrs Valeria, by common consent of both parties?'

The tone in which he put the question was not at all to my liking. The look he fixed on me was a look which unpleasantly suggested that I had trusted myself alone with him, and that he might end in taking advantage of it. I reminded him quietly, by my manner more than by my words, of the respect which he owed to me.

'You are entirely mistaken,' I said. 'There is no anger – there is not even a misunderstanding between us. Our parting has cost bitter sorrow, Mr Dexter, to him and to me.'

He submitted to be set right with ironical resignation. 'I am all attention,' he said, threading his needle. 'Pray go on; I won't interrupt you again.' Acting on this invitation, I told him the truth about my husband and myself quite unreservedly; taking care, however, at the same time, to put Eustace's motives in the best light that they would bear. Miserrimus Dexter laid aside his embroidery on the chair, and laughed softly to himself, with an impish enjoyment of my poor little narrative, which set every nerve in me on edge as I looked at him.

'I see nothing to laugh at,' I said, sharply.

His beautiful blue eyes rested on me with a look of innocent surprise.

'Nothing to laugh at,' he repeated, 'in such an exhibition of human folly as you have described!' His expression suddenly changed; his face darkened and hardened very strangely. 'Stop!' he cried, before I could answer him. 'There can be only one reason for your taking it as seriously as you do. Mrs Valeria, you are fond of your husband.'

'Fond of him isn't strong enough to express it,' I retorted. 'I love him with my whole heart.'

Miserrimus Dexter stroked his magnificent beard, and contemplatively repeated my words. 'You love him with your whole heart? Do you know why?'

'Because I can't help it,' I answered, doggedly.

He smiled satirically, and went on with his embroidery. 'Curious!' he said to himself; 'Eustace's first wife loved him, too. There are some men whom the women all like; and there are other men whom the women never care for. Without the least reason for it in either case. The one man is just as good as the other; just as handsome, as agreeable, as honourable, and as high in rank as the other. And yet, for Number One, they will go through fire and water; and for Number Two, they won't so much as turn their heads to look at him. Why? They don't know themselves – as Mrs Valeria has just said! Is there a physical reason for it? Is there some potent magnetic emanation[1] from Number One, which Number Two doesn't possess? I must investigate this when I have the time, and when I find myself in the humour.' Having so far settled the question to his own entire satisfaction, he looked up at me again. 'I am still in the dark about you and your motives,' he said. 'I am still as far as ever from understanding what your interest is in investigating that hideous tragedy at Gleninch. Clever Mrs Valeria, please take me by the hand, and lead me into the light. You're not offended with me – are you? Make it up; and I will give you this pretty piece of embroidery when I have done it. I am only a poor solitary deformed wretch, with a quaint turn of mind; I mean no harm. Forgive me! indulge me! enlighten me!'

He resumed his childish ways; he recovered his innocent smile, with the odd little puckers and wrinkles accompanying it at the corners of his eyes. I began to doubt whether I might not have been unreasonably hard on him. I penitently resolved to be more considerate towards his infirmities of mind and body, during the remainder of my visit.

'Let me go back for a moment, Mr Dexter, to past times at Gleninch,' I said. 'You agree with me in believing Eustace to be absolutely innocent of the crime for which he was tried. Your evidence at the Trial tells me that.'

He paused over his work, and looked at me with a grave and stern attention which presented his face in quite a new light.

'That is *our* opinion,' I resumed. 'But it was not the opinion of the Jury. Their verdict, you remember, was Not Proven. In plain English, the Jury who tried my husband declined to express their opinion, positively and publicly, that he was innocent. Am I right?'

Instead of answering, he suddenly put his embroidery back in the basket, and moved the machinery of his chair, so as to bring it close by mine.

'Who told you this?' he asked.

'I found it for myself, in a book.'

Thus far, his face had expressed steady attention – and no more. Now, for the first time, I thought I saw something darkly passing over him which betrayed itself to my mind as rising distrust.

'Ladies are not generally in the habit of troubling their heads about dry questions of law,' he said. 'Mrs Eustace Macallan the Second, you must have some very powerful motive for turning your studies that way.'

'I have a very powerful motive, Mr Dexter. My husband is resigned to the Scotch Verdict. His mother is resigned to it. His friends (so far as I know) are resigned to it—'

'Well?'

'Well! I don't agree with my husband, or his mother, or his friends. I refuse to submit to the Scotch Verdict.'

The instant I said those words, the madness in him which I had hitherto denied, seemed to break out. He suddenly stretched himself over his chair: he pounced on me, with a hand on each of my shoulders; his wild eyes questioned me fiercely, frantically, within a few inches of my face.

'What do you mean?' he shouted, at the utmost pitch of his ringing and resonant voice.

A deadly fear of him shook me. I did my best to hide the outward betrayal of it. By look and word, I showed him, as firmly as I could, that I resented the liberty he had taken with me.

'Remove your hands, sir,' I said. 'And retire to your proper place.'

He obeyed me mechanically. He apologised to me mechanically. His whole mind was evidently still filled with the words that I had spoken to him, and still bent on discovering what those words meant.

'I beg your pardon,' he said; 'I humbly beg your pardon. The subject excites me, frightens me, maddens me. You don't know what a difficulty I have in controlling myself. Never mind. Don't take me seriously. Don't be frightened at me. I am so ashamed of myself – I feel so small and so miserable at having offended you. Make me suffer for it. Take a stick and beat me. Tie me down in my chair. Call up Ariel, who is as strong as a horse, and tell her to hold me. Dear Mrs Valeria! Injured Mrs Valeria! I'll endure anything in the way of punishment, if you will only tell me what you mean by not submitting to the Scotch Verdict?' He backed his chair penitently, as he made that entreaty. 'Am I far enough away yet?' he asked, with a rueful look. 'Do I still frighten you? I'll drop out of sight, if you prefer it, in the bottom of the chair.'

He lifted the sea-green coverlid. In another moment he would have disappeared like a puppet in a show, if I had not stopped him.

'Say nothing more, and do nothing more; I accept your apologies,' I said. 'When I tell you that I refuse to submit to the opinion of the Scotch Jury, I mean exactly what my words express. That Verdict has left a stain on my husband's character. He feels the stain bitterly. How bitterly no one knows so well as I do. His sense of his degradation is the sense that has parted him from me. It is not enough for *him* that I am persuaded of his innocence. Nothing will bring him back to me – nothing will persuade Eustace that I think him worthy to be the guide and companion of my life – but the proof of his innocence, set before the Jury which doubts it, and the public which doubts it, to this day. He, and his friends, and his lawyers all despair of ever finding that proof, now. But I am his wife; and none of you love him as I love him. I alone refuse to despair; I alone refuse to listen to reason. If God spares me, Mr Dexter, I dedicate my life to the vindication of my husband's innocence. You are his old friend – I am here to ask you to help me.'

It appeared to be now my turn to frighten *him*. The colour left his face. He passed his hand restlessly over his forehead, as if he was trying to brush some delusion out of his brain.

'Is this one of my dreams?' he asked, faintly. 'Are you a vision of the night?'

'I am only a friendless woman,' I said, 'who has lost all that she loved and prized, and who is trying to win it back again.'

He began to move his chair nearer to me once more. I lifted my hand. He stopped the chair directly. There was a moment of silence. We sat watching one another. I saw his hands tremble as he laid them on the coverlid; I saw his face grow paler and paler, and his under lip drop. What dead and buried remembrances had I brought to life in him, in all their olden horror?

He was the first to speak again.

'So this is your interest,' he said, 'in clearing up the mystery of Mrs Eustace Macallan's death?'

'Yes.'

'And you believe that I can help you?'

'I do.'

He slowly lifted one of his hands, and pointed at me with his long forefinger.

'You suspect somebody,' he said.

The tone in which he spoke was low and threatening: it warned me to be careful. At the same time, if I now shut him out of my confidence, I should lose the reward that might yet be to come, for all that I had suffered and risked at that perilous interview.

'You suspect somebody,' he repeated.

'Perhaps!' was all I said in return.

'Is the person within your reach?'

'Not yet.'

'Do you know where the person is?'

'No.'

He laid his head languidly on the back of his chair, with a trembling long-drawn sigh. Was he disappointed? Or was he relieved? or was he simply exhausted in mind and body alike? Who could fathom him? Who could say?

'Will you give me five minutes?' he asked, feebly and wearily, without raising his head. 'You know already how any reference to events at Gleninch excites and shakes me. I shall be fit for it again, if you will kindly give me a few minutes to myself. There are books in the next room. Please excuse me.'

I at once retired to the circular ante-chamber. He followed me in his chair, and closed the door between us.

CHAPTER XXIX

In the Light

A little interval of solitude was a relief to me, as well as to Miserrimus Dexter.

Startling doubts beset me as I walked restlessly backwards and forwards, now in the ante-room, and now in the corridor outside. It was plain that I had (quite innocently) disturbed the repose of some formidable secrets in Miserrimus Dexter's mind. I confused and wearied my poor brains in trying to guess what the secrets might be. All my ingenuity – as after events showed me – was wasted on speculations not one of which even approached the truth. I was on surer ground, when I arrived at the conclusion that Dexter had really kept every mortal creature out of his confidence. He could never have betrayed such serious signs of disturbance as I had noticed in him, if he had publicly acknowledged at the Trial, or if he had privately communicated to any chosen friend, all that he knew of the tragic and terrible drama acted in the bedchamber at Gleninch. What powerful influence had induced him to close his lips? Had he been silent in mercy to others? or in dread of consequences to himself? Impossible to tell! Could I hope that he would confide to Me what he had kept secret from Justice and Friendship alike? When he knew what I really wanted of him, would he arm me, out of his own stores of knowledge, with the weapon that would win me victory in the struggle to come? The chances were all against it – there was no denying that. Still, the end was worth trying for. The caprice of the moment might yet stand my friend, with such a wayward being as Miserrimus Dexter. My plans and projects were sufficiently strange, sufficiently wide of the ordinary limits of a woman's thoughts and actions, to attract his sympathies. 'Who knows' (I thought to myself), 'if I may not take his confidence by surprise, by simply telling him the truth!'

The interval expired; the door was thrown open; the voice of my host summoned me again to the inner room.

'Welcome back!' said Miserrimus Dexter. 'Dear Mrs Valeria, I am quite myself again. How are you?'

He looked and spoke with the easy cordiality of an old friend. During the period of my absence, short as it was, another change had passed over this most multiform of living beings. His eyes sparkled with good humour; his cheeks were flushing under a new excitement of some sort. Even his dress had undergone alteration since I had seen it last. He now wore an extemporised cap of white paper; his ruffles were tucked up; a clean apron was thrown over the sea-green coverlid. He backed his chair before me, bowing and smiling; and waved me to a seat with the grace of a dancing-master, chastened by the dignity of a lord in waiting.

'I am going to cook,' he announced, with the most engaging simplicity. 'We both stand in need of refreshment, before we return to the serious business of our interview. You see me in my cook's dress – forgive it. There is a form in these things; I am a great stickler for forms. I have been taking some wine. Please sanction that proceeding by taking some wine too.'

He filled a goblet of ancient Venetian glass with a purple-red liquor, beautiful to see.

'Burgundy!' he said. 'The King of Wines. And this is the King of Burgundies – Clos Vougeot.[1] I drink to your health and happiness!'

He filled a second goblet for himself, and honoured the toast by draining it to the bottom. I now understood the sparkle in his eyes and the flush in his cheeks! It was my interest not to offend him. I drank a little of his wine – and I quite agreed with him; I thought it delicious.

'What shall we eat?' he asked. 'It must be something worthy of our Clos Vougeot. Ariel is good at roasting and boiling joints, poor wretch! But I don't insult your taste by offering you Ariel's cookery. Plain joints!' he exclaimed, with an expression of refined disgust. 'Bah! A man who eats a plain joint is only one remove from a cannibal – or a butcher. Will you leave it to me to discover something more worthy of us? Let us go to the kitchen.'

He wheeled his chair round; and invited me to accompany him with a courteous wave of his hand.

I followed the chair to some closed curtains at one end of the room, which I had not hitherto noticed. Drawing aside the curtains, he revealed to view an alcove, in which stood a neat little gas stove for cooking. Drawers and cupboards, plates, dishes, and saucepans were ranged round the alcove – all on a miniature scale, all scrupulously bright and clean. 'Welcome to the kitchen!' said Miserrimus Dexter. He drew out of a recess in the wall a marble slab which served as a table, and reflected profoundly with his hand to his head. 'I have it!' he cried – and opening one of the cupboards next, took from it a black bottle of a form that was new to me. Sounding this bottle with a spike, he pierced and produced to view some little irregularly-formed black objects, which might have been familiar enough to a woman accustomed to the luxurious tables of the rich; but which were a new revelation to a person like myself, who had led a simple country life in the house of a clergyman with small means. When I saw my host carefully lay out these occult substances, of uninviting appearance, on a clean napkin, and then plunge once more into profound reflection at the sight of them, my curiosity could be no longer restrained. I ventured to say, 'What are those things, Mr Dexter? and are we really going to eat them?'

He started at the rash question, and looked at me, with hands outspread in irrepressible astonishment.

'Where is our boasted progress?' he cried. 'What is education but a name? Here is a cultivated person who doesn't know Truffles when she sees them!'

'I have heard of truffles,' I answered, humbly. 'But I never saw them before. We had no such foreign luxuries as those, Mr Dexter, at home in the North.'

Miserrimus Dexter lifted one of the truffles tenderly on his spike, and held it up to me in a favourable light.

'Make the most of one of the few first sensations in this life, which has no ingredient of disappointment lurking under the surface,' he said. 'Look at it; meditate over it. You shall eat it, Mrs Valeria, stewed in Burgundy!'

He lit the gas for cooking, with the air of a man who was about to offer me an inestimable proof of his good will.

'Forgive me if I observe the most absolute silence,' he said, 'dating from the moment when I take this in my hand.' He produced a bright little stew-pan from his collection of culinary utensils as he spoke. 'Properly pursued, the Art of Cookery allows of no divided attention,' he continued, gravely. 'In that observation you will find the reason why no woman ever has reached, or ever will reach, the highest distinction as a cook. As a rule, women are incapable of absolutely concentrating their attention on any one occupation, for any given time. Their minds will run on something else – say typically, for the sake of illustration, their sweetheart, or their new bonnet. The one obstacle, Mrs Valeria, to your rising equal to the men in the various industrial processes of life is not raised, as the women vainly suppose, by the defective institutions of the age they live in. No! the obstacle is in themselves. No institutions that can be devised to encourage them, will ever be strong enough to contend successfully with the sweetheart and the new bonnet. A little while ago, for instance, I was instrumental in getting women employed in our local post-office here. The other day I took the trouble – a serious business to me – of getting downstairs, and wheeling myself away to the office to see how they were getting on. I took a letter with me to register. It had an unusually long address. The registering-woman began copying the address on the receipt-form, in a business-like manner cheering and delightful to see. Half-way through, a little child, sister of one of the other women employed, trotted into the office, and popped under the counter to go and speak to her relative. The registering-woman's mind instantly gave way. Her pencil stopped; her eyes wandered off to the child, with a charming expression of interest. "Well, Lucy!" she said, "how-d'ye-do?" Then she remembered business again, and returned to her receipt. When I took it across the counter, an important line in the address of my letter was left out in the copy. Thanks to Lucy. Now a man in the same position would not have seen Lucy – he would have been too closely occupied with what he was about at the moment. There is the whole difference between the mental constitution of the sexes, which no legislation will ever alter as long as the world lasts! What does it matter? Women are infinitely superior to men in the moral qualities which are the true adornments of humanity. Be content – oh, my mistaken sisters, be content with that!'

He twisted his chair round towards the stove. It was useless to dispute the question with him, even if I had felt inclined to do so. He absorbed himself in his stew-pan.

I looked about me in the room.

The same insatiable relish for horrors exhibited downstairs by the pictures in the hall, was displayed again here. The photographs hanging on the wall, represented the various forms of madness taken from the life. The plaster casts ranged on the shelf opposite, were casts (after death) of the heads of famous murderers. A frightful little skeleton of a woman hung in a cupboard, behind a glazed door, with this cynical inscription placed above the skull – 'Behold the scaffolding on which beauty is built!' In a corresponding cupboard, with the door wide open, there hung in loose folds a shirt (as I took it to be) of chamois leather. Touching it (and finding it to be far softer than any chamois leather that my fingers had ever felt before), I disarranged the folds, and disclosed a ticket pinned among them, describing the thing in these horrid lines: 'Skin of a French Marquis, tanned in the Revolution of Ninety Three. Who says the nobility are not good for something? They make good leather.'

After this last specimen of my host's taste in curiosities, I pursued my investigation no further. I returned to my chair, and waited for the Truffles.

After a brief interval, the voice of the poet-painter-composer-and-cook summoned me back to the alcove.

The gas was out. The stew-pan and its accompaniments had vanished. On the marble slab were two plates, two napkins, two rolls of bread – and a dish, with another napkin in it, on which reposed two quaint little black balls. Miserrimus Dexter, regarding me with a smile of benevolent interest, put one of the balls on my plate, and took the other himself. 'Compose yourself, Mrs Valeria,' he said. 'This is an epoch in your life. Your first Truffle! Don't touch it with the knife. Use the fork alone. And – pardon me; this is most important – eat slowly.'

I followed my instructions, and assumed an enthusiasm which I honestly confess I did not feel. I privately thought the new vegetable a great deal too rich, and, in other respects, quite unworthy of the fuss that had been made about it. Miserrimus Dexter lingered and languished over his truffles, and sipped his wonderful Burgundy, and sang his own praises as a cook – until I was really almost mad with impatience to return to the real object of my visit. In the reckless state of mind which this feeling produced, I abruptly reminded my host that he was wasting our time, by the most dangerous question that I could possibly put to him.

'Mr Dexter,' I said, 'have you heard anything lately of Mrs Beauly?'

The easy sense of enjoyment expressed in his face left it at those rash words, and went out like a suddenly-extinguished light. That furtive distrust of me which I had already noticed, instantly made itself felt again in his manner and in his voice.

'Do you know Mrs Beauly?' he asked.

'I only know her,' I answered, 'by what I have read of her in the Trial.'

He was not satisfied with that reply.

'You must have an interest of some sort in Mrs Beauly,' he said, 'or you would not have asked me about her. Is it the interest of a friend? or the interest of an enemy?'

Rash as I might be, I was not quite reckless enough yet, to meet that plain question by an equally plain reply. I saw enough in his face to warn me to be careful with him before it was too late.

'I can only answer you in one way,' I rejoined. 'I must return to a subject which is very painful to you – the subject of the Trial.'

'Go on!' he said, with one of his grim outbursts of humour. 'Here I am at your mercy – a martyr at the stake. Poke the fire! poke the fire!'

'I am only an ignorant woman,' I resumed; 'and I daresay I am quite wrong. But there is one part of my husband's trial which doesn't at all satisfy me. The defence set up for him seems to me to have been a complete mistake.'

'A complete mistake?' he repeated. 'Strange language, Mrs Valeria, to say the least of it!' He tried to speak lightly; he took up his goblet of wine. But I could see that I had produced an effect on him. His hand trembled as it carried the glass to his lips.

'I don't doubt that Eustace's first wife really asked him to buy the arsenic,' I continued. 'I don't doubt that she used it secretly to improve her complexion. But what I do *not* believe is – that she died of an overdose of the poison, taken by mistake.'

He put back the goblet of wine on the table near him, so unsteadily that he spilt the greater part of it. For a moment, his eyes met mine; then looked down again.

'How do you believe she died?' he enquired, in tones so low that I could hardly hear them.

'By the hand of a poisoner,' I answered.

He made a movement as if he was about to start up in the chair, and sank back again, seized apparently with a sudden faintness.

'Not my husband!' I hastened to add. 'You know that I am satisfied of *his* innocence.'

I saw him shudder. I saw his hands fasten their hold convulsively on the arms of his chair.

'Who poisoned her?' he asked – still lying helplessly back in the chair.

At the critical moment, my courage failed me. I was afraid to tell him in what direction my suspicions pointed.

'Can't you guess?' I said.

There was a pause. I supposed him to be secretly following his own train of thought. It was not for long. On a sudden, he started up in his chair. The prostration which had possessed him appeared to vanish in an instant. His eyes recovered their wild light; his hands were steady again; his colour was brighter than ever. Had he been pondering over the secret of my interest in Mrs Beauly, and had he guessed? He had!

'Answer me on your word of honour!' he cried. 'Don't attempt to deceive me. Is it a woman?'

'It is.'

'What is the first letter of her name? Is it one of the first three letters of the alphabet?'

'Yes.'

'B.?'

'Yes.'

'Beauly?'

'Beauly.'

He threw his hands up above his head, and burst into a frantic fit of laughter.

'I have lived long enough!' he broke out, wildly. 'At last I have discovered one other person in the world who sees it as plainly as I do. Cruel Mrs Valeria! why did you torture me? Why didn't you own it before?'

'What!' I exclaimed, catching the infection of his excitement. 'Are *your* ideas, *my* ideas? Is it possible that *you* suspect Mrs Beauly, too?'

He made this remarkable reply:

'Suspect?' he repeated, contemptuously. 'There isn't the shadow of a doubt about it. Mrs Beauly poisoned her.'

END OF THE SECOND VOLUME

VOLUME III

CHAPTER XXX

The Indictment of Mrs Beauly

I started to my feet, and looked at Miserrimus Dexter. I was too much agitated to be able to speak to him.

My utmost expectations had not prepared me for the tone of absolute conviction in which he had spoken. At the best, I had anticipated that he might, by the barest chance, agree with me in suspecting Mrs Beauly. And now, his own lips had said it, without hesitation or reserve! 'There isn't the shadow of a doubt; Mrs Beauly poisoned her.'

'Sit down,' he said, quietly. 'There's nothing to be afraid of. Nobody can hear us in this room.'

I sat down again, and recovered myself a little.

'Have you never told anyone else what you have told me?' was the first question that I put to him.

'Never. No one else suspected her.'

'Not even the lawyers?'

'Not even the lawyers. There is no legal evidence against Mrs Beauly. There is nothing but moral certainty.'

'Surely you might have found the evidence, if you had tried?'

He laughed at the idea.

'Look at me!' he said. 'How is a man to hunt up evidence who is tied to this chair? Besides, there were other difficulties in my way. I am not generally in the habit of needlessly betraying myself – I am a cautious man, though you may not have noticed it. But my immeasurable hatred of Mrs Beauly was not to be concealed. If eyes can tell secrets, she must have discovered, in my eyes, that I hungered and thirsted[1] to see her in the hangman's hands. From first to last, I tell you, Mrs Borgia-Beauly[2] was on her guard against me. Can I describe her cunning? All my resources of language are not equal to the task. Take the degrees of comparison to give you a faint idea of it. I am positively cunning; the devil is comparatively cunning; Mrs Beauly is superlatively cunning. No! no! If she is ever discovered, at this distance of time, it will not be done by a man – it will be done by a woman; a woman whom she doesn't suspect; a woman who can watch her with the patience of a tigress in a state of starvation—'

'Say a woman like Me!' I broke out. 'I am ready to try.'

His eyes glittered; his teeth showed themselves viciously under his moustache; he drummed fiercely with both hands on the arms of his chair.

'Do you really mean it?' he asked.

'Put me in your position,' I answered. 'Enlighten me with your moral certainty (as you call it) – and you shall see!'

'I'll do it!' he said. 'Tell me one thing first. How did an outside stranger, like you, come to suspect her?'

I set before him, to the best of my ability, the various elements of suspicion which I had collected from the evidence at the Trial; and I laid especial stress on the fact (sworn to by the nurse) that Mrs Beauly was missing, exactly at the time when Christina Ormsay had left Mrs Eustace Macallan alone in her room.

'You have hit it!' cried Miserrimus Dexter. 'You are a wonderful woman! What was she doing on the morning of the day when Mrs Eustace Macallan died poisoned? And where was she, during the dark hours of the night? I can tell you where she was *not*: – she was not in her own room.'

'Not in her own room?' I repeated. 'Are you really sure of that?'

'I am sure of everything that I say, when I am speaking of Mrs Beauly. Mind that; and now listen! This is a drama; and I excel in dramatic narrative. You shall judge for yourself. Date, the twentieth of October. Scene, The Corridor, called The Guests' Corridor, at Gleninch. On one side, a row of windows looking out into the garden. On the other, a row of four bedrooms, with dressing-rooms attached. First bedroom (beginning from the staircase), occupied by Mrs Beauly. Second bedroom, empty. Third bedroom occupied by Miserrimus Dexter. Fourth bedroom empty. So much for the Scene! The time comes next – the time is eleven at night. Dexter discovered in his bedroom, reading. Enter to him Eustace Macallan. Eustace speaks: – "My dear fellow, be particularly careful not to make any noise; don't bowl your chair up and down the corridor to-night." Dexter enquires, "Why?" Eustace answers, "Mrs Beauly has been dining with some friends in Edinburgh, and has come back terribly fatigued; she has gone up to her room to rest." Dexter makes another enquiry (satirical enquiry, this time): – "How does she look when she is terribly fatigued? As beautiful as ever?" Answer: – "I don't know; I have not seen her; she slipped upstairs, without speaking to anybody." Third enquiry by Dexter (logical enquiry, on this occasion): – "If she spoke to nobody, how do you know she is fatigued?" Eustace hands me a morsel of paper, and answers, "Don't be a fool! I found this on the hall table. Remember what I have told you about keeping quiet: good night!" Eustace retires. Dexter looks at the paper, and reads these lines in pencil: – "Just returned. Please forgive me for going to bed without saying good night. I have over-exerted myself; I am dreadfully fatigued. (Signed) HELENA." Dexter is by nature suspicious; Dexter suspects Mrs Beauly. Never mind his reasons; there is no time to enter into his reasons now. He puts the case to himself thus: – "A weary woman would never have given herself the trouble to write this. She would have found it much less fatiguing to knock at the drawing-room door as she passed, and to make her apologies by word of mouth. I see something here out of the ordinary way: I shall make a night of it in my chair." Very good. Dexter proceeds to make a night of it. He opens his door; wheels himself softly into the corridor; locks the doors of the two empty bedrooms, and returns (with the keys in his pocket) to his own room. "Now," says D. to himself, "if I hear a door softly opened in this part of the house, I shall know for certain it is Mrs Beauly's door!" Upon that, he closes his own door, leaving the tiniest little chink to look through; puts out his light; and waits and watches at his tiny little chink, like a cat at a mousehole. The corridor is the only place he wants to see; and a lamp burns there all night. Twelve o'clock strikes; he hears the doors below bolted and locked, and nothing happens. Half-past twelve – and nothing still. The house is as silent as the grave. One o'clock; two o'clock – same silence. Half-past two – and something happens at last. Dexter hears a sound close by, in the corridor. It is the sound of a handle turning very softly in a door – in the only door that can be opened, the door of Mrs Beauly's room. Dexter drops noiselessly from his chair, on to his hands; lies flat on the floor at his chink; and listens. He hears the handle closed again;

he sees a dark object flit by him; he pops his head out of his door, down on the floor where nobody would think of looking for him. And, what does he see? Mrs Beauly! There she goes, with the long brown cloak over her shoulders which she wears when she is driving, floating behind her. In a moment more, she disappears, past the fourth bed-room, and turns at a right angle, into a second corridor, called the South Corridor. What rooms are in the South Corridor? There are three rooms. First room, the little study, mentioned in the nurse's evidence. Second room, Mrs Eustace Macallan's bedchamber. Third room, her husband's bedchamber. What does Mrs Beauly (supposed to be worn out by fatigue) want in that part of the house, at half-past two in the morning? Dexter decides on running his risk of being seen – and sets forth on a voyage of discovery. Do you know how he gets from place to place, without his chair? Have you seen the poor deformed creature hop on his hands? Shall he show you how he does it, before he goes on with his story?'

I hastened to stop the proposed exhibition.

'I saw you hop last night,' I said. 'Go on! pray go on with your story!'

'Do you like my dramatic style of narrative?' he asked. 'Am I interesting?'

'Indescribably interesting, Mr Dexter. I am eager to hear more.'

He smiled in high approval of his own abilities.

'I am equally good at the autobiographical style,' he said. 'Shall we try that next, by way of variety?'

'Anything you like,' I cried, losing all patience with him, 'if you will only go on!'

'Part Two: Autobiographical Style,' he announced, with a wave of his hand. 'I hopped along the Guests' Corridor, and turned into the South Corridor. I stopped at the little study. Door open; nobody there. I crossed the study to the second door, communicating with Mrs Macallan's bedchamber. Locked! I looked through the keyhole. Was there something hanging over it, on the other side? I can't say – I only know there was nothing to be seen, but blank darkness. I listened. Nothing to be heard. Same blank darkness, same absolute silence, inside the locked second door of Mrs Eustace's room, opening on the corridor. I went on to her husband's bedchamber. I had the worst possible opinion of Mrs Beauly – I should not have been in the least surprised if I had caught her in Eustace's room. I looked through the keyhole. In this case, the key was out of it – or was turned the right way for me – I don't know which. Eustace's bed was opposite the door. No discovery. I could see him, by his nightlight, innocently asleep. I reflected a little. The back staircase was at the end of the corridor, beyond me. I slid down the stairs, and looked about me on the lower floor, by the light of the night-lamp. Doors all fast locked, and keys outside, so that I could try them myself. House door barred and bolted. Door leading into the servants' offices barred and bolted. I got back to my own room, and thought it out quietly. Where could she be? Certainly *in* the house, somewhere. Where? I had made sure of the other rooms; the field of search was exhausted. She could only be in Mrs Macallan's room – the *one* room which had baffled my investigations; the *only* room which had not lent itself to examination. Add to this, that the key of the door in the study, communicating with Mrs Macallan's room, was stated in the nurse's evidence to be missing; and don't forget that the dearest object of Mrs Beauly's life (on the showing of her own letter, read at the Trial) was to be Eustace Macallan's happy wife. Put these things together in your own mind, and you will know what my thoughts were, as I sat waiting for events in my chair, without my telling you. Towards four o'clock, strong as I am, fatigue got the better of me. I fell asleep. Not for long. I woke with a start and looked at my watch. Twenty-five minutes past four. Had she got back to her room while I was asleep? I hopped to her door, and listened. Not a sound. I softly opened the door. The room was empty. I went back again to my own room to wait and watch. It was hard work to keep my eyes open. I drew up the window to let the cool air refresh me; I fought hard with exhausted nature; and exhausted nature won. I fell asleep again. This time it was eight in the morning when I woke. I have goodish ears, as you may have noticed. I heard women's voices talking under my open window. I peeped out. Mrs Beauly and her maid, in close confabulation! Mrs Beauly and her maid, looking guiltily about them to make sure that they were neither seen nor heard! "Take care, ma'am," I heard the maid say; "that horrid deformed monster is as sly as a fox. Mind he doesn't discover you." Mrs Beauly answered, "You go first, and look out in front; I will follow you; and make sure there is nobody behind us." With that, they disappeared round the corner of the house. In five minutes more I heard the door of Mrs Beauly's room softly opened and closed again. Three hours later, the nurse met her in the corridor, innocently on her way to make enquiries at Mrs Eustace Macallan's door. What do you think of these circumstances? What do you think of Mrs Beauly and her maid having something to say to each other, which they didn't dare say in the house – for fear of my being behind some door listening to them? What do you think of these discoveries of mine being made, on the very morning when Mrs Eustace was taken ill – on the very day when she died by a poisoner's hand? Do you see your way to the guilty person? And has mad Miserrimus Dexter been of some assistance to you, so far?'

I was too violently excited to answer him. The way to the vindication of my husband's innocence was opened to me at last!

'Where is she?' I cried. 'And where is that servant who is in her confidence?'

'I can't tell you,' he said. 'I don't know.'

'Where can I enquire? Can you tell me that?'

He considered a little.

'There is one man who must know where she is – or who could find it out for you,' he said.

'Who is he? What is his name?'

'He is a friend of Eustace's. Major Fitz-David.'

'I know him! I am going to dine with him next week. He has asked you to dine too.'

Miserrimus Dexter laughed contemptuously.

'Major Fitz-David may do very well for the ladies,' he said. 'The ladies can treat him as a species of elderly human lap-dog. I don't dine with lap-dogs; I have said, No. You go. He, or some of his ladies, may be of use to you. Who are the guests? Did he tell you?'

'There was a French lady whose name I forget,' I said, 'and Lady Clarinda—'

'That will do! She is a friend of Mrs Beauly's. She is sure to know where Mrs Beauly is. Come to me, the moment you have got your information. Find out if the maid is with her: she is the easiest to deal with of the two. Only make the maid open her lips; and we have got Mrs Beauly. We crush her,' he cried, bringing his hand down like lightning on the last languid fly of the season, crawling over the arm of his chair, 'we crush her as I crush this fly. Stop! A question; a most important question in dealing with the maid. Have you got any money?'

'Plenty of money.'

He snapped his fingers joyously.

'The maid is ours!' he cried. 'It's a matter of pounds, shillings, and pence, with the maid. Wait! Another question. About your name? If you approach Mrs Beauly in your own character as Eustace's wife, you approach her as the woman who has taken her place – you make a mortal enemy of her at starting. Beware of that!'

My jealousy of Mrs Beauly, smouldering in me all through the interview, burst into flame at those words. I could resist it no longer – I was obliged to ask him if my husband had ever loved her.

'Tell me the truth,' I said. 'Did Eustace really—?'

He burst out laughing maliciously; he penetrated my jealousy, and guessed my question almost before it had passed my lips.

'Yes,' he said, 'Eustace did really love her – and no mistake about it. She had every reason to believe (before the Trial) that the wife's death would put her in the wife's place. But the Trial made another man of Eustace. Mrs Beauly had been a witness of the public degradation of him. That was enough to prevent his marrying Mrs Beauly. He broke off with her at once and for ever – for the same reason precisely which has led him to separate himself from you. Existence with a woman who knew that he had been tried for his life as a murderer, was an existence that he was not hero enough to face. You wanted the truth. There it is! You have need to be cautious of Mrs Beauly – you have no need to be jealous of her. Take the safe course. Arrange with the Major, when you meet Lady Clarinda at his dinner, that you meet her under an assumed name.'

'I can go to the dinner,' I said, 'under the name in which Eustace married me. I can go as "Mrs Woodville." '

'The very thing!' he exclaimed. 'What would I not give to be present when Lady Clarinda introduces you to Mrs Beauly! Think of the situation. A woman with a hideous secret, hidden in her inmost soul: and another woman who knows of it – another woman who is bent, by fair means or foul, on dragging that secret into the light of day. What a struggle! What a plot for a novel! I am in a fever when I think of it. I am beside myself when I look into the future, and see Mrs Borgia-Beauly brought to her knees at last. Don't be alarmed!' he cried, with the wild light flashing once more in his eyes. 'My brains are beginning to boil again in my head. I must take refuge in physical exercise. I must blow off the steam, or I shall explode in my pink jacket on the spot!'

The old madness seized on him again. I made for the door, to secure my retreat in case of necessity – and then ventured to look round at him.

He was off on his furious wheels – half man, half chair – flying like a whirlwind to the other end of the room. Even this exercise was not violent enough for him, in his present mood. In an instant he was down on the floor; poised on his hands, and looking in the distance like a monstrous frog. Hopping down the room, he overthrew, one after another, all the smaller and lighter chairs as he passed them. Arrived at the end, he turned, surveyed the prostrate chairs, encouraged himself with a scream of triumph, and leapt rapidly over chair after chair, on his hands – his limbless body, now thrown back from the shoulders, and now thrown forward to keep the balance, in a manner at once wonderful and horrible to behold. 'Dexter's Leapfrog!' he cried, cheerfully, perching himself, with his birdlike lightness, on the last of the prostrate chairs, when he had reached the further end of the room. 'I'm pretty active, Mrs Valeria, considering I'm a cripple. Let us drink to the hanging of Mrs Beauly, in another bottle of Burgundy!'

I seized desperately on the first excuse that occurred to me for getting away from him.

'You forget,' I said – 'I must go at once to the Major. If I don't warn him in time, he may speak of me to Lady Clarinda by the wrong name.'

Ideas of hurry and movement were just the ideas to take his fancy, in his present state. He blew furiously on the whistle that summoned Ariel from the kitchen regions, and danced up and down on his hands in the full frenzy of his delight.

'Ariel shall get you a cab!' he cried. 'Drive at a gallop to the Major's. Set the trap for her without losing a moment. Oh, what a day of days this has been! Oh, what a relief to get rid of my dreadful secret, and share it with You! I am suffocating with happiness – I am like the Spirit of the Earth in Shelley's poem.' He broke out with the magnificent lines in 'Prometheus Unbound,' in which the Earth feels the Spirit of Love, and bursts into speech. '"The joy, the triumph, the delight, the madness! The boundless, overflowing, bursting gladness, The vaporous exultation not to be confined! Ha! ha! the animation of delight, Which wraps me like an atmosphere of light, And bears me as a cloud is borne by its own wind."[3] That's how I feel, Valeria! that's how I feel!'

I crossed the threshold while he was still speaking. The last I saw of him, he was pouring out that glorious flood of words – his deformed body, poised on the overthrown chair, his face lifted in rapture to some fantastic Heaven of his own making. I slipped out softly into the antechamber. Even as I crossed the room, he changed once more. I heard his ringing cry; I heard the soft thump-thump of his hands on the floor. He was going down the room again, in 'Dexter's Leapfrog,' flying over the prostrate chairs!

In the hall, Ariel was on the watch for me.

As I approached her, I happened to be putting on my gloves. She stopped me; and taking my right arm, lifted my hand towards her face. Was she going to kiss it? or to bite it? Neither. She smelt it like a dog – and dropped it again with a hoarse chuckling laugh.

'You don't smell of his perfumes,' she said. 'You *haven't* touched his beard. *Now* I believe you. Want a cab?'

'Thank you. I'll walk till I meet a cab.'

She was bent on being polite to me – now I had *not* touched his beard.

'I say!' she burst out, in her deepest notes.

'Yes?'

'I'm glad I didn't upset you in the canal. There now!'

She gave me a friendly smack on the shoulder which nearly knocked me down – relapsed, the instant after, into her leaden stolidity of look and manner – and led the way out by the front door. I heard her hoarse chuckling laugh as she locked the gate behind me. My star was at last in the ascendant! In one and the same day, I had found my way into the confidence of Ariel, and Ariel's Master!

CHAPTER XXXI

The Defence of Mrs Beauly

The days that elapsed before Major Fitz-David's dinner-party were precious days to me.

My long interview with Miserrimus Dexter had disturbed me far more seriously than I suspected at the time. It was not until some hours after I had left him, that I really began to feel how my nerves had been tried by all that I had seen and heard, during my visit at his house. I started at the slightest noises; I dreamed of dreadful things; I was ready to cry without reason, at one moment, and to fly into a passion without reason, at another. Absolute rest was what I wanted, and (thanks to my good Benjamin) was what I got. The dear old man controlled his anxieties on my account, and spared me the questions which his fatherly interest in my welfare made him eager to ask. It was tacitly understood between us that all conversation on the subject of my visit to Miserrimus Dexter (of which, it is needless to say, he strongly disapproved), should be deferred until repose had restored my energies of body and mind. I saw no visitors. Mrs Macallan came to the cottage, and Major Fitz-David came to the cottage – one of them to hear what had passed between Miserrimus Dexter and myself: the other to amuse me with the latest gossip about the guests at the forthcoming dinner. Benjamin took it on himself to make my apologies, and to spare me the exertion of receiving my visitors. We hired a little open carriage, and took long drives in the pretty country lanes, still left flourishing within a few miles of the northern suburb of London. At home, we sat and talked quietly of old times, or played at back-gammon and dominoes – and so, for a few happy days, led the peaceful, unadventurous life which was good for me. When the day of the dinner arrived, I felt restored to my customary health. I was ready again, and eager again, for the introduction to Lady Clarinda, and the discovery of Mrs Beauly.

Benjamin looked a little sadly at my flushed face, as we drove to Major Fitz-David's house.

'Ah, my dear,' he said, in his simple way, 'I see you are well again! You have had enough of our quiet life already.'

My recollection of events and persons, in general, at the dinner-party, is singularly indistinct. I remember that we were very merry, and as easy and familiar with one another as if we had been old friends. I remember that Madame Mirliflore was unapproachably superior to the other women present, in the perfect beauty of her dress, and in the ample justice which she did to the luxurious dinner set before us. I remember the Major's young prima-donna, more round-eyed, more over-dressed, more shrill and strident as the coming 'Queen of Song,' than ever. I remember the Major himself, always kissing our hands, always luring us to indulge in dainty dishes and drinks, always making love, always detecting resemblances between us, always 'under the charm,' and never once out of his character as elderly Don Juan, from the beginning of the evening to the end. I remember dear old Benjamin completely bewildered, shrinking into corners, blushing when he was personally drawn into the conversation, frightened at Madame Mirliflore, bashful with Lady Clarinda, submissive to the Major, suffering under the music, and, from the bottom of his honest old heart, wishing himself home again. And there, as to the members of that cheerful little gathering, my memory finds its limits – with one exception. The appearance of Lady Clarinda is as present to me as if I had met her yesterday; and of the memorable conversation which we two held together privately, towards the close of the evening, it is no exaggeration to say that I can still call to mind almost every word.

I see her dress, I hear her voice again, while I write.

She was attired, I remember, with that extreme assumption of simplicity which always defeats its own end, by irresistibly suggesting art. She wore plain white muslin, over white silk, without trimming or ornament of any kind. Her rich brown hair, dressed in defiance of the prevailing fashion, was thrown back from her forehead, and gathered into a simple knot behind, without adornment of any sort. A little white ribbon encircled her neck, fastened by the only article of jewellery that she wore – a tiny diamond brooch. She was unquestionably handsome; but her beauty was of the somewhat hard and angular type which is so often seen in English women of her race: the nose and chin too prominent and too firmly shaped; the well-opened grey eyes full of spirit and dignity, but wanting in tenderness and mobility of expression. Her manner had all the charm which fine breeding can confer – exquisitely polite, easily cordial; showing that perfect yet unobtrusive confidence in herself, which (in England) seems to be the natural outgrowth of pre-eminent social rank. If you had accepted her for what she was, on the surface, you would have said, Here is the model of a noble woman who is perfectly free from pride. And if you had taken a liberty with her, on the strength of that conviction, she would have made you remember it to the end of your life.

We got on together admirably. I was introduced as 'Mrs Woodville,' by previous arrangement with the Major, effected through Benjamin. Before the dinner was over, we had promised to exchange visits. Nothing but the opportunity was wanting to lead Lady Clarinda into talking, as I wanted her to talk, of Mrs Beauly.

Late in the evening, the opportunity came.

I had taken refuge from the terrible bravura singing of the Major's strident prima-donna, in the back drawing-room. As I had hoped and anticipated, after a while, Lady Clarinda (missing me from the group around the piano) came in search of me. She seated herself by my side, out of sight and out of hearing of our friends in the front room; and, to my infinite relief and delight, touched on the subject of Miserrimus Dexter, of her own accord. Something I had said of him, when his name had been accidentally mentioned at dinner, remained in her memory, and led us, by perfectly natural gradations, into speaking of Mrs Beauly. 'At last,' I thought to myself, 'the Major's little dinner will bring me my reward!'

And what a reward it was, when it came! My heart sinks in me again – as it sank on that never-to-be-forgotten evening – while I sit at my desk, thinking of it.

'So Dexter really spoke to you of Mrs Beauly!' exclaimed Lady Clarinda. 'You have no idea how you surprise me.'

'May I ask why?'

'He hates her! The last time I saw him, he wouldn't allow me to mention her name. It is one of his innumerable oddities. If any such feeling as sympathy is a possible feeling in such a nature as his, he ought to like Helena Beauly. She is the most completely unconventional person I know. When she does break out, poor dear, she says things and does things, which are almost reckless enough to be worthy of Dexter himself. I wonder whether you would like her?'

'You have kindly asked me to visit you, Lady Clarinda. Perhaps I may meet her at your house?'

Lady Clarinda laughed as if the idea amused her.

'I hope you will not wait until *that* is likely to happen,' she said. 'Helena's last whim is to fancy that she has got – the gout, of all the maladies in the world! She is away at some wonderful baths in Hungary, or Bohemia (I don't remember which) – and where she will go, or what she will do, next, it is perfectly impossible to say. Dear Mrs Woodville! is the heat of the fire too much for you? You are looking quite pale.'

I *felt* that I was looking pale. The discovery of Mrs Beauly's absence from England was a shock for which I was quite unprepared. For the moment, it unnerved me.

'Shall we go into the other room?' asked Lady Clarinda.

To go into the other room would be to drop the conversation. I was determined not to let that catastrophe happen. It was just possible that Mrs Beauly's maid might have quitted her service, or might have been left behind in England. My information would not be complete, until I knew what had become of the maid. I pushed my chair back a little from the fire-place, and took a hand-screen from a table near me. It might be made useful in hiding my face, if any more disappointments were in store for me.

'Thank you, Lady Clarinda: I was only a little too near the fire. I shall do admirably here. You surprise me about Mrs Beauly. From what Mr Dexter said to me, I had imagined—'

'Oh, you must not believe anything Dexter tells you!' interposed Lady Clarinda. 'He delights in mystifying people; and he purposely misled you, I have no doubt. If all that I hear is true, *he* ought to know more of Helena Beauly's strange freaks and fancies than most people. He all but discovered her, in one of her adventures (down in Scotland), which reminds me of the story in Auber's charming opera – what is it called? I shall forget my own name next! I mean the opera in which the two nuns slip out of the convent, and go to the ball. Listen! how very odd! That vulgar girl is singing the castanet song in the second act, at this moment. Major! What opera is the young lady singing from?'

The Major was scandalised at the interruption. He bustled into the back room – whispered 'Hush! hush! my dear lady. The *Domino Noir*[1] – and bustled back again to the piano.

'Of course!' said Lady Clarinda. 'How stupid of me! The *Domino Noir*. And how strange that you should forget it too!'

I had remembered it perfectly; but I could not trust myself to speak. If, as I believed, the 'adventure' mentioned by Lady Clarinda was connected, in some way, with Mrs Beauly's mysterious proceedings on the morning of the twenty-first of October, I was on the brink of the very discovery which it was the one interest of my life to make! I held the screen so as to hide my face; and I said in the steadiest voice that I could command at the moment,

'Pray go on! Pray tell me what the adventure was!'

Lady Clarinda was quite flattered by my eager desire to hear the coming narrative.

'I hope my story will be worthy of the interest which you are so good as to feel in it,' she said. 'If you only knew Helena – it is *so* like her! I have it, you must know, from her maid. She has taken a woman who speaks foreign languages with her to Hungary, and she has left the maid with me. A perfect treasure! I should only be too glad if I

could keep her in my service: she has but one defect, a name I hate
– Phœbe.[2] Well! Phœbe and her mistress were staying at a place near
Edinburgh, called (I think) Gleninch. The house belonged to that Mr
Macallan, who was afterwards tried – you remember it, of course? –
for poisoning his wife. A dreadful case; but don't be alarmed – my
story has nothing to do with it; my story has to do with Helena Beauly.
One evening (while she was staying at Gleninch) she was engaged to
dine with some English friends visiting Edinburgh. The same night –
also in Edinburgh – there was a masked ball, given by somebody
whose name I forget. The ball (almost an unparalleled event in
Scotland!) was reported to be not at all a reputable affair. All sorts of
amusing people were to be there. Ladies of doubtful virtue, you know;
and gentlemen on the outlying limits of society, and so on. Helena's
friends had contrived to get cards, and were going, in spite of the
objections – in the strictest incognito, of course; trusting to their masks.
And Helena herself was bent on going with them, if she could only
manage it without being discovered at Gleninch. Mr Macallan was
one of the strait-laced people who disapproved of the ball. No lady,
he said, could show herself at such an entertainment, without com-
promising her reputation. What stuff! Well, Helena, in one of her
wildest moments, hit on a way of going to the ball without discovery,
which was really as ingenious as a plot in a French play. She went to
the dinner in the carriage from Gleninch, having sent Phœbe to
Edinburgh before her. It was not a grand dinner – a little friendly
gathering; no evening dress. When the time came for going back to
Gleninch, what do you think Helena did? She sent her maid back in
the carriage, instead of herself! Phœbe was dressed in her mistress's
cloak and bonnet and veil. She was instructed to run upstairs the
moment she got to the house; leaving on the hall-table a little note of
apology (written by Helena of course!) pleading fatigue as an excuse
for not saying good night to her host. The mistress and the maid were
about the same height; and the servants naturally never discovered
the trick. Phœbe got up to her mistress's room, safely enough. There,
her instructions were to wait until the house was quiet for the night,
and then to steal up to her own room. While she was waiting, the girl
fell asleep. She only woke at two in the morning, or later. It didn't

much matter, as she thought. She stole out on tip-toe, and closed the door behind her. Before she was at the end of the corridor, she fancied she heard something. She waited till she was safe on the upper storey, and then she looked over the banisters. There was Dexter – so like him! – hopping about on his hands (did you ever see it? the most grotesquely-horrible exhibition you can imagine!) – there was Dexter, hopping about, and looking through keyholes – evidently in search of the person who had left her room at two in the morning; and no doubt taking Phœbe for her mistress, seeing that she had forgotten to take her mistress's cloak off her shoulders. The next morning early, Helena came back in a hired carriage from Edinburgh, with a hat and mantle borrowed from her English friends. She left the carriage in the road; and got into the house by way of the garden – without being discovered, this time, by Dexter, or by anybody. Clever and daring, wasn't it? And, as I said just now, quite a new version of the *Domino Noir*. You will wonder, as I did, how it was that Dexter didn't make mischief in the morning? He would have done it no doubt. But even *he* was silenced (as Phœbe told me) by the dreadful event that happened in the house on the same day.—My dear Mrs Woodville! the heat of this room is certainly too much for you. Take my smelling-bottle. Let me open the window.'

I was just able to answer, 'Pray say nothing! Let me slip out into the air!'

I made my way unobserved to the landing, and sat down on the stairs to compose myself, where nobody could see me. In a moment more, I felt a hand laid gently on my shoulder, and discovered good Benjamin looking at me in dismay. Lady Clarinda had considerately spoken to him, and had assisted him in quietly making his retreat from the room, while his host's attention was still absorbed by the music.

'My dear child!' he whispered, 'what is the matter?'

'Take me home, and I will tell you,' was all that I could say.

CHAPTER XXXII

A Specimen of My Wisdom

The scene must follow my erratic movements – the scene must close on London for a while, and open in Edinburgh.

Two days had passed since Major Fitz-David's dinner-party. I was able to breathe again freely, after the utter destruction of all my plans for the future, and of all the hopes that I had founded on them. I could now see that I had been trebly in the wrong – wrong in hastily and cruelly suspecting an innocent woman; wrong in communicating my suspicions (without an attempt to verify them previously) to another person; wrong in accepting the flighty inferences and conclusions of Miserrimus Dexter as if they had been solid truths. I was so ashamed of my folly, when I thought of the past; so completely discouraged, so rudely shaken in my confidence in myself, when I thought of the future, that, for once in a way, I accepted sensible advice when it was offered to me. 'My dear,' said good old Benjamin, after we had thoroughly talked over my discomfiture on our return from the dinner-party, 'judging by what you tell me of him, I don't fancy Mr Dexter. Promise me that you will not go back to him, until you have first consulted some person who is fitter to guide you through this dangerous business than I am.'

I gave him my promise, on one condition. 'If I fail to find the person,' I said, 'will you undertake to help me?'

Benjamin pledged himself to help me, cheerfully.

The next morning, when I was brushing my hair, and thinking over my affairs, I called to mind a forgotten resolution of mine, at the time when I first read the Report of my husband's Trial. I mean the resolution – if Miserrimus Dexter failed me – to apply to one of the two agents (or solicitors, as we should term them) who had prepared Eustace's defence, namely, Mr Playmore. This gentleman, it may be remembered, had especially recommended himself to my confidence by his friendly interference, when the sheriff's officers were in search of my husband's papers. Referring back to the evidence of 'Isaiah

Schoolcraft,' I found that Mr Playmore had been called in to assist and advise Eustace, by Miserrimus Dexter. He was therefore not only a friend on whom I might rely, but a friend who was personally acquainted with Dexter as well. Could there be a fitter man to apply to for enlightenment in the darkness that had now gathered round me? Benjamin, when I put the question to him, acknowledged that I had made a sensible choice on this occasion, and at once exerted himself to help me. He discovered (through his own lawyer) the address of Mr Playmore's London agents; and from these gentlemen he obtained for me a letter of introduction to Mr Playmore himself. I had nothing to conceal from my new adviser; and I was properly described in the letter as Eustace Macallan's second wife.

The same evening, we two set forth (Benjamin refused to let me travel alone) by the night mail for Edinburgh.

I had previously written to Miserrimus Dexter (by my old friend's advice), merely saying that I had been unexpectedly called away from London for a few days, and that I would report to him the result of my interview with Lady Clarinda on my return. A characteristic answer was brought back to the cottage by Ariel. 'Mrs Valeria, I happen to be a man of quick perceptions; and I can read the *unwritten* part of your letter. Lady Clarinda has shaken your confidence in me. Very good. I pledge myself to shake your confidence in Lady Clarinda. In the meantime, I am not offended. In serene composure I wait the honour and the happiness of your visit. Send me word by telegraph, whether you would like Truffles again, or whether you would prefer something simpler and lighter – say that incomparable French dish, Pig's Eyelids and Tamarinds. Believe me always your ally and admirer, your poet and cook – DEXTER.'

Arrived in Edinburgh, Benjamin and I had a little discussion. The question in dispute between us was, whether I should go with him, or go alone, to Mr Playmore. I was all for going alone.

'My experience of the world is not a very large one,' I said. 'But I have observed that, in nine cases out of ten, a man will make concessions to a woman, if she approaches him by herself, which he would hesitate even to consider, if another man was within hearing. I don't know how it is – I only know that it is so. If I find that I get on badly with

Mr Playmore, I will ask him for a second appointment, and, in that case, you shall accompany me. Don't think me self-willed. Let me try my luck alone, and let us see what comes of it.'

Benjamin yielded, with his customary consideration for me. I sent my letter of introduction to Mr Playmore's office – his private house being in the neighbourhood of Gleninch. My messenger brought back a polite answer, inviting me to visit him at an early hour in the afternoon. At the appointed time to the moment, I rang the bell at the office door.

CHAPTER XXXIII

A Specimen of My Folly

The incomprehensible submission of Scotchmen to the ecclesiastical tyranny of their Established Church, has produced – not unnaturally as I think – a very mistaken impression of the national character in the popular mind.

Public opinion looks at the institution of 'The Sabbath' in Scotland; finds it unparalleled in Christendom for its senseless and savage austerity; sees a nation content to be deprived by its priesthood of every social privilege on one day in every week – forbidden to travel; forbidden to telegraph; forbidden to eat a hot dinner; forbidden to read a newspaper; in short, allowed the use of two liberties only, the liberty of exhibiting oneself at the Church and the liberty of secluding oneself over the bottle – public opinion sees this, and arrives at the not unreasonable conclusion that the people who submit to such social laws as these are the most stolid, stern, and joyless people on the face of the earth. Such are Scotchmen supposed to be, when viewed at a distance. But how do Scotchmen appear when they are seen under a closer light, and judged by the test of personal experience? There are no people more cheerful, more companionable, more hospitable, more liberal in their ideas, to be found on the face of the civilised globe than the very people who submit to the Scotch Sunday! On the six days of the week, there is an atmosphere of quiet humour, a radiation of genial common sense, about Scotchmen in general, which is simply delightful to feel. But on the seventh day, these same men will hear one of their ministers seriously tell them that he views taking a walk on the Sabbath in the light of an act of profanity, and will be the only people in existence who can let a man talk downright nonsense without laughing at him.

I am not clever enough to be able to account for this anomaly in the national character; I can only notice it by way of necessary preparation for the appearance in my little narrative of a personage not frequently seen, in writing – a cheerful Scotchman.

In all other respects I found Mr Playmore only negatively remarkable. He was neither old nor young, neither handsome nor ugly; he was personally not in the least like the popular idea of a lawyer; and he spoke perfectly good English, touched with only the slightest possible flavour of a Scotch accent.

'I have the honour to be an old friend of Mr Macallan,' he said, cordially shaking hands with me; 'and I am honestly happy to become acquainted with Mr Macallan's wife. Where will you sit? Near the light? You are young enough not to be afraid of the daylight, just yet. Is this your first visit to Edinburgh? Pray let me make it as pleasant to you as I can. I shall be delighted to present Mrs Playmore to you. We are staying in Edinburgh for a little while. The Italian opera is here; and we have a box for to-night. Will you kindly waive all ceremony, and dine with us and go to the music afterwards?'

'You are very kind,' I answered. 'But I have some anxieties just now which will make me a very poor companion for Mrs Playmore at the opera. My letter to you mentions, I think, that I have to ask your advice on matters which are of very serious importance to me.'

'Does it?' he rejoined. 'To tell you the truth I have not read the letter through. I observed your name in it, and I gathered from your message that you wished to see me here. I sent my note to your hotel – and then went on with something else. Pray pardon me. Is this a professional consultation? For your own sake, I sincerely hope not.'

'It is hardly a professional consultation, Mr Playmore. I find myself in a very painful position; and I come to you to advise me, under very unusual circumstances. I shall greatly surprise you when you hear what I have to say; and I am afraid I shall occupy more than my fair share of your time.'

'I, and my time, are entirely at your disposal,' he said. 'Tell me what I can do for you – and tell it in your own way.'

The kindness of his language was more than matched by the kindness of his manner. I spoke to him freely and fully – I told him my strange story, exaggerating nothing, and suppressing nothing.

He showed the varying impressions that I produced on his mind, without the slightest concealment. My separation from Eustace distressed him. My resolution to dispute the Scotch Verdict, and my unjust suspicions of Mrs Beauly, first amused, then surprised him. It was not, however, until I had described my extraordinary interview with Miserrimus Dexter, and my hardly less remarkable conversation with Lady Clarinda, that I produced the greatest effect on the lawyer's mind. I saw him change colour for the first time. He started, and muttered to himself, as if he had completely forgotten me. 'Good God!' I heard him say – 'Can it be possible? Does the truth lie *that* way, after all?'

I took the liberty of interrupting him. I had no idea of allowing him to keep his thoughts to himself.

'I seem to have surprised you?' I said.

He started at the sound of my voice.

'I beg ten thousand pardons!' he exclaimed. 'You have not only surprised me, you have opened an entirely new view to my mind. I see a possibility, a really startling possibility, in connection with the poisoning at Gleninch, which never occurred to me until the present moment. This is a nice state of things,' he added, falling back again into his ordinary humour. 'Here is the client leading the lawyer. My dear Mrs Eustace, which is it – do you want my advice? or do I want yours?'

'May I hear the new idea?' I asked.

'Not just yet, if you will excuse me,' he answered. 'Make allowances for my professional caution. I don't want to be professional with You – my great anxiety is to avoid it. But the lawyer gets the better of the man, and refuses to be suppressed. I really hesitate to realise what is passing in my own mind, without some further enquiry. Do me a great favour. Let us go over a part of the ground again, and let me ask you some questions as we proceed. Do you feel any objection to obliging me in this matter?'

'Certainly not, Mr Playmore. How far shall we go back?'

'To your visit to Dexter, with your mother-in-law. When you first asked him if he had any ideas of his own, on the subject of Mrs Macallan's death, did I understand you to say that he looked at you suspiciously?'

'Very suspiciously.'

'And his face cleared up again, when you told him that your question was only suggested by what you had read in the Report of the Trial?'

'Yes.'

He drew a slip of paper out of the drawer in his desk, dipped his pen in the ink, considered a little, and placed a chair for me close at his side.

'The lawyer disappears,' he said, 'and the man resumes his proper place. There shall be no professional mysteries between you and me. As your husband's old friend, Mrs Eustace, I feel no common interest in you. I see a serious necessity for warning you before it is too late; and I can only do so to any good purpose, by running a risk on which few men in my place would venture. Personally and professionally, I am going to trust you – though I *am* a Scotchman and a lawyer! Sit here, and look over my shoulder while I make my notes. You will see what is passing in my mind, if you see what I write.'

I sat down by him and looked over his shoulder, without the smallest pretence of hesitation.

He began to write as follows: –

'The poisoning at Gleninch. Queries: In what position does Miserrimus Dexter stand towards the poisoning? And what does he (presumably) know about that matter?

'He has ideas which are secrets. He suspects that he has betrayed them, or that they have been discovered in some way, inconceivable to himself. He is palpably relieved when he finds that this is not the case.'

The pen stopped; and the questions went on.

'Let us advance to your second visit,' said Mr Playmore, 'when you saw Dexter alone. Tell me again what he did, and how he looked, when you informed him that you were not satisfied with the Scotch Verdict.'

I repeated what I have already written. The pen went back to the paper again, and added these lines: –

'He hears nothing more remarkable than that a person visiting him, who is interested in the case, refuses to accept the verdict at the Macallan Trial, as a final verdict, and proposes to re-open the enquiry. What does he do upon that?

'He exhibits all the symptoms of a panic of terror; he sees himself in some incomprehensible danger; he is frantic at one moment, and servile at the next; he must and will know what this disturbing person really means. And when he is informed on that point, he first turns pale and doubts the evidence of his own senses; and next, with nothing said to justify it, gratuitously accuses his visitor of suspecting somebody. Query, here: When a small sum of money is missing in a household, and the servants in general are called together to be informed of the circumstance, what do we think of the one servant, in particular, who speaks first, and who says, "Do you suspect *me*?"'

He laid down the pen again.

'Is that right?' he asked.

I began to see the end to which the notes were drifting. Instead of answering his question, I entreated him to enter into the explanations that were still wanting to convince my own mind. He held up a warning forefinger, and stopped me.

'Not yet,' he said. 'Once again, am I right – so far?'

'Quite right.'

'Very well. Now tell me what Dexter did next. Don't mind repeating yourself. Give me all the details, one after another, to the end.'

I gave him all the details, exactly as I remembered them. Mr Playmore returned to his writing for the third and last time. Thus the notes ended: –

'He is indirectly assured that *he* at least is not the person suspected. He sinks back in his chair; he draws a long breath; he asks to be left awhile by himself, under the pretence that the subject excites him. When the visitor returns, Dexter has been drinking in the interval. The visitor resumes the subject – not Dexter. The visitor is convinced that Mrs Eustace Macallan died by the hand of a poisoner, and openly says so. Dexter sinks back in his chair like a man fainting. What is the horror that has got possession of him? It is easy to understand, if we call it guilty horror. It is beyond all understanding if we call it anything else. And how does it leave him? He flies from one extreme to another; he is indescribably delighted when he discovers that the visitor's suspicions are all fixed on an absent person. And then, and then only, he takes refuge in the declaration that he has been of one mind with his guest, in the matter of suspicion, from the first! These are facts. To what plain conclusion do they point?'

He shut up his notes, and, steadily watching my face, waited for me to speak first.

'I understand you, Mr Playmore,' I began, impetuously. 'You believe that Mr Dexter—'

His warning forefinger stopped me there.

'Tell me,' he interposed, 'what Dexter said to you when he was so good as to confirm your opinion of poor Mrs Beauly?'

'He said, "There isn't a doubt about it. Mrs Beauly poisoned her."'

'I can't do better than follow so good an example – with one trifling difference. I say too, There isn't a doubt about it! Dexter poisoned her.'

'Are you joking, Mr Playmore?'

'I never was more in earnest in my life. Your rash visit to Dexter, and your extraordinary imprudence in taking him into your confidence, have led to astonishing results. The light which the whole machinery of the Law was unable to throw on the poisoning case at Gleninch, has been accidentally let in on it, by a Lady who refuses to listen to reason and who insists on having her own way. Quite incredible, and nevertheless quite true!'

'Impossible!' I exclaimed.

'What is impossible?' he asked, coolly.

'That Dexter poisoned my husband's first wife.'

'And why is that impossible, if you please?'

I began to be almost enraged with Mr Playmore.

'Can you ask the question?' I replied, indignantly. 'I have told you that I heard him speak of her, in terms of respect and affection of which any woman might be proud. He lives in the memory of her. I owe his friendly reception of me to some resemblance which he fancies he sees between my figure and hers. I have seen tears in his eyes, I have heard his voice falter and fail him, when he spoke of her. He may be the falsest of men in all besides; but he is true to *her* – he has not misled me in that one thing. There are signs that never deceive a woman, when a man is talking to her of what is really near his heart. I saw those signs. It is as true that I poisoned her, as that he did. I am ashamed to set my opinion against yours, Mr Playmore; but I really cannot help it. I declare I am almost angry with you!'

He seemed to be pleased, instead of offended, by the bold manner in which I expressed myself.

'My dear Mrs Eustace, you have no reason to be angry with me! In one respect, I entirely share your view – with this difference, that I go a little further than you do.'

'I don't understand you.'

'You will understand me directly. You describe Dexter's feeling for the late Mrs Eustace, as a happy mixture of respect and affection. I can tell you, it was a much warmer feeling towards her than that. I have my information from the poor lady herself – who honoured me with her confidence and friendship for the best part of her life. Before she married Mr Macallan – she kept it a secret from him, and you had better keep it a secret too – Miserrimus Dexter was in love with her. Miserrimus Dexter asked her – deformed as he was, seriously asked her – to be his wife.'

'And in the face of that,' I cried, 'you say that he poisoned her!'

'I do. I see no other conclusion possible, after what happened during your visit to him. You all but frightened him into a fainting-fit. What was he afraid of?'

I tried hard to find an answer to that. I even embarked on an answer, without quite knowing where my own words might lead me.

'Mr Dexter is an old and true friend of my husband's,' I began.

'When he heard me say I was not satisfied with the Verdict, he might have felt alarmed—'

'He might have felt alarmed at the possible consequences to your husband of re-opening the enquiry,' said Mr Playmore, ironically finishing the sentence for me. 'Rather far-fetched, Mrs Eustace! and not very consistent with your faith in your husband's innocence! Clear your mind of one mistake,' he continued, seriously, 'which may fatally mislead you, if you persist in pursuing your present course. Miserrimus Dexter, you may take my word for it, ceased to be your husband's friend on the day when your husband married his first wife. Dexter has kept up appearances, I grant you – both in public and in private. His evidence in his friend's favour at the Trial, was given with the deep feeling which everybody expected from him. Nevertheless I firmly believe, looking under the surface, that Mr Macallan has no bitterer enemy living than Miserrimus Dexter.'

He turned me cold. I felt that here, at least, he was right. My husband had wooed and won the woman who had refused Dexter's offer of marriage. Was Dexter the man to forgive that? My own experience answered me – and said, No.

'Bear in mind what I have told you,' Mr Playmore proceeded. 'And now let us get on to your own position in this matter, and to the interests that you have at stake. Try to adopt my point of view for the moment; and let us enquire what chance we have of making any further advance towards a discovery of the truth. It is one thing to be morally convinced (as I am) that Miserrimus Dexter is the man who ought to have been tried for the murder at Gleninch; and it is another thing, at this distance of time, to lay our hands on the plain evidence which can alone justify anything like a public assertion of his guilt. There, as I see it, is the insuperable difficulty in the case. Unless I am completely mistaken, the question is now narrowed to this plain issue: The public assertion of your husband's innocence depends entirely on the public assertion of Dexter's guilt. How are you to arrive at that result? There is not a particle of evidence against him. You can only convict Dexter, on Dexter's own confession. Are you listening to me?'

I was listening, most unwillingly. If he was right, things had indeed come to that terrible pass. But I could not – with all my respect for his superior knowledge and experience – I could not persuade myself that he *was* right. And I owned it, with the humility which I really felt.

He smiled good-humouredly.

'At any rate,' he said, 'you will admit that Dexter has not freely opened his mind to you, thus far? He is still keeping something from your knowledge, which you are interested in discovering?'

'Yes. I admit that.'

'Very good. What applies to your view of the case, applies to mine. I say, he is keeping from you the confession of his guilt. You say, he is keeping from you information which may fasten the guilt on some other person. Let us start from that point. Confession, or information, how are you to get at what he is now withholding from you? What influence can you bring to bear on him, when you see him again?'

'Surely, I might persuade him?'

'Certainly. And if persuasion fails – what then? Do you think you can entrap him into speaking out? or terrify him into speaking out?'

'If you will look at your notes, Mr Playmore, you will see that I have already succeeded in terrifying him – though I am only a woman, and though I didn't mean to do it.'

'Very well answered! You mark the trick. What you have done once, you think you can do again. Well! as you are determined to try the experiment, it can do you no harm to know a little more of Dexter than you know now. Before you go back to London, suppose we apply for information to somebody who can help us?'

I started, and looked round the room. He made me do it: he spoke as if the person who was to help us was close at our elbows.

'Don't be alarmed,' he said. 'The oracle is silent; and the oracle is here.'

He unlocked one of the drawers of his desk; produced a bundle of letters; and picked out one.

'When we were arranging your husband's defence,' he said, 'we felt some difficulty about including Miserrimus Dexter among our witnesses. We had not the slightest suspicion of him – I need hardly tell you. But we were all afraid of his eccentricity; and some among us even feared that the excitement of appearing at the Trial might drive him completely out of his mind. In this emergency we applied to a doctor to help us. Under some pretext which I forget now, we introduced him to Dexter. And in due course of time we received his report. Here it is.'

He opened the letter; and, marking a certain passage in it with a pencil, handed it to me.

'Read the lines which I have marked,' he said; 'they will be quite sufficient for our purpose.'

I read these words: –

'Summing up the results of my observation, I may give it as my opinion that there is undoubtedly latent insanity in this case; but that no active symptoms of madness have presented themselves as yet. You may, I think, produce him at the Trial, without fear of consequences. He may say and do all sorts of odd things; but he has his mind under the control of his will, and you may trust his self-esteem to exhibit him in the character of a substantially intelligent witness.

'As to the future, I am, of course, not able to speak positively. I can only state my views.

'That he will end in madness (if he lives), I entertain little or no doubt. The question of *when* the madness will show itself, depends entirely on the state of his health. His nervous system is highly sensitive; and there are signs that his way of life has already damaged it. If he conquers the bad habits to which I have alluded in an earlier part of my report, and if he passes many hours of every day quietly in the open air, he may last as a sane man for years to come. If he persists in his present way of life – or, in other words, if further mischief occurs to that sensitive nervous system – his lapse into insanity must infallibly take place when the mischief has reached its culminating point. Without warning to himself or to others, the whole mental structure will give way; and, at a moment's notice, while he is acting as quietly or speaking as intelligently as at his best time, the man will drop (if I may use the expression) into madness or idiocy. In either case, when the catastrophe has happened, it is only due to his friends to add, that they can (as I believe) entertain no hope of his cure. The balance once lost, will be lost for life.'

There it ended. Mr Playmore put the letter back in his drawer.

'You have just read the opinion of one of our highest living authorities,' he said. 'Does Dexter strike you as a likely man to give his nervous system a chance of recovery? Do you see no obstacles and no perils in your way?'

My silence answered him.

'Suppose you go back to Dexter,' he proceeded. 'And suppose that the doctor's opinion exaggerates the peril, in his case. What are you to do? The last time you saw him, you had the immense advantage of taking him by surprise. Those sensitive nerves of his gave way; and he betrayed the fear that you roused in him. Can you take him by surprise again? Not you! He is prepared for you now; and he will be on his guard. If you encounter nothing worse, you will have his cunning to deal with, next. Are you his match at that? But for Lady Clarinda he would have hopelessly misled you on the subject of Mrs Beauly.'

There was no answering this, either. I was foolish enough to try to answer it, for all that.

'He told me the truth, so far as he knew it,' I rejoined. 'He really saw, what he said he saw, in the corridor at Gleninch.'

'He told you the truth,' returned Mr Playmore, 'because he was cunning enough to see that the truth would help him in irritating your suspicions. You don't really believe that he shared your suspicions?'

'Why not?' I said. 'He was as ignorant of what Mrs Beauly was really doing on that night, as I was – until I met Lady Clarinda. It remains to be seen, whether he will not be as much astonished as I was, when I tell him what Lady Clarinda told me.'

This smart reply produced an effect which I had not anticipated.

To my surprise, Mr Playmore abruptly dropped all further discussion on his side. He appeared to despair of convincing me, and he owned it indirectly in his next words.

'Will nothing that I can say to you,' he asked, 'induce you to think as I think in this matter?'

'I have not your ability, or your experience,' I answered. 'I am sorry to say, I can't think as you think.'

'And are you really determined to see Miserrimus Dexter again?'

'I have engaged myself to see him again.'

He waited a little, and thought over it.

'You have honoured me by asking for my advice,' he said. 'I earnestly advise you, Mrs Eustace, to break your engagement. I go even further than that. I *entreat* you not to see Dexter again.'

Just what my mother-in-law had said! just what Benjamin and Major Fitz-David had said! They were all against me. And still I held out. I wonder, when I look back at it, at my own obstinacy. I am almost ashamed to relate that I made Mr Playmore no reply. He waited, still looking at me. I felt irritated by that fixed look. I rose, and stood before him with my eyes on the floor.

He rose in his turn. He understood that the conference was over.

'Well! well!' he said, with a kind of sad good-humour, 'I suppose it is unreasonable of me to expect that a young woman like you should share any opinion with an old lawyer like me. Let me only remind you that our conversation must remain strictly confidential, for the present – and then let us change the subject. Is there anything that I can do for you? Are you alone in Edinburgh?'

'No. I am travelling with an old friend of mine, who has known me from childhood.'

'And do you stay here to-morrow?'

'I think so.'

'Will you do me one favour? Will you think over what has passed between us, and will you come back to me in the morning?'

'Willingly, Mr Playmore, if it is only to thank you again for your kindness.'

On that understanding we parted. He sighed – the cheerful man sighed – as he opened the door for me. Women are contradictory creatures. That sigh affected me more than all his arguments. I felt myself blush for my own headstrong resistance to him, as I took my leave and turned away into the street.

CHAPTER XXXIV

Gleninch

I found Benjamin at the hotel, poring over a cheap periodical; absorbed in guessing one of the weekly 'Enigmas' which the Editor presented to his readers. My old friend was a great admirer of these verbal 'puzzles,' and had won all sorts of cheap prizes by his ingenuity in arriving at the right solution of the problems submitted to him. On ordinary occasions, it was useless to attempt to attract his attention, while he was occupied with his favourite amusement. But his interest in hearing the result of my interview with the lawyer proved to be even keener than his interest in solving the problem before him. He shut up his journal the moment I entered the room, and asked, eagerly, 'What news, Valeria? What news?'

In telling him what had happened, I of course respected Mr Playmore's confidence in me. Not a word relating to the lawyer's horrible suspicion of Miserrimus Dexter passed my lips.

'Aha!' said Benjamin, complacently. 'So the lawyer thinks as I do. You will listen to Mr Playmore (won't you), though you wouldn't listen to me?'

'You must forgive me, my old friend,' I replied. 'I am afraid it has come to this – try as I may, I can listen to nobody who advises me. On our way here, I honestly meant to be guided by Mr Playmore – we should never have taken this long journey, if I had *not* honestly meant it. I have tried, tried hard, to be a teachable, reasonable woman. But there is something in me that won't be taught. I am afraid I shall go back to Dexter.'

Even Benjamin lost all patience with me, this time.

'What is bred in the bone,' he said, quoting the old proverb, 'will never come out of the flesh. In years gone by, you were the most obstinate child that ever made a mess in a nursery. Oh, dear me, we might as well have stayed in London!'

'No,' I replied, 'now we have travelled to Edinburgh, we will see something (interesting to *me* at any rate), which we should never have seen if we had not left London. My husband's country house is within a few miles of us, here. To-morrow we will go to Gleninch.'

'Where the poor lady was poisoned?' asked Benjamin, with a look of dismay. 'You mean that place?'

'Yes. I want to see the room in which she died; I want to go all over the house.'

Benjamin crossed his hands resignedly on his lap. 'I try to understand the new generation,' said the old man, sadly. 'But I can't manage it. The new generation beats me.'

I sat down to write to Mr Playmore about the visit to Gleninch. The house in which the tragedy had occurred that had blighted my husband's life, was, to my mind, the most interesting house on the habitable globe. The prospect of visiting Gleninch had, indeed (to tell the truth), strongly influenced my resolution to consult the Edinburgh lawyer. I sent my note to Mr Playmore by a messenger, and received the kindest reply in return. If I would wait until the afternoon, he would get the day's business done, and would take us to Gleninch in his own carriage.

Benjamin's obstinacy – in its own quiet way, and on certain occasions only – was quite a match for mine. He had privately determined, as one of the old generation, to have nothing to do with Gleninch. Not a word on the subject escaped him, until Mr Playmore's carriage was at the hotel door. At that appropriate moment, Benjamin remembered an old friend of his in Edinburgh. 'Will you please to excuse me, Valeria? My friend's name is Saunders – and he will take it unkindly of me, if I don't dine with him to-day.'

Apart from the associations that I connected with it, there was nothing to interest a traveller at Gleninch.

The country round was pretty and well cultivated, and nothing more. The park was, to an English eye, wild and badly kept. The house had been built within the last seventy or eighty years. Outside, it was as bare of all ornament as a factory, and as gloomily heavy in effect as a prison. Inside, the deadly dreariness, the close oppressive solitude, of a deserted dwelling wearied the eye and weighed on the mind, from the roof to the basement. The house had been shut up since the time of the Trial. A lonely old couple, man and wife, had the keys, and the charge of it. The man shook his head in silent and sorrowful disapproval of our intrusion, when Mr Playmore ordered him to open the doors and shutters, and let the light in on the dark, deserted place. Fires were burning in the library and the picture gallery, to preserve the treasures which they contained from the damp. It was not easy, at first, to look at the cheerful blaze, without fancying that the inhabitants of the house must surely come in and warm themselves! Ascending to the upper floor, I saw the rooms made familiar to me by the Report of the Trial. I entered the little study, with the old books on the shelves, and the key still missing from the locked door of communication with the bedchamber. I looked into the room in which the unhappy mistress of Gleninch had suffered and died. The bed was left in its place; the sofa on which the nurse had snatched her intervals of repose was at its foot: the Indian cabinet, in which the crumpled paper with the grains of arsenic had been found, still held its little collection of curiosities. I moved on its pivot the invalid table on which she had taken her meals, and written her poems, poor soul. The place was dreary and dreadful; the heavy air felt as if it was still burdened with its horrid load of misery and distrust. I was glad to get out (after a passing glance at the room which Eustace had occupied, in those days) into the Guests' Corridor. There was the bedroom, at the door of which Miserrimus Dexter had waited and watched! There was the oaken floor along which he had hopped, in his horrible way, following the footsteps of the servant disguised in her mistress's clothes! Go where I might, the ghosts of the dead and the absent went with me, step by step. Go where I might, the lonely horror of the house had its still and awful voice for Me: – '*I* keep the secret of the Poison! *I* hide the mystery of the death!'

The oppression of the place became unendurable. I longed for the pure sky, and the free air. My companion noticed and understood me.

'Come!' he said. 'We have had enough of the house. Let us look at the grounds.'

In the grey quiet of the evening, we roamed about the lonely gardens, and threaded our way through the rank, neglected shrubberies. Wandering here and wandering there, we drifted into the kitchen garden – with one little patch still sparely cultivated by the old man and his wife, and all the rest a wilderness of weeds. Beyond the far end of the garden, divided from it by a low paling of wood, there stretched a piece of waste ground, sheltered on three sides by trees. In one lost corner of the ground, an object, common enough elsewhere, attracted my attention here. The object was a dust-heap.[1] The great size of it, and the curious situation in which it was placed, roused a moment's languid curiosity in me. I stopped, and looked at the dust and ashes, at the broken crockery and the old iron. Here, there was a torn hat; and there, some fragments of rotten old boots; and, scattered round, a small attendant litter of waste paper and frowsy rags.

'What are you looking at?' asked Mr Playmore.

'At nothing more remarkable than the dust-heap,' I answered.

'In tidy England, I suppose you would have all that carted away, out of sight,' said the lawyer. 'We don't mind in Scotland, as long as the dust-heap is far enough away not to be smelt at the house. Besides, some of it, sifted, comes in usefully as manure for the garden. Here, the place is deserted, and the rubbish in consequence has not been disturbed. Everything at Gleninch, Mrs Eustace (the big dust-heap included), is waiting for the new mistress to set it to rights. One of these days, you may be queen here – who knows?'

'I have done with Gleninch, Mr Playmore, when I leave it to-day!'

'Don't be too sure of that,' returned my companion. 'Time has its surprises in store for all of us.'

We turned away, and walked back in silence to the park gate, at which the carriage was waiting.

On the return to Edinburgh, Mr Playmore directed the conversation to topics entirely unconnected with my visit to Gleninch. He saw that my mind stood in need of relief; and he most goodnaturedly, and successfully, exerted himself to amuse me. It was not until we were close to the city that he touched on the subject of my return to London.

'Have you decided yet on the day when you leave Edinburgh?' he asked.

'We leave Edinburgh,' I replied, 'by the train of to-morrow morning.'

'Do you still see no reason to alter the opinions which you expressed yesterday? Does your speedy departure mean that?'

'I am afraid it does, Mr Playmore. When I am an older woman, I may be a wiser woman. In the meantime, I can only trust to your indulgence if I still blindly blunder on, in my own way.'

He smiled pleasantly, and patted my hand – then changed on a sudden, and looked at me gravely and attentively, before he opened his lips again.

'This is my last opportunity of speaking to you before you go,' he said. 'May I speak freely?'

'As freely as you please, Mr Playmore! Whatever you may say to me, will only add to my grateful sense of your kindness.'

'I have very little to say, Mrs Eustace – and that little begins with a word of caution. You told me yesterday that, when you paid your last visit to Miserrimus Dexter, you went to him alone. Don't do that again. Take somebody with you.'

'Do you think I am in any danger, then?'

'Not in the ordinary sense of the word. I only think that a friend may be useful in keeping Dexter's audacity (he is one of the most impudent men living) within proper limits. Then, again, in case anything worth remembering and acting on *should* fall from him in his talk, a friend may be valuable as witness. In your place, I should have a witness with me who could take notes – but then I am a lawyer, and my business is to make a fuss about trifles. Let me only say – go with a companion, when you next visit Dexter; and be on your guard against yourself, when the talk turns on Mrs Beauly.'

'On my guard against myself? What do you mean?'

'Practice, my dear Mrs Eustace, has given me an eye for the little weaknesses of human nature. You are (quite naturally) disposed to be jealous of Mrs Beauly; and you are, in consequence, not in full possession of your excellent common sense, when Dexter uses that lady as a means of blindfolding you. Am I speaking too freely?'

'Certainly not! It is very degrading to me to be jealous of Mrs Beauly. My vanity suffers dreadfully when I think of it. But my common sense yields to conviction. I dare say you are right.'

'I am delighted to find that we agree on one point,' he rejoined, drily. 'I don't despair yet of convincing you, in that far more serious matter which is still in dispute between us. And, what is more, if you will throw no obstacles in the way, I look to Dexter himself to help me.'

This roused my curiosity. How Miserrimus Dexter could help him, in that or in any other way, was a riddle beyond my reading.

'You propose to repeat to Dexter all that Lady Clarinda told you about Mrs Beauly,' he went on. 'And you think it is likely that Dexter will be overwhelmed, as you were overwhelmed, when he hears the story. I am going to venture on a prophecy. I say that Dexter will disappoint you. Far from showing any astonishment, he will boldly tell you that you have been duped by a deliberately false statement of facts, invented and set afloat, in her own guilty interests, by Mrs Beauly. Now tell me – if he really tries, in that way, to renew your unfounded suspicion of an innocent woman, will *that* shake your confidence in your own opinion?'

'It will entirely destroy my confidence in my own opinion, Mr Playmore.'

'Very good. I shall expect you to write to me, in any case; and I believe we shall be of one mind, before the week is out. Keep strictly secret all that I said to you yesterday about Dexter. Don't even mention my name, when you see him. Thinking of him as I think now, I would as soon touch the hand of the hangman as the hand of that monster! God bless you. Good bye.'

So he said his farewell words, at the door of the hotel. Kind, genial, clever – but oh, how easily prejudiced, how shockingly obstinate in holding to his own opinion! And *what* an opinion! I shuddered as I thought of it.

CHAPTER XXXV

Mr Playmore's Prophecy

We reached London between eight and nine in the evening. Strictly methodical in all his habits, Benjamin had telegraphed to his housekeeper, from Edinburgh, to have supper ready for us by ten o'clock, and to send the cabman whom he always employed to meet us at the station.

Arriving at the villa, we were obliged to wait for a moment to let a pony-chaise get by us before we could draw up at Benjamin's door. The chaise passed very slowly, driven by a rough-looking man, with a pipe in his mouth. But for the man, I might have doubted whether the pony was quite a stranger to me. As things were, I thought no more of the matter.

Benjamin's respectable old housekeeper opened the garden gate, and startled me by bursting into a devout ejaculation of gratitude at the sight of her master. 'The Lord be praised, Sir!' she cried. 'I thought you would never come back!'

'Anything wrong?' asked Benjamin, in his own impenetrably quiet way.

The housekeeper trembled at the question, and answered in these enigmatical words: –

'My mind's upset, Sir; and whether things are wrong or whether things are right, is more than I can say. Hours ago, a strange man came in and asked' – she stopped as if she was completely bewildered – looked for a moment vacantly at her master – and suddenly addressed herself to me. 'And asked,' she proceeded, 'when *you* was expected back, ma'am. I told him what my master had telegraphed, and the man says upon that, "Wait a bit" (he says); "I'm coming back." He came back in a minute or less; and he carried a Thing in his arms which curdled my blood – it did! – and set me shaking from the crown of my head to the sole of my foot. I know I ought to have stopped it; but I couldn't stand upon my legs – much less put the man out of the house. In he went, without *with* your leave, or *by* your leave, Mr

Benjamin, Sir – in he went with the Thing in his arms, straight through to your library. And there It has been all these hours. And there It is now. I've spoken to the Police; but they wouldn't interfere – and what to do next, is more than my poor head can tell. Don't you go in by yourself, ma'am! You'll be frightened out of your wits – you will!'

I persisted in entering the house, for all that. Aided by the pony, I easily solved the mystery of the housekeeper's otherwise unintelligible narrative. Passing through the dining-room (where the supper table was already laid for us), I looked through the half-opened library door.

Yes; there was Miserrimus Dexter, arrayed in his pink jacket, fast asleep in Benjamin's favourite arm-chair! No coverlid hid his horrible deformity. Nothing was sacrificed to conventional ideas of propriety, in his extraordinary dress. I could hardly wonder that the poor old housekeeper trembled from head to foot when she spoke of him!

'Valeria!' said Benjamin, pointing to the Portent in the chair. 'Which is it – an Indian idol? or a man?'

I have already described Miserrimus Dexter as possessing the sensitive ear of a dog. He now showed that he also slept the light sleep of a dog. Quietly as Benjamin had spoken, the strange voice roused him on the instant. He rubbed his eyes, and smiled as innocently as a waking child.

'How do you do, Mrs Valeria?' he said. 'I have had a nice little sleep. You don't know how happy I am to see you again. Who is this?'

He rubbed his eyes once more, and looked at Benjamin. Not knowing what else to do in this extraordinary emergency, I presented my visitor to the master of the house.

'Excuse my getting up, Sir,' said Miserrimus Dexter. 'I can't get up – I have got no legs. You look as if you thought I was occupying your chair? If I am committing an intrusion, be so good as to put your umbrella under me, and give me a jerk. I shall fall on my hands, and I shan't be offended with you. I will submit to a tumble and a scolding – but please don't break my heart by sending me away. That beautiful woman, there, can be very cruel sometimes, Sir, when the fit takes her. She went away when I stood in the sorest need of a little talk with her – she went away, and left me to my loneliness and my suspense.

I am a poor deformed wretch, with a warm heart, and (perhaps) an insatiable curiosity as well. Insatiable curiosity (have you ever felt it?) is a curse. I bore it till my brains began to boil in my head; and then I sent for my gardener, and made him drive me here. I like being here. The air of your library soothes me; the sight of Mrs Valeria is balm to my wounded heart. She has something to tell me – something that I am dying to hear. If she is not too tired after her journey, and if you will let her tell it, I promise to have myself taken away when she has done. Dear Mr Benjamin, you look like the refuge of the afflicted. I am afflicted. Shake hands like a good Christian, and take me in.'

He held out his hand. His soft blue eyes melted into an expression of piteous entreaty. Completely stupefied by the amazing harangue of which he had been made the object, Benjamin took the offered hand, with the air of a man in a dream. 'I hope I see you well, Sir,' he said, mechanically – and then looked round at me to know what he was to do next.

'I understand Mr Dexter,' I whispered. 'Leave him to me.'

Benjamin stole a last bewildered look at the Object in the chair; bowed to it, with the instinct of politeness which never failed him; and (still with the air of a man in a dream) withdrew into the next room.

Left together, we looked at each other, for the first moment, in silence.

Whether I unconsciously drew on that inexhaustible store of indulgence which a woman always keeps in reserve for a man who owns that he has need of her – or whether, resenting as I did Mr Playmore's horrible suspicion of him, my heart was especially accessible to feelings of compassion, in his unhappy case – I cannot tell. I only know that I pitied Miserrimus Dexter, at that moment, as I had never pitied him yet; and that I spared him the reproof which I should certainly have administered to any other man, who had taken the liberty of establishing himself, uninvited, in Benjamin's house.

He was the first to speak.

'Lady Clarinda has destroyed your confidence in me!' he began, wildly.

'Lady Clarinda has done nothing of the sort,' I replied. 'She has not attempted to influence my opinion. I was really obliged to leave London, as I told you.'

He sighed, and closed his eyes contentedly, as if I had relieved him of a heavy weight of anxiety.

'Be merciful to me,' he said; 'and tell me something more. I have been so miserable in your absence.' He suddenly opened his eyes again, and looked at me with an appearance of the greatest interest. 'Are you very much fatigued by travelling?' he proceeded. 'I am hungry for news of what happened at the Major's dinner-party. Is it cruel of me to tell you so, when you have not rested after your journey? Only one question to-night! and I will leave the rest till to-morrow. What did Lady Clarinda say about Mrs Beauly? All that you wanted to hear?'

'All, and more,' I answered.

'What? what? what?' he cried, wild with impatience in a moment.

Mr Playmore's last prophetic words were vividly present to my mind. He had declared, in the most positive manner, that Dexter would persist in misleading me, and would show no signs of astonishment when I repeated what Lady Clarinda had told me of Mrs Beauly. I resolved to put the lawyer's prophecy – so far as the question of astonishment was concerned – to the sharpest attainable test. I said not a word to Miserrimus Dexter, in the way of preface or preparation; I burst on him with my news as abruptly as possible.

'The person you saw in the corridor was *not* Mrs Beauly,' I said. 'It was the maid, dressed in her mistress's cloak and hat. Mrs Beauly herself was not in the house at all. Mrs Beauly herself was dancing at a masked ball in Edinburgh. There is what the maid told Lady Clarinda; and there is what Lady Clarinda told *me*.'

In the absorbing interest of the moment, I poured out those words one after another as fast as they could pass my lips. Miserrimus Dexter completely falsified the lawyer's prediction. He shuddered under the shock. His eyes opened wide with amazement. 'Say it again!' he cried. 'I can't take it all in at once. You stun me.'

I was more than contented with this result – I triumphed in my victory. For once, I had really some reason to feel satisfied with myself.

I had taken the Christian and merciful side in my discussion with Mr Playmore; and I had won my reward. I could sit in the same room with Miserrimus Dexter, and feel the blessed conviction that I was not breathing the same air with a poisoner. Was it not worth the visit to Edinburgh to have made sure of that?

In repeating, at his own desire, what I had already said to him, I took care to add the details which made Lady Clarinda's narrative coherent and credible. He listened throughout with breathless attention – here and there repeating the words after me to impress them the more surely and the more deeply on his mind.

'What is to be said? what is to be done?' he asked, with a look of blank despair. 'I can't disbelieve it. From first to last, strange as it is, it sounds true.'

(How would Mr Playmore have felt, if he had heard those words? I did him the justice to believe that he would have felt heartily ashamed of himself!)

'There is nothing to be said,' I rejoined; 'except that Mrs Beauly is innocent, and that you and I have done her a grievous wrong. Don't you agree with me?'

'I entirely agree with you,' he answered, without an instant's hesitation. 'Mrs Beauly is an innocent woman. The defence at the Trial was the right defence after all.'

He folded his arms complacently; he looked perfectly satisfied to leave the matter there.

I was not of his mind. To my own amazement, I now found myself the least reasonable person of the two!

Miserrimus Dexter (to use the popular phrase) had given me more than I had bargained for. He had not only done all that I had anticipated, in the way of falsifying Mr Playmore's prediction – he had actually advanced beyond my limits. I could go the length of recognising Mrs Beauly's innocence; but at that point I stopped. If the Defence at the Trial was the right defence – farewell to all hope of asserting my husband's innocence! I held to that hope, as I held to my love and my life.

'Speak for yourself,' I said. 'My opinion of the Defence remains unchanged.'

He started and knit his brows as if I had disappointed and displeased him.

'Does that mean that you are determined to go on?'

'It does.'

He was downright angry with me. He cast his customary politeness to the winds.

'Absurd! Impossible!' he cried, contemptuously. 'You have yourself declared that we wronged an innocent woman, when we suspected Mrs Beauly. Is there anyone else whom we can suspect? It is ridiculous to ask the question! There is no alternative left but to accept the facts as they are, and to stir no further in the matter of the poisoning at Gleninch. It is childish to dispute plain conclusions. You *must* give up.'

'You may be angry with me, if you will, Mr Dexter. Neither your anger nor your arguments will make me give up.'

He controlled himself by an effort – he was quiet and polite again, when he next spoke to me.

'Very well. Pardon me for a moment, if I absorb myself in my own thoughts. I want to do something which I have not done yet.'

'What may that be, Mr Dexter?'

'I am going to put myself into Mrs Beauly's skin, and to think with Mrs Beauly's mind. Give me a minute. Thank you.'

What did he mean? What new transformation of him was passing before my eyes? Was there ever such a puzzle of a man as this? Who that saw him now, intently pursuing his new train of thought, would have recognised him as the childish creature who had woke up so innocently, and who had amazed Benjamin by the infantine nonsense which he talked? It is said, and said truly, that there are many sides to every human character. Dexter's many sides were developing themselves at such a rapid rate of progress, that they were already beyond my counting!

He lifted his head, and fixed a look of keen enquiry on me.

'I have come out of Mrs Beauly's skin,' he announced. 'And I have arrived at this result: – We are two impetuous people; and we have been a little hasty in rushing at a conclusion.'

He stopped. I said nothing. Was the shadow of a doubt of him beginning to rise in my mind? I waited, and listened.

'I am as fully satisfied as ever of the truth of what Lady Clarinda told you,' he proceeded. 'But I see, on consideration, what I failed to see at the time. The story admits of two interpretations. One on the surface, and another under the surface. I look under the surface, in your interests; and I say, it is just possible that Mrs Beauly may have been cunning enough to forestall suspicion, and to set up an Alibi.'

I am ashamed to own that I did not understand what he meant by the last word – Alibi.[1] He saw that I was not following him, and spoke out more plainly.

'Was the maid something more than her mistress's passive accomplice?' he said. 'Was she the Hand that her mistress used? Was she on her way to give the first dose of poison, when she passed me in the corridor? Did Mrs Beauly spend the night in Edinburgh – so as to have her defence ready, if suspicion fell upon her?'

My shadowy doubt of him became substantial doubt, when I heard that. Had I absolved him a little too readily? Was he really trying to renew my suspicions of Mrs Beauly, as Mr Playmore had foretold? This time I was obliged to answer him. In doing so, I unconsciously employed one of the phrases which the lawyer had used to me, during my first interview with him.

'That sounds rather far-fetched, Mr Dexter,' I said.

To my relief, he made no attempt to defend the new view that he had advanced.

'It *is* far-fetched,' he admitted. 'When I said it was just possible – though I didn't claim much for my idea – I said more for it perhaps than it deserved. Dismiss my view as ridiculous; what are you to do next? If Mrs Beauly is not the poisoner (either by herself or by her maid), who is? She is innocent, and Eustace is innocent. Where is the other person whom you can suspect? Have *I* poisoned her?' he cried, with his eyes flashing, and his voice rising to its highest notes. 'Do you, does anybody, suspect Me? I loved her; I adored her; I have never been the same man since her death. Hush! I will trust you with a secret. (Don't tell your husband; it might be the destruction of our friendship.) I would have married her, before she met with Eustace, if she would have taken me. When the doctors told me she had died poisoned – ask Doctor Jerome what I suffered! *he* can tell you! All through that horrible night, I was awake; watching my opportunity until I found my way to her! I got into the room, and took my last leave of the cold remains of the angel whom I loved. I cried over her. I kissed her, for the first and last time. I stole one little lock of her hair. I have worn it ever since; I have kissed it night and day. Oh, God! the room comes back to me! the dead face comes back to me! Look! look!'

He tore from its place of concealment in his bosom a little locket, fastened by a ribbon round his neck. He threw it to me where I sat; and burst into a passion of tears.

A man in my place might have known what to do. Being only a woman, I yielded to the compassionate impulse of the moment.

I got up and crossed the room to him. I gave him back his locket, and put my hand, without knowing what I was about, on the poor wretch's shoulder. 'I am incapable of suspecting you, Mr Dexter,' I said, gently. 'No such idea ever entered my head. I pity you from the bottom of my heart.'

He caught my hand in his, and devoured it with kisses. His lips burnt me like fire. He twisted himself suddenly in the chair, and wound his arm round my waist. In the terror and indignation of the moment, vainly struggling with him, I cried out for help.

The door opened, and Benjamin appeared on the threshold. Dexter let go his hold of me.

I ran to Benjamin and prevented him from advancing into the room. In all my long experience of my fatherly old friend, I had never seen him really angry yet. I saw him more than angry now. He was pale – the patient, gentle old man was pale with rage! I held him at the door with all my strength.

'You can't lay your hand on a cripple,' I said. 'Send for his servant outside to take him away.'

I drew Benjamin out of the room, and closed and locked the library door. The housekeeper was in the dining-room. I sent her out to call the driver of the pony-chaise into the house.

The man came in – the rough man whom I had noticed when we were approaching the garden gate. Benjamin opened the library door in stern silence. It was perhaps unworthy of me – but I could *not* resist the temptation to look in.

Miserrimus Dexter had sunk down in the chair. The rough man lifted his master with a gentleness that surprised me. 'Hide my face,' I heard Dexter say to him, in broken tones. He opened his coarse pilot jacket, and hid his master's head under it, and so went silently out – with the deformed creature held to his bosom, like a woman sheltering her child.

CHAPTER XXXVI

Ariel

I passed a sleepless night.

The outrage that had been offered to me was bad enough in itself. But consequences were associated with it which might affect me more seriously still. In so far as the attainment of the one object of my life might yet depend on my personal association with Miserrimus Dexter, an insurmountable obstacle appeared to be now placed in my way. Even in my husband's interests, ought I to permit a man who had grossly insulted me, to approach me again? Although I was no prude, I recoiled from the thought of it.

I rose late, and sat down at my desk, trying to summon energy enough to write to Mr Playmore – and trying in vain.

Towards noon (while Benjamin happened to be out for a little while), the housekeeper announced the arrival of another strange visitor at the gate of the villa.

'It's a woman this time, ma'am – or something like one,' said this worthy person, confidentially. 'A great, stout, awkward, stupid creature, with a man's hat on, and a man's stick in her hand. She says she has got a note for you, and she won't give it to anybody *but* you. I'd better not let her in – had I?'

Recognising the original of the picture, I astonished the housekeeper by consenting to receive the messenger immediately.

Ariel entered the room – in stolid silence, as usual. But I noticed a change in her which puzzled me. Her dull eyes were red and bloodshot. Traces of tears (as I fancied) were visible on her fat, shapeless cheeks. She crossed the room, on her way to my chair, with a less determined tread than was customary with her. Could Ariel (I asked myself) be woman enough to cry? Was it within the limits of possibility that Ariel should approach me in sorrow and in fear?

'I hear you have brought something for me?' I said. 'Won't you sit down?'

She handed me a letter – without answering, and without taking a chair. I opened the envelope. The letter inside was written by Miserrimus Dexter. It contained these lines: –

'Try to pity me, if you have any pity left for a miserable man; I have bitterly expiated the madness of a moment. If you could see me – even you would own that my punishment has been heavy enough. For God's sake, don't abandon me! I was beside myself when I let the feeling that you have awakened in me get the better of my control. It shall never show itself again; it shall be a secret that dies with me. Can I expect you to believe this? No. I won't ask you to believe me; I won't ask you to trust me in the future. If you ever consent to see me again, let it be in the presence of any third person whom you may appoint to protect you. I deserve that – I will submit to it; I will wait till time has composed your angry feeling against me. All I ask now, is leave to hope. Say to Ariel, "I forgive him; and one day I will let him see me again." She will remember it, for love of me. If you send her back without a message, you send me to the madhouse. Ask her, if you don't believe me. – MISERRIMUS DEXTER.'

I finished the strange letter, and looked at Ariel.

She stood with her eyes on the floor, and held out to me the thick walking-stick which she carried in her hand.

'Take the stick' – were the first words she said to me.

'Why am I to take it?' I asked.

She struggled a little with her sluggishly-working mind, and slowly put her thoughts into words.

'You're angry with the Master,' she said. 'Take it out on Me. Here's the stick. Beat me.'

'Beat you!' I exclaimed.

'My back's broad,' said the poor creature. 'I won't make a row. I'll bear it. Drat you, take the stick! Don't vex *him*. Whack it out on my back. Beat *me*.'

She roughly forced the stick into my hand; she turned her poor shapeless shoulders to me, waiting for the blow. It was at once dreadful and touching to see her. The tears rose in my eyes. I tried, gently and patiently, to reason with her. Quite useless! The idea of taking the Master's punishment on herself was the one idea in her mind. 'Don't vex *him*,' she repeated. 'Beat *me*.'

'What do you mean by "vexing him"?' I asked.

She tried to explain, and failed to find the words. She showed me by imitation, as a savage might have shown me, what she meant. Striding to the fireplace, she crouched on the rug, and looked into the fire with a horrible vacant stare. Then she clasped her hands over her forehead, and rocked slowly to and fro, still staring into the fire. 'There's how he sits!' she said, with a sudden burst of speech. 'Hours on hours, there's how he sits! Notices nobody. Cries about *you*.'

The picture she presented recalled to my memory the Report of Dexter's health, and the doctor's plain warning of peril waiting for him in the future. Even if I could have resisted Ariel, I must have yielded to the vague dread of consequences which now shook me in secret.

'Don't do that!' I cried. She was still rocking herself in imitation of the 'Master,' and still staring into the fire with her hands to her head. 'Get up, pray! I am not angry with him now. I forgive him.'

She rose on her hands and knees, and waited, looking up intently into my face. In that attitude – more like a dog than a human being – she repeated her customary petition, when she wanted to fix words that interested her in her mind.

'Say it again!'

I did as she bade me. She was not satisfied.

'Say it as it is in the letter,' she went on. 'Say it as the Master said it to Me.'

I looked back at the letter, and repeated the form of message contained in the latter part of it, word for word: 'I forgive him; and one day I will let him see me again.'

She sprang to her feet at a bound. For the first time since she had entered the room, her dull face began to break slowly into light and life.

'That's it!' she cried. 'Hear if I can say it, too! Hear if I've got it by heart.'

Teaching her, exactly as I should have taught a child, I slowly fastened the message, word by word, on her mind.

'Now rest yourself,' I said; 'and let me give you something to eat and drink, after your long walk.'

I might as well have spoken to one of the chairs! She snatched up her stick from the floor, and burst out with a hoarse shout of joy. 'I've got it by heart!' she cried. 'This will cool the Master's head! Hooray!' She dashed out into the passage, like a wild animal escaping from its cage. I was just in time to see her tear open the garden gate, and set forth on her walk back, at a pace which made it hopeless to attempt to follow and stop her.

I returned to the sitting-room, pondering on a question which has perplexed wiser heads than mine. Could a man who was hopelessly and entirely wicked, have inspired such devoted attachment to him as Dexter had inspired in the faithful woman who had just left me – in the rough gardener, who had carried him out so gently on the previous night? Who can decide? The greatest scoundrel living always has a friend – in a woman, or a dog.

I sat down again at my desk, and made another attempt to write to Mr Playmore.

Recalling, for the purpose of my letter, all that Miserrimus Dexter had said to me, my memory dwelt, with special interest, on the strange outbreak of feeling which had led him to betray the secret of his infatuation for Eustace's first wife. I saw again the ghastly scene in the death-chamber – the deformed creature crying over the corpse, in the stillness of the first dark hours of the new day. The horrible picture took a strange hold on my mind. I rose, and walked up and down, and tried to turn my thoughts some other way. It was not to be done:

the scene was too familiar to be easily dismissed. I had myself walked in the corridor which Dexter had crossed, on his way to take his last leave of her.

The corridor? I stopped. My thoughts suddenly took a new direction, uninfluenced by any effort of my will.

What other association, besides the associations with Dexter, did I connect with the corridor? Was it something I had seen, during my visit to Gleninch? No. Was it something I had read? I snatched up the Report of the Trial to see. It opened at a page which contained the nurse's evidence. I read the evidence through again, without recovering the lost remembrance, until I came to these lines close at the end: –

'Before bedtime I went upstairs to prepare the remains of the deceased lady for the coffin. The room in which she lay was locked; the door leading into Mr Macallan's room being secured, as well as the door leading into the corridor. The keys had been taken away by Mr Gale. Two of the men-servants were posted outside the bedroom to keep watch. They were to be relieved at four in the morning – that was all they could tell me.'

There was my lost association with the corridor! There was what I ought to have remembered, when Miserrimus Dexter was telling me of his visit to the dead!

How had he got into the bedroom – the doors being locked, and the keys being taken away by Mr Gale? There was but one of the locked doors, of which Mr Gale had not got the key: the door of communication between the study and the bedroom. The key was missing from this. Had it been stolen? And was Dexter the thief? He might have passed by the men on the watch, while they were asleep; or he might have crossed the corridor, in an unguarded interval while the men were being relieved. But how could he have got into the bedchamber, except by way of the locked study door? He *must* have had the key! And he *must* have secreted it, weeks before Mrs Eustace Macallan's death! When the nurse first arrived at Gleninch, on the seventh of the month, her evidence declared the key of the door of communication to be then missing.

To what conclusion did these considerations and discoveries point?

Had Miserrimus Dexter, in a moment of ungovernable agitation, unconsciously placed the clue in my hands? Was the pivot on which turned the whole mystery of the poisoning at Gleninch, the missing key?

I went back for the third time to my desk. The one person who might be trusted to find the answer to those questions was Mr Playmore. I wrote him a full and careful account of all that had happened; I begged him to forgive and forget my ungracious reception of the advice which he had so kindly offered to me; and I promised beforehand to do nothing, without first consulting his opinion, in the new emergency which now confronted me.

The day was fine, for the time of year; and by way of getting a little wholesome exercise, after the surprises and occupations of the morning, I took my letter to Mr Playmore to the post.

Returning to the villa, I was informed that another visitor was waiting to see me: a civilised visitor this time, who had given her name. My mother-in law – Mrs Macallan.

CHAPTER XXXVII

At the Bedside

Before she had uttered a word, I saw in my mother-in-law's face that she brought bad news.

'Eustace?' I said.

She answered me by a look.

'Let me hear it at once!' I cried. 'I can bear anything but suspense.'

Mrs Macallan lifted her hand, and showed me a telegraphic despatch which she had hitherto kept concealed in the folds of her dress.

'I can trust your courage,' she said. 'There is no need, my child, to prevaricate with you. Read that.'

I read the telegram. It was sent by the chief surgeon of a field-hospital; and it was dated from a village in the north of Spain.

'Mr Eustace severely wounded in a skirmish, by a stray shot. Not in danger, so far. Every care taken of him. Wait for another telegram.'

I turned away my face, and bore as best I might the pang that wrung me when I read those words. I thought I knew how dearly I loved him. I had never known it till that moment.

My mother-in-law put her arm round me, and held me to her tenderly. She knew me well enough not to speak to me at that moment.

I rallied my courage, and pointed to the last sentence in the telegram. 'Do you mean to wait?' I asked.

'Not a day!' she answered. 'I am going to the Foreign Office about my passport – I have some interest there: they can give me letters; they can advise and assist me. I leave to-night by the mail train to Calais!'

'*You* leave?' I said. 'Do you suppose I will let you go without me? Get my passport when you get yours. At seven this evening, I will be at your house.'

She attempted to remonstrate; she spoke of the perils of the journey. At the first words, I stopped her. 'Don't you know yet, mother, how obstinate I am? They may keep you waiting at the Foreign Office. Why do you waste the precious hours here?'

She yielded with a gentleness that was not in her everyday character. 'Will my poor Eustace ever know what a wife he has got!' That was all she said. She kissed me, and went away in her carriage.

My remembrances of our journey are strangely vague and imperfect.

As I try to recall them, the memory of those more recent and more interesting events which occurred after my return to England, gets between me and my adventures in Spain, and seems to force these last into a shadowy background, until they look like adventures that happened many years since. I confusedly recollect delays and alarms that tried our patience and our courage. I remember our finding friends (thanks to our letters of recommendation) in a Secretary to the Embassy, and in a Queen's Messenger, who assisted and protected us at a critical point in the journey. I recall to mind a long succession of men, in our employment as travellers, all equally remarkable for their dirty cloaks and their clean linen, for their highly-civilised courtesy to women, and their utterly-barbarous cruelty to horses. Last, and most important of all, I see again, more clearly than I can see anything else, the one wretched bedroom of a squalid village-inn, in which we found our poor darling, prostrate between life and death, insensible to everything that passed in the narrow little world that lay round his bedside.

There was nothing romantic or interesting in the accident which had put my husband's life in peril.

He had ventured too near the scene of the conflict (a miserable affair) to rescue a poor lad who lay wounded on the field – mortally wounded as the event proved. A rifle-bullet had struck him in the body. His brethren of the field-hospital had carried him back to their quarters, at the risk of their lives. He was a great favourite with all of them; patient, and gentle, and brave; only wanting a little more judgment to be the most valuable recruit who had joined the brotherhood.

In telling me this, the surgeon kindly and delicately added a word of warning as well.

The fever caused by the wound had brought with it delirium as usual. My poor husband's mind, in so far as his wandering words might interpret it, was filled by the one image of his wife. The medical attendant had heard enough, in the course of his ministrations at the bedside, to satisfy him that any sudden recognition of me by Eustace (if he recovered) might be attended by the most lamentable results. As things were at that sad time, I might take my turn at nursing him, without the slightest chance of his discovering me, perhaps for weeks and weeks to come. But on the day when he was declared out of danger – if that happy day ever arrived – I must resign my place at his bedside, and must wait to show myself until the surgeon gave me leave.

My mother-in-law and I relieved each other regularly, day and night, in the sick room.

In the hours of his delirium – hours that recurred with a pitiless regularity – my name was always on my poor darling's fevered lips. The ruling idea in him was the one dreadful idea which I had vainly combated at our last interview. In the face of the verdict pronounced at the Trial, it was impossible even for his wife to be really and truly persuaded that he was an innocent man. All the wild pictures which his distempered imagination drew, were equally inspired by that one obstinate conviction. He fancied himself to be still living with me, under those dreaded conditions. Do what he might, I was always recalling to him the terrible ordeal through which he had passed. He acted his part, and he acted mine. He gave me a cup of tea; and I said to him, 'We quarrelled yesterday, Eustace. Is it poisoned?' He kissed me, in token of our reconciliation; and I laughed, and said, 'It's morning now, my dear. Shall I die by nine o'clock to-night?' I was ill in bed, and he gave me my medicine. I looked at him with a doubting eye. I said to him, 'You are in love with another woman. Is there anything in the medicine that the doctor doesn't know of?' Such was the horrible drama which now perpetually acted itself in his mind. Hundreds and hundreds of times I heard him repeat it, almost always in the same words. On other occasions, his thoughts wandered away to my desperate project of proving him to be an innocent man. Sometimes, he laughed at it. Sometimes, he mourned over it. Sometimes, he devised cunning schemes for placing unsuspected obstacles in my way. He was especially hard on me when he was inventing his preventive stratagems – he cheerfully instructed the visionary people who assisted him, not to hesitate at offending or distressing me. 'Never mind if you make her angry; never mind if you make her cry. It's all for her good; it's all to save the poor fool from dangers she doesn't dream of. You mustn't pity her when she says she does it for my sake. See! she is going to be insulted; she is going to be deceived; she is going to disgrace herself without knowing it. Stop her! stop her!' It was weak of me I know; I ought to have kept the plain fact that he was out of his senses always present to my mind. Still, it is true that my hours passed at my husband's pillow were many of them hours of mortification and misery of which he, poor dear, was the innocent and only cause.

The weeks passed; and he still hovered between life and death.

I kept no record of the time, and I cannot now recall the exact date on which the first favourable change took place. I only remember that it was towards sunrise on a fine winter morning, when we were relieved at last of our heavy burden of suspense. The surgeon happened to be by the bedside, when his patient woke. The first thing he did, after looking at Eustace, was to caution me by a sign to be silent, and to keep out of sight. My mother-in-law and I both knew what this meant. With full hearts, we thanked God together for giving us back the husband and the son.

The same evening, being alone, we ventured to speak of the future – for the first time since we had left home.

'The surgeon tells me,' said Mrs Macallan, 'that Eustace is too weak to be capable of bearing anything in the nature of a surprise, for some days to come. We have time to consider whether he is, or is not, to be told that he owes his life as much to your care as to mine. Can you find it in your heart to leave him, Valeria, now that God's mercy has restored him to you and to me?'

'If I only consulted my own heart,' I answered, 'I should never leave him again.'

Mrs Macallan looked at me in grave surprise.

'What else have you to consult?' she asked.

'If we both live,' I replied, 'I have to think of the happiness of his life, and the happiness of mine, in the years that are to come. I can bear a great deal, mother, but I cannot endure the misery of his leaving me for the second time.'

'You wrong him, Valeria – I firmly believe you wrong him – in thinking it possible that he can leave you again!'

'Dear Mrs Macallan, have you forgotten what we have both heard him say of me, while we have been sitting by his bedside?'

'We have heard the ravings of a man in delirium. It is surely hard to hold Eustace responsible for what he said when he was out of his senses?'

'It is harder still,' I said, 'to resist his mother when she is pleading for him. Dearest and best of friends! I don't hold Eustace responsible for what he said in the fever – but I *do* take warning by it. The wildest words that fell from him were, one and all, the faithful echo of what he said to me in the best days of his health and his strength. What hope have I that he will recover with an altered mind towards me? Absence has not changed it; suffering has not changed it. In the delirium of fever, and in the full possession of his reason, he has the same dreadful doubt of me. I see but one way of winning him back. I must destroy at its root his motive for leaving me. It is hopeless to persuade him that I believe in his innocence: I must show him that belief is no longer necessary; I must prove to him that his position towards me has become the position of an innocent man.'

'Valeria! Valeria! you are wasting time and words. You have tried the experiment; and you know as well as I do, the thing is not to be done.'

I had no answer to that. I could say no more than I had said already.

'Suppose you go back to Dexter, out of sheer compassion for a mad and miserable wretch who has already insulted you,' proceeded my mother-in-law. 'You can only go back, accompanied by me, or by some other trustworthy person. You can only stay long enough to humour the creature's wayward fancy, and to keep his crazy brain quiet for a time. That done, all is done – you leave him. Even supposing Dexter to be still capable of helping you, how can you make use of him but by admitting him to terms of confidence and familiarity – by treating him, in short, on the footing of an intimate friend? Answer me honestly: can you bring yourself to do that, after what happened at Mr Benjamin's house?'

I had told her of my last interview with Miserrimus Dexter, in the natural confidence that she inspired in me as relative and fellow-traveller; and this was the use to which she turned her information! I suppose I had no right to blame her; I suppose the motive sanctioned everything. At any rate, I had no choice but to give offence, or to give an answer. I gave it. I acknowledged that I could never again permit Miserrimus Dexter to treat me on terms of familiarity, as a trusted and intimate friend.

Mrs Macallan pitilessly pressed the advantage that she had won.

'Very well,' she said, 'that resource being no longer open to you, what hope is left? Which way are you to turn next?'

There was no meeting those questions, in my present situation, by any adequate reply. I felt strangely unlike myself – I submitted in silence. Mrs Macallan struck the last blow that completed her victory.

'My poor Eustace is weak and wayward,' she said; 'but he is not an ungrateful man. My child! you have returned him good for evil[1] – you have proved how faithfully and how devotedly you love him, by suffering hardships and by risking dangers for his sake. Trust me, and trust him! He cannot resist you. Let him see the dear face that he has been dreaming of, looking at him again with all the old love in it; and he is yours once more, my daughter – yours for life.' She rose and touched my forehead with her lips; her voice sank to tones of tenderness which I had never heard from her yet. 'Say yes, Valeria,' she whispered; 'and be dearer to me and dearer to him than ever!'

My heart sided with her. My energies were worn out. No letter had arrived from Mr Playmore, to guide and to encourage me. I had resisted so long and so vainly; I had tried and suffered so much; I had met with such cruel disasters and such reiterated disappointments – and *he* was in the room beneath me, feebly finding his way back to consciousness and to life – how could I resist? It was all over! In saying Yes (if Eustace confirmed his mother's confidence in him), I was saying adieu to the one cherished ambition, the one dear and noble hope of my life. I knew it – and I said Yes.

And so good-bye to the grand struggle! And so welcome to the new resignation which owned that I had failed!

My mother-in-law and I slept together under the only shelter that the inn could offer to us – a sort of loft at the top of the house. The night that followed our conversation was bitterly cold. We felt the chilly temperature, in spite of the protection of our dressing-gowns and our travelling wrappers. My mother-in-law slept; but no rest came to me. I was too anxious and too wretched, thinking over my changed position and doubting how my husband would receive me, to be able to sleep.

Some hours, as I suppose, must have passed, and I was still absorbed in my own melancholy thoughts – when I suddenly became conscious of a new and strange sensation which astonished and alarmed me. I started up in the bed, breathless and bewildered. The movement awakened Mrs Macallan. 'Are you ill?' she asked. 'What is the matter with you?' I tried to tell her, as well as I could. She seemed to understand me before I had done; she took me tenderly in her arms, and pressed me to her bosom. 'My poor innocent child,' she said, 'is it possible you don't know? Must I really tell you?' She whispered her next words. Shall I ever forget the tumult of feelings which the whisper aroused in me – the strange medley of joy and fear, and wonder and relief, and pride and humility, which filled my whole being, and made a new woman of me from that moment? Now, for the first time, I knew it! If God spared me for a few months more, the most enduring and the most sacred of all human joys might be mine – the joy of being a mother.

I don't know how the rest of the night passed. I only found my memory again, when the morning came, and when I went out by myself to breathe the crisp wintry air on the open moor behind the inn.

I have said that I felt like a new woman. The morning found me with a new resolution and a new courage. When I thought of the future, I had not only my husband to consider now. His good name was no longer his own and mine – it might soon become the most precious inheritance that he could leave to his child. What had I done, while I was in ignorance of this? I had resigned the hope of cleansing his name from the stain that had rested on it – a stain still, no matter how little it might look in the eye of the Law. Our child might live to hear malicious tongues say, 'Your father was tried for the vilest of all murders, and was never absolutely acquitted of the charge.' Could I face the glorious perils of childbirth, with that possibility present to my mind? No! not until I had made one more effort to lay the conscience of Miserrimus Dexter bare to my view! not until I had once again renewed the struggle, and brought the truth that vindicated the husband and the father to the light of day!

I went back to the house, with my new courage to sustain me. I opened my heart to my friend and mother, and told her frankly of the change that had come over me, since we had last spoken of Eustace.

She was more than disappointed, she was almost offended with me. The one thing needful had happened, she said. The happiness that was coming to us would form a new tie between my husband and me. Every other consideration but this, she treated as purely fanciful. If I left Eustace now, I did a heartless thing and a foolish thing. I should regret, to the end of my days, having thrown away the one golden opportunity of my married life.

It cost me a hard struggle, it oppressed me with many a painful doubt; but I held firm, this time. The honour of the father, the inheritance of the child – I kept those thoughts as constantly as possible before my mind. Sometimes they failed me, and left me nothing better than a poor fool who had some fitful bursts of crying, and was ashamed of herself afterwards. But my native obstinacy (as Mrs Macallan said) carried me through. Now and then, I had a peep at Eustace, while he was asleep, and that helped me too. Though they made my heart ache and shook me sadly at the time, those furtive visits to my husband fortified me afterwards. I cannot explain how this happened (it seems so contradictory); I can only repeat it as one of my experiences at that troubled time.

I made one concession to Mrs Macallan – I consented to wait for two days, before I took any steps for returning to England, on the chance that my mind might change in the interval.

It was well for me that I yielded so far. On the second day, the director of the field-hospital sent to the post-office, at our nearest town, for letters addressed to him or to his care. The messenger brought back a letter for me. I thought I recognised the handwriting, and I was right. Mr Playmore's answer had reached me at last!

If I had been in any danger of changing my mind, the good lawyer would have saved me in the nick of time. The extract that follows contains the pith of his letter; and shows how he encouraged me, when I stood in sore need of a few cheering and friendly words.

'Let me now tell you' (he wrote) 'what I have done towards verifying the conclusion to which your letter points.

'I have traced one of the servants who was appointed to keep watch in the corridor, on the night when the first Mrs Eustace died at Gleninch. The man perfectly remembers that Miserrimus Dexter appeared before him and his fellow-servant (in his chair), after the house was quiet for the night. Dexter said to them, "I suppose there is no harm in my going into the study to read? I can't sleep after what has happened; I must relieve my mind somehow." The men had no orders to keep anyone out of the study. They knew that the door of communication with the bedchamber was locked, and that the keys of the two other doors of communication were in the possession of Mr Gale. They accordingly permitted Dexter to go into the study. He closed the door (the door that opened on the corridor), and remained absent for some time – in the study as the men supposed; in the bedchamber as *we* know, from what he let out at his interview with you. Now, he could enter that room, as you rightly imagine, in but one way – by being in possession of the missing key. How long he remained there, I cannot discover. The point is of little consequence. The servant remembers that he came out of the study again "as pale as death," and that he passed on without a word, on his way back to his own room.

'These are facts. The conclusion to which they lead is serious in the last degree. It justifies everything that I confided to you in my office at Edinburgh. You remember what passed between us. I say no more.

'As to yourself next. You have innocently aroused in Miserrimus Dexter a feeling towards you, which I need not attempt to characterise. There is a certain something – I saw it myself – in your figure, and in some of your movements, which does recall the late Mrs Eustace to those who knew her well, and which has evidently had its effect on Dexter's morbid mind. Without dwelling further on this subject, let me only remind you that he has shown himself (as a consequence of your influence over him) to be incapable, in his moments of agitation, of thinking before he speaks, while he is in your presence. It is not merely possible, it is highly probable, that he may betray himself far more seriously than he has betrayed himself yet, if you give him the opportunity. I owe it to you (knowing what your interests are) to express myself plainly on this point. I have no sort of doubt that you have advanced one step nearer to the end which you have in view, in the brief interval since you left Edinburgh. I see in your letter (and in my discoveries) irresistible evidence that Dexter must have been in secret communication with the deceased lady (innocent communication, I am certain, so far as *she* was concerned), not only at the time of her death, but probably for weeks before it. I cannot disguise from myself, or from you, my own strong persuasion that, if you succeed in discovering the nature of this communication, in all human likelihood you prove your husband's innocence by the discovery of the truth. As an honest man, I am bound not to conceal this. And, as an honest man also, I am equally bound to add that, not even with your reward in view, can I find it in my conscience to advise you to risk what you must risk, if you see Miserrimus Dexter again. In this difficult and delicate matter, I cannot, and will not, take the responsibility. The final decision must rest with yourself. One favour only I entreat you to grant – let me hear what you resolve to do as soon as you know it yourself.'

The difficulties which my worthy correspondent felt were no difficulties to me. I did not possess Mr Playmore's judicial mind. My resolution (come what might of it) to see Miserrimus Dexter again, was settled before I had read his letter to the end.

The mail to France crossed the frontier the next day. There was a place for me under the protection of the conductor, if I chose to take it. Without consulting a living creature – rash as usual, headlong as usual – I took it.

CHAPTER XXXVIII
On the Journey Back

If I had been travelling homeward in my own carriage, the remaining chapters of this narrative would never have been written. Before we had been an hour on the road, I should have called to the driver, and should have told him to turn back.

Who can be always resolute?

In asking that question, I speak of the women, not of the men. I had been resolute in turning a deaf ear to Mr Playmore's doubts and cautions; resolute in holding out against my mother-in-law; resolute in taking my place by the French mail. Until ten minutes after we had driven away from the inn my courage held out – and then it failed me; then I said to myself, 'You wretch, you have deserted your husband!' For hours afterwards, if I could have stopped the mail, I would have done it. I hated the conductor, the kindest of men. I hated the Spanish ponies that drew us, the cheeriest animals that ever jingled a string of bells. I hated the bright day that *would* make things pleasant, and the bracing air that forced me to feel the luxury of breathing, whether I liked it or not. Never was a journey more miserable than my safe and easy journey to the frontier! But one little comfort helped me to bear my heart-ache resignedly – a stolen morsel of Eustace's hair. We had started at an hour of the morning, when he was still sound asleep. I could creep into his room, and kiss him, and cry over him softly, and cut off a stray lock of his hair, without danger of discovery. How I summoned resolution enough to leave him is, to this hour, not clear to my mind. I think my mother-in-law must have helped me, without meaning to do it. She came into the room with an erect head, and a cold eye; she said, with an unmerciful emphasis on the word, 'If you *mean* to go, Valeria, the carriage is here.' Any woman with a spark of spirit in her would have 'meant' it under those circumstances. I meant it – and did it.

And then I was sorry for it. Poor humanity!

Time has got all the credit of being the great consoler of afflicted mortals. In my opinion, Time has been over-rated in this matter. Distance does the same beneficent work, far more speedily, and (when assisted by Change) far more effectually as well. On the railroad to Paris, I became capable of taking a sensible view of my position. I could now remind myself that my husband's reception of me – after the first surprise and the first happiness had passed away – might not have justified his mother's confidence in him. Admitting that I ran a risk in going back to Miserrimus Dexter, should I not have been equally rash, in another way, if I had returned, uninvited, to a husband who had declared that our conjugal happiness was impossible, and that our married life was at an end? Besides, who could say that the events of the future might not yet justify me – not only to myself, but to him? I might yet hear him say, 'She was inquisitive when she had no business to enquire; she was obstinate when she ought to have listened to reason; she left my bedside when other women would have remained: but in the end she atoned for it all – she turned out to be right!'

I rested a day at Paris, and wrote three letters.

One to Benjamin, telling him to expect me the next evening. One to Mr Playmore, warning him, in good time, that I meant to make a last effort to penetrate the mystery at Gleninch. One to Eustace (of a few lines only), owning that I had helped to nurse him through the dangerous part of his illness; confessing the one reason which had prevailed with me to leave him; and entreating him to suspend his opinion of me, until time had proved that I loved him more dearly than ever. This last letter I enclosed to my mother-in-law; leaving it to her discretion to choose the right time for giving it to her son. I positively forbade Mrs Macallan, however, to tell Eustace of the new tie between us. Although he *had* separated himself from me, I was determined that he should not hear of it from other lips than mine. Never mind why! There are certain little matters which I must keep to myself; and this is one of them.

My letters being written, my duty was done. I was free to play my last card in the game – the darkly-doubtful game which was neither quite for me, nor quite against me, as the chances now stood.

CHAPTER XXXIX

On the Way to Dexter

'I declare to Heaven, Valeria, I believe that monster's madness is infectious – and you have caught it!'

This was Benjamin's opinion of me (on my arrival at the villa); after I had announced my intention of returning Miserrimus Dexter's visit, in his company.

Being determined to carry my point, I could afford to try the influence of mild persuasion. I begged my good friend to have a little patience with me. 'And do remember what I have already told you,'

I added. 'It is of serious importance to me to see Dexter again.'

I only heaped fuel on the fire. 'See him again?' Benjamin repeated, indignantly. 'See him, after he grossly insulted you, under my roof, in this very room? I can't be awake; I must be asleep and dreaming.'

It was wrong of me, I know. But Benjamin's virtuous indignation was so very virtuous that it let the spirit of mischief loose in me. I really could not resist the temptation to outrage his sense of propriety, by taking an audaciously liberal view of the whole matter.

'Gently, my good friend, gently!' I said. 'We must make allowances for a man who suffers under Dexter's infirmities, and lives Dexter's life. And really we must not let our modesty lead us beyond reasonable limits. I begin to think that I took rather a prudish view of the thing myself, at the time. A woman who respects herself, and whose whole heart is with her husband, is not so very seriously injured when a wretched crippled creature is rude enough to put his arm round her waist. Virtuous indignation (if I may venture to say so) is sometimes very cheap indignation. Besides, I have forgiven him – and you must forgive him, too. There is no fear of his forgetting himself again, while you are with me. His house is quite a curiosity; it is sure to interest you; the pictures alone are worth the journey. I will write to him to-day, and we will go and see him together to-morrow. We owe it to ourselves (if we don't owe it to Mr Dexter) to pay this visit. If you will look about you, Benjamin, you will see that benevolence towards everybody is the great virtue of the time we live in. Poor Mr Dexter must have the benefit of the prevailing fashion. Come, come, march with the age! Open your mind to the new ideas!'

Instead of accepting this polite invitation, worthy old Benjamin flew at the age we lived in, like a bull at a red cloth.

'Oh, the new ideas! the new ideas! By all manner of means, Valeria, let us have the new ideas! The old morality's all wrong, the old ways are all worn out. Let's march with the age we live in. Nothing comes amiss to the age we live in. The wife in England and the husband in Spain, married or not married, living together or not living together – it's all one to the new ideas. I'll go with you, Valeria; I'll be worthy of the generation I live in. When we have done with Dexter, don't let's do things by halves. Let's go and get crammed with ready-made science at a lecture – let's hear the last new professor, the man who has been behind the scenes at Creation, and knows to a T how the world was made, and how long it took to make it. There's the other fellow, too: mind we don't forget the modern Solomon who has left his proverbs behind him – the bran-new philosopher who considers the consolations of religion in the light of harmless playthings, and who is kind enough to say that he might have been all the happier if he could only have been childish enough to play with them himself. Oh, the new ideas, the new ideas, what consoling, elevating, beautiful discoveries have been made by the new ideas! We were all monkeys before we were men, and molecules before we were monkeys![1] And what does it matter? And what does anything matter to anybody? I'm with you, Valeria – I'm ready! The sooner the better. Come to Dexter! Come to Dexter!'

'I am so glad you agree with me,' I said. 'But let us do nothing in a hurry. Three o'clock to-morrow will be time enough for Mr Dexter. I will write at once and tell him to expect us. – Where are you going?'

'I am going to clear my mind of cant,' said Benjamin, sternly. 'I am going into the library.'

'What are you going to read?'

'I am going to read—"Puss in Boots," and "Jack and the Bean-Stalk," and anything else I can find that doesn't march with the age we live in.'

With that parting shot at the new ideas, my old friend left me for a time.

Having despatched my note, I found myself beginning to revert, with a certain feeling of anxiety, to the subject of Miserrimus Dexter's health. How had he passed through the interval of my absence from England? Could anybody, within my reach, tell me news of him? To enquire of Benjamin would only be to provoke a new outbreak. While I was still considering, the housekeeper entered the room on some domestic errand. I asked, at a venture, if she had heard anything more, while I had been away, of the extraordinary person who had so seriously alarmed her on a former occasion.

The housekeeper shook her head, and looked as if she thought it in bad taste to mention the subject at all.

'About a week after you had gone away, ma'am,' she said, with extreme severity of manner, and with excessive carefulness in her choice of words, 'the Person you mention had the impudence to send a letter to you. The messenger was informed, by my master's orders, that you had gone abroad, and he and his letter were both sent about their business together. Not long afterwards, ma'am, I happened, while drinking tea with Mrs Macallan's housekeeper, to hear of the Person again. He himself called in his chaise, at Mrs Macallan's, to enquire about you there. How he can contrive to sit, without legs to balance him, is beyond my understanding – but that is neither here nor there. Legs or no legs, the housekeeper saw him, and she says, as I say, she will never forget him to her dying day. She told him (as soon as she recovered herself) of Mr Eustace's illness, and of you and Mrs Macallan being in foreign parts nursing him. He went away, so the housekeeper told me, with tears in his eyes, and oaths and curses on his lips – a sight shocking to see. That's all I know about the Person, ma'am, and I hope to be excused if I venture to say that the subject is (for good reasons) extremely disagreeable to me.'

She made a formal curtsey, and quitted the room.

Left by myself, I felt more anxious and more uncertain than ever, when I thought of the experiment that was to be tried on the next day. Making due allowance for exaggeration, the description of Miserrimus Dexter, on his departure from Mrs Macallan's house, suggested that he had not endured my long absence very patiently, and that he was still as far as ever from giving his shattered nervous system its fair chance of repose.

The next morning brought me Mr Playmore's reply to the letter which I had addressed to him from Paris.

He wrote very briefly, neither approving nor blaming my decision, but strongly reiterating his opinion that I should do well to choose a competent witness as my companion at my coming interview with Dexter. The most interesting part of the letter was at the end. 'You must be prepared,' Mr Playmore wrote, 'to see a change for the worse in Dexter. A friend of mine was with him on a matter of business a few days since, and was struck by the alteration in him. Your presence is sure to have its effect one way or another. I can give you no instructions for managing him – you must be guided by the circum-stances. Your own tact will tell you whether it is wise, or not, to encourage him to speak of the late Mrs Eustace. The chances of his betraying himself all revolve (as I think) round that one topic: keep him to it if you can.' To this was added, in a postscript: 'Ask Mr Benjamin if he was near enough to the library door to hear Dexter tell you of his entering the bedchamber, on the night of Mrs Eustace Macallan's death.'

I put the question to Benjamin when we met at the luncheon-table, before setting forth for the distant suburb in which Miserrimus Dexter lived. My old friend disapproved of the contemplated expedition as strongly as ever. He was unusually grave and unusually sparing of words, when he answered me.

'I am no listener,' he said. 'But some people have voices which insist on being heard. Mr Dexter is one of them.'

'Does that mean that you heard him?' I asked.

'The door couldn't muffle him, and the wall couldn't muffle him,' Benjamin rejoined. 'I heard him – and I thought it infamous. There!'

'I may want you to do more than hear him, this time,' I ventured to say. 'I may want you to make notes of our conversation, while Mr Dexter is speaking to me. You used to write down what my father said, when he was dictating his letters to you. Have you got one of your little note-books to spare?'

Benjamin looked up from his plate with an aspect of stern surprise.

'It is one thing,' he said, 'to write under the dictation of a great merchant, conducting a vast correspondence by which thousands of pounds change hands in due course of post. And it's another thing to take down the gibberish of a maundering mad monster who ought to be kept in a cage. Your good father, Valeria, would never have asked me to do that.'

'Forgive me, Benjamin: I must really ask you to do it. It is Mr Playmore's idea, mind! – not mine. Come! give way this once, dear, for my sake.'

Benjamin looked down again at his plate, with a rueful resignation which told me that I had carried my point.

'I have been tied to her apron-string all my life,' I heard him grumble to himself. 'And it's too late in the day to get loose from her now.' He looked up again at me. 'I thought I had retired from business,' he said. 'But it seems I must turn clerk again. Well? What is the new stroke of work that's expected from me, this time?'

The cab was announced to be waiting for us at the gate, as he asked the question. I rose and took his arm, and gave him a grateful kiss on his rosy old cheek.

'Only two things,' I said. 'Sit down behind Mr Dexter's chair, so that he can't see you. But take care to place yourself, at the same time, so that you can see me.'

'The less I see of Mr Dexter, the better I shall be pleased,' growled Benjamin. 'What am I to do, after I have taken my place behind him?'

'You are to wait until I make you a sign; and when you see it you are to begin writing down in your note-book what Mr Dexter is saying – and you are to go on, until I make another sign which means, Leave off!'

'Well?' said Benjamin, 'What's the sign for, Begin? and what's the sign for, Leave off?'

I was not quite prepared with an answer to this. I asked him to help me with a hint. No! Benjamin would take no active part in the matter. He was resigned to be employed in the capacity of passive instrument – and there all concession ended, so far as he was concerned.

Left to my own resources, I found it no easy matter to invent a telegraphic system which should sufficiently inform Benjamin, without awakening Dexter's quick suspicion. I looked into the glass to see if I could find the necessary suggestion in anything that I wore. My earrings supplied me with the idea of which I was in search.

'I shall take care to sit in an arm-chair,' I said. 'When you see me rest my elbow on the chair, and lift my hand to my earring, as if I was playing with it – write down what he says; and go on until – well, suppose we say, until you hear me move my chair. At that sound, stop. You understand me?'

'I understand you.'

We started for Dexter's house.

CHAPTER XL

Nemesis[1] *at Last!*

The gardener opened the gate to us on this occasion. He had evidently received his orders, in anticipation of my arrival.

'Mrs Valeria?' he asked.

'Yes.'

'And friend?'

'And friend.'

'Please to step upstairs. You know the house.'

Crossing the hall, I stopped for a moment, and looked at a favourite walking-cane which Benjamin still kept in his hand.

'Your cane will only be in your way,' I said. 'Had you not better leave it here?'

'My cane may be useful upstairs,' retorted Benjamin, gruffly. '*I* haven't forgotten what happened in the library.'

It was no time to contend with him. I led the way up the stairs.

Arriving at the upper flight of steps, I was startled by hearing a sudden cry from the room above. It was like the cry of a person in pain; and it was twice repeated, before we entered the circular antechamber. I was the first to approach the inner room, and to see the many-sided Miserrimus Dexter in another new aspect of his character.

The unfortunate Ariel was standing before a table, with a dish of little cakes placed in front of her. Round each of her wrists was tied a string, the free end of which (at a distance of a few yards) was held in Miserrimus Dexter's hands. 'Try again, my beauty!' I heard him say, as I stopped on the threshold of the door. 'Take a cake.' At the word of command, Ariel submissively stretched out one arm towards the dish. Just as she touched a cake with the tips of her fingers, her hand was jerked away by a pull at the string, so savagely cruel in the nimble and devilish violence of it, that I felt inclined to snatch Benjamin's cane out of his hand, and break it over Miserrimus Dexter's back. Ariel suffered the pain this time in Spartan silence. The position

in which she stood enabled her to be the first to see me at the door.
She had discovered me. Her teeth were set; her face was flushed under
the struggle to restrain herself. Not even a sigh escaped her in my
presence.

'Drop the strings!' I called out, indignantly. 'Release her, Mr Dexter,
or I shall leave the house.'

At the sound of my voice he burst out with a shrill cry of welcome.
His eyes fastened on me with a fierce, devouring delight.

'Come in! come in!' he cried. 'See what I am reduced to, in the
maddening suspense of waiting for you. See how I kill the time when
the time parts us. Come in! come in! I am in one of my malicious
humours this morning, caused entirely, Mrs Valeria, by my anxiety
to see you. When I am in my malicious humours I must tease something.
I am teasing Ariel. Look at her! She has had nothing to eat all day,
and she hasn't been quick enough to snatch a morsel of cake yet. You
needn't pity her. Ariel has no nerves – I don't hurt her.'

'Ariel has no nerves,' echoed the poor creature, frowning at me for
interfering between her master and herself. 'He doesn't hurt me.'

I heard Benjamin beginning to swing his cane behind me.

'Drop the strings!' I reiterated, more vehemently than ever. 'Drop
them – or I shall instantly leave you.'

Miserrimus Dexter's delicate nerves shuddered at my violence.
'What a glorious voice!' he exclaimed – and dropped the strings. 'Take
the cakes,' he added, addressing Ariel in his most imperial manner.

She passed me, with the strings hanging from her swollen wrists,
and the dish of cakes in her hand. She nodded her head at me defiantly.

'Ariel has got no nerves,' she repeated, proudly. 'He doesn't hurt
me.'

'You see,' said Miserrimus Dexter, 'there is no harm done – and I
dropped the strings when you told me. Don't *begin* by being hard on
me, Mrs Valeria, after your long, long absence.' He paused. Benjamin,
standing silent in the doorway, attracted his attention for the first time.
'Who is this?' he asked; and wheeled his chair suspiciously nearer to
the door. 'I know!' he cried, before I could answer. 'This is the
benevolent gentleman who looked like the refuge of the afflicted, when
I saw him last. You have altered for the worse since then, Sir. You

have stepped into quite a new character – you personify Retributive Justice, now. Your new protector, Mrs Valeria – I understand!' He bowed low to Benjamin, with ferocious irony. 'Your humble servant, Mr Retributive Justice! I have deserved you – and I submit to you. Walk in, Sir! I will take care that your new office shall be a sinecure. This lady is the Light of my Life. Catch me failing in respect towards her, if you can!' He backed his chair before Benjamin (who listened to him in contemptuous silence) until he reached the part of the room in which I was standing. 'Your hand, Light of my Life!' he murmured, in his gentlest tones. 'Your hand – only to show you have forgiven me!' I gave him my hand. 'One?' he whispered, entreatingly. 'Only one?' He kissed my hand once, respectfully – and dropped it with a heavy sigh. 'Ah, poor Dexter!' he said, pitying himself with the whole sincerity of his egotism. 'A warm heart, wasted in solitude, mocked by deformity. Sad! sad! Ah, poor Dexter!' He looked round again at Benjamin, with another flash of his ferocious irony. 'A beautiful day, Sir,' he said, with mock-conventional courtesy. 'Seasonable weather indeed after the late long-continued rains. Can I offer you any refreshment? Won't you sit down? Retributive Justice, when it is no taller than you are, looks best in a chair.'

'And a monkey looks best in a cage,' rejoined Benjamin, enraged at the satirical reference to his shortness of stature. 'I was waiting, Sir, to see you get into your swing.'

The retort produced no effect on Miserrimus Dexter: it appeared to have passed by him unheard. He had changed again; he was thoughtful, he was subdued; his eyes were fixed on me with a sad and rapt attention. I took the nearest arm-chair; first casting a glance at Benjamin, which he immediately understood. He placed himself behind Dexter, at an angle which commanded a view of my chair. Ariel, silently devouring her cakes, crouched on a stool at 'the Master's' feet, and looked up at him like a faithful dog. There was an interval of quiet and repose. I was able to observe Miserrimus Dexter uninterruptedly, for the first time since I had entered the room.

I was not surprised – I was nothing less than alarmed by the change for the worse in him, since we had last met. Mr Playmore's letter had not prepared me for the serious deterioration in him which I could now discern.

His features were pinched and worn; the whole face seemed to have wasted strangely in substance and size, since I had last seen it. The softness in his eyes was gone. Blood-red veins were intertwined all over them now; they were set in a piteous and vacant stare. His once firm hands looked withered; they trembled as they lay on the coverlid. The paleness of his face (exaggerated, perhaps, by the black velvet jacket that he wore) had a sodden and sickly look – the fine outline was gone. The multitudinous little wrinkles at the corners of his eyes had deepened. His head sank into his shoulders when he leaned forward in his chair. Years appeared to have passed over him, instead of months, while I had been absent from England. Remembering the medical report which Mr Playmore had given me to read – recalling the doctor's positively-declared opinion that the preservation of Dexter's sanity depended on the healthy condition of his nerves – I could not but feel that I had done wisely (if I might still hope for success) in hastening my return from Spain. Knowing what I knew, fearing what I feared, I believed that his time was near. I felt, when our eyes met by accident, that I was looking at a doomed man.

I pitied him.

Yes! yes! I know that compassion for him was utterly inconsistent with the motive which had taken me to his house – utterly inconsistent with the doubt, still present to my mind, whether Mr Playmore had really wronged him in believing that his was the guilt which had compassed the first Mrs Eustace's death. I felt this: I knew him to be cruel; I believed him to be false. And yet, I pitied him! Is there a common fund of wickedness in us all? Is the suppression or the development of that wickedness a mere question of training and temptation? And is there something in our deeper sympathies which mutely acknowledges this, when we feel for the wicked; when we crowd to a criminal trial; when we shake hands at parting (if we happen to be present officially) with the vilest monster that ever swung on a gallows?[2] It is not for me to decide. I can only say that I pitied Miserrimus Dexter – and that he found it out.

'Thank you,' he said, suddenly. 'You see I am ill, and you feel for me. Dear and good Valeria!'

'This lady's name, Sir, is Mrs Eustace Macallan,' interposed Benjamin, speaking sternly behind him. 'The next time you address her, remember, if you please, that you have no business with her Christian name.'

Benjamin's rebuke passed, like Benjamin's retort, unheeded and unheard. To all appearance, Miserrimus Dexter had completely forgotten that there was such a person in the room.

'You have delighted me with the sight of you,' he went on. 'Add to the pleasure by letting me hear your voice. Talk to me of yourself. Tell me what you have been doing since you left England.'

It was necessary to my object to set the conversation afloat; and this was as good a way of doing it as any other. I told him plainly how I had been employed during my absence.

'So you are still fond of Eustace?' he said, bitterly.

'I love him more dearly than ever.'

He lifted his hands, and hid his face. After waiting awhile, he went on; speaking in an odd, muffled manner, still under cover of his hands.

'And you leave Eustace in Spain?' he said; 'and you return to England by yourself! What made you do that?'

'What made me first come here, and ask you to help me, Mr Dexter?'

He dropped his hands, and looked at me. I saw in his eyes, not amazement only, but alarm.

'Is it possible,' he exclaimed, 'that you won't let that miserable matter rest even yet? Are you still determined to meddle with the mystery at Gleninch?'

'I am still determined, Mr Dexter; and I still hope that you may be able to help me.'

The old distrust that I remembered so well, darkened again over his face the moment I said those words.

'How can I help you?' he asked. 'Can I alter facts?' He stopped. His face brightened again, as if some sudden sense of relief had come to him. 'I *did* try to help you,' he went on. 'I told you that Mrs Beauly's absence was a device to screen herself from suspicion; I told you that the poison might have been given by Mrs Beauly's maid. Has reflection convinced you? Do you see something in the idea?'

This return to Mrs Beauly gave me my first chance of leading the talk to the right topic.

'I see nothing in the idea,' I answered. 'I see no motive. Had the maid any reason to be an enemy to the late Mrs Eustace?'

'Nobody had any reason to be an enemy to the late Mrs Eustace!' he broke out, loudly and vehemently. 'She was all goodness, all kindness; she never injured any human creature in thought or deed. She was a saint upon earth. Respect her memory! Let the martyr rest in her grave!' He covered his face again with his hands, and shook and shuddered under the paroxysm of emotion that I had roused in him.

Ariel suddenly and softly left her stool, and approached me.

'Do you see my ten claws?' she whispered, holding out her hands. 'Vex the Master again – and you will feel my ten claws on your throat!'

Benjamin rose from his seat: he had seen the action, without hearing the words. I signed to him to keep his place. Ariel returned to her stool, and looked up again at the Master.

'Don't cry,' she said. 'Come on. Here are the strings. Tease me again. Make me screech with the smart of it.'

He never answered, and never moved.

Ariel bent her slow mind to meet the difficulty of attracting his attention. I saw it in her frowning brows, in her colourless eyes looking at me vacantly. On a sudden, she joyfully struck the open palm of one of her hands with the fist of the other. She had triumphed. She had got an idea.

'Master!' she cried. 'Master! You haven't told me a story for ever so long. Puzzle my thick head. Make my flesh creep. Come on. A good long story. All blood and crimes.'

Had she accidentally hit on the right suggestion to strike his wayward fancy? I knew his high opinion of his own skill in 'dramatic narrative.' I knew that one of his favourite amusements was to puzzle Ariel by telling her stories that she could not understand. Would he wander away into the region of wild romance? Or would he remember that my obstinacy still threatened him with re-opening the enquiry into the tragedy at Gleninch? and would he set his cunning at work to mislead me by some new stratagem? This latter course was the course which my past experience of him suggested that he would take. But, to my surprise and alarm, I found my past experience at fault. Ariel succeeded in diverting his mind from the subject which had been in full possession of it the moment before she spoke! He showed his face again. It was overspread by a broad smile of gratified self-esteem. He was weak enough now to let even Ariel find her way to his vanity! I saw it, with a sense of misgiving, with a doubt whether I had not delayed my visit until too late, which turned me cold, from head to foot.

Miserrimus Dexter spoke – to Ariel, not to me.

'Poor devil!' he said, patting her head complacently. 'You don't understand a word of my stories, do you? And yet I can make the flesh creep on your great clumsy body – and yet I can stir your stagnant mind, and make you like it! Poor devil!' He leaned back serenely in his chair, and looked my way again. Would the sight of me remind him of the words that had passed between us, not a minute since? No! There was the pleasantly-tickled self-conceit smiling at me exactly as it had smiled at Ariel. 'I excel in dramatic narrative, Mrs Valeria,' he said. 'And this creature here on the stool, is a remarkable proof of it. She is quite a psychological study, when I tell her one of my stories. It is really amusing to see the half-witted wretch's desperate efforts to understand me. You shall have a specimen. I have been out of spirits, while you were away – I haven't told her a story for weeks past; I will tell her one now. Don't suppose it's any effort to me! My invention is inexhaustible. You are sure to be amused – you are naturally serious – but you are sure to be amused. I am naturally serious, too: and I always laugh at her.'

Ariel clapped her great shapeless hands. 'He always laughs at me!' she said, with a proud look of superiority, directed straight at Me.

I was at a loss, seriously at a loss, what to do. The outbreak which I had provoked in leading him to speak of the late Mrs Eustace warned me to be careful, and to wait for my opportunity, before I reverted to *that* subject. How else could I turn the conversation, so as to lead him, little by little, towards the betrayal of the secrets which he was keeping from me? In this uncertainty, one thing only seemed to be plain. To let him tell his story, would be simply to let him waste the precious minutes. With a vivid remembrance of Ariel's 'ten claws,' I decided nevertheless on discouraging Dexter's new whim, at every opportunity and by every means in my power.

'Now, Mrs Valeria!' he began, loudly and loftily. 'Listen. Now, Ariel! Bring your brains to a focus. I improvise poetry; I improvise fiction. We will begin with the good old formula of the fairy stories. Once upon a time—'

I was waiting for my opportunity to interrupt him, when he interrupted himself. He stopped, with a bewildered look. He put his hand to his head, and passed it backwards and forwards over his forehead. He laughed feebly.

'I seem to want rousing,' he said.

Was his mind gone? There had been no signs of it, until I had unhappily stirred his memory of the dead mistress of Gleninch. Was the weakness which I had already noticed, was the bewilderment which I now saw, attributable to the influence of a passing disturbance only? In other words, had I witnessed nothing more serious than a first warning to him, and to us? Would he soon recover himself, if we were patient, and gave him time? Even Benjamin was interested at last; I saw him trying to look at Dexter round the corner of the chair. Even Ariel was surprised and uneasy. She had no dark glances to cast at me now.

We all waited to see what he would do, to hear what he would say, next.

'My harp!' he cried. 'Music will rouse me.'

Ariel brought him his harp.

'Master!' she said, wonderingly. 'What's come to you?' He waved his hand, commanding her to be silent.

'Ode to Invention,' he announced loftily, addressing himself to me. 'Poetry and music improvised by Dexter. Silence! Attention!'

His fingers wandered feebly over the harp-strings; awakening no melody, suggesting no words. In a little while, his hand dropped; his head sank forward gently, and rested on the frame of the harp. I started to my feet and approached him. Was it a sleep? or was it a swoon?

I touched his arm, and called to him by his name.

Ariel instantly stepped between us, with a threatening look at me. At the same moment, Miserrimus Dexter raised his head. My voice had reached him. He looked at me with a curious, contemplative quietness in his eyes, which I had never seen in them before.

'Take away the harp,' he said to Ariel, speaking in languid tones, like a man who was very weary.

The mischievous half-witted creature – in sheer stupidity, or in downright malice towards me, I am not sure which – irritated him once more.

'Why, Master?' she asked, staring at him with the harp hugged in her arms. 'What has come to you? Where is the story?'

'We don't want the story,' I interposed. 'I have many things to say to Mr Dexter which I have not said yet.'

Ariel lifted her heavy hand. 'You *will* have it!' she said, and advanced towards me. At the same moment the Master's voice stopped her.

'Put away the harp, you fool!' he repeated, sternly. 'And wait for the story until I choose to tell it.'

She took the harp submissively back to its place at the end of the room. Miserrimus Dexter moved his chair a little closer to mine. 'I know what will rouse me,' he said, confidentially. 'Exercise will do it. I have had no exercise lately. Wait a little, and you will see.'

He put his hands on the machinery of the chair, and started on his customary course down the room. Here again, the ominous change in him showed itself under a new form. The pace at which he travelled was not the furious pace that I remembered; the chair no longer rushed under him on rumbling and whistling wheels. It went, but it went slowly. Up the room, and down the room, he painfully urged it – and then he stopped, for want of breath.

We followed him. Ariel was first, and Benjamin was by my side. He motioned impatiently to both of them to stand back, and to let me approach him alone.

'I'm out of practice,' he said, faintly. 'I hadn't the heart to make the wheels roar, and the floor tremble, while you were away.'

Who would not have pitied him? Who would have remembered his misdeeds at that moment? Even Ariel felt it. I heard her beginning to whine and whimper behind me. The magician who alone could rouse the dormant sensibilities in her nature had awakened them now by his neglect. Her fatal cry was heard again, in mournful, moaning tones.

'What's come to you, Master? Have you forgot me? Where's the story?'

'Never mind her,' I whispered to him. 'You want the fresh air. Send for the gardener. Let us take a drive in your pony-chaise.'

It was useless. Ariel would be noticed. The mournful cry came once more.

'Where's the story? Where's the story?'

The sinking spirit leapt up in Dexter again.

'You wretch! you fiend!' he cried, whirling his chair round, and facing her. 'The story is coming. I *can* tell it! I *will* tell it! Wine! You whimpering idiot, get me the wine. Why didn't I think of it before? The kingly Burgundy! that's what I want, Valeria, to set my invention alight and flaming in my head. Glasses for everybody! Honour to the King of the Vintages – the Royal Clos Vougeot!'

Ariel opened the cupboard in the alcove, and produced the wine and the high Venetian glasses. Dexter drained his goblet full of Burgundy at a draught; he forced us to drink (or at least pretend to drink) with him. Even Ariel had her share, this time, and emptied her glass in rivalry with her master. The powerful wine mounted almost instantly to her weak head. She began to sing hoarsely a song of her own devising, in imitation of Dexter. It was nothing but the repetition, the endless mechanical repetition, of her demand for the story. 'Tell us the story. Master! master! tell us the story!' Absorbed over his wine, the Master silently filled his goblet for the second time. Benjamin whispered to me, while his eye was off us, 'Take my advice, Valeria, for once; let us go.'

'One last effort,' I whispered back. 'Only one!'

Ariel went drowsily on with her song.

'Tell us the story. Master! master! tell us the story.'

Miserrimus Dexter looked up from his glass. The generous stimulant was beginning to do its work. I saw the colour rising in his face. I saw the bright intelligence flashing again in his eyes. The Burgundy *had* roused him! The good wine offered me a last chance!

'Now for the story!' he cried.

'No story!' I said. 'I want to talk to you, Mr Dexter. I am not in the humour for a story.'

'Not in the humour?' he repeated, with a gleam of the old impish irony showing itself again in his face. 'That's an excuse. I see what it is! You think my invention is gone – and you are not frank enough to confess it. I'll show you you're wrong. I'll show you that Dexter is himself again. Silence, you Ariel, or you shall leave the room! I have got it, Mrs Valeria, all laid out here, with scenes and characters complete.' He touched his forehead, and looked at me with a furtive and smiling cunning, before he added his next words. 'It's the very thing to interest *you*, my fair friend. It's the story of a Mistress and a Maid. Come back to the fire and hear it.'

The Story of a Mistress and a Maid? If that meant anything, it meant the story of Mrs Beauly and her maid, told in disguise!

The title, and the look which had escaped him when he announced it, revived the hope that was well-nigh dead in me. He had rallied at last. He was again in possession of his natural foresight and his natural cunning. Under pretence of telling Ariel her story, he was evidently about to make the attempt to mislead me, for the second time. The conclusion was irresistible. To use his own words – Dexter was himself again.

I took Benjamin's arm as we followed him back to the fireplace in the middle of the room. 'There is a chance for me yet,' I whispered. 'Don't forget the signals.'

We returned to the places which we had already occupied. Ariel cast another threatening look at me. She had just sense enough left, after emptying her goblet of wine, to be on the watch for a new interruption on my part. I took care of course that nothing of the sort should happen. I was now as eager as Ariel to hear the story. The subject was full of snares for the narrator. At any moment, in the excitement of speaking, Dexter's memory of the true events might show itself reflected in the circumstances of the fiction. At any moment, he might betray himself.

He looked round him, and began.

'My public, are you seated? My public, are you ready?' he asked, gaily. 'Your face a little more this way,' he added, in his softest and tenderest tones, motioning to me to turn my full face towards him. 'Surely I am not asking too much? You look at the meanest creature that crawls – look at Me. Let me find my inspiration in your eyes. Let me feed my hungry admiration on your form. Come! have one little pitying smile left for the man whose happiness you have wrecked. Thank you. Light of my Life, thank you!' He kissed his hand to me, and threw himself back luxuriously in his chair. 'The story,' he resumed. 'The story at last! In what form shall I cast it? In the dramatic form – the oldest way, the truest way, the shortest way of telling a story! Title, first. A short title, a taking title: "Mistress and Maid." Scene, the land of romance – Italy. Time, the age of romance – the fifteenth century. Ha! look at Ariel. She knows no more about the fifteenth century than the cat in the kitchen, and yet she is interested already. Happy Ariel!'

Ariel looked at me again, in the double intoxication of the wine and the triumph.

'I know no more than the cat in the kitchen,' she repeated, with a broad grin of gratified vanity. 'I am "happy Ariel!" What are You?'

Miserrimus Dexter laughed uproariously.

'Didn't I tell you?' he said. 'Isn't she fun? Persons of the Drama,' he resumed: – 'Three in number. Women only. Angelica, a noble lady; noble alike in spirit and in birth. Cunegonda, a beautiful devil, in woman's form. Damoride, her unfortunate maid. First scene. A dark vaulted chamber in a castle. Time, evening. The owls are hooting in the wood; the frogs are croaking in the marsh. Look at Ariel! Her flesh creeps; she shudders audibly. Admirable Ariel!'

My rival in the Master's favour eyed me defiantly. 'Admirable Ariel!' she repeated, in drowsy accents. Miserrimus Dexter paused to take up his goblet of Burgundy – placed close at hand on a little sliding table attached to his chair. I watched him narrowly, as he sipped the wine. The flush was still mounting in his face; the light was still brightening in his eyes. He set down his glass again, with a jovial smack of his lips – and went on.

'Persons present in the vaulted chamber: – Cunegonda and Damoride. Cunegonda speaks. "Damoride!" "Madam?" "Who lies ill in the chamber above us?" "Madam, the noble lady, Angelica." (A pause. Cunegonda speaks again.) "Damoride!" "Madam?" "How does Angelica like you?" "Madam, the noble lady, sweet and good to all who approach her, is sweet and good to me." "Have you attended on her, Damoride?" "Sometimes, madam, when the nurse was weary." "Has she taken her healing medicine from your hand?" "Once or twice, madam, when I happened to be by." "Damoride, take this key, and open the casket on the table there." (Damoride obeys.) "Do you see a green vial in the casket?" "I see it, madam." "Take it out." (Damoride obeys.) "Do you see a liquid in the green vial? can you guess what it is?" "No, madam." "Shall I tell you?" (Damoride bows respectfully.) "Poison is in the vial." (Damoride starts; she shrinks from the poison; she would fain put it aside. Her mistress signs to her to keep it in her hand; her mistress speaks.) "Damoride, I have told you one of my secrets; shall I tell you another?" (Damoride waits, fearing what is to come. Her mistress speaks.) "I hate the Lady Angelica. Her life stands between me and the joy of my heart. You hold her life in your hand." (Damoride drops on her knees; she is a devout person; she crosses herself, and then she speaks.) "Mistress, you terrify me. Mistress, what do I hear?" (Cunegonda advances, stands over her, looks down on her with terrible eyes, whispers the next words.) "Damoride, the Lady Angelica must die – and I must not be suspected. The Lady Angelica must die – and by your hand."'

He paused again. To sip the wine once more? No; to drink a deep draught of it, this time.

Was the stimulant beginning to fail him already?

I looked at him attentively, as he laid himself back again in his chair, to consider for a moment before he went on.

The flush on his face was as deep as ever; but the brightness in his eyes was beginning to fade already. I had noticed that he spoke more and more slowly as he advanced to the later dialogue of the scene.

Was he feeling the effort of invention already? Had the time come when the wine had done all that the wine could do for him?

We waited. Ariel sat watching him, with vacantly-staring eyes and vacantly-open mouth. Benjamin, impenetrably expecting the signal, kept his open note-book on his knee, covered by his hand.

Miserrimus Dexter went on.

'Damoride hears those terrible words; Damoride clasps her hands in entreaty. "Oh, madam! madam! how can I kill the dear and noble lady? What motive have I for harming her?" Cunegonda answers, "You have the motive of obeying Me." Damoride falls with her face on the floor, at her mistress's feet. "Madam, I cannot do it! Madam, I dare not do it!" Cunegonda answers, "You run no risk: I have my plan for diverting discovery from myself, and my plan for diverting discovery from you." Damoride repeats, "I cannot do it! I dare not do it!" Cunegonda's eyes flash lightnings of rage. She takes from its place of concealment in her bosom—'

He stopped in the middle of the sentence, and put his hand to his head. Not like a man in pain, but like a man who had lost his idea.

Would it be well if I tried to help him to recover his idea? or would it be wiser (if I could only do it) to keep silence?

I could see the drift of his story plainly enough. His object, under the thin disguise of the Italian romance, was to meet my unanswerable objection to suspecting Mrs Beauly's maid – the objection that the woman had no motive for committing herself to an act of murder. If he could practically contradict this, by discovering a perfectly reasonable and perfectly probable motive, his end would be gained. Those enquiries which I had pledged myself to pursue – those enquiries which might, at any moment, take a turn that directly concerned him – would, in that case, be successfully diverted from the right to the wrong person. The innocent maid would set my strictest scrutiny at defiance; and Dexter would be safely shielded behind her.

I determined to give him time. Not a word passed my lips.

The minutes followed each other. I waited in the deepest anxiety. It was a trying and a critical moment. If he succeeded in inventing a probable motive, and in shaping it neatly to suit the purpose of his story, he would prove, by that act alone, that there were reserves of mental power still left in him, which the practised eye of the Scotch doctor had failed to see. But the question was – would he do it?

He did it! Not in a new way; not in a convincing way; not without a painfully-evident effort. Still, well done, or ill done, he found a motive for the maid.

'Cunegonda,' he resumed, 'takes from its place of concealment in her bosom a written paper, and unfolds it. "Look at this," she says. Damoride looks at the paper, and sinks again at her mistress's feet in a paroxysm of horror and despair. Cunegonda is in possession of a shameful secret in the maid's past life. Cunegonda can say to her, "Choose your alternative. Either submit to an exposure which disgraces you, and disgraces your parents, for ever – or make up your mind to obey Me." Damoride might submit to the disgrace if it only affected herself. But her parents are honest people; she cannot disgrace her parents. She is driven to her last refuge – there is no hope of melting the hard heart of Cunegonda. Her only resource is to raise difficulties; she tries to show that there are obstacles between her and the crime. "Madam! madam!" she cries, "how can I do it, when the nurse is there to see me?" Cunegonda answers, "Sometimes the nurse sleeps; sometimes the nurse is away." Damoride still persists. "Madam! madam! the door is kept locked, and the nurse has got the key."'

The key! I instantly thought of the missing key at Gleninch. Had *he* thought of it too? He certainly checked himself as the word escaped him. I resolved to make the signal! I rested my elbow on the arm of my chair, and played with my earring. Benjamin took out his pencil, and arranged his note-book, so that Ariel could not see what he was about, if she happened to look his way.

We waited, until it pleased Miserrimus Dexter to proceed. The interval was a long one. His hand went up again to his forehead. A duller and duller look was palpably stealing over his eyes. When he did speak, it was not to go on with the narrative, but to put a question.

'Where did I leave off?' he asked.

My hopes sank again as rapidly as they had risen. I managed to answer him, however, without showing any change in my manner.

'You left off,' I said, 'where Damoride was speaking to Cunegonda—'

'Yes! yes!' he interposed. 'And what did she say?'

'She said, "The door is kept locked, and the nurse has got the key." '

He instantly leaned forward in his chair.

'No!' he answered, vehemently. 'You're wrong. "Key?" Nonsense! I never said "Key." '

'I thought you did, Mr Dexter.'

'I never did! I said something else; and you have forgotten it.'

I refrained from disputing with him, in fear of what might follow. We waited again. Benjamin, sullenly submitting to my caprices, had taken down the questions and answers that had passed between Dexter and myself. He still mechanically kept his page open, and still held his pencil in readiness to go on. Ariel, quietly submitting to the drowsy influence of the wine while Dexter's voice was in her ears, felt uneasily the change to silence. She glanced round her restlessly; she lifted her eyes to 'the Master.'

There he sat, silent, with his hand to his head, still struggling to marshal his wandering thoughts; still trying to see light through the darkness that was closing round him.

'Master!' cried Ariel, piteously. 'What's become of the story?'

He started as if she had awakened him out of a sleep: he shook his head impatiently, as though he wanted to throw off some oppression that weighed upon it.

'Patience! patience!' he said. 'The story is going on again.'

He dashed at it desperately: he picked up the first lost thread that fell in his way, reckless whether it was the right thread or the wrong one.

'Damoride fell on her knees. She burst into tears. She said—'

He stopped, and looked about him with vacant eyes.

'What name did I give the other woman?' he asked; not putting the question to me, or to either of my companions: asking it of himself, or asking it of the empty air.

'You called the other woman, Cunegonda,' I said.

At the sound of my voice, his eyes turned slowly – turned on me, and yet failed to look at me. Dull and absent, still and changeless, they were eyes that seemed to be fixed on something far away. Even his voice was altered when he spoke next. It had dropped to a quiet, vacant, monotonous tone. I had heard something like it while I was watching by my husband's bedside, at the time of his delirium – when Eustace's mind appeared to be too weary to follow his speech. Was the end so near as this?

'I called her Cunegonda,' he repeated. 'And I called the other—' He stopped once more.

'And you called the other Damoride,' I said.

Ariel looked up at him with a broad stare of bewilderment. She pulled impatiently at the sleeve of his jacket, to attract his notice.

'Is this the story, Master?' she asked.

He answered without looking at her; his changeless eyes still fixed, as it seemed, on something far away.

'This is the story,' he said, absently. 'But why Cunegonda? why Damoride? Why not Mistress and Maid? It's easier to remember Mistress and Maid—'

He hesitated; he shivered as he tried to raise himself in his chair. Then he seemed to rally. 'What did the Maid say to the Mistress?' he muttered. 'What? what? what?' He hesitated again. Then, something seemed to dawn upon him, unexpectedly. Was it some new thought that had struck him? Or some lost thought that he had recovered? Impossible to say! He went on, suddenly and rapidly went on, in these strange words.

'"The letter." The Maid said, "The letter." Oh, my heart! Every word a dagger. A dagger in my heart. Oh, you letter. Horrible, horrible, horrible letter.'

What, in God's name, was he talking about? What did those words mean?

Was he unconsciously pursuing his faint and fragmentary recollections of a past time at Gleninch, under the delusion that he was going on with the story? In the wreck of the other faculties, was memory the last to sink? Was the truth, the dreadful truth, glimmering on me dimly, through the awful shadow cast before it by the advancing eclipse of the brain? My breath failed me; a nameless horror crept through my whole being.

Benjamin, with his pencil in his hand, cast one warning look at me.

Ariel was quiet and satisfied. 'Go on, Master,' was all she said. 'I like it! I like it! Go on with the story.'

He went on – like a man sleeping with his eyes open, and talking in his sleep.

'The Maid said to the Mistress. No: the Mistress said to the Maid. The Mistress said, "Show him the letter. Must, must, must do it." The Maid said, "No. Mustn't do it. Shan't show it. Stuff. Nonsense. Let him suffer. We can get him off. Show it? No. Let the worst come to the worst. Show it then." The Mistress said—' He paused, and waved his hand rapidly to and fro before his eyes, as if he was brushing away some visionary confusion or entanglement. 'Which was it last?' he said, 'Mistress or Maid? Mistress? No. Maid speaks, of course. Loud. Positive. "You scoundrels. Keep away from that table. The Diary's there. Number Nine, Caldershaws. Ask for Dandie. You shan't have the Diary. A secret in your ear. The Diary will hang him. I won't have him hanged. How dare you touch my chair? My chair is Me. How dare you touch Me?'

The last words burst on me like a gleam of light! I had read them in the Report of the Trial – in the evidence of the sheriff's officer. Miserrimus Dexter had spoken in those very terms, when he had tried vainly to prevent the men from seizing my husband's papers, and when the men had pushed his chair out of the room. There was no doubt now of what his memory was busy with. The mystery at Gleninch! His last backward flight of thought circled, feebly and more feebly, nearer and nearer to the mystery at Gleninch!

Ariel roused him again. She had no mercy on him; she insisted on hearing the whole story.

'Why do you stop, Master? Get along with it! get along with it! Tell us quick – what did the Missus say to the Maid?'

He laughed feebly, and tried to imitate her.

'What did the Missus say to the Maid?' he repeated. His laugh died away. He went on speaking, more and more vacantly, more and more rapidly. 'The Mistress said to the Maid, "We've got him off. What about the letter? Burn it now. No fire in the grate. No matches in the box. House topsy-turvy. Servants all gone. Tear it up. Shake it up in the basket. Along with the rest. Shake it up. Waste paper. Throw it away. Gone for ever. Oh, Sara, Sara, Sara. Gone for ever."'

Ariel clapped her hands, and mimicked him, in her turn.

'"Oh, Sara, Sara, Sara,"' she repeated. '"Gone for ever." That's prime, Master! Tell us – who was Sara?'

His lips moved. But his voice sank so low that I could barely hear him. He began again, with the old melancholy refrain.

'The Maid said to the Mistress. No: the Mistress said to the Maid—' He stopped abruptly, and raised himself erect in the chair; he threw up both his hands above his head; and burst into a frightful screaming laugh. 'Aha-ha-ha-ha! How funny! Why don't you laugh? Funny, funny, funny, funny. Aha-ha-ha-ha-ha—'

He fell back in the chair. The shrill and dreadful laugh died away into a low sob. Then there was one long, deep, wearily-drawn breath. Then, nothing but a mute vacant face turned up to the ceiling, with eyes that looked blindly, with lips parted in a senseless, changeless grin. Nemesis at last! The foretold doom had fallen on him. The night had come.

But one feeling animated me, when the first shock was over. Even the horror of that fearful sight seemed only to increase the pity that I felt for the stricken wretch. I started impulsively to my feet. Seeing nothing, thinking of nothing, but the helpless figure in the chair, I sprang forward to raise him; to revive him; to recall him (if such a thing might be possible) to himself. At the first step that I took, I felt hands on me – I was violently drawn back. 'Are you blind?' cried Benjamin, dragging me nearer and nearer to the door. 'Look there!'

He pointed; and I looked.

Ariel had been beforehand with me. She had raised her master in the chair; she had got one arm round him. In her free hand she brandished an Indian club, torn from a 'trophy' of Oriental weapons that ornamented the wall over the fireplace. The creature was transfigured! Her dull eyes glared like the eyes of a wild animal. She gnashed her teeth in the frenzy that possessed her. 'You have done this!' she shouted to me, waving the club furiously round and round over her head. 'Come near him; and I'll dash your brains out! I'll mash you till there's not a whole bone left in your skin!' Benjamin, still holding me with one hand, opened the door with the other. I let him do with me as he would; Ariel fascinated me; I could look at nothing but Ariel. Her frenzy vanished as she saw us retreating. She dropped the club; she threw both arms round him, and nestled her head on his bosom, and sobbed and wept over him. 'Master! Master! They shan't vex you any more. Look up again. Laugh at me as you used to do. Say, "Ariel; you're a fool." Be like yourself again!' I was forced into the next room. I heard a long, low, wailing cry of misery from the poor creature who loved him with a dog's fidelity and a woman's devotion. The heavy door was closed between us. I was in the quiet antechamber; crying over that piteous sight; clinging to my kind old friend, as helpless and as useless as a child.

Benjamin turned the key in the lock.

'There's no use in crying about it,' he said, quietly. 'It would be more to the purpose, Valeria, if you thanked God that you have got out of that room, safe and sound. Come with me.'

He took the key out of the lock, and led me downstairs into the hall. After a little consideration, he opened the front door of the house. The gardener was still quietly at work in the grounds.

'Your master is taken ill,' Benjamin said; 'and the woman who attends upon him has lost her head – if she ever had a head to lose. Where does the nearest doctor live?'

The man's devotion to Dexter showed itself as the woman's devotion had shown itself – in the man's rough way. He threw down the spade, with an oath.

'The Master taken bad?' he said. 'I'll fetch the doctor. I shall find him sooner than you will.'

'Tell the doctor to bring a man with him,' Benjamin added. 'He may want help.'

The gardener turned round sternly.

'*I'm* the man,' he said. 'Nobody shall help but me.'

He left us. I sat down on one of the chairs in the hall, and did my best to compose myself. Benjamin walked to and fro, deep in thought. 'Both of them fond of him,' I heard my old friend say to himself. 'Half monkey, half man – and both of them fond of him. *That* beats me.'

The gardener returned with the doctor – a quiet, dark, resolute

323

man. Benjamin advanced to meet them. 'I have got the key,' he said. 'Shall I go upstairs with you?'

Without answering, the doctor drew Benjamin aside into a corner of the hall. The two talked together in low voices. At the end of it, the doctor said, 'Give me the key. You can be of no use; you will only irritate her.'

With those words, he beckoned to the gardener. He was about to lead the way up the stairs, when I ventured to stop him.

'May I stay in the hall, Sir?' I said. 'I am very anxious to hear how it ends.'

He looked at me for a moment before he replied.

'You had better go home, Madam,' he said. 'Is the gardener acquainted with your address?'

'Yes, Sir.'

'Very well. I will let you know how it ends, by means of the gardener. Take my advice. Go home.'

Benjamin placed my arm in his. I looked back, and saw the doctor and the gardener ascending the stairs together, on their way to the locked-up room.

'Never mind the doctor!' I whispered. 'Let's wait in the garden.'

Benjamin would not hear of deceiving the doctor. 'I mean to take you home,' he said. I looked at him in amazement. My old friend, who was all meekness and submission, so long as there was no emergency to try him, now showed the dormant reserve of manly spirit and decision in his nature, as he had never (in my experience) shown it yet. He led me into the garden. We had kept our cab: it was waiting for us at the gate.

On our way home, Benjamin produced his note-book.

'What's to be done, my dear, with the gibberish that I have written here?' he said.

'Have you written it all down?' I asked, in surprise.

'When I undertake a duty I do it,' he answered. 'You never gave me the signal to leave off – you never moved your chair. I have written every word of it. What shall I do? Throw it out of the cab-window?'

'Give it to me!'

'What are you going to do with it?'

'I don't know yet. I will ask Mr Playmore.'

CHAPTER XLI

Mr Playmore in a New Character

By that night's post – although I was far from being fit to make the exertion – I wrote to Mr Playmore, to tell him what had taken place, and to beg for his earliest assistance and advice.

The notes in Benjamin's book were partly written in short-hand, and were, on that account, of no use to me in their existing condition. At my request, he made two fair copies. One of the copies I enclosed in my letter to Mr Playmore. The other I laid by me, on my bedside table, when I went to rest.

Over and over again, through the long hours of the wakeful night, I read and re-read the last words which had dropped from Miserrimus Dexter's lips. Was it possible to interpret them to any useful purpose? At the very outset, they seemed to set interpretation at defiance. After trying vainly to solve the hopeless problem, I did at last what I might as well have done at first – I threw down the paper in despair. Where were my bright visions of discovery and success, now? Scattered to the winds! Was there the faintest chance of the stricken man's return to reason? I remembered too well what I had seen to hope for it. The closing lines of the medical report which I had read in Mr Playmore's office recurred to my memory, in the stillness of the night. 'When the catastrophe has happened, his friends can entertain no hope of his cure: the balance once lost, will be lost for life.'

The confirmation of that terrible sentence was not long in reaching me. The next morning the gardener brought a note, containing the information which the doctor had promised to give me on the previous day.

Miserrimus Dexter and Ariel were still where Benjamin and I had left them together – in the long room. They were watched by skilled attendants; waiting the decision of Dexter's nearest relative (a younger brother), who lived in the country, and who had been communicated with by telegraph. It had been found impossible to part the faithful Ariel from her Master, without using the bodily restraints adopted in cases of raging insanity. The doctor and the gardener (both unusually strong men) had failed to hold the poor creature, when they first attempted to remove her on entering the room. Directly they permitted her to return to her Master, the frenzy vanished: she was perfectly quiet and contented, so long as they let her sit at his feet and look at him.

Sad as this was, the report of Miserrimus Dexter's condition was more melancholy still.

'My patient is in a state of absolute imbecility' – those were the words in the doctor's letter; and the gardener's simple narrative confirmed them as the truest words that could have been used. Dexter was unconscious of poor Ariel's devotion to him – he did not even appear to know that she was present in the room. For hours together, he remained in a state of utter lethargy in his chair. He showed an animal interest in his meals, and a greedy animal enjoyment of eating and drinking as much as he could get – and that was all. 'This morning,' the honest gardener said to me at parting, 'we thought he seemed to wake up a bit. Looked about him, you know, and made queer signs with his hands. I couldn't make out what he meant; no more could the doctor. *She* knew, poor thing – she did. Went and got him his harp, and put his hand up to it. Lord bless you, no use! He couldn't play, no more than I can. Twanged at it anyhow, and grinned and gabbled to himself. No: he'll never come right again. Any person can see that, without the doctor to help 'em. Enjoys his meals, as I told you; and that's all. It would be the best thing that could happen, if it would please God to take him. There's no more to be said. I wish you good morning, Ma'am.'

He went away with the tears in his eyes; and left me, I own it, with the tears in mine.

An hour later, there came some news which revived me. I received a telegram from Mr Playmore, expressed in these welcome words: 'Obliged to go to London by to-night's mail train. Expect me to breakfast to-morrow morning.'

The appearance of the lawyer at our breakfast-table duly followed the appearance of his telegram. His first words cheered me. To my infinite surprise and relief, he was far from sharing the despondent view which I took of my position.

'I don't deny,' he said, 'that there are some serious obstacles in your way. But I should never have called here before I attend to my professional business in London, if Mr Benjamin's notes had not produced a very strong impression on my mind. For the first time, as *I* think – you really have a prospect of success. For the first time, I feel justified in offering (under certain restrictions) to help you. That miserable wretch, in the collapse of his intelligence, has done what he would never have done in the possession of his sense and cunning – he has let us see the first precious glimmerings of the light of truth.'

'Are you sure it *is* the truth?' I asked.

'In two important particulars,' he answered, 'I know it to be the truth. Your idea about him is the right one. His memory (as you suppose) was the least injured of his faculties, and was the last to give way, under the strain of trying to tell that story. I believe his memory to have been speaking to you (unconsciously to himself) in all that he said – from the moment when the first reference to "the letter" escaped him, to the end.'

'But what does the reference to the letter mean?' I asked. 'For my part, I am entirely in the dark about it.'

'So am I,' he answered, frankly. 'The chief one among the obstacles which I mentioned just now, is the obstacle presented by that same "letter." The late Mrs Eustace must have been connected with it in some way – or Dexter would never have spoken of it as "a dagger in his heart"; Dexter would never have coupled her name with the words which describe the tearing up of the letter, and the throwing of it away. I can arrive with some certainty at this result, and I can get no further. I have no more idea than you have of who wrote the letter, or of what was written in it. If we are ever to make that discovery – probably the most important discovery of all – we must despatch our first enquiries a distance of three thousand miles. In plain English, my dear lady, we must send to America.'

This, naturally enough, took me completely by surprise. I waited eagerly to hear why we were to send to America.

'It rests with you,' he proceeded, 'when you hear what I have to tell you, to say whether you will go to the expense of sending a man to New York, or not. I can find the right man for the purpose; and I estimate the expense (including a telegram)—'

'Never mind the expense!' I interposed, losing all patience with the eminently Scotch view of the case which put my purse in the first place of importance. 'I don't care for the expense; I want to know what you have discovered.'

He smiled. 'She doesn't care for the expense,' he said to himself, pleasantly. 'How like a woman!'

I might have retorted, 'He thinks of the expense, before he thinks of anything else. How like a Scotchman!' As it was, I was too anxious to be witty. I only drummed impatiently with my fingers on the table; and said, 'Tell me! tell me!'

He took out the fair copy from Benjamin's note-book, which I had sent to him, and showed me these among Dexter's closing words: 'What about the letter? Burn it now. No fire in the grate. No matches in the box. House topsy-turvy. Servants all gone.'

'Do you really understand what those words mean?' I asked.

'I look back into my own experience,' he answered; 'and I understand perfectly what the words mean.'

'And can you make me understand them too?'

'Easily. In those incomprehensible sentences, Dexter's memory has correctly recalled certain facts. I have only to tell you the facts; and you will be as wise as I am. At the time of the Trial, your husband surprised and distressed me by insisting on the instant dismissal of all the household servants at Gleninch. I was instructed to pay them a quarter's wages in advance; to give them the excellent written charac- ters which their good conduct thoroughly deserved, and to see the house clear of them at an hour's notice. Eustace's motive for this summary proceeding was much the same motive which animated his conduct towards you. "If I am ever to return to Gleninch," he said, "I cannot face my honest servants, after the infamy of having stood my trial for murder." There was his reason! Nothing that I could say to him, poor fellow, shook his resolution. I dismissed the servants accordingly. At an hour's notice, they quitted the house, leaving their work for the day all undone. The only persons placed in charge of

Gleninch were persons who lived on the outskirts of the park – that is to say, the lodge-keeper and his wife and daughter. On the last day of the Trial, I instructed the daughter to do her best to make the rooms tidy. She was a good girl enough; but she had no experience as a housemaid: it would never enter her head to lay the bedroom fires ready for lighting, or to replenish the empty match-boxes. Those chance words that dropped from Dexter would, no doubt, exactly describe the state of his room, when he returned to Gleninch, with the prisoner and his mother, from Edinburgh. That he tore up the mysterious letter in his bedroom, and (finding no means immediately at hand for burning it) that he threw the fragments into the empty grate, or into the waste-paper basket, seems to be the most reasonable conclusion that we can draw from what we know. In any case, he would not have much time to think about it. Everything was done in a hurry on that day. Eustace and his mother, accompanied by Dexter, left for England the same evening by the night-train. I myself locked up the house, and gave the keys to the lodge-keeper. It was understood that he was to look after the preservation of the reception-rooms on the ground floor; and that his wife and daughter were to perform the same service, between them, in the rooms upstairs. On receiving your letter, I drove at once to Gleninch, to question the old woman on the subject of the bedrooms, and of Dexter's room especially. She remembered the time when the house was shut up, by associating it with the time when she was confined to her bed by an attack of sciatica. She had not crossed the lodge-door, she was sure, for at least a week (if not longer) after Gleninch had been left in charge of her husband and herself. Whatever was done in the way of keeping the bedrooms aired and tidy, during her illness, was done by her daughter. She, and she only, must have disposed of any litter which might have been lying about in Dexter's room. Not a vestige of torn paper, as I can myself certify, is to be discovered in any part of the room, now. Where did the girl find the fragments of the letter? and what did she do with them? Those are the questions (if you approve of it) which we must send three thousand miles away to ask – for this sufficient reason, that the lodge-keeper's daughter was married more than a year since, and that she is settled with her husband in business at New York. It rests with you to decide what is to be done. Don't let me mislead you with false hopes! Don't let me tempt you to throw away your money! Even if this woman does remember what she did with the torn paper, the chances, at this distance of time, are enormously against our ever recovering a single morsel of it. Be in no haste to decide. I have my work to do in the City – I can give you the whole day to think it over.'

'Send the man to New York by the next steamer,' I said. 'There is my decision, Mr Playmore, without keeping you waiting for it!'

He shook his head, in grave disapproval of my impetuosity. In my former interview with him, we had never once touched on the question of money. I was now, for the first time, to make acquaintance with Mr Playmore on the purely Scotch side of his character!

'Why, you don't even know what it will cost you!' he exclaimed, taking out his pocket-book with the air of a man who was equally startled and scandalised. 'Wait till I tot it up,' he said, 'in English and American money.'

'I can't wait! I want to make more discoveries!'

He took no notice of my interruption: he went on impenetrably with his calculations.

'The man will go second-class, and will take a return-ticket. Very well. His ticket includes his food; and (being, thank God, a tee-totaller) he won't waste your money in buying liquor on board. Arrived at New York, he will go to a cheap German house, where he will, as I am credibly informed, be boarded and lodged at the rate—'

By this time (my patience being completely worn out) I had taken my cheque-book from the table-drawer; had signed my name; and had handed the blank cheque across the table to my legal adviser.

'Fill it in with whatever the man wants,' I said. 'And for Heaven's sake let us get back to Dexter!'

Mr Playmore fell back in his chair, and lifted his hands and eyes to the ceiling. I was not in the least impressed by that solemn appeal to the unseen powers of arithmetic and money. I insisted positively on being fed with more information.

'Listen to this,' I went on; reading from Benjamin's notes. 'What did Dexter mean, when he said, "Number Nine, Caldershaws. Ask for Dandie. You shan't have the Diary. A secret in your ear. The Diary will hang him"? How came Dexter to know what was in my husband's Diary? And what does he mean by "Number Nine, Caldershaws," and the rest of it? Facts again?'

'Facts again!' Mr Playmore answered, 'muddled up together, as you may say – but positive facts for all that. Caldershaws, you must know, is one of the most disreputable districts in Edinburgh. One of my clerks (whom I am in the habit of employing confidentially) volunteered to enquire for "Dandie," at "Number nine." It was a ticklish business, in every way; and my man wisely took a person with him who was known in the neighbourhood. "Number nine" turned out to be (ostensibly) a shop for the sale of rags and old iron; and "Dandie" was suspected of trading now and then, additionally, as a receiver of stolen goods. Thanks to the influence of his companion, backed by a bank-note (which can be repaid, by the way, out of the fund for the American expenses), my clerk succeeded in making the fellow speak. Not to trouble you with needless details, the result in substance was this. A fortnight or more before the date of Mrs Eustace's death, "Dandie" made two keys from wax models supplied to him by a new customer. The mystery observed in the matter by the agent who managed it, excited Dandie's distrust. He had the man privately watched before he delivered the keys; and he ended in discovering that his customer was – Miserrimus Dexter. Wait a little! I have not done yet. Add to this information Dexter's incomprehensible knowledge of the contents of your husband's Diary; and the product is – that the wax models sent to the old iron shop in Caldershaws, were models taken by theft from the key of the Diary and the key of the table-drawer in which it was kept. I have my own idea of the revelations that are still to come, if this matter is properly followed up. Never mind going into that, at present. Dexter (I tell you again) is answerable for the late Mrs Eustace's death. *How* he is answerable, I believe you are in a fair way of finding out. And, more than that, I say now, what I could not venture to say before – it is a duty towards Justice, as well as a duty towards your husband, to bring the truth to light. As for the difficulties to be encountered, I don't think they need daunt you. The greatest difficulties give way in the end, when they are attacked by the united alliance of patience, resolution, – *and* economy.'

With a strong emphasis on the last words, my worthy adviser, mindful of the flight of time and the claims of business, rose to take his leave.

'One word more,' I said, as he held out his hand. 'Can you manage to see Miserrimus Dexter before you go back to Edinburgh? From what the gardener told me, his brother must be with him by this time. It would be a relief to me to hear the latest news of him, and to hear it from you.'

'It is part of my business in London to see him,' said Mr Playmore. 'But, mind! I have no hope of his recovery: I only wish to satisfy myself that his brother is able and willing to take care of him. So far as *we* are concerned, Mrs Eustace, that unhappy man has said his last words.'

He opened the door – stopped – considered – and came back to me.

'With regard to that matter of sending the agent to America,' he resumed. 'I propose to have the honour of submitting to you a brief abstract—'

'Oh, Mr Playmore!'

'A brief abstract in writing, Mrs Eustace, of the estimated expenses of the whole proceeding. You will be good enough maturely to consider the same; making any remarks on it, tending to economy, which may suggest themselves to your mind at the time. And you will further oblige me, if you approve of the abstract, by yourself filling in the blank space on your cheque with the needful amount in words and figures. No, Madam! I really cannot justify it to my conscience to carry about my person any such loose and reckless document as a blank cheque. There's a total disregard of the first claims of prudence and economy, implied in this small slip of paper, which is nothing less than a flat contradiction of the principles that have governed my whole life. I can't submit to flat contradiction. Good morning, Mrs Eustace – good morning.'

He laid my cheque on the table with a low bow, and left me. Among the curious developments of human stupidity which occasionally present themselves to view, surely the least excusable is the stupidity which, to this day, persists in wondering why the Scotch succeed so well in life!

CHAPTER XLII

More Surprises!

The same evening I received my 'abstract' by the hands of a clerk.

It was an intensely characteristic document. My expenses were remorselessly calculated down to shillings and even to pence; and our unfortunate messenger's instructions, in respect of his expenditure, were reduced to a nicety which must have made his life in America nothing less than a burden to him. In mercy to the man, I took the liberty, when I wrote back to Mr Playmore, of slightly increasing the indicated amount of the figures which were to appear on the cheque. I ought to have better known the correspondent whom I had to deal with. Mr Playmore's reply (informing me that our emissary had started on his voyage) returned a receipt in due form – and the whole of the surplus money, to the last farthing!

A few hurried lines accompanied the 'abstract,' and stated the result of the lawyer's visit to Miserrimus Dexter.

There was no change for the better – there was no change at all. Mr Dexter (the brother) had arrived at the house, accompanied by a medical man accustomed to the charge of the insane. The new doctor declined to give any definite opinion on the case until he had studied it carefully with plenty of time at his disposal. It had been accordingly arranged that he should remove Miserrimus Dexter to the asylum of which he was the proprietor, as soon as the preparations for receiving the patient could be completed. The one difficulty that still remained to be met, related to the disposal of the faithful creature who had never left her master, night or day, since the catastrophe had happened. Ariel had no friends, and no money. The proprietor of the asylum could not be expected to receive her without the customary payment; and Mr Dexter's brother 'regretted to say that he was not rich enough to find the money.' A forcible separation from the one human being whom she loved, and a removal in the character of a pauper to a public asylum – such was the prospect which awaited the unfortunate creature, unless some one interfered in her favour before the end of the week.

Under these sad circumstances, good Mr Playmore – passing over the claims of economy in favour of the claims of humanity – suggested that we should privately start a Subscription, and offered to head the list liberally himself.

I must have written all these pages to very little purpose, if it is necessary for me to add that I instantly sent a letter to Mr Dexter (the brother), undertaking to be answerable for whatever money was required, while the subscriptions were being collected, and only stipulating that when Miserrimus Dexter was removed to the asylum, Ariel should accompany him. This was readily conceded. But serious objections were raised, when I further requested that she might be permitted to attend on her master in the asylum, as she had attended on him in the house. The rules of the establishment forbade it, and the universal practice in such cases forbade it, and so on, and so on. However, by dint of perseverance, and persuasion, I so far carried my point as to gain a reasonable concession. During certain hours in the day, and under certain wise restrictions, Ariel was to be allowed the privilege of waiting on the Master in his room, as well as of accompanying him when he was brought out in his chair to take the air in the garden. For the honour of humanity, let me add, that the liability which I had undertaken made no very serious demands on my resources. Placed in Benjamin's charge, our subscription list prospered. Friends, and even strangers sometimes, opened their hearts and their purses when they heard Ariel's melancholy story.

The day which followed the day of Mr Playmore's visit brought me news from Spain, in a letter from my mother-in-law. To describe what

I felt, when I broke the seal, and read the first lines, is simply impossible. Let Mrs Macallan be heard on this occasion in my place.

Thus she wrote: –

'Prepare yourself, my dearest Valeria, for a delightful surprise. Eustace has justified my confidence in him. When he returns to England, he returns – if you will let him – to his wife.

'This resolution, let me hasten to assure you, has not been brought about by any persuasions of mine. It is the natural outgrowth of your husband's gratitude and your husband's love. The first words he said to me, when he was able to speak, were these: "If I live to return to England, and if I go to Valeria, do you think she will forgive me?" We can only leave it to you, my dear, to give the answer. If you love us, answer us by return of post.

'Having now told you what he said, when I first informed him that you had been his nurse – and remember, if it seems very little, that he is still too weak to speak, except with difficulty – I shall purposely keep my letter back for a few days. My object is to give him time to think, and to frankly tell you of it, if the interval produces any change in his resolution.

'Three days have passed; and there is no change. He has but one feeling now – he longs for the day which is to unite him again to his wife.

'But there is something else connected with Eustace, that you ought to know, and that I ought to tell you.

'Greatly as time and suffering have altered him, in many respects, there is no change, Valeria, in the aversion – the horror I may even say – with which he views your design of enquiring anew into the circumstances which attended the lamentable death of his first wife. I dare not give him your letter: if I touch on the subject, I irritate and distress him. "Has she given up that idea? Can you positively say she has given up that idea?" Over and over again, he has put those questions to me. I have answered – what else could I do, in the miserably feeble state in which he still lies? – I have answered in such a manner as to soothe and satisfy him. I have said: "Relieve your mind of all anxiety on that subject: Valeria has no choice but to give up the idea; the obstacles in her way have proved to be insurmountable

– the obstacles have conquered her." This, if you remember, was what I really believed would happen when you and I spoke of that painful topic; and I have heard nothing from you since which has tended to shake my opinion in the smallest degree. If I am right (as I pray God I may be) in the view that I take, you have only to confirm me in your reply, and all will be well. In the other event – that is to say, if you are still determined to persevere in your hopeless project – then make up your mind to face the result. Set Eustace's prejudices at defiance in this particular; and you lose your hold on his gratitude, his penitence, and his love – you will, in my belief, never see him again.

'I express myself strongly, in your own interests, my dear, and for your own sake. When you reply write a few lines to Eustace, enclosed in your letter to me.

'As for the date of our departure, it is still impossible for me to give you any definite information. Eustace recovers very slowly: the doctor has not yet allowed him to leave his bed. And when we do travel, we must journey by easy stages. It will be at least six weeks, at the earliest, before we can hope to be back again in dear Old England.

'Affectionately yours,

'CATHERINE MACALLAN.'

I laid down the letter, and did my best (vainly enough for some time) to compose my spirits. To understand the position in which I now found myself, it is only necessary to remember one circumstance. The messenger to whom we had committed our enquiries was, at that moment, crossing the Atlantic on his way to New York.

What was to be done?

I hesitated. Shocking as it may seem to some people, I hesitated. There was really no need to hurry my decision. I had the whole day before me.

I went out, and took a wretched, lonely walk, and turned the matter over in my mind. I came home again, and turned the matter over once more, by the fireside. To offend and repel my darling when he was returning to me, penitently returning of his own free will, was what no woman in my position, and feeling as I did, could under any earthly circumstances have brought herself to do. And yet, on the other hand, how in Heaven's name could I give up my grand enterprise, at the very time when even wise and prudent Mr Playmore saw such a prospect of succeeding in it that he had actually volunteered to help me? Placed between those two cruel alternatives, which could I choose? Think of your own frailties; and have some mercy on mine. I turned my back on both the alternatives. Those two agreeable fiends, Prevarication and Deceit, took me as it were softly by the hand: 'Don't commit yourself either way, my dear,' they said, in their most persuasive manner. 'Write just enough to compose your mother-in-law, and to satisfy your husband. You have got time before you. Wait and see if Time doesn't stand your friend, and get you out of the difficulty.'

Infamous advice! And yet, I took it – I, who had been well brought up, and who ought to have known better. You who read this shameful confession, would have known better, I am sure. *You* are not included, in the Prayer Book category, among the 'miserable sinners.'[1]

Well! well! let me have virtue enough to tell the truth. In writing to my mother-in-law, I informed her that it had been found necessary to remove Miserrimus Dexter to an asylum – and I left her to draw her own conclusions from that fact, unenlightened by so much as one word of additional information. In the same way, I told my husband a part of the truth, and no more. I said I forgave him with all my heart – and I did! I said he had only to come to me, and I would receive him with open arms – and so I would! As for the rest, let me say, with Hamlet: 'The rest is silence.'[2]

Having despatched my unworthy letters, I found myself growing restless, and feeling the want of a change. It would be necessary to wait at least eight or nine days before we could hope to hear by telegraph from New York. I bade farewell for a time to my dear and admirable Benjamin, and betook myself to my old home in the North, at the Vicarage of my Uncle Starkweather. My journey to Spain to nurse Eustace had made my peace with my worthy relatives; we had exchanged friendly letters; and I had promised to be their guest as soon as it was possible for me to leave London.

I passed a quiet, and (all things considered) a happy time, among the old scenes. I visited once more the bank by the river side, where Eustace and I had first met. I walked again on the lawn, and loitered through the shrubbery – those favourite haunts in which we had so often talked over our troubles, and so often forgotten them in a kiss. How sadly and strangely had our lives been parted since that time! How uncertain still was the fortune which the future had in store for us!

The associations amid which I was now living, had their softening effect on my heart, their elevating influence over my mind. I reproached myself, bitterly reproached myself, for not having written more fully and frankly to Eustace. Why had I hesitated to sacrifice to him my hopes and my interests in the coming investigation? *He* had not hesitated, poor fellow – *his* first thought was the thought of his wife!

I had passed a fortnight with my uncle and aunt, before I heard again from Mr Playmore. When a letter from him arrived at last, it disappointed me indescribably. A telegram from our messenger informed us that the lodge-keeper's daughter and her husband had left New York, and that he was still in search of a trace of them.

There was nothing to be done but to wait as patiently as we could, on the chance of hearing better news. I remained in the North, by Mr Playmore's advice, so as to be within an easy journey to Edinburgh – in case it might be necessary for me to consult him personally. Three more weeks of weary expectation passed, before a second letter reached me. This time it was impossible to say whether the news was good or bad. It might have been either – it was simply bewildering. Even Mr Playmore himself was taken by surprise. These were the last wonderful words – limited, of course, by considerations of economy – which reached us (by telegram) from our agent in America: –

'*Open the dust-heap at Gleninch.*'

CHAPTER XLIII

At Last!

My letter from Mr Playmore, enclosing the agent's extraordinary telegram, was not inspired by the sanguine view of our prospects which he had expressed to me when we met at Benjamin's house.

'If the telegram means anything,' he wrote, 'it means that the fragments of the torn letter have been cast into the housemaid's bucket (along with the dust, the ashes, and the rest of the litter in the room), and have been emptied on the dust-heap at Gleninch. Since this was done, the accumulated refuse collected from the periodical cleansings of the house, during a term of nearly three years – including, of course, the ashes from the fires kept burning, for the greater part of the year, in the library and the picture gallery – have been poured upon the heap, and have buried the precious morsels of paper deeper and deeper, day by day. Even if we have a fair chance of finding these fragments, what hope can we feel, at this distance of time, of recovering them with the writing in a state of preservation? I shall be glad to hear, by return of post, if possible, how the matter strikes you. If you could make it convenient to consult with me personally in Edinburgh, we should save time, when time may be of serious importance to us. While you are at Doctor Starkweather's, you are within easy reach of this place. Please think of it.'

I thought of it seriously enough. The foremost question which I had to consider was the question of my husband.

The departure of the mother and son from Spain had been so long delayed, by the surgeon's orders, that the travellers had only advanced on their homeward journey as far as Bordeaux, when I had last heard from Mrs Macallan three or four days since. Allowing for an interval of repose at Bordeaux, and for the slow rate at which they would be compelled to move afterwards, I might still expect them to arrive in England some time before a letter from the agent in America could reach Mr Playmore. How, in this position of affairs, I could contrive to join the lawyer in Edinburgh, after meeting my husband in London, it was not easy to see. The wise way and the right way, as I thought, was to tell Mr Playmore frankly that I was not mistress of my own movements, and that he had better address his next letter to me at Benjamin's house.

Writing to my legal adviser in this sense, I had a word of my own to add, about the dust-heap and the torn letter.

In the last years of my father's life I had travelled with him in Italy; and I had seen in the Museum at Naples the wonderful relics of a bygone time discovered among the ruins of Pompeii. By way of encouraging Mr Playmore, I now reminded him that the eruption which had overwhelmed the town had preserved, for more than sixteen hundred years, such perishable things as the straw in which pottery had been packed; the paintings on house walls; the dresses worn by the inhabitants; and (most noticeable of all, in our case) a piece of ancient paper, still attached to the volcanic ashes which had fallen over it. If these discoveries had been made after a lapse of sixteen centuries, under a layer of dust and ashes on a large scale, surely we might hope to meet with similar cases of preservation, after a lapse of three or four years only, under a layer of dust and ashes on a small scale? Taking for granted (what was perhaps doubtful enough) that the fragments of the letter could be recovered, my own conviction was that the writing on them, though it might be faded, would certainly still be legible. The very accumulations which Mr Playmore deplored would be the means of preserving them from the rain and the damp. With these modest hints I closed my letter; and thus for once, thanks to my Continental experience, I was able to instruct my lawyer!

Another day passed; and I heard nothing of the travellers.

I began to feel anxious. I made my preparations for the journey southward, over night; and I resolved to start for London the next day – unless I heard of some change in Mrs Macallan's travelling arrangements in the interval.

The post of the next morning decided my course of action. It brought me a letter from my mother-in-law, which added one more to the memorable dates in my domestic calendar.

Eustace and his mother had advanced as far as Paris on their homeward journey, when a cruel disaster had befallen them. The fatigues of travelling, and the excitement of his anticipated meeting with me, had proved together to be too much for my husband. He had held out as far as Paris with the greatest difficulty; and he was now confined to his bed again, struck down by a relapse. The doctors, this time, had no fear for his life; provided that his patience would support him through a lengthened period of the most absolute repose.

'It now rests with you, Valeria,' Mrs Macallan wrote, 'to fortify and comfort Eustace under this new calamity. Do not suppose that he has ever blamed, or thought of blaming, you, for leaving him in Spain, when the surgeon had pronounced him to be out of danger. "It was *I* who left *her*," he said to me, when we first talked about it; "and it is my wife's right to expect that I should go back to her." Those were his words, my dear; and he has done all he can to abide by them. Helpless in his bed, he now asks you to take the will for the deed, and to join him in Paris. I think I know you well enough, my child, to be sure that you will do this; and I need only add one word of caution, before I close my letter. Avoid all reference, not only to the Trial (you will do that of your own accord), but even to our house at Gleninch. You will understand how he feels, in his present state of nervous depression, when I tell you that I should never have ventured on asking you to join him here, if your letter had not informed me that your visits to Dexter were at an end. Would you believe it? – his horror of anything which recalls our past troubles is still so vivid, that he has actually asked me to give my consent to selling Gleninch!'

So Eustace's mother wrote of him. But she had not trusted entirely to her own powers of persuasion. A slip of paper was enclosed in her letter, containing these two lines, traced in pencil – oh, so feebly and so wearily! – by my poor darling himself: 'I am too weak to travel any further, Valeria. Will you come to me and forgive me?' A few pencil-marks followed; but they were illegible. The writing of those two short sentences had exhausted him.

It is not saying much for myself, I know – but, having confessed it when I was wrong, let me at least record it when I did what was right – I decided instantly on giving up all further connection with the recovery of the torn letter. If Eustace asked me the question, I was resolved to be able to answer truly: 'I have made the sacrifice that assures your tranquillity. When resignation was hardest, I have given way for my husband's sake.'

The motive which had determined me on returning to England, when I first knew that I was mother as well as wife, was still present to my mind when I arrived at this resolution. The one change in me was, that I now treated my husband's tranquillity as the first and foremost consideration. In making this concession, I was not without hope to sustain me. Eustace might yet see the duty of asserting his innocence, in a new light – he might see it as a duty which the father owed to the child.

That morning, I wrote again to Mr Playmore; telling him what my position was, and withdrawing, definitely, from all share in investigating the mystery which lay hidden under the dust-heap at Gleninch.

CHAPTER XLIV

Our New Honeymoon

It is not to be disguised or denied that my spirits were depressed, on my journey to London.

To resign the one cherished purpose of my life, when I had suffered so much in pursuing it, and when I had (to all appearance) so nearly reached the realisation of my hopes, was putting to a hard trial a woman's fortitude, and a woman's sense of duty. Still, even if the opportunity had been offered to me, I would not have recalled my letter to Mr Playmore. 'It is done, and well done,' I said to myself; 'and I have only to wait a day to be reconciled to it – when I give my husband my first kiss.'

I had planned and hoped to reach London, in time to start for Paris by the night-mail. But the train was twice delayed on the long journey from the North; and there was no help for it but to sleep at Benjamin's villa, and to defer my departure until the morning.

It was, of course, impossible for me to warn my old friend of the change in my plans. My arrival took him by surprise. I found him alone in his library, with a wonderful illumination of lamps and candles; absorbed over some morsels of torn paper scattered on the table before him.

'What in the world are you about?' I asked.

Benjamin blushed – I was going to say, like a young girl. But young girls have given up blushing in these latter days of the age we live in.

'Oh, nothing, nothing!' he said, confusedly. 'Don't notice it.'

He stretched out his hand to brush the morsels of paper off the table. Those morsels raised a sudden suspicion in my mind. I stopped him.

'You have heard from Mr Playmore!' I said. 'Tell me the truth, Benjamin. Yes, or No?'

Benjamin blushed a shade deeper, and answered 'Yes.'

'Where is the letter?'

'I mustn't show it to you, Valeria.'

This (need I say it?) made me determined to see the letter. My best way of persuading Benjamin to show it to me was to tell him of the sacrifice that I had made to my husband's wishes. 'I have no further voice in the matter,' I added, when I had done. 'It now rests entirely with Mr Playmore to go on or to give up; and this is my last opportunity of discovering what he really thinks about it. Don't I deserve some little indulgence? Have I no claim to look at the letter?'

Benjamin was too much surprised, and too much pleased with me, when he heard what had happened, to be able to resist my entreaties. He gave me the letter.

Mr Playmore wrote, to appeal confidentially to Benjamin as a commercial man. In the long course of his occupation in business, it was just possible that he might have heard of cases in which documents had been put together again, after having been torn up, by design or by accident. Even if his experience failed in this particular, he might be able to refer to some authority in London who would be capable of giving an opinion on the subject. By way of explaining his strange request, Mr Playmore reverted to the notes which Benjamin had taken at Miserrimus Dexter's house, and informed him of the serious importance of 'the gibberish' which he had reported under protest. The letter closed by recommending that any correspondence which ensued should be kept a secret from me – on the ground that it might excite false hopes in my mind if I was informed of it.

I now understood the tone which my worthy adviser had adopted in writing to me. His interest in the recovery of the letter was evidently so overpowering that common prudence compelled him to conceal it from me, in case of ultimate failure. This did not look as if Mr Playmore was likely to give up the investigation, on my withdrawal from it. I glanced again at the fragments of paper on Benjamin's table, with an interest in them which I had not felt yet.

'Has anything been found at Gleninch?' I asked.

'No,' said Benjamin. 'I have only been trying experiments with a little note of my own, before I wrote to Mr Playmore.'

'Oh! you have torn up your little note yourself, then?'

'Yes. And, to make it all the more difficult to put them together again, I shook up the pieces in a basket. It's a childish thing to do, my dear, at my age—'

He stopped, looking very much ashamed of himself.

'Well,' I went on; 'and have you succeeded in putting the pieces together again?'

'It's not very easy, Valeria. But I have made a beginning. It's the same principle as the principle in the "Puzzles" which we used to put together when I was a boy. Only get one central bit of it right, and the rest of the Puzzle falls into its place in a longer or a shorter time. Please don't tell anybody, my dear. People might say I was in my dotage.'

People might have said that, who did not know Benjamin as I knew him. I remembered my old friend's delight in guessing riddles in the columns of the cheap periodicals – and I perfectly understood the strong hold that the new 'Puzzle' had taken on his fancy. 'It's almost as interesting as solving Enigmas – isn't it?' I said, slyly.

'Enigmas!' Benjamin repeated, contemptuously. 'It's better than any Enigma I ever guessed yet. To think of that gibberish in my note-book having a meaning in it, after all! I only got Mr Playmore's letter this morning; and – I am really almost ashamed to mention it

– I have been trying experiments, off and on, ever since. You won't tell upon me, will you?'

I answered the dear old man by a hearty embrace. Now that he had lost his steady moral balance, and had caught the infection of my enthusiasm, I loved him better than ever!

But I was not quite happy, though I tried to appear so. Struggle against it as I might, I felt a little mortified, when I remembered that I had resigned all further connection with the search for the letter at such a time as this. My one comfort was to think of Eustace. My one encouragement was to keep my mind fixed as constantly as possible on the bright change for the better that now appeared in the domestic prospect. Here, at least, there was no disaster to fear; here I could honestly feel that I had triumphed. My husband had come back to me of his own free will; he had not given way, under the hard weight of evidence – he had yielded to the nobler influences of his gratitude and his love. And I had taken him to my heart again – not because I had made discoveries which left him no other alternative than to live with me, but because I believed in the better mind that had come to him, and loved and trusted him without reserve. Was it not worth some sacrifice to have arrived at this result! True – most true! And yet I was a little out of spirits. Ah, well! well! the remedy was within a day's journey. The sooner I was with Eustace the better.

Early the next morning, I left London for Paris, by the tidal-train.[1] Benjamin accompanied me to the Terminus.

'I shall write to Edinburgh by to-day's post,' he said, in the interval before the train moved out of the station. 'I think I can find the man Mr Playmore wants to help him, if he decides to go on. Have you any message to send, Valeria?'

'No. I have done with it, Benjamin; I have nothing more to say.'

'Shall I write and tell you how it ends, if Mr Playmore does really try the experiment at Gleninch?'

I answered, as I felt, a little bitterly.

'Yes,' I said. 'Write and tell me, if the experiment fails.'

My old friend smiled. He knew me better than I knew myself.

'All right!' he said, resignedly. 'I have got the address of your banker's correspondent in Paris. You will have to go there for money, my dear; and you *may* find a letter waiting for you in the office, when you least expect it. Let me hear how your husband goes on. Good-bye – and God bless you!'

That evening, I was restored to Eustace.

He was too weak, poor fellow, even to raise his head from the pillow. I knelt down at the bedside and kissed him. His languid, weary eyes kindled with a new life, as my lips touched his. 'I must try to live now,' he whispered, 'for your sake.'

My mother-in-law had delicately left us together. When he said those words, the temptation to tell him of the new hope that had come to brighten our lives was more than I could resist.

'You must try to live now, Eustace,' I said, 'for some one else, besides me.'

His eyes looked wonderingly into mine.

'Do you mean my mother?' he asked.

I laid my head on his bosom, and whispered back,

'I mean your child.'

I had all my reward for all that I had given up! I forgot Mr Playmore; I forgot Gleninch. Our new honeymoon dates, in my remembrance, from that day.

The quiet time passed, in the bye street in which we lived. The outer stir and tumult of Parisian life ran its daily course around us, unnoticed and unheard. Steadily, though slowly, Eustace gained strength. The doctors, with a word or two of caution, left him almost entirely to me. 'You are his physician,' they said; 'the happier you make him, the sooner he will recover.' The quiet, monotonous round of my new life was far from wearying me. I, too, wanted repose – I had no interests, no pleasures, out of my husband's room.

Once, and once only, the placid surface of our lives was just gently ruffled by an allusion to the past. Something that I accidentally said, reminded Eustace of our last interview at Major Fitz-David's house. He referred, very delicately, to what I had then said of the Verdict pronounced on him at the Trial; and he left me to infer that a word from my lips, confirming what his mother had already told him, would quiet his mind at once and for ever.

My answer involved no embarrassments or difficulties: I could, and did, honestly tell him that I had made his wishes my law. But it was hardly in womanhood, I am afraid, to be satisfied with merely replying, and to leave it there. I thought it due to me that Eustace too should concede something, in the way of an assurance which might quiet *my* mind. As usual with me, the words followed the impulse to speak them. 'Eustace,' I asked, 'are you quite cured of those cruel doubts which once made you leave me?'

His answer (as he afterwards said) made me blush with pleasure. 'Ah, Valeria, I should never have gone away, if I had known you then as well as I know you now!'

So the last shadows of distrust melted away out of our lives.

The very remembrance of the turmoil and the trouble of my past days in London seemed now to fade from my memory. We were lovers again; we were absorbed again in each other; we could almost fancy that our marriage dated back once more to only a day or two since. But one last victory over myself was wanting to make my happiness complete. I still felt secret longings, in those dangerous moments when I was left to myself, to know whether the search for the torn letter had, or had not, taken place. What wayward creatures we are! With everything that a woman could want to make her happy, I was ready to put that happiness in peril, rather than remain ignorant of what was going on at Gleninch! I actually hailed the day, when my empty purse gave me an excuse for going to my banker's correspondent on business, and so receiving any letters waiting for me which might be placed in my hands.

I applied for my money without knowing what I was about; wondering all the time whether Benjamin had written to me or not. My eyes wandered over the desks and tables in the office, looking for letters furtively. Nothing of the sort was visible. But a man appeared from an inner office: an ugly man, who was yet beautiful to my eyes, for this sufficient reason – he had a letter in his hand, and he said, 'Is this for you, Ma'am?'

A glance at the address showed me Benjamin's handwriting.

Had they tried the experiment of recovering the letter? and had they failed?

Somebody put my money in my bag, and politely led me out to the little hired carriage which was waiting for me at the door. I remember nothing distinctly, until I looked at my news from Benjamin on my way home. His first words told me that the dust-heap had been examined, and that the fragments of the torn letter had been found!

CHAPTER XLV

The Dust-heap Disturbed

My head turned giddy. I was obliged to wait and let my overpowering agitation subside, before I could read any more.

Looking at the letter again, after an interval, my eyes fell accidentally on a sentence near the end, which surprised and startled me.

I stopped the driver of the carriage, at the entrance to the street in which our lodgings were situated, and told him to take me to the beautiful Park of Paris – the famous Bois de Boulogne. My object was to gain time enough, in this way, to read the letter carefully through by myself, and to ascertain whether I ought, or ought not, to keep the receipt of it a secret, before I confronted my husband and his mother, at home.

This precaution taken, I read the narrative which my good Benjamin had so wisely and so thoughtfully written for me. Treating the various incidents methodically, he began with the Report which had arrived, in due course of mail, from our agent in America.

Our man had successfully traced the lodge-keeper's daughter and her husband to a small town in one of the Western States. Mr Playmore's letter of introduction at once secured him a cordial reception from the married pair, and a patient hearing when he stated the object of his voyage across the Atlantic.

His first questions led to no very encouraging results. The woman was confused and surprised, and was apparently quite unable to exert her memory to any useful purpose. Fortunately, her husband proved to be a very intelligent man. He took the agent privately aside, and said to him: 'I understand my wife, and you don't. Tell me exactly what it is you want to know, and leave it to me to discover how much she remembers, and how much she forgets.'

This sensible suggestion was readily accepted. The agent waited for events, a day and a night.

Early the next morning, the husband said to him: 'Talk to my wife now, and you will find she has something to tell you. Only mind this! Don't laugh at her when she speaks of trifles. She is half ashamed to speak of trifles, even to me. Thinks men are above such matters, you know. Listen quietly, and let her talk – and you will get at it all in that way.'

The agent followed his instructions, and 'got at it' as follows: –

The woman remembered, perfectly well, being sent to clean the bedrooms and put them tidy, after the gentlefolks had all left Gleninch. Her mother had a bad hip at the time, and could not go with her and help her. She did not much fancy being alone in the great house, after what had happened in it. On her way to her work, she passed two of the cottagers' children in the neighbourhood, at play in the park. Mr Macallan was always kind to his poor tenants, and never objected to the young ones round about having a run on the grass. The two children idly followed her to the house. She took them inside, along with her; not liking the place, as already mentioned, and feeling that they would be company in the solitary rooms.

She began her work in the Guests' Corridor – leaving the room in the other Corridor, in which the death had happened, to the last.

There was very little to do in the first two rooms. There was not litter enough, when she had swept the floors and cleaned the grates, to even half fill the housemaid's bucket which she carried with her. The children followed her about; and, all things considered, were 'very good company,' in the lonely place.

The third room (that is to say, the bedchamber which had been occupied by Miserrimus Dexter) was in a much worse state than the other two, and wanted a great deal of tidying. She did not much notice the children here, being occupied with her work. The litter was swept up from the carpet, and the cinders and ashes were taken out of the grate, and the whole of it was in the bucket, when her attention was recalled to the children by hearing one of them cry.

She looked about the room without at first discovering them.

A fresh outburst of crying led her in the right direction, and showed her the children under a table in a corner of the room. The youngest of the two had got into a waste-paper basket. The eldest had found an old bottle of gum, with a brush fixed in the cork, and was gravely painting the face of the smaller child with what little remained of the contents of the bottle. Some natural struggles, on the part of the little creature, had ended in the overthrow of the basket, and the usual outburst of crying had followed as a matter of course.

In this state of things the remedy was soon applied. The woman took the bottle away from the eldest child, and gave it a 'box on the ear.' The younger one she set on its legs again, and she put the two 'in the corner' to keep them quiet. This done, she swept up such fragments of the torn paper in the basket as had fallen on the floor; threw them back again into the basket, along with the gum-bottle; fetched the bucket, and emptied the basket into it; and then proceeded to the fourth and last room in the Corridor, where she finished her work for that day.

Leaving the house, with the children after her, she took the filled bucket to the dust-heap, and emptied it in a hollow place among the rubbish, about halfway up the mound. Then she took the children home; and there was an end of it, for the day.

Such was the result of the appeal made to the woman's memory of domestic events at Gleninch.

The conclusion at which Mr Playmore arrived, from the facts submitted to him, was, that we might now hope to recover the letter. Thrown on the refuse ashes in the housemaid's bucket, and afterwards covered by the litter from the fourth room, the torn morsels would be protected above as well as below, when they were emptied on the dust-heap.

Succeeding weeks and months would add to that protection, by adding to the accumulated refuse. In the neglected condition of the grounds, the dust-heap had not been disturbed in search of manure. There it stood, untouched, from the time when the family left Gleninch, to the present day. And there, hidden deep somewhere in the mound, the fragments of the letter must be!

Such were the lawyer's conclusions. He had written immediately to communicate them to Benjamin. And, thereupon, what had Benjamin done?

After having tried his powers of reconstruction on his own correspondence, the prospect of experimenting on the mysterious letter itself, had proved to be a temptation too powerful for the old man to resist. 'I almost fancy, my dear, this business of yours has bewitched me,' he wrote. 'You see I have the misfortune to be an idle man. I have time to spare and money to spare. And the end of it is, that I am here at Gleninch, engaged on my own responsibility (with good Mr Playmore's permission), in searching the dust-heap!'

Benjamin's description of his first view of the field of action at Gleninch followed these characteristic lines of apology.

I passed over the description, without ceremony. My remembrance of the scene was too vivid to require any prompting of that sort. I saw again, in the dim evening light, the unsightly mound which had so strangely attracted my attention at Gleninch. I heard again the words in which Mr Playmore had explained to me the custom of the dust-heap in Scotch country-houses. What had Benjamin and Mr Playmore done? What had Benjamin and Mr Playmore found? For me, the true interest of the narrative was there – and to that portion of it I eagerly turned next.

They had proceeded methodically, of course, with one eye on the pounds, shillings, and pence, and the other on the object in view. In Benjamin, the lawyer had found what he had not met with in me – a sympathetic mind, alive to the value of 'an abstract of the expenses,' and conscious of that most remunerative of human virtues, the virtue of economy.

At so much a week, they had engaged men to dig into the mound and to sift the ashes. At so much a week, they had hired a tent to shelter the open dust-heap from wind and weather. At so much a week, they had engaged the services of a young man (personally known to Benjamin), who was employed in a laboratory under a professor of chemistry, and who had distinguished himself by his skilful manipulation of paper in a recent case of forgery on a well-known London firm. Armed with these preparations, they had begun the work; Benjamin and the young chemist living at Gleninch, and taking it in turns to superintend the proceedings.

Three days of labour with the spade and the sieve produced no results of the slightest importance. However, the matter was in the hands of two quietly-determined men. They declined to be discouraged. They went on.

On the fourth day, the first morsels of paper were found.

Upon examination, they proved to be the fragments of a tradesman's prospectus. Nothing dismayed, Benjamin and the young chemist still persevered. At the end of the day's work, more pieces of paper were turned up. These proved to be covered with written characters. Mr Playmore (arriving at Gleninch, as usual, every evening on the conclusion of his labours in the law) was consulted as to the handwriting. After careful examination, he declared that the mutilated portions of sentences submitted to him had been written, beyond all doubt, by Eustace Macallan's first wife!

This discovery roused the enthusiasm of the searchers to fever height.

Spades and sieves were from that moment forbidden utensils. However unpleasant the task might be, hands alone were used in the further examination of the mound. The first and foremost necessity was to place the morsels of paper (in flat cardboard boxes prepared for the purpose), in their order as they were found. Night came; the labourers were dismissed; Benjamin and his two colleagues worked on by lamplight. The morsels of paper were turned up by dozens, instead of by ones and twos. For awhile the search prospered in this way; and then the morsels appeared no more. Had they all been recovered? or would renewed hand-digging yield more yet? The next light layers of rubbish were carefully removed – and the grand discovery of the day followed. There (upside down) was the gum-bottle, which the lodge-keeper's daughter had spoken of! And, more precious still, under it, were more fragments of written paper, all stuck together in a little lump, by the last drippings from the gum-bottle dropping upon them as they lay in the dust-heap!

The scene now shifted to the interior of the house. When the searchers next assembled, they met at the great table in the library at Gleninch.

Benjamin's experience with the 'Puzzles' which he had put together in the days of his boyhood proved to be of some use to his companions. The fragments accidentally stuck together, would, in all probability, be found to fit each other, and would certainly (in any case) be the easiest fragments to reconstruct, as a centre to start from.

The delicate business of separating these pieces of paper, and of preserving them in the order in which they had adhered to each other, was assigned to the practised fingers of the chemist. But the difficulties of his task did not end here. The writing was (as usual in letters) traced on both sides of the paper, and it could only be preserved for the purpose of reconstruction by splitting each morsel into two – so as artificially to make a blank side, on which could be spread the fine cement used for reuniting the fragments in their original form.

To Mr Playmore and Benjamin, the prospect of successfully putting the letter together, under these disadvantages, seemed to be almost hopeless. Their skilled colleague soon satisfied them that they were wrong.

He drew their attention to the thickness of the paper – note-paper of the strongest and best quality – on which the writing was traced. It was of more than twice the substance of the last paper on which he had operated, when he was engaged in the forgery case; and it was, on that account, comparatively easy for him (aided by the mechanical appliances which he had brought from London) to split the morsels of the torn paper, within a given space of time which might permit them to begin the reconstruction of the letter that night.

With these explanations, he quietly devoted himself to his work. While Benjamin and the lawyer were still poring over the scattered morsels of the letter which had been first discovered, and trying to piece them together again, the chemist had divided the greater part of the fragments specially confided to him into two halves each; and had correctly put together some five or six sentences of the letter, on the smooth sheet of cardboard prepared for that purpose.

They looked eagerly at the reconstructed writing, so far.

It was correctly done: the sense was perfect. The first result gained by examination was remarkable enough to reward them for all their exertions. The language used, plainly identified the person to whom the late Mrs Eustace had addressed her letter.

That person was – my husband.

And the letter thus addressed – if the plainest circumstantial evidence could be trusted – was identical with the letter which Miserrimus Dexter had suppressed until the Trial was over, and had then destroyed by tearing it up.

These were the discoveries that had been made, at the time when Benjamin wrote to me. He had been on the point of posting his letter, when Mr Playmore had suggested that he should keep it by him for a few days longer, on the chance of having more still to tell me.

'We are indebted to her for these results,' the lawyer had said. 'But for her resolution, and her influence over Miserrimus Dexter, we should never have discovered what the dust-heap was hiding from us – we should never have seen so much as a glimmering of the truth. She has the first claim to the fullest information. Let her have it.'

The letter had been accordingly kept back for three days. That interval being at an end, it was hurriedly resumed and concluded in terms which indescribably alarmed me.

'The chemist is advancing rapidly with his part of the work' (Benjamin wrote); 'and I have succeeded in putting together a separate portion of the torn writing which makes sense. Comparison of what he has accomplished with what I have accomplished has led to startling conclusions. Unless Mr Playmore and I are entirely wrong (and God grant we may be so!) there is a serious necessity for your keeping the reconstruction of the letter strictly secret from everybody about you. The disclosures suggested by what has come to light are so heart-rending and so dreadful, that I cannot bring myself to write about them, until I am absolutely obliged to do so. Please forgive me for disturbing you with this news. We are bound, sooner or later, to consult with you in the matter; and we think it right to prepare your mind for what may be to come.'

To this there was added a postscript in Mr Playmore's handwriting.

'Pray observe strictly the caution which Mr Benjamin impresses on you. And bear this in mind, as a warning from *me*. If we succeed in reconstructing the entire letter, the last person living who ought (in my opinion) to be allowed to see it, is – your husband.'

I read those startling words; and I asked myself what I was to do next.

As matters now stood, my husband's tranquillity was, so to speak, committed to my charge. It was surely due to *him* that I should not receive Benjamin's letter and Mr Playmore's postscript in silence. At the same time, it was due to myself that I should honestly tell Eustace I was in correspondence with Gleninch – only waiting to speak, until I knew more than I knew now.

Thus I reasoned with myself. And, to this day, I am not quite sure whether I was right or wrong.

CHAPTER XLVI

The Crisis Deferred

'Take care, Valeria!' said Mrs Macallan. 'I ask you no questions; I only caution you, for your own sake. Eustace has noticed, what I have noticed – Eustace has seen a change in you. Take care!'

So my mother-in-law spoke to me, later in the day, when we happened to be alone. I had done my best to conceal all traces of the effect produced on me by the strange and terrible news from Gleninch. But who could read what I had read, who could feel what I now felt, and still maintain an undisturbed serenity of look and manner? If I had been the vilest hypocrite living, I doubt, even then, if my face could have kept my secret, while my mind was full of Benjamin's letter.

Having spoken her word of caution, Mrs Macallan made no further advance to me. I dare say she was right. Still, it seemed hard to be left, without a word of advice or of sympathy, to decide for myself what it was my duty to my husband to do next.

To show him Benjamin's narrative, in his state of health, and in the face of the warning addressed to me, was simply out of the question. At the same time, it was equally impossible, after I had already betrayed myself, to keep him entirely in the dark. I thought over it anxiously in the night. When the morning came, I decided to appeal to my husband's confidence in me.

I went straight to the point in these terms: –

'Eustace, your mother said yesterday that you noticed a change in me, when I came back from my drive. Is she right?'

'Quite right, Valeria,' he answered – speaking in lower tones than usual, and not looking at me.

'We have no concealments from each other, now,' I answered. 'I ought to tell you, and I do tell you, that I found a letter from England waiting at the banker's, which has caused me some agitation and alarm. Will you leave it to me to choose my own time for speaking more plainly? And will you believe, love, that I am really doing my duty towards you, as a good wife, in making this request?'

I paused. He made no answer: I could see that he was secretly struggling with himself. Had I ventured too far? Had I over-estimated the strength of my influence? My heart beat fast, my voice faltered – but I summoned courage enough to take his hand, and to make a last appeal to him. 'Eustace!' I said. 'Don't you know me, yet, well enough to trust me?'

He turned towards me for the first time. I saw a last vanishing trace of doubt in his eyes as they looked into mine.

'You promise, sooner or later, to tell me the whole truth?' he said.

'I promise with all my heart!'

'I trust you, Valeria!'

His brightening eyes told me that he really meant what he said. We sealed our compact with a kiss. Pardon me for mentioning these trifles – I am still writing (if you will kindly remember it) of our new honeymoon.

By that day's post I answered Benjamin's letter, telling him what I had done, and entreating him, if he and Mr Playmore approved of my conduct, to keep me informed of any future discoveries which they might make at Gleninch.

After an interval – an endless interval, as it seemed to me – of ten days more, I received a second letter from my old friend; with another postscript added by Mr Playmore.

'We are advancing steadily and successfully with the putting together of the letter,' Benjamin wrote. 'The one new discovery which we have made is of serious importance to your husband. We have reconstructed certain sentences, declaring, in the plainest words, that the arsenic which Eustace procured was purchased at the request of his wife, and was in her possession at Gleninch. This, remember, is in the handwriting of the wife, and is signed by the wife – as we have also found out. Unfortunately, I am obliged to add, that the objection to taking your husband into our confidence, mentioned when I last wrote, still remains in force – in greater force, I may say, than ever. The more we make out of the letter, the more inclined we are (if we only studied our own feelings) to throw it back into the dust-heap, in mercy to the memory of the unhappy writer. I shall keep this open for a day or two. If there is more news to tell you, by that time, you will hear of it from Mr Playmore.'

Mr Playmore's postscript followed, dated three days later.

'The concluding part of the late Mrs Macallan's letter to her husband,' the lawyer wrote, 'has proved accidentally to be the first part which we have succeeded in piecing together. With the exception of a few gaps still left, here and there, the writing of the closing paragraphs has been perfectly reconstructed. I have neither the time nor the inclination to write to you on this sad subject, in any detail. In a fortnight more, at the longest, we shall, I hope, send you a copy of the letter, complete from the first line to the last. Meanwhile, it is my duty to tell you that there is one bright side to this otherwise deplorable and shocking document. Legally speaking, as well as morally speaking, it absolutely vindicates your husband's innocence. And it may be lawfully used for this purpose – if he can reconcile it to his conscience, and to the mercy due to the memory of the dead, to permit the public exposure of the letter in Court. Understand me, he cannot be tried again on what we call the criminal charge – for certain technical reasons with which I need not trouble you. But, if the facts which were involved at the criminal trial, can also be shown to be involved in a civil case (and, in this case, they can), the entire matter may be made the subject of a new legal enquiry; and the verdict of a second jury, completely vindicating your husband, may be thus obtained. Keep this information to yourself for the present. Preserve the position which you have so sensibly adopted towards Eustace, until you have read the restored letter. When you have done this, my own idea is that you will shrink, in pity to *him*, from letting him see it. How he is to be kept in ignorance of what we have discovered is another question, the discussion of which must be deferred until we can consult together. Until that time comes, I can only repeat my advice, – Wait till the next news reaches you from Gleninch.'

I waited. What I suffered, what Eustace thought of me, does not matter. Nothing matters now but the facts.

In less than a fortnight more, the task of restoring the letter was completed. Excepting certain instances, in which the morsels of the torn paper had been irretrievably lost – and in which it had been necessary to complete the sense, in harmony with the writer's intention – the whole letter had been put together; and the promised copy of it was forwarded to me in Paris.

Before you, too, read that dreadful letter, do me one favour. Let me briefly remind you of the circumstances under which Eustace Macallan married his first wife.

Remember that the poor creature fell in love with him, without awakening any corresponding affection on his side. Remember that he separated himself from her, and did all he could to avoid her, when he found this out. Remember that she presented herself at his residence in London, without a word of warning; that he did his best to save her reputation; that he failed, through no fault of his own; and that he ended, rashly ended in a moment of despair, by marrying her, to silence the scandal that must otherwise have blighted her life as a woman for the rest of her days. Bear all this in mind (it is the sworn testimony of respectable witnesses); and pray do not forget – however foolishly and blameably he may have written about her in the secret pages of his Diary – that he was proved to have done his best to conceal from his wife the aversion which the poor soul inspired in him; and that he was (in the opinion of those who could best judge him) at least a courteous and a considerate husband, if he could be no more.

And now take the letter. It asks but one favour of you; it asks to be read by the light of Christ's teaching: 'Judge not, that ye be not judged.'[1]

CHAPTER XLVII

The Wife's Confession

'Gleninch, October 19, 18—.

'My Husband: –

'I have something very painful to tell you, about one of your oldest friends.

'You have never encouraged me to come to you with any confidences of mine. If you had allowed me to be as familiar with you as some wives are with their husbands, I should have spoken to you personally, instead of writing. As it is, I don't know how you might receive what I have to say to you, if I said it by word of mouth. So I write.

'The man against whom I warn you is still a guest in this house – Miserrimus Dexter. No falser or wickeder creature walks the earth. Don't throw my letter aside! I have waited to say this until I could find proof that might satisfy you. I have got the proof.

'You may remember that I ventured to express some disapproval, when you first told me you had asked this man to visit us. If you had allowed me time to explain myself, I might have been bold enough to give you a good reason for the aversion I felt towards your friend. But you would not wait. You hastily (and most unjustly) accused me of feeling prejudiced against the miserable creature on account of his deformity. No other feeling than compassion for deformed persons has ever entered my mind. I have indeed almost a fellow-feeling for them; being that next worst thing myself to a deformity – a plain woman. I objected to Mr Dexter as your guest, because he had asked me to be his wife in past days, and because I had reason to fear that he still regarded me (after my marriage) with a guilty and a horrible love. Was it not my duty, as a good wife, to object to his being your guest at Gleninch? And was it not your duty, as a good husband, to encourage me to say more?

'Well! Mr Dexter has been your guest for many weeks; and Mr Dexter has dared to speak to me again of his love. He has insulted me, and insulted you, by declaring that *he* adores me, and that *you* hate me. He has promised me a life of unalloyed happiness, in a foreign country with my lover. And he has prophesied for me a life of unendurable misery, at home with my husband.

'Why did I not make my complaint to you, and have this monster dismissed from the house at once and for ever?

'Are you sure you would have believed me, if I had complained, and if your bosom friend had denied all intention of insulting me? I heard you once say (when you were not aware that I was within hearing) that the vainest women were always the ugly women. You might have accused *me* of vanity. Who knows?

'But I have no desire to shelter myself under this excuse. I am a jealous, unhappy creature; always doubtful of your affection for me; always fearing that another woman has got my place in your heart. Miserrimus Dexter has practised on this weakness of mine. He has declared he can prove to me (if I will permit him) that I am, in your secret heart, an object of loathing to you; that you shrink from touching me; that you curse the hour when you were foolish enough to make me your wife. I have struggled as long as I could against the temptation to let him produce his proofs. It was a terrible temptation, to a woman who was far from feeling sure of the sincerity of your love for her; and it has ended in getting the better of my resistance. I wickedly concealed the disgust which the wretch inspired in me; I wickedly gave him leave to explain himself; I wickedly permitted this enemy of yours and of mine to take me into his confidence. And why? Because I loved you and you only; and because Miserrimus Dexter's proposal did, after all, echo a doubt of you that had long been gnawing secretly at my heart.

'Forgive me, Eustace! This is my first sin against you. It shall be my last.

'I will not spare myself; I will write a full confession of what I said to him and of what he said to me. You may make me suffer for it, when you know what I have done; but you will at least be warned in time; you will see your false friend in his true light.

'I said to him: "How can you prove to me that my husband hates me in secret?"

'He answered: "I can prove it, under his own handwriting; you shall see it in his Diary."

'I said: "His Diary has a lock; and the drawer in which he keeps it has a lock. How can you get at the Diary and the drawer?"

'He answered: "I have my own way of getting at both of them, without the slightest risk of being discovered by your husband. All you have to do is to give me the opportunity of seeing you privately. I will engage, in return, to bring the open Diary with me to your room."

'I said: "How can I give you the opportunity? What do you mean?"

'He pointed to the key, in the door of communication between my room and the little study.

'He said: "With my infirmity, I may not be able to profit by the next opportunity of visiting you here, unobserved: I must be able to choose my own time and my own way of getting to you secretly. Let me take the key; leaving the door locked. When the key is missed, if *you* say it doesn't matter – if *you* point out that the door is locked, and tell the servants not to trouble themselves about finding the key – there will be no disturbance in the house; and I shall be in secure possession of a means of communication with you which no one will suspect. Will you do this?"

'I have done it.

'Yes! I have become the accomplice of this double-faced villain. I have degraded myself, and outraged you, by making an appointment to pry into your Diary. I know how base my conduct is. I can make no excuse. I can only repeat that I love you, and that I am sorely afraid you don't love me. And Miserrimus Dexter offers to end my doubts by showing me the most secret thoughts of your heart, in your own writing.

'He is to be here, after many delays (while you are out), some time in the course of the next two hours. I shall decline to be satisfied with only once looking at your Diary; and I shall make an appointment with him to bring it to me again, at the same time to-morrow. Before then, you will receive these lines, by the hand of my nurse. Go out as usual, after reading them. But return privately, and unlock the table drawer in which you keep your book. You will find it gone. Post yourself quietly in the little study; and you will discover the Diary (when Miserrimus Dexter leaves me), in the hands of your friend.*

'October 20.

'I have read your Diary.

'At last I know what you really think of me. I have read what Miserrimus Dexter promised I should read – the confession of your loathing for me, in your own handwriting.

'You will not receive what I wrote to you yesterday, at the time, or in the manner, which I had proposed. Long as my letter is, I have still (after reading your Diary) some more words to add. After I have closed and sealed the envelope, and addressed it to you, I shall put it under my pillow. It will be found there when I am laid out for the grave – and then, Eustace (when it is too late for hope or help), my letter will be given to you.

'Yes: I have had enough of my life. Yes: I mean to die.

'I have already sacrificed everything but my life to my love for you. Now I know that my love is not returned, the last sacrifice left is easy. My death will set you free to marry Mrs Beauly.

---

* Note by Mr Playmore: – The greatest difficulties of reconstruction occurred in this first portion of the torn letter. In the fourth paragraph from the beginning, we have been obliged to supply lost words in no less than three places. In the ninth, tenth, and seventeenth paragraphs the same proceeding was, in a greater or less degree, found to be necessary. In all these cases, the utmost pains have been taken to supply the deficiency in exact accordance with what appeared to be the meaning of the writer, as indicated in the existing pieces of the manuscript.

'You don't know what it cost me to control my hatred of her, and to beg her to pay her visit here, without minding my illness. I could never have done it if I had not been so fond of you, and so fearful of irritating you against me by showing my jealousy. And how did you reward me? Let your Diary answer! "I tenderly embraced her, this very morning: and I hope, poor soul, she did not discover the effort that it cost me."

'Well; I have discovered it now. I know that you privately think your life with me "a purgatory." I know that you have compassionately hidden from me the "sense of shrinking that comes over you when you are obliged to submit to my caresses." I am nothing but an obstacle – an "utterly distasteful" obstacle – between you and the woman whom you love so dearly that you "adore the earth which she touches with her foot." Be it so! I will stand in your way no longer. It is no sacrifice and no merit on my part. Life is unendurable to me, now I know that the man whom I love with all my heart and soul, secretly shrinks from me whenever I touch him.

'I have got the means of death close at hand.

'The arsenic that I twice asked you to buy for me is in my dressing-case. I deceived you when I mentioned some common-place reasons for wanting it. My true reason was to try if I could not improve my ugly complexion – not from any vain feeling of mine: only to make myself look better and more lovable in your eyes. I have taken some of it for that purpose; but I have got plenty left to kill myself with. The poison will have its use at last. It might have failed to improve my complexion. It will not fail to relieve you of your ugly wife.

'Don't let me be examined after death. Show this letter to the doctor who attends me. It will tell him that I have committed suicide; it will prevent any innocent person from being suspected of poisoning me. I want nobody to be blamed or punished. I shall remove the chemist's label, and carefully empty the bottle containing the poison, so that he may not suffer on my account.

'I must wait here, and rest a little while – then take up my letter again. It is far too long already. But these are my farewell words. I may surely dwell a little on my last talk with you!

'October 21. Two o'clock in the morning.

'I sent you out of the room yesterday, when you came in to ask how I had passed the night. And I spoke of you shamefully, Eustace, after you had gone, to the hired nurse who attends on me. Forgive me. I am almost beside myself now. You know why.

'Half-past three.

'Oh, my husband, I have done the deed which will relieve you of the wife whom you hate! I have taken the poison – all of it that was left in the paper packet, which was the first that I found. If this is not enough to kill me, I have more left in the bottle.

'Ten minutes past five.

'You have just gone, after giving me my composing draught. My courage failed me at the sight of you. I thought to myself, "If he looks at me kindly, I will confess what I have done, and let him save my life." You never looked at me at all. You only looked at the medicine. I let you go, without saying a word.

'Half-past five.

'I begin to feel the first effects of the poison. The nurse is asleep at the foot of my bed. I won't call for assistance; I won't wake her. I will die.

'Half-past nine.

'The agony was beyond my endurance – I woke the nurse. I have seen the doctor.

'Nobody suspects anything. Strange to say, the pain has left me; I have evidently taken too little of the poison. I must open the bottle which contains the larger quantity. Fortunately, you are not near me – my resolution to die, or rather, my loathing of life, remains as bitterly unaltered as ever. To make sure of my courage, I have forbidden the nurse to send for you. She has just gone downstairs by my orders. I am free to get the poison out of my dressing-case.

'Ten minutes to ten.

'I had just time to hide the bottle (after the nurse had left me), when you came into my room.

'I had another moment of weakness when I saw you. I determined to give myself a last chance of life. That is to say, I determined to offer you a last opportunity of treating me kindly. I asked you to get me a cup of tea. If, in paying me this little attention, you only encouraged me by one fond word or one fond look, I resolved not to take the second dose of poison.

'You obeyed my wishes; but you were not kind. You gave me my tea, Eustace, as if you were giving a drink to your dog. And then you wondered in a languid way (thinking, I suppose, of Mrs Beauly all the time), at my dropping the cup in handing it back to you. I really could not help it; my hand *would* tremble. In my place, your hand might have trembled, too – with the arsenic under the bedclothes. You politely hoped, before you went away, that the tea would do me good – and, oh God! you could not even look at me when you said that! You looked at the broken bits of the tea-cup.

'The instant you were out of the room I took the poison – a double dose this time.

'I have a little request to make here, while I think of it.

'After removing the label from the bottle, and putting it back, clean, in my dressing-case, it struck me that I had failed to take the same precaution (in the early morning) with the empty paper-packet, bearing on it the name of the other chemist. I threw it aside on the counterpane of the bed, among some other loose papers. My ill-tempered nurse complained of the litter, and crumpled them all up, and put them away somewhere. I hope the chemist will not suffer through my carelessness. Pray bear it in mind to say that he is not to blame.

'Dexter – something reminds me of Miserrimus Dexter. He has put your Diary back again in the drawer, and he presses me for an answer to his proposals. Has this false wretch any conscience? If he has, even *he* will suffer – when my death answers him.

'The nurse has been in my room again. I have sent her away. I have told her I want to be alone.

'How is the time going? I cannot find my watch. Is the pain coming back again, and paralysing me? I don't feel it keenly yet.

'It may come back, though, at any moment. I have still to close my letter, and to address it to you. And, besides, I must save up my strength to hide it under the pillow, so that nobody may find it until after my death.

'Farewell, my dear. I wish I had been a prettier woman. A more loving woman (towards you) I could not be. Even now, I dread the sight of your dear face. Even now, if I allowed myself the luxury of looking at you, I don't know that you might not charm me into confessing what I have done – before it is too late to save me.

'But you are not here. Better as it is! better as it is!

'Once more, farewell! Be happier than you have been with me. I love you, Eustace – I forgive you. When you have nothing else to think about, think sometimes, as kindly as you can, of your poor, ugly

'SARA MACALLAN.'*

---

* Note by Mr Playmore: – The lost words and phrases supplied in this concluding portion of the letter are so few in number that it is needless to mention them. The fragments which were found accidentally stuck together by the gum, and which represent the part of the letter first completely reconstructed, being at the phrase, 'I spoke of you shamefully, Eustace'; and end with the broken sentence, 'If, in paying me this little attention, you only encouraged me by one fond word or one fond look, I resolved not to take—' With the assistance thus afforded to us, the labour of putting together the concluding half of the letter (dated 'October 20') was trifling, compared with the almost insurmountable difficulties which we encountered in dealing with the scattered wreck of the preceding pages.

CHAPTER XLVIII

What Else Could I Do?

As soon as I could dry my eyes and compose my spirits, after reading the wife's pitiable and dreadful farewell, my first thought was of Eustace – my first anxiety was to prevent him from ever reading what I had read.

Yes! to this end it had come. I had devoted my life to the attainment of one object; and that object I had gained. There, on the table before me, lay the triumphant vindication of my husband's innocence; and, in mercy to him, in mercy to the memory of his dead wife, my one hope was that he might never see it! My one desire was to hide it from the public view!

I looked back at the strange circumstances under which the letter had been discovered.

It was all my doing – as the lawyer had said. And yet, what I had done, I had, so to speak, done blindfold. The merest accident might have altered the whole course of later events. I had over and over again interfered to check Ariel, when she entreated the Master to 'tell her a story.' If she had not succeeded, in spite of my opposition, Miserrimus Dexter's last effort of memory might never have been directed to the tragedy at Gleninch. And again, if I had only remembered to move my chair, and so to give Benjamin the signal to leave off, he would never have written down the apparently senseless words which have led us to the discovery of the truth.

Looking back at events in this frame of mind, the very sight of the letter sickened and horrified me. I cursed the day which had disinterred the fragments of it from their foul tomb. Just at the time when Eustace had found his weary way back to health and strength; just at the time when we were united again and happy again – when a month or two more might make us father and mother, as well as husband and wife – that frightful record of suffering and sin had risen against us like an avenging spirit. There it faced me on the table, threatening my husband's tranquillity; nay, for all I knew (if he read it at the present critical stage of his recovery), even threatening his life!

The hour struck from the clock on the mantelpiece. It was Eustace's time for paying me his morning visit, in my own little room. He might come in at any moment; he might see the letter; he might snatch the letter out of my hand. In a frenzy of terror and loathing, I caught up the vile sheets of paper, and threw them into the fire.

It was a fortunate thing that a copy only had been sent to me. If the original letter had been in its place, I believe I should have burnt the original at that moment.

The last morsel of paper had been barely consumed by the flames when the door opened, and Eustace came in.

He glanced at the fire. The black cinders of the burnt paper were still floating at the back of the grate. He had seen the letter brought to me at the breakfast-table. Did he suspect what I had done? He said nothing – he stood gravely looking into the fire. Then he advanced and fixed his eyes on me. I suppose I was very pale. The first words he spoke were words which asked me if I felt ill.

I was determined not to deceive him, even in the merest trifle.

'I am feeling a little nervous, Eustace,' I answered. 'That is all!'

He looked at me again, as if he expected me to say something more. I remained silent. He took a letter out of the breast-pocket of his coat, and laid it on the table before me – just where the Confession had lain before I destroyed it!

'I have had a letter, too, this morning,' he said. 'And *I*, Valeria, have no secrets from *you*.'

I understood the reproach which those words conveyed; but I made no attempt to answer him.

'Do you wish me to read it?' was all I said, pointing to the envelope which he had laid on the table.

'I have already said that I have no secrets from you,' he repeated. 'The envelope is open. See for yourself what is enclosed in it.'

I took out – not a letter, but a printed paragraph, cut from a Scotch newspaper.

'Read it,' said Eustace.

I read, as follows: –

'STRANGE DOINGS AT GLENINCH. – A romance in real life seems to be in course of progress at Mr Macallan's country-house. Private excavations are taking place – if our readers will pardon us the unsavoury allusion? – at the dust-heap, of all places in the world! Something has assuredly been discovered; but nobody knows what. This alone is certain: – For weeks past, two strangers from London (superintended by our respected fellow-citizen, Mr Playmore) have been at work night and day in the library at Gleninch, with the door locked. Will the secret ever be revealed? And will it throw any light on a mysterious and shocking event, which our readers have learnt to associate with the past history of Gleninch? Perhaps, when Mr Macallan returns, he may be able to answer these questions. In the meantime, we can only await events.'

I laid the newspaper slip on the table, in no very Christian frame of mind towards the persons concerned in producing it. Some reporter in search of news had evidently been prying about the grounds at Gleninch, and some busybody in the neighbourhood had in all probability sent the published paragraph to Eustace. Entirely at a loss what to do, I waited for my husband to speak. He did not keep me in suspense – he questioned me instantly.

'Do you understand what it means, Valeria?'

I answered honestly. I owned that I understood what it meant.

He waited again as if he expected me to say more. I still kept the only refuge left to me – the refuge of silence.

'Am I to know no more than I know now?' he proceeded, after an interval. 'Are you not bound to tell me what is going on in my own house?'

It is a common remark that people, if they can think at all, think quickly in emergencies. There was but one way out of the embarrassing position in which my husband's last words had placed me. My instincts showed me the way, I suppose. At any rate, I took it.

'You have promised to trust me,' I began.

He admitted that he had promised.

'I must ask you, for your own sake, Eustace, to trust me for a little while longer. I will satisfy you, if you will only give me time.'

His face darkened. 'How much longer must I wait?' he asked.

I saw that the time had come for trying some stronger form of persuasion than words.

'Kiss me,' I said, 'before I tell you!'

He hesitated (so like a husband!). And I persisted (so like a wife!). There was no choice for him but to yield. Having given me my kiss (not over-graciously), he insisted once more on knowing how much longer I wanted him to wait.

'I want you to wait,' I answered, 'until our child is born.'

He started. My condition took him by surprise. I gently pressed his hand, and gave him a look. He returned the look (warmly enough, this time, to satisfy me). 'Say you consent,' I whispered.

He consented.

So I put off the day of reckoning once more. So I gained time to consult with Benjamin and Mr Playmore.

While Eustace remained with me in the room, I was composed, and capable of talking to him. But, when he left me, after a time, to think over what had passed between us, and to remember how kindly he had given way to me, my heart turned pityingly to those other wives (better women, some of them, than I am), whose husbands, under similar circumstances, would have spoken hard words to them; would perhaps even have acted more cruelly still. The contrast thus suggested between their fate and mine quite overcame me. What had I done to deserve my happiness? What had *they* done, poor souls, to deserve their misery? My nerves were overwrought, I dare say, after reading the dreadful confession of Eustace's first wife. I burst out crying – and I was all the better for it afterwards!

CHAPTER XLIX

Past and Future

I write from memory unassisted by notes or diaries; and I have no distinct recollection of the length of our residence abroad. It certainly extended over a period of some months. Long after Eustace was strong enough to take the journey to London, the doctors persisted in keeping him in Paris. He had shown symptoms of weakness in one of his lungs, and his medical advisers, seeing that he prospered in the dry atmosphere of France, warned him to be careful of breathing too soon the moist air of his own country.

Thus it happened that we were still in Paris, when I received my next news from Gleninch.

This time, no letters passed on either side. To my surprise and delight, Benjamin quietly made his appearance, one morning, in our pretty French drawing-room. He was so preternaturally smart in his dress, and so incomprehensibly anxious (while my husband was in the way) to make us understand that his reasons for visiting Paris were holiday reasons only, that I at once suspected him of having crossed the Channel in a double character – say, as tourist in search of pleasure, when third persons were present: as ambassador from Mr Playmore, when he and I had the room to ourselves.

Later in the day I contrived that we should be left together, and I soon found that my anticipations had not misled me. Benjamin had set out for Paris, at Mr Playmore's express request, to consult with me as to the future, and to enlighten me as to the past. He presented me with his credentials, in the shape of a little note from the lawyer.

'There are some few points' (Mr Playmore wrote) 'which the recovery of the letter does not seem to clear up. I have done my best, with Mr Benjamin's assistance, to find the right explanation of these debatable matters, and I have treated the subject, for the sake of brevity, in the form of Questions and Answers. Will you accept me as interpreter, after the mistakes I made when you consulted me in Edinburgh? Events, I admit, have proved that I was entirely wrong in trying to prevent you from returning to Dexter – and partially wrong in suspecting Dexter of being directly, instead of indirectly, answerable for the first Mrs Eustace's death! I frankly make my confession, and leave you to tell Mr Benjamin whether you think my new Catechism worthy of examination or not.'

I thought his 'new Catechism' (as he called it) decidedly worthy of examination. If you don't agree with this view, and if you are dying to be done with me and my narrative, pass on to the next chapter by all means!

Benjamin produced the Questions and Answers, and read them to me, at my request, in these terms: –

'Questions suggested by the letter discovered at Gleninch. First Group: Questions relating to the Diary. First Question: – In obtaining access to Mr Macallan's private journal, was Miserrimus Dexter guided by any previous knowledge of its contents?

'Answer: – It is doubtful if he had any such knowledge. The probabilities are that he noticed how carefully Mr Macallan secured his Diary from observation; that he inferred therefrom the existence of dangerous domestic secrets in the locked-up pages; and that he speculated on using those secrets for his own purpose, when he caused the false keys to be made.

'Second Question: – To what motive are we to attribute Miserrimus Dexter's interference with the sheriff's officers, on the day when they seized Mr Macallan's Diary, along with his other papers?

'Answer: – In replying to this question, we must first do justice to Dexter himself. Infamously as we now know him to have acted, the man was not a downright fiend. That he secretly hated Mr Macallan, as his successful rival in the affections of the woman whom he loved – and that he did all he could to induce the unhappy lady to desert her husband – are, in this case, facts not to be denied. On the other hand, it is fairly to be doubted whether he was additionally capable of permitting the friend who trusted him to be tried for murder, through his fault, without making an effort to save the innocent man. It had naturally never occurred to Mr Macallan (being guiltless of his wife's death) to destroy his Diary and his letters, in the fear that they might be used against him. Until the prompt and secret action of the Fiscal took him by surprise, the idea of his being charged with the murder of his wife was an idea which we know, from his own statement, had never even entered his mind. But Dexter must have looked at the matter from another point of view. In his last wandering words (spoken when his mind broke down) he refers to the Diary in these terms, "The Diary will hang him; I won't have him hanged." If he could have found his opportunity of getting at it in time – or if the sheriff's officers had not been too quick for him – there can be no reasonable doubt that Dexter would have himself destroyed the Diary, foreseeing the consequences of its production in Court. So strongly does he appear to have felt these considerations, that he even resisted the officers in the execution of their duty. His agitation, when he sent for Mr Playmore to interfere, was witnessed by that gentleman, and (it may not be amiss to add) was genuine agitation beyond dispute.

'Questions of the Second Group: relating to the Wife's Confession. First Question: – What prevented Dexter from destroying the letter, when he first discovered it under the dead woman's pillow?

'Answer: – The same motives which led him to resist the seizure of the Diary, and to give his evidence in the prisoner's favour at the Trial, induced him to preserve the letter, until the verdict was known. Looking back once more at his last words (as taken down by Mr Benjamin), we may infer that if the verdict had been Guilty, he would not have hesitated to save the innocent husband by producing the wife's confession. There are degrees in all wickedness. Dexter was wicked enough to suppress the letter, which wounded his vanity by revealing him as an object for loathing and contempt – but he was not wicked enough deliberately to let an innocent man perish on the scaffold. He was capable of exposing the rival whom he hated to the infamy and torture of a public accusation of murder; but, in the event of an adverse verdict, he shrank before the direr cruelty of letting him be hanged. Reflect, in this connection, on what he must have suffered, villain as he was, when he first read the wife's confession. He had calculated on undermining her affection for her husband – and whither had his calculations led him? He had driven the woman whom he loved to the last dreadful refuge of death by suicide! Give these

373

considerations their due weight; and you will understand that some little redeeming virtue might show itself, as the result even of *this* man's remorse.

'Second Question: – What motive influenced Miserrimus Dexter's conduct, when Mrs (Valeria) Macallan informed him that she proposed reopening the enquiry into the poisoning at Gleninch?

'Answer: – In all probability, Dexter's guilty fears suggested to him that he might have been watched, on the morning when he secretly entered the chamber in which the first Mrs Eustace lay dead. Feeling no scruples himself, to restrain him from listening at doors and looking through keyholes, he would be all the more ready to suspect other people of the same practices. With this dread in him, it would naturally occur to his mind that Mrs Valeria might meet with the person who had watched him, and might hear all that the person had discovered – unless he led her astray at the outset of her investigations. Her own jealous suspicions of Mrs Beauly offered him the chance of easily doing this. And he was all the readier to profit by the chance, being himself animated by the most hostile feeling towards that lady. He knew her, as the enemy who destroyed the domestic peace of the mistress of the house: he loved the mistress of the house, and he hated her enemy, accordingly. The preservation of his guilty secret, and the persecution of Mrs Beauly: there you have the greater and the lesser motive of his conduct, in his relations with Mrs Eustace the second!'*

Benjamin laid down his notes, and took off his spectacles.

'We have not thought it necessary to go further than this,' he said. 'Is there any point you can think of that is still left unexplained?'

I reflected. There was no point of any importance left unexplained that I could remember. But there was one little matter (suggested by the recent allusions to Mrs Beauly) which I wished, if possible, to have thoroughly cleared up.

'Have you and Mr Playmore ever spoken together on the subject

---

* Note by the writer of the narrative: – Look back for a further illustration of this point of view to the scene at Benjamin's house (Chapter XXXV), where Dexter, in a moment of ungovernable agitation, betrays his secret (or, rather, a part of his secret) to Valeria.

of my husband's former attachment to Mrs Beauly?' I asked. 'Has Mr Playmore ever told you why Eustace did not marry her, after the Trial?'

'I put that question to Mr Playmore myself,' said Benjamin. 'He answered it easily enough. Being your husband's confidential friend and adviser, he was consulted when Mr Eustace wrote to Mrs Beauly, after the Trial; and he repeated the substance of the letter, at my request. Would you like to hear what I remember of it, in my turn?'

I owned that I should like to hear it. What Benjamin thereupon told me, exactly coincided with what Miserrimus Dexter had told me – as related in the thirtieth chapter of my narrative. Mrs Beauly had been a witness of the public degradation of my husband. That was enough in itself to prevent him from marrying her. He broke off with *her*, for the same reason which had led him to separate himself from *me*. Existence with a woman who knew that he had been tried for his life as a murderer, was an existence which he had not resolution enough to face. The two accounts agreed in every particular. At last my jealous curiosity was pacified; and Benjamin was free to dismiss the past from further consideration, and to approach the more critical and more interesting topic of the future.

His first enquiries related to Eustace. He asked if my husband had any suspicion of the proceedings which had taken place at Gleninch.

I told him what had happened, and how I had contrived to put off the inevitable disclosure for a time.

My old friend's face cleared up as he listened to me.

'This will be good news for Mr Playmore,' he said. 'Our excellent friend, the lawyer, is sorely afraid that our discoveries may compromise your position with your husband. On the one hand, he is naturally anxious to spare Mr Eustace the distress which he must certainly feel, if he reads his first wife's confession. On the other hand, it is impossible, in justice (as Mr Playmore puts it) to the unborn children of your marriage, to suppress a document which vindicates the memory of their father from the aspersion that the Scotch Verdict might otherwise cast on it.'

I listened attentively. In referring to our future, Benjamin had touched on a trouble which had been long secretly preying on my mind.

'How does Mr Playmore propose to meet the difficulty?' I asked.

'He can only meet it in one way,' Benjamin replied. 'He proposes to seal up the original manuscript of the letter, and to add to it a plain statement of the circumstances under which it was discovered; supported by your signed attestation and mine, as witnesses to the facts. This done, he must leave it to you to take your husband into your confidence, at your own time. It will then be for Mr Eustace to decide whether he will open the enclosure – or whether he will leave it, with the seal unbroken, as an heirloom to his children, to be made public or not, at their discretion, when they are of an age to think for themselves. Do you consent to this, my dear? or would you prefer that Mr Playmore should see your husband, and act for you in the matter?'

I decided, without hesitation, to take the responsibility on myself. Where the question of guiding Eustace's decision was concerned, I considered my influence to be decidedly superior to the influence of Mr Playmore. My choice met with Benjamin's full approval. He arranged to write to Edinburgh, and relieve the lawyer's anxieties by that day's post.

The one last thing now left to be settled, related to our plans for returning to England. The doctors were the authorities on this subject. I promised to consult them about it, at their next visit to Eustace.

'Have you anything more to say to me?' Benjamin enquired, as he opened his writing-case.

I thought of Miserrimus Dexter and Ariel; and I enquired if he had heard any news of them lately. My old friend sighed, and warned me that I had touched on a painful subject.

'The best thing that can happen to that unhappy man, is likely to happen,' he said. 'The one change in him is a change that threatens paralysis. You may hear of his death before you get back to England.'

'And Ariel?' I asked.

'Quite unaltered,' Benjamin answered. 'Perfectly happy so long as she is with "the Master." From all I can hear of her, poor soul, she doesn't reckon Dexter among mortal beings. She laughs at the idea of his dying; and she waits patiently, in the firm persuasion that he will recognise her again.'

Benjamin's news saddened and silenced me. I left him to his letter.

CHAPTER L

The Last of the Story

In ten days more we returned to England, accompanied by Benjamin.

Mrs Macallan's house in London offered us ample accommodation. We gladly availed ourselves of her proposal, when she invited us to stay with her until our child was born, and our plans for the future were arranged.

The sad news from the asylum (for which Benjamin had prepared my mind at Paris) reached me soon after our return to England. Miserrimus Dexter's release from the burden of life had come to him, by slow degrees. A few hours before he breathed his last, he rallied for a while, and recognised Ariel at his bedside. He feebly pronounced her name, and looked at her, and asked for me. They thought of sending for me, but it was too late. Before the messenger could be despatched, he said with a touch of his old self-importance: 'Silence all of you! my brains are weary; I am going to sleep.' He closed his eyes in slumber, and never woke again. So for this man, too, the end came mercifully, without grief or pain! So that strange and many-sided life – with its guilt and its misery, its fitful flashes of poetry and humour, its fantastic gaiety, cruelty, and vanity – ran its destined course, and faded out like a dream!

Alas for Ariel! She had lived for the Master – what more could she do, now the Master was gone? She could die for him.

They had mercifully allowed her to attend the funeral of Miserrimus Dexter – in the hope that the ceremony might avail to convince her of his death. The anticipation was not realised; she still persisted in denying that 'the Master' had left her. They were obliged to restrain the poor creature by force, when the coffin was lowered into the grave; and they could only remove her from the cemetery, by the same means, when the burial service was over. From that time, her life alternated, for a few weeks, between fits of raving delirium, and intervals of lethargic repose. At the annual ball given in the asylum, when the strict superintendence of the patients was in some degree relaxed, the alarm was raised, a little before midnight, that Ariel was missing. The nurse in charge had left her asleep, and had yielded to the temptation of going downstairs to look at the dancing. When the woman returned to her post, Ariel was gone. The presence of strangers, and the confusion incidental to the festival, offered her facilities for escaping which would not have presented themselves at any other time. That night the search for her proved to be useless. The next morning brought with it the last touching and terrible tidings of her. She had strayed back to the burial-ground; and she had been found towards sunrise, dead of cold and exposure, on Miserrimus Dexter's grave. Faithful to the last, Ariel had followed the Master! Faithful to the last, Ariel had died on the Master's grave!

Having written these sad words, I turn willingly to a less painful theme.

Events had separated me from Major Fitz-David, after the date of the dinner-party which had witnessed my memorable meeting with Lady Clarinda. From that time, I heard little or nothing of the Major; and I am ashamed to say I had almost entirely forgotten him – when I was reminded of the modern Don Juan, by the amazing appearance of wedding-cards, addressed to me at my mother-in-law's house! The Major had settled in life at last. And, more wonderful still, the Major had chosen as the lawful ruler of his household and himself – 'the future Queen of Song'; the round-eyed, over-dressed young lady with the strident soprano voice!

We paid our visit of congratulation in due form; and we really did feel for Major Fitz-David.

The ordeal of marriage had so changed my gay and gallant admirer of former times, that I hardly knew him again. He had lost all his pretensions to youth: he had become, hopelessly and undisguisedly, an old man. Standing behind the chair on which his imperious young wife sat enthroned, he looked at her submissively between every two words that he addressed to me, as if he waited for her permission to open his lips and speak. Whenever she interrupted him – and she did it, over and over again, without ceremony – he submitted with a senile docility and admiration, at once absurd and shocking to see.

'Isn't she beautiful?' he said to me (in his wife's hearing!). 'What a figure, and what a voice! You remember her voice? It's a loss, my dear lady, an irretrievable loss, to the operatic stage![1] Do you know, when I think what that grand creature might have done, I sometimes ask myself if I really had any right to marry her. I feel, upon my honour I feel, as if I had committed a fraud on the public!'

As for the favoured object of this quaint mixture of admiration and regret, she was pleased to receive me graciously, as an old friend. While Eustace was talking to the Major, the bride drew me aside out of their hearing, and explained her motives for marrying, with a candour which was positively shameless.

'You see we are a large family at home, quite unprovided for!' this odious young woman whispered in my ear. 'It's all very well to talk about my being a "Queen of Song" and the rest of it. Lord bless you, I have been often enough to the opera, and I have learnt enough of my music-master, to know what it takes to make a fine singer. I haven't the patience to work at it as those foreign women do: a parcel of brazen-faced Jezebels – I hate them. No! no! between you and me, it was a great deal easier to get the money by marrying the old gentleman. Here I am, provided for – and there's my family provided for, too, – and nothing to do but to spend the money. I am fond of my family; I'm a good daughter and sister – *I* am! See how I'm dressed; look at the furniture: I haven't played my cards badly, have I? It's a great advantage to marry an old man – you can twist him round your little finger. Happy? Oh, yes! I'm quite happy; and I hope you are, too. Where are you living now? I shall call soon, and have a long gossip with you. I always had a sort of liking for you, and (now I'm as good as you are) I want to be friends.'

I made a short and civil reply to this; determining inwardly that when she did visit me, she should get no further than the house-door. I don't scruple to say that I was thoroughly disgusted with her. When a woman sells herself to a man, that vile bargain is none the less infamous (to my mind), because it happens to be made under the sanction of the Church and the Law.

As I sit at the desk thinking, the picture of the Major and his wife vanishes from my memory – and the last scene in my story comes slowly into view.

The place is my bedroom. The persons (both, if you will be pleased to excuse them, in bed), are myself and my son. He is already three weeks old; and he is now lying fast asleep by his mother's side. My good Uncle Starkweather is coming to London to baptise him. Mrs Macallan will be his godmother; and his godfathers will be Benjamin and Mr Playmore. I wonder whether my christening will pass off more merrily than my wedding?

The doctor has just left the house, in some little perplexity about me. He has found me reclining as usual (latterly) in my arm-chair; but, on this particular day, he has detected symptoms of exhaustion, which he finds quite unaccountable under the circumstances, and which warn him to exert his authority by sending me back to my bed.

The truth is, that I have not taken the doctor into my confidence. There are two causes for those signs of exhaustion which have surprised my medical attendant – and the names of them are: Anxiety and Suspense.

On this day, I have at last summoned courage enough to perform the promise which I made to my husband in Paris. He is informed, by this time, how his wife's confession was discovered. He knows (on Mr Playmore's authority), that the letter may be made the means, if he so wills it, of publicly vindicating his innocence in a Court of Law. And, last and most important of all, he is now aware that the Confession itself has been kept a sealed secret from him, out of compassionate regard for his own peace of mind, as well as for the memory of the unhappy woman who was once his wife.

These necessary disclosures I have communicated to my husband – not by word of mouth; when the time came, I shrank from speaking to him personally of his first wife – but by a written statement of the circumstances, taken mainly out of my letters received in Paris, from Benjamin and Mr Playmore. He has now had ample time to read all that I have written to him, and to reflect on it in the retirement of his own study. I am waiting, with the fatal letter in my hand – and my mother-in-law is waiting in the next room to me – to hear from his own lips whether he decides to break the seal or not.

The minutes pass; and still we fail to hear his footstep on the stairs. My doubts as to which way his decision may turn, affect me more and more uneasily the longer I wait. The very possession of the letter, in the present excited state of my nerves, oppresses and revolts me. I shrink from touching it, or looking at it. I move it about restlessly from place to place on the bed, and still I cannot keep it out of my mind. At last, an odd fancy strikes me. I lift up one of the baby's hands, and put the letter under it – and so associate that dreadful record of sin and misery with something innocent and pretty that seems to hallow and to purify it.

The minutes pass; the half-hour longer strikes from the clock on the chimney-piece; and at last I hear him! He knocks softly, and opens the door.

He is deadly pale: I fancy I can detect traces of tears on his cheeks. But no outward signs of agitation escape him, as he takes his seat by my side. I can see that he has waited until he could control himself – for my sake.

He takes my hand, and kisses me tenderly.

'Valeria!' he says. 'Let me once more ask you to forgive what I said, and did, in the bygone time. If I understand nothing else, my love, I understand this: – The proof of my innocence has been found; and I owe it entirely to the courage and the devotion of my wife!'

I wait a little, to enjoy the full luxury of hearing him say those words – to revel in the love and the gratitude that moisten his dear eyes as they look at me. Then, I rouse my resolution, and put the momentous question on which our future depends.

'Do you wish to see the letter, Eustace?'

Instead of answering directly, he questions me in his turn.

'Have you got the letter here?'

'Yes.'

'Sealed up?'

'Sealed up.'

He waits a little, considering what he is going to say next, before he says it.

'Let me be sure that I know exactly what it is I have to decide,' he proceeds. 'Suppose I insist on reading the letter——?'

There I interrupt him. I know it is my duty to restrain myself. But I cannot do my duty.

'My darling, don't talk of reading the letter! Pray, pray spare yourself——'

He holds up his hand for silence.

'I am not thinking of myself,' he says.

'I am thinking of my dead wife. If I give up the public vindication of my innocence, in my own lifetime – if I leave the seal of the letter unbroken – do you say, as Mr Playmore says, that I shall be acting mercifully and tenderly towards the memory of my wife?'

'Oh, Eustace, there cannot be the shadow of a doubt of it!'

'Shall I be making some little atonement for any pain that I may have thoughtlessly caused her to suffer in her lifetime?'

'Yes! yes!'

'And, Valeria – shall I please You?'

'My darling, you will enchant me!'

'Where is the letter?'

'In your son's hand, Eustace.'

He goes round to the other side of the bed, and lifts the baby's little pink hand to his lips. For a while, he waits so, in sad and secret communion with himself. I see his mother softly open the door, and watch him as I am watching him. In a moment more, our suspense is at an end. With a heavy sigh, he lays the child's hand back again on the sealed letter; and, by that one little action, says (as if in words) to his son: 'I leave it to You!'

And so it ended! Not as I thought it would end; not perhaps as you thought it would end. What do we know of our own lives? What do we know of the fulfilment of our dearest wishes? God knows – and that is best.

Must I shut up the paper? Yes. There is nothing more for you to read, or for me to say.

Except this – as a postscript. Don't bear hardly, good people, on the follies and the errors of my husband's life. Abuse *me* as much as you please. But pray think kindly of Eustace, for my sake.

THE END

Abbreviation   Taylor: explanatory notes by Jenny Bourne Taylor to her edition of the novel in World's Classics, 1992.

DEDICATION

1. *Regnier (Of the Théâtre Français, Paris)*: François-Joseph Régnier, a friend of Collins and in 1866–7 a collaborator in the dramatization of *Armadale* for the French stage.

VOLUME I

CHAPTER I: *The Bride's Mistake*

1. *For after this manner . . . amazement*: 1 Peter 3:5–6.
2. *Valeria*: Strong, healthy, resolute.
3. *like the hair of the Venus de' Medici*: The reputation of this famous sculpture from the Roman period as the most perfect representation of female beauty had not yet been overtaken by that of the earlier Venus de Milo, which came to be considered to have a poise and serenity lacking in its more sexually provocative rival.
4. *coupé*: A compartment in a railway carriage, with seats on one side only.

CHAPTER VII: *On the Way to the Major*

1. *pearl powder*: A cosmetic used to make the skin look white and glowing. Many people associated the use of cosmetics with prostitution. Additional disrepute had recently fallen on cosmetics with the condemnation to five years' penal servitude in 1868 of a fraudster, 'Madame Rachel', who claimed that her products were made from such ingredients as water from the River Jordan, and could make women 'beautiful for ever'.

CHAPTER VIII: *The Friend of the Women*

1. *a camellia in the buttonhole*: The camelia or camellia was often used as a symbol of the falseness of appearances, or what would later be called worthless glamour, because it looked impressive but was unscented. In the 'language of flowers' of the day, it signified 'beauty is your only attraction' (Beverley Seaton, *The Language of Flowers: a History*, University Press of Virginia, 1995, p. 173). Thanks to *La Dame aux camélias* by Alexandre Dumas the younger (published in English as *The Lady with the Camelias* in 1856), it was associated with illicit sex.

CHAPTER IX: *The Defeat of the Major*

1. *Come per me sereno*: 'How clear to me today is the day reborn', Amina's famous cavatina from Act I, scene i of Bellini's opera *La Sonnambula* (1831). The role of Amina, which was made popular in London by Jenny Lind (1847) and Adelina Patti (1861), was famous as a vehicle for sopranos in 'the florid style', and rises to top E-flat.

CHAPTER X: *The Search*

1. *reproductions . . . of the Venus Milo and the Venus Callipyge*: These two classical nude sculptures were among the erotic images which were socially permitted, although perhaps only in a bachelor's rooms. In a letter written in 1887, Collins reveals his lifelong enthusiasm for 'the Venus of the beautiful buttocks': 'My beau ideal is the "Venus Callipyge" – holding up her robe, and looking over her shoulder at her own divine back view . . . and my life has been passed in trying to find a living woman who is like her – and never succeeding' (letter to Baron Sarony, 19 March 1887, quoted in Catherine Peters, *The King of Inventors: A Life of Wilkie Collins*, London, Secker & Warburg, 1991, p. 119).

2. *Voltaire in red morocco; Shakespeare in blue; Walter Scott in green; the History of England in brown; the Annual Register in yellow calf*: This is clearly a library consisting of large uniform sets, which may suggest that its owner has them as suitable decoration to a gentleman's apartments, but himself actually reads lighter literature such as French novels. The collected works of Voltaire are extensive: 30 volumes in the *Collection Complette* of 1768–77, for example, and 38 volumes in Smollett's English translation of 1761–74; in Victorian Britain Voltaire's name stands for atheism and scepticism. Given the age of the other collections, the *History of England* is less likely to be Macaulay's four-volume *History* of 1849–55 than the eighteenth-century work by David Hume, which was continued by Smollett and then T. S. Hughes, and published in 21 volumes, 1834–6. *The Annual Register, or a View of the History, Politicks and Literature of the Year* was first published in 1759, and was edited by Edmund Burke until 1791. It ran until 1953.

3. *Clémence. Idole de mon âme. Toujours fidèle. Hélas: 2me Avril, 1840*: 'Clémence. Idol of my soul. Ever faithful. Alas! 2nd April, 1840' (French). For many Englishmen, including Collins and Dickens, France was the chosen country for sexual adventures.

CHAPTER XI: *The Return to Life*

1. *My name is Hoighty – Miss Hoighty*: The *Oxford English Dictionary* gives one meaning of 'hoity-toity' as 'frolicsome, giddy; assuming, haughty, petulant'.

CHAPTER XIV: *The Woman's Answer*

1. *Ogilvie's Imperial Dictionary*: The *Imperial Dictionary, English, technological, and scientific, adapted to the present state of literature, science and art*, edited by John Ogilvie, Glasgow, 1850, with a supplement in 1855.

2. *My own little fortune . . . had been settled on myself when I married*: Although the Married Women's Property Acts of 1870 and 1874 had materially increased a married woman's control over property which she had brought to her marriage, it was not until 1882 that the law recognized a married woman's property as hers separately. Before that date a legal settlement was required to give her rights over her own property. An income of £800 a year was sufficient to maintain a respectable but not fashionable middle-class existence for a family, and would have been very comfortable for a single person.

3. *lawyers in petticoats*: University College, London had just admitted women to its Jurisprudence class in 1873, though the first woman law graduate from the College was not to take her degree until 1917, and there were no women barristers or solicitors until the two branches of the legal profession were compelled by the Sex Disqualification (Removal) Act of 1919 to admit them.

VOLUME II

CHAPTER XV: *The Story of the Trial. The Preliminaries*

1. *W. S.*: Writer to the Signet, or a member of the ancient Scottish society of law agents able to conduct cases at the Court of Session, and to prepare Crown writs, charters, etc.

CHAPTER XVIII: *Third Question – What Was His Motive?*

1. *judicial separation*: A judgment given in a civil court, which under a law of 1857 had replaced the earlier divorce *a mensa et thoro* ('from bed and board'), granted only by an ecclesiastical court. Judicial separation was a form of divorce distinct from annulment, which established the invalidity of the marriage.

CHAPTER XIX: *The Evidence for the Defence*

1. *the practice of eating arsenic, among the Styrian peasantry . . . health*: Styria is a mountainous province of south-east Austria, bordering on Hungary and Slovenia. Taylor points out that articles concerning the eating of arsenic there for cosmetic purposes were quoted in 1857 at the trial for poisoning of Madeleine Smith, whose defence was that she had obtained the poison for cosmetic use. An article, 'The Poison-Eaters', which Taylor quotes from *Chambers's Edinburgh Journal* 16 (1851), states that in Styria 'the youthful poison-eaters . . . are generally speaking, distinguished by a blooming complexion, and an appearance of exuberant health'. The 'book' relating to Styrian arsenic-eating practices has not been identified, and it is possible that one or more of the articles from *Chambers's* or *Blackwood's* were reissued in pamphlet form.

CHAPTER XX: *The End of the Trial*

1. *coverlid*: A variant of 'coverlet' or 'cover-lit', normally meaning bedcover or bedspread.

2. *their timid and trimming Scotch Verdict . . . Not Proven*: The suggestion (from the political sense of 'trimming') is that the 'not proven' verdict is the result of inclining to alternate sides of an argument as one's interest or cowardice dictates.

CHAPTER XXIII: *My Mother-in-law Surprises Me*

1. *he is off to the war in Spain with a red cross on his arm*: The International Conference of the Red Cross, founded in 1863, was active during the Carlist War of 1872–6. The Carlists had opposed the accession of Isabella II to the Spanish throne in 1833, on the grounds that the Salic Law excluded female succession. The Don Carlos of the period of this novel was the nephew of the original claimant. Wilkie Collins avoids making the issues of the Spanish conflict relevant to the novel, and Eustace's mission to Navarre is purely humanitarian, with no characters having opinions on the question of Spanish liberalism and its opponents. Carlist volunteers from Navarre later fought for Franco during the Spanish Civil War of 1936–9. Taylor points out that illustrations of the war appeared in the *Graphic* while *The Law and the Lady* was being serialized there.

CHAPTER XXIV: *Miserrimus Dexter – First View*

1. *oyster-shells*: Oysters still provided cheap portable food for building-workers in the nineteenth century, as they had since ancient times.

2. *Dexter's cousin is an idiot*: In mid-Victorian literature on mental health, a connection is made between eccentricity, idiocy and madness. See, for example, the entry 'Insanity', *Encyclopaedia Britannica* (9th ed., 1881), viii, 96, quoted in the Introduction.

3. *I am Napoleon, at the sunrise of Austerlitz*: One of Napoleon's greatest victories, the Battle of Austerlitz was fought on 2 December 1805 near what is now the village of Slavkov in the Czech Republic, between a French army of 68,000 and an Austro-Russian army of nearly 90,000.

CHAPTER XXV: *Miserrimus Dexter – Second View*

1. *the Caliban's, rather than the Ariel's voice*: Dexter's use of the name 'Ariel' for his cousin is of course ironic. Prospero's two slaves in *The Tempest* have often been taken to represent the earthbound and ethereal aspects of human nature respectively.

2. *pilot jacket*: Otherwise known as a pea-jacket: a short coat of coarse woollen fabric, commonly worn by sailors.

3. *a physiognomist's, point of view*: Physiognomy, or the study of human character as revealed in the face, was an ancient practice, whose best-established modern authority was Johann Caspar Lavater; his *Essays in Physiognomy* were published in an English translation by Thomas Holcroft in 1789, with illustrations by Henry Fuseli.

4. *the severer harmonies of the old Gregorian chants*: Strictly speaking Gregorian chants have no harmony, their characteristic sound deriving from 'organum', or the parallel movement of musical lines at perfect intervals. This unfamiliar modal music would have sounded 'severe' to ears accustomed to the rich and changing harmonies of Romantic music.

CHAPTER XXVII: *Mr Dexter at Home*

1. *the painter considered the Flying Dutchman to be no other than the Wandering Jew, pursuing his interminable journey by sea*: In their respective legends the Flying Dutchman is doomed to sail for ever around the Cape of Good Hope (or in some versions the North Sea) as a punishment for blasphemy, while the Wandering Jew is condemned to wander the earth until the Second Coming, having refused to allow Jesus to rest at his door on his way to Calvary. The former was currently most familiar from Richard Wagner's opera of 1843, and the latter (a recurring vehicle for anti-Semitism) from Eugène Sue's novel of 1844–5.

CHAPTER XXVIII: *In the Dark*

1. *some potent magnetic emanation*: These questions show the intersection of two important ideas of the day: the non-Darwinian idea that socio-sexual attraction between human beings was a part of the mechanism of evolutionary natural selection; and 'animal magnetism', the name given by the Austrian physician

Franz Mesmer (1734–1815) to a supposed magnetic force having a powerful influence on the human mind and body (for example in hypnosis), and which his followers (including Charles Dickens) used in suggestive therapy and psychotherapy. Though not as successful as a hypnotist as Dickens, Wilkie Collins was an enthusiastic witness of experiments in 'animal magnetism', and published a series of letters entitled 'Magnetic Evenings at Home' in the *Leader* from January to April 1852, covering clairvoyance as well as hypnotism. The later development of the notion that sexual attraction was the expression of 'the life force' is seen clearly (in terms of Lamarckian, purposive evolution rather than Darwinian random selection) in George Bernard Shaw's *Man and Superman* (published 1903 and first performed 1905).

CHAPTER XXIX: *In the Light*

1. *the King of Burgundies – Clos Vougeot*: Historically one of the most admired *premier cru* burgundies, it has the reputation of being unreliable, because of a multiplicity of producers on its 125 acres.

VOLUME III

CHAPTER XXX: *The Indictment of Mrs Beauly*

1. *hungered and thirsted*: See the fourth beatitude, Matthew 5:6: 'Blessed are they which do hunger and thirst after righteousness: for they shall be filled'.

2. *Mrs Borgia-Beauly*: The name of Lucrezia Borgia (1480–1519) is probably spuriously connected with poisoning. An important Italian patron of the arts during the Renaissance, she achieved notoriety by association with the ruthless exercise of power by her brother, Cesare Borgia, who was much praised by Machiavelli in *The Prince*. Her reputation as murderess and voluptuary was sealed by Donizetti's popular opera *Lucrezia Borgia* (1833), with which Collins was familiar, making the evil Count Fosco in *The Woman in White* heartily applaud a performance of it.

3. *as a cloud is borne by its own wind*: Shelley, *Prometheus Unbound*, IV, 319–24.

CHAPTER XXXI: *The Defence of Mrs Beauly*

1. The *Domino Noir*: Comic opera by the leading French exponent of the genre, D. F. E. Auber, to a libretto by Eugène Scribe (1837; in English, 1838).

2. *Phœbe*: It is not clear whether Lady Clarinda hates her maid's name because it is unfashionable, or because it is associated with virginity, being one of the names of the goddess Artemis as the Moon.

CHAPTER XXXIV: *Gleninch*

1. *a dust-heap*: A domestic dust-heap, like the large communal ones portrayed by Dickens in *Our Mutual Friend* (1864–5), would consist of household refuse and the mixture of earth and excrement ('night earth') removed from earth closets.

CHAPTER XXXV: *Mr Playmore's Prophecy*

1. *I did not understand what he meant by the last word – Alibi*: According to the *Oxford English Dictionary*, the word had then been in use for a century as a noun ('a plea of having been elsewhere'), and for fifty years more as an adverb ('elsewhere'), having an even longer history in legal Latin.

CHAPTER XXXVII: *At the Bedside*

1. *you have returned him good for evil*: Similar phrases of the contrary import occur in Psalm 35:12, as to 'reward' or 'render' evil for good'; while in Romans 12:17, 1 Thessalonians 5:15 and 1 Peter 3:9 we find the injunction not to 'recompense' or 'render' 'evil for evil'. The well-established variant 'return good for evil' is a favourite of Collins's which occurs at least once in *The Woman in White* and three times in *The Moonstone*.

CHAPTER XXXIX: *On the Way to Dexter*

1. *We were all monkeys before we were men, and molecules before we were monkeys*: The most likely objects of Benjamin's attack on modern ideas are John Stuart Mill (1806–73), the philosopher, whose *Autobiography* had recently appeared in 1873, and Thomas Henry Huxley (1825–95), the champion of Darwin, along with evolutionism itself; with a possible reference to Professor Sir Richard Owen (1804–92), the comparative anatomist and popular lecturer, and Herbert Spencer (1820–1903), the philosopher. The evolution of *homo sapiens* was highly topical again, with the publication of Darwin's *The Descent of Man* in 1871.

CHAPTER XL: *Nemesis at Last!*

1. *Nemesis*: The Greek goddess of Retributive Justice.

2. *when we shake hands at parting (if we happen to be present officially) with the vilest monster that ever swung on a gallows*: The narrator is presumably identifying with men of the class of her author at this point, since women were not often 'officially present' at hangings. For the habit of shaking hands with the condemned person before execution, see Wemmick's remark in Dickens's *Great Expectations*: ' "You're in the habit of shaking hands? . . . I have got so out of it!" said Mr Wemmick – "except at last. Very glad, I'm sure, to make your acquaintance" ' (Chapter 21).

CHAPTER XLII: *More Surprises!*

1. *miserable sinners*: In the Litany or General Supplication in the Book of Common Prayer, the words 'have mercy upon us miserable sinners' occur eight times.

2. *The rest is silence*: Hamlet's dying words; *Hamlet*, V.ii.359.

CHAPTER XLIV: *Our New Honeymoon*

1. *the tidal-train*: A train timed to catch a steamer sailing on the tide, in this case out of one of the Channel ports.

CHAPTER XLVI: *The Crisis Deferred*

1. *Judge not, that ye be not judged*: Matthew 7:1.

CHAPTER L: *The Last of the Story*

1. *an irretrievable loss . . . to the operatic stage*: A woman opera singer would have to give up her career on marrying a 'respectable' husband.

READ MORE IN PENGUIN

READ MORE IN PENGUIN

A CHOICE OF CLASSICS

Francis Bacon	**The Essays**
Aphra Behn	**Love-Letters between a Nobleman and His Sister**
	Oroonoko, The Rover and Other Works
George Berkeley	**Principles of Human Knowledge/Three Dialogues between Hylas and Philonous**
James Boswell	**The Life of Samuel Johnson**
Sir Thomas Browne	**The Major Works**
John Bunyan	**The Pilgrim's Progress**
Edmund Burke	**Reflections on the Revolution in France**
Frances Burney	**Evelina**
Margaret Cavendish	**The Blazing World and Other Writings**
William Cobbett	**Rural Rides**
William Congreve	**Comedies**
Thomas de Quincey	**Confessions of an English Opium Eater**
	Recollections of the Lakes and the Lake Poets
Daniel Defoe	**A Journal of the Plague Year**
	Moll Flanders
	Robinson Crusoe
	Roxana
	A Tour Through the Whole Island of Great Britain
Henry Fielding	**Amelia**
	Jonathan Wild
	Joseph Andrews
	The Journal of a Voyage to Lisbon
	Tom Jones
John Gay	**The Beggar's Opera**
Oliver Goldsmith	**The Vicar of Wakefield**
Lady Gregory	**Selected Writings**

READ MORE IN PENGUIN

A CHOICE OF CLASSICS

William Hazlitt	**Selected Writings**
George Herbert	**The Complete English Poems**
Thomas Hobbes	**Leviathan**
Samuel Johnson/	
James Boswell	**A Journey to the Western Islands of Scotland** and **The Journal of a Tour of the Hebrides**
Charles Lamb	**Selected Prose**
George Meredith	**The Egoist**
Thomas Middleton	**Five Plays**
John Milton	**Paradise Lost**
Samuel Richardson	**Clarissa**
	Pamela
Earl of Rochester	**Complete Works**
Richard Brinsley Sheridan	**The School for Scandal and Other Plays**
Sir Philip Sidney	**Selected Poems**
Christopher Smart	**Selected Poems**
Adam Smith	**The Wealth of Nations** (Books I–III)
Tobias Smollett	**The Adventures of Ferdinand Count Fathom**
	Humphrey Clinker
	Roderick Random
Laurence Sterne	**The Life and Opinions of Tristram Shandy**
	A Sentimental Journey Through France and Italy
Jonathan Swift	**Gulliver's Travels**
	Selected Poems
Thomas Traherne	**Selected Poems and Prose**
Henry Vaughan	**Complete Poems**

READ MORE IN PENGUIN

A CHOICE OF CLASSICS

Sylvia's Lovers   Elizabeth Gaskell

In an atmosphere of unease the rivalries of two men, the sober tradesman Philip Hepburn, who has been devoted to his cousin Sylvia since her childhood, and the gallant, charming whaleship harpooner Charley Kinraid, are played out.

The Republic   Plato

The best-known of Plato's dialogues, *The Republic* is also one of the supreme masterpieces of Western philosophy, whose influence cannot be overestimated.

Ethics   Benedict de Spinoza

'Spinoza (1632–77),' wrote Bertrand Russell, 'is the noblest and most lovable of the great philosophers. Intellectually, some others have surpassed him, but ethically he is supreme.'

Virgil in English

From Chaucer to Auden, Virgil is a defining presence in English poetry. Penguin Classics' new series, Poets in Translation, offers the best translations in English, through the centuries, of the major Classical and European poets.

What is Art?   Leo Tolstoy

Tolstoy wrote prolifically in a series of essays and polemics on issues of morality, social justice and religion. These culminated in *What is Art?*, published in 1898, in which he rejects the idea that art reveals and reinvents through beauty.

An Autobiography   Anthony Trollope

A fascinating insight into a writer's life, in which Trollope also recorded his unhappy youth and his progress to prosperity and social recognition.

READ MORE IN PENGUIN

A CHOICE OF CLASSICS

Kate Chopin	**The Awakening and Selected Stories**
	A Vocation and a Voice
James Fenimore Cooper	**The Last of the Mohicans**
	The American Democrat
Stephen Crane	**The Red Badge of Courage**
Frederick Douglass	**Narrative of the Life of Frederick Douglass, An American Slave**
Ralph Waldo Emerson	**Selected Essays**
Nathaniel Hawthorne	**The Blithedale Romance**
	The House of the Seven Gables
	The Scarlet Letter and Selected Tales
William Dean Howells	**The Rise of Silas Lapham**
Henry James	**The Ambassadors**
	The American Scene
	The Aspern Papers/The Turn of the Screw
	The Awkward Age
	The Bostonians
	The Critical Muse
	Daisy Miller
	The Europeans
	The Figure in the Carpet
	The Golden Bowl
	An International Episode
	The Jolly Corner and Other Tales
	A Landscape Painter and Other Tales
	The Portrait of a Lady
	The Princess Casamassima
	Roderick Hudson
	The Sacred Fount
	The Spoils of Poynton
	The Tragic Muse
	Washington Square
	What Maisie Knew
	The Wings of the Dove

READ MORE IN PENGUIN

A CHOICE OF CLASSICS

Sarah Orne Jewett	**The Country of the Pointed Firs**
Herman Melville	**Billy Budd, Sailor and Other Stories**
	The Confidence-Man
	Moby-Dick
	Pierre
	Redburn
	Typee
Thomas Paine	**Common Sense**
	The Rights of Man
Edgar Allan Poe	**Comedies and Satires**
	The Fall of the House of Usher
	The Narrative of Arthur Gordon Pym of Nantucket
	The Science Fiction of Edgar Allan Poe
Harriet Beecher Stowe	**Uncle Tom's Cabin**
Henry David Thoreau	**Walden/Civil Disobedience**
	A Year in Thoreau's Journal: 1851
Mark Twain	**The Adventures of Huckleberry Finn**
	The Adventures of Tom Sawyer
	A Connecticut Yankee at King Arthur's Court
	Life on the Mississippi
	Pudd'nhead Wilson
	Roughing It
	Short Stories
	Tales, Speeches, Essays and Sketches
Walt Whitman	**The Complete Poems**
	Leaves of Grass

READ MORE IN PENGUIN

A CHOICE OF CLASSICS

Charles Dickens	**American Notes for General Circulation**
	Barnaby Rudge
	Bleak House
	The Christmas Books (in two volumes)
	David Copperfield
	Dombey and Son
	Great Expectations
	Hard Times
	Little Dorrit
	Martin Chuzzlewit
	The Mystery of Edwin Drood
	Nicholas Nickleby
	The Old Curiosity Shop
	Oliver Twist
	Our Mutual Friend
	The Pickwick Papers
	Selected Short Fiction
	A Tale of Two Cities
Elizabeth Gaskell	**Cranford/Cousin Phillis**
	The Life of Charlotte Brontë
	Mary Barton
	North and South
	Ruth
	Sylvia's Lovers
	Wives and Daughters
Edward Gibbon	**The Decline and Fall of the Roman Empire** (in three volumes)
George Gissing	**New Grub Street**
	The Odd Women
William Godwin	**Caleb Williams**

READ MORE IN PENGUIN

A CHOICE OF CLASSICS

Thomas Hardy	**Desperate Remedies**
	The Distracted Preacher and Other Tales
	Far from the Madding Crowd
	Jude the Obscure
	The Hand of Ethelberta
	A Laodicean
	The Mayor of Casterbridge
	A Pair of Blue Eyes
	The Return of the Native
	Selected Poems
	Tess of the d'Urbervilles
	The Trumpet-Major
	Two on a Tower
	Under the Greenwood Tree
	The Well-Beloved
	The Woodlanders
Lord Macaulay	**The History of England**
Henry Mayhew	**London Labour and the London Poor**
John Stuart Mill	**The Autobiography**
	On Liberty
William Morris	**News from Nowhere** and **Other Writings**
John Henry Newman	**Apologia Pro Vita Sua**
Robert Owen	**A New View of Society and Other Writings**
Walter Pater	**Marius the Epicurean**
John Ruskin	**Unto This Last and Other Writings**
Walter Scott	**Ivanhoe**
	Heart of Mid-Lothian
	Old Mortality
	Rob Roy
	Waverley

READ MORE IN PENGUIN

A CHOICE OF CLASSICS

READ MORE IN PENGUIN

A CHOICE OF CLASSICS